THE
STOLEN
CHILD

THE
STOLEN
CHILD

COLIN CHEONG

Marshall Cavendish
Editions

© 1989 Times Editions Pte Ltd
© 2003 Times Media Pte Ltd
© 2011 Marshall Cavendish International (Asia) Private Limited

Published by Marshall Cavendish Editions
An imprint of Marshall Cavendish International
1 New Industrial Road, Singapore 536196

Cover art by OpalWorks

The publisher makes no representation or warranties with respect to the contents
of this book, and specifically disclaims any implied warranties or merchantability or
fitness for any particular purpose, and shall in no events be liable for any loss of profit
or any other commercial damage, including but not limited to special, incidental,
consequential, or other damages.

Other Marshall Cavendish Offices
Marshall Cavendish Ltd. PO Box 65829, London EC1P 1NY, UK • Marshall
Cavendish Corporation. 99 White Plains Road, Tarrytown NY 10591-9001,
USA • Marshall Cavendish International (Thailand) Co Ltd. 253 Asoke, 12th Flr,
Sukhumvit 21 Road, Klongtoey Nua, Wattana, Bangkok 10110, Thailand • Marshall
Cavendish (Malaysia) Sdn Bhd, Times Subang, Lot 46, Subang Hi-Tech Industrial
Park, Batu Tiga, 40000 Shah Alam, Selangor Darul Ehsan, Malaysia

Marshall Cavendish is a trademark of Times Publishing Limited

National Library Board Singapore Cataloguing in Publication Data
Cheong, Colin.
The stolen child / Colin Cheong. – Singapore : Marshall Cavendish Editions, c2011.
p. cm.
ISBN : 978-981-4346-64-1

I. Title.

PR9570.S53
S823 -- dc22   OCN719409735

Printed in Singapore by Fabulous Printers Pte Ltd

For
Matthew and Celeste

"Come away, O human child!
To the waters and the wild
With a faery hand in hand,
For the world's more full of weeping than you
can understand."

(WB Yeats, *The Stolen Child*)

PART ONE

Snapshots

"A lovely boy, stolen from an Indian king;
She never had so sweet a changeling;
And jealous Oberon would have the child
Knight of his train, to trace the forest wild;"

(Shakespeare, *A Midsummer Night's Dream, II.I.22-25*)

1

IT was late afternoon, warm and quiet. The sun's rays slanted through wide, open windows, specks of dust dancing in the warm light. Outside, a tame breeze rustled through the leaves of the mango and rambutan trees and slipped between the tall, dry stalks of lallang grass that grew on the little hills behind the wire fences surrounding little houses. Flocks of sparrows darted about in the pale, open skies, while a canary in a cage somewhere rolled out a single plaintive call and was silent again. The avenue in front of the house was quiet. Row upon row of neat little terrace houses stood along the other avenues and they too were quiet.

From one of the houses along the avenues, the silence was broken by the sound of a C-major scale being played on a piano. A finger slipped and a wrong note was struck, a slight faltering, and the fingers continued.

The boy looked up from the keyboard with a sigh and watched the dust specks floating in the sunlight. The light came through the thin yellow curtains, through tiny gaps in the material, as they moved gently back and forth with the breeze. Like waves, the boy thought as he watched them. His eyes turned to the clock on the piano top. He had been at the keyboard for ten minutes. There were twenty more long minutes to go before his time was up and freedom was his. The hands of the clock were moving painfully slowly, edging reluctantly towards liberation. The clock was a wretched piece of machinery, with a sadistic personality matched only by the metronome. He took a deep breath of warm, sleepy air and began thumping out his scales again.

It was all his kid sister's fault. If she had not wanted to play the piano, this would not have happened. But the little girl had proven herself talented to their relatives and their parents' friends, and when the girl next door had got a piano, the kid sister had immediately wanted one too. She got it and within a week, both started to take lessons. The boy had protested, but Mother had waved his protests aside for his own good because she had once wanted to play the piano too. She was not going to let her son miss out on it.

His half hour was up. He was now free. He lifted the lid of the piano bench and dumped in his books with a feeling of great satisfaction. He shot an irreverent smirk at the scowling bust of Beethoven sitting on the far end of the piano top. Then his eyes turned to the metronome, still ticking away the beats. For half an hour everyday, it ruled his life and fingers and caused him great misery. Now, at the end of that half hour, he was once again the master and the metronome was at his mercy. He reached out for it slowly, savouring every moment of his revenge, and silenced it. It was the climax of his daily ritual. And he went out to play.

The lookout sat in the back of an abandoned pickup, waiting for his friends to come back. On the floor of the flatbed lay a walkie-talkie and a pair of plastic binoculars. In his hands, he held a Schmeisser sub-machinegun, permanently loaded and ready, plastic and made in Hong Kong. An empty canteen was slung over his shoulder. It was late afternoon, almost evening. The canteen had been empty since midday and the boy was thirsty.

He had done a lot of fighting that day, all by himself. The abandoned pickup was his prize and the men who had towed it there in their Land Rover — he had killed them all and they now lay dead in a trench a hundred feet away. They had since risen from the dead and driven away.

He did not know if it had been worth it, because the pickup looked like a piece of junk. He had looked under the bonnet — there had not even been an engine. There was only one seat in the cab and the truck's tailgate was missing.

An evening breeze was blowing and the boy enjoyed its coolness as it gently ruffled his hair and dried his sweat. It was a nice evening. Barren ground stretched out before him. To him, it was infinite, stretching on and on, further and further, until Earth met Sky, although in reality, a highway and a secondary forest formed the horizon. But it did not bother him. He was watching the sun as it slowly came down. The sky was yellow and orange and red with streaks of purple in its higher parts. If only I could paint a sunset, he thought. He watched and wished that it would last forever.

His solitude was broken by the sound of running feet. He looked up and saw the returning patrol.

"Hi there!" a boy called out to him. He waved back and watched as three boys ran towards him.

"Hey, what's this?" one of them asked.

"Enemy carrier. Captured it just now," the boy in the pickup said proudly.

"That's great! Let's get in," said Eddie, the biggest and oldest boy in the group. The three boys climbed in.

"Oh wow," Keith said. "Our own truck!"

"Got an engine?" Mike asked.

"No," answered Wings. "I checked already."

"Too bad, otherwise we could have driven it."

"How did you capture it?" Eddie asked. "You told me over the radio there were troops on board."

"I shot one, grenaded three and stabbed one."

"That's cool."

"What are we going to do with it?" Keith asked.

"Ya, how we going to hide it?" Mike asked. Eddie thought for a moment.

"Well, since we can't drive it to some cave…"

"There are no caves…"

"We'll camouflage it, so that the enemy won't find it," he said at last.

They began in earnest. They pushed the truck behind a little knoll. Wings steered because he had captured the truck. They pulled up shrubs and long grass and scooped up handfuls of dirt, all of which they threw on the truck in an attempt to hide it from enemy eyes.

Eddie was nine, a year older than the other boys and he lived next door to Wings. He was strong, brave and had the wisdom that came with age, so he was their leader. Keith lived across the street from Wings. He was Eurasian and had a very pretty older sister named Anna-Maria. He was the best behaved of the lot and was the quietest. Mike lived along another avenue. He was tough, and if there was a fight, he would stay and slug it out, even if all the odds were against him. Wings was the boy who played the piano.

At last, the camouflage was complete.

"Not so bad," Eddie said.

"Can still see some of it," Keith noted.

"Ya, but it looks so bad nobody would want it," Mike said.

"Hope nobody even thinks of looking for it," Wings said.

"They won't. Let's go home. It's getting late," Eddie suggested. He stuck a candy cigarette between his lips.

"When's our next mission?" Wings asked him.

"Next Saturday," he replied. Their missions were always on Saturdays because they had to go to school in the afternoon on weekdays.

"'Where?" Wings asked.

"Behind the football field at Kalidasa. Do your parents let you go there?"

"No."

Wings' mother had set up boundaries for his play area and the best parts were not within them. He could go anywhere within the boundaries of the estate, except the outlying areas, where all the fun was. In fact, he could only ride his bicycle along their own avenue.

The others had not told their mothers how far they were going on their first mission because instinct had told them not to. The instinct had not developed in Wings yet, so he told his mother and was promptly rewarded with a set of boundaries. She would be lifting his bicycle boundary soon and he would be able to ride anywhere he wished, because after some long and hard reasoning, he had finally convinced her that he could look after himself. He also reasoned that if he could ride anywhere, he could similarly, play anywhere. But of course, he did not tell her that. He did not want to push his luck. But all that, all paradise would be his only after he had come of age.

"When do you become eight?" Eddie asked.

"In a month. Wish it was faster," Wings murmured wistfully.

"Okay, listen, when you become eight years old, you can come along with us on missions. You won't have to be lookout anymore. Deal?"

"Deal!" Wings grinned. Eddie had created the lookout post for Wings so that he could play within his mother's boundaries while still having a part in the game. Eddie offered Wings a candy cigarette. It was his way of saying that a deal had been made. And as the patrol trudged homeward, the boy took a long drag on his cigarette and felt happy.

Wings saw his father's car's headlights on the porch wall and heard the gate squeaking open. The tiny Fiat rumbled up the driveway and Wings got up to open the front door for his father.

"Hi, Daddy," he said as the little schoolteacher got out of his car.

"Hello, son, have you been good?" the man smiled and patted the boy's back.

"Ya. Could you make my airplane for me tonight?"

The man looked at his son and shook his head.

"Sorry, boy, I've got to go to a co-op meeting. Daddy can't make that plane for you tonight."

"Why do you always have to go?"

"It's my work." He looked at the boy and spoke again, "Try and understand, eh?" The boy nodded and they went in.

"How's your piano?"

"Yuck."

"Oh, come on now, it's not that bad. Besides, you should try to make your mother happy, right?"

"I think I'll watch the cartoons."

The man smiled and said, "Okay, I'm taking a bath."

He had not been gone long when Wings heard them yelling at each other again upstairs. He kept his eyes on the television screen. He was not really watching the cartoon. He stared because there was nothing else he could do. His talented kid sister was already crying and their nanny was comforting her. The kindly old lady put one hand on Wings' shoulder. He did not move, but was reassured. She was someone he could depend on.

Upstairs, a door slammed and Wings heard his father's heavy steps as he came down. He walked past the dining table where his dinner was growing cold and to the door. As he opened it, he glanced for a moment at Wings. His face softened a little and he said, "I'll do your plane later, son." Wings nodded and his father closed the door.

As he drove out of the porch, she came down the stairs crying and stopped halfway. She wanted to talk to all of them in her room. She turned and went up again.

The old lady got up with the sister in her arms, but Wings did not move.

"Your mother is calling you. You must come," the lady said gently. Wings felt helpless. He did not want to hear his mother speak against his father, as he knew she was going to now. Father never spoke ill of Mother, so why? Wings did not understand. All he knew was that his mother would be in tears at the moment and highly emotional. He hated situations like that. If he could have, he would have simply run out of the house into the cool night air, but he had nowhere to run to. He gave his hand to the lady and she gently led him upstairs, his sister in her other arm.

It was Monday and he was back in school. Wings went to school in the afternoon and he found afternoons in school unbearably long. The light of the afternoon sun depressed him and made him feel sleepy and lethargic. The dreary yellow light angled in through half-opened shutters and louvres, casting long shadows and a feeling of gloom throughout the room. Often, the boy would watch the tiny specks of dust playing in the slanting yellow rays, wishing he could be as free to do the same; and for those few minutes that he watched the dust specks, the rest of the world would slowly recede from his awareness, reduced to the background droning of a teacher and he would soar with his fellow dust specks.

When he was not with his fellow dust specks, his mind would float around the classroom (once a dust speck, always a dust speck) and settle on his classmates or on objects around the room. He always noticed how the light fell on their young faces; young, clear-skinned faces with their white facial fuzz now visible, and created shadows and highlights that made everyone look so unreal. He would also notice the way the light passed through a clear brown eye, and how beautifully transparent it was. Until the teacher caught him in mid-reverie.

"Pay attention, Nicholas, don't dream!"

Dream, Sir? No, Sir! But he always went back to it.

It was Monday and he was back in school. Wings the Dustspeck was floating around the classroom and his mind, like a weightless, transparent veil, fell softly over a classmate. Her hair was brown in the light and locks floated up and down in the gentle breeze made by the ceiling fan. There was light in her eyes and around her sweet profile. It looked to Wings like she was giving out her own radiance, lighting up her face like a faint halo glowing against the gloom of the classroom. And then she turned to look at him with her brown almond-shaped eyes and for a moment, she smiled and then turned back.

Wings could not move. He sat there transfixed by the vision that he had just beheld, unable to do or say anything. He could not understand the feeling that was surging through his mind and senses because he had never felt it before. It was a beautiful sensation and yet it frightened him, perhaps because of its suddenness or perhaps because of its immensity and intensity. What was it? Wings had no answer. All he could do was sit there and gaze in wonder.

"Nicholas, what are you doing?"

He was startled and looked up to meet his teacher's questioning and stern unfriendly eye.

"N-nothing, Sir…"

"So I noticed. You're supposed to do the sums on the board, not stare at pretty young things. You're too young for that, boy!" And the class dissolved into helpless giggles.

"Y-yes, Sir."

"Good, let's not see you do it again."

Suddenly feeling very hot, Wings quietly reached into his bag for his exercise book. He opened it to a new page and began his work, trying hard not to look her way or meet his teacher's knowing eye. Soon, he became entangled in long division and slowly, the heat left his cheeks as he forgot.

It was a Friday afternoon. She was standing in the playground with a group of girls. All of them were watching and cheering with delight at the stunts and tricks some of the boys were doing on the monkey bars. Wings stood in a corner of the playground watching them. He could not even make himself go up to her to say hello. He could not make his jelly-legs obey. His courage had left him. He had failed. Tomorrow, Wings thought, there's always tomorrow. But in the back of his mind, he knew that every tomorrow had its own tomorrow. He felt relief because he could always put it off and at the same time, frustration, because if that kept on, he was not going to get anywhere. Right now, he could not do anything because of his jelly-legs, so he stayed in his corner of the playground and watched her.

"Hi," said a voice behind him. He looked around. It was Keith.

"Oh, hi, Keith," Wings smiled back, but his heart was somewhere else.

"What you watching?" Keith asked quietly.

"Nothing."

He looked at the group at the monkey bars and saw the distant look in Wings' eyes.

"Maybe."

Wings looked at his dark face and Keith looked back at him.

"Let's go have a drink," he suggested. Wings nodded and they went.

"Do you want a birthday party this year, son?"

Wings turned round to face her when she asked. She gave him a tired look and Wings knew she was tired; tired from her work, her part in the housekeeping and her squabbles with his father. But Wings knew that whatever answer he gave, he would get what he wanted.

"No."

"Alright, son, no big party with lots of friends, but we'll have a few relatives over, like Grandad and Grandma, Auntie Janice and Uncle Boon and a few of your friends. Small tea-party, okay?"

"Okay."

It had not only been the tired sound of her voice and her weary look that had given her away. She would have had the party if Wings had wanted it, but Wings knew that she did not. She did not want him to say yes and he could tell by the very fact that she had asked. She was the kind of mother who would just go ahead and do something like that without anyone's opinion and simply expect her children to appreciate the effort.

"You're getting a bit too big for that kind of thing too, right?"

"1 guess so."

The big party was out then, but she had to keep the little one, because it was her son's eighth birthday and she had to give him a party of some kind. It was, after all, her fault that he was not getting his big party and she had to make up for it in some way. She knew the boy had said no because he had looked at her and in a brief moment, her eyes and face had betrayed their weariness to his.

"You're sure you don't mind not having one?"

"Yes."

"I'll get you a really big present instead."

"Okay."

"Thank you, son." And she retired to her room.

It was night, after dinner. The relatives and friends were gone. Wings sat alone in the living room downstairs, beside his little stack of presents. There were lots of model planes this year, more books too. It was as if everyone had tacitly agreed that he was older now and needed a different kind of present, the kind that was more mature, more suitable for his age. There were labels on the boxes and books with phrases like, "For eight years and above", "For the Intermediate Reading Level" and there was even one that said, "For ages twelve and above". Wings did not know what some of them meant, but he knew that he was getting somewhere.

It felt strange for Wings. He was glad to hear people say that he had grown so much, or how mature he looked, or how fast it had all been, it seemed so short a time ago when he had been cradled in someone's arms as a baby. But at the same time, he was sorry. Growing up opened a whole new world for him, but it also meant that he would have to leave the old one behind. There was still so much in the old one that he had not yet seen, heard, touched, tasted and felt and soon he would not be allowed to. He would be too old. He would not be able to have the toys marked "For ages three to seven", or "Recommended for children below eight", which he still liked. Maybe they would even make him give up his furry, yellow duck, the one that he had cuddled in bed at night all these years. "They are for children. You are too old for that now, Wings."

He looked round at his presents, the planes, the books, the big model car kit with the engine which his mother had given him and he could sense them beckoning to him, calling him to join them, enticing him with the promise of the glamour of maturity. Hey, big boy, we're waiting for you. Being grown up lets you command respect, young man. Mature and worldly-wise. But I want my furry toys, he thought. I want the toys that I'm too old for. I want to be looked after, I'd feel better. Hey, big boy, you can't have everything, you know. When you grow up, you have to leave a lot behind and some of it will hurt. But you're grown up, you can handle it.

You don't need to be looked after — and that's not the word for it — you want to be babied, kid. Hey, you can look after yourself. You've got to be independent, you know. You can't always depend on Mummy, dear. Besides, you're going to get a girlfriend, right? At that thought, the heat rushed to his face and he felt ashamed. Oh, please. Oh, yes, you're in love. Do you think she's going to love a Mummy's boy who won't grow up? No way, kid. You've got to act mature. You've got to impress her, you know. I know, I know, I know, Wings agreed. Maybe it's not such a bad idea after all. Being grown up makes me feel important and useful. Why not? So I'm grown up. It was not that he did not like being grown-up. He just missed being young.

Behind the kitchen, in the little study which had once been his great-grandmother's room and where she had died one night, his father was typing out a comprehension passage. Being night, it was quiet, and the typewriter's clack clack clack seemed louder than usual. Wings got up and pattered through the dark kitchen up to the study door. In the yellow light, he saw his father referring to an old, battered copy of *Julius Caesar*, cursive scrawls sprawled over its ageing yellow pages. He stood there and waited. Then his father leaned back in his chair and reached for a mug of coffee.

"Hello, Daddy."

"Hello, son, how's my birthday boy?"

"Okay. Want to see my presents?"

"Sorry, son, I can't. I've got finish all this."

"Oh."

"How many presents did you get?"

"Fifteen."

"Oh well, that's not too bad. What did your mum give you?"

"A car with an engine."

Father nodded his head.

"Come here, son." He gave the boy a hug. It was rare.

"Don't you think it's time you went to bed?"

"What time is it?"

"Ten to ten."

"Goodnight, Daddy."

"Goodnight, son." He patted the boy's back and ruffled his hair. He waited till he could not hear his son's footsteps before he turned back to his typewriter.

In the living room, Wings checked his bicycle one last time for the night. Early tomorrow morning, he was going to ride the dawn patrol alone and he would be able to go anywhere he wanted to. He checked his tyres, then his brakes. He took a last look at his machine before he began the task of ferrying all his gifts upstairs to his bedroom.

In bed, he sighed at the coolness of his pillow and the bedsheets and squeezed his bolster harder. He shut his eyes and a little smile lit up his face as he fell asleep and began a dream of Dawn Patrols and her.

Once upon a time, a little boy fell in love with a little girl. He fell in love with her one warm, dull afternoon during mathematics. He loved her very much and thought about her a lot. But he did not dare to tell her, nor did he dare to talk to her. So he looked at her as often as he could and loved her. And the little girl, she never knew that the little boy loved her.

One day, he finally decided that he would talk to the little girl and be friends with her. And later, he would tell her all about how much he loved her. He would even ask her to marry him. The little boy made his plans. He would try to catch her attention in the playground. He would then try to talk to her. He would try to win her heart. He could hardly wait for tomorrow to come, when he would go to school again.

The next day, he found his lessons very long. He always found his lessons long, but this time, he found his lessons very, very, very long and he could not stand it. I am going to die, the little boy said to himself. But he did not. And slowly, the lessons finally finished and it was recess. Everybody rushed out to the playground to play as much as possible before lessons began again.

Little good friend, he said to his little good friend, I am going to swing from the bars today and hang upside-down. When his little good friend heard this, he was very scared and said no, no, don't, you will fall down. You will die if you fall down on your head. But the little boy was going to do it. I will go, he said firmly. No little girl is worth your head, the little good friend said. This one is, the little boy said, and I will go. And he went.

The little boy went to the bars and climbed up. There were some boys there already and they were doing many daring tricks. The little girls and the less brave little boys stood around watching. It was suddenly very quiet. The little boy was not a Brave. He was a Less Brave and he was climbing the bars. Some of the Braves laughed at him, but they made way for him. It seemed a very long way up and he was suddenly very scared. He began to think. Is it worth it? What if I fail? What if I die? Will she cry for me? I want to come down. But he could not come down because everybody would laugh at him and he would be called a Coward. I must go on. And he went on.

The little boy began his tricks. First, he swung from the bars. Higher, higher, they shouted, faster, faster. His arms were aching and he felt like he had to let go but he held on and went on. He crossed from bar to bar and climbed from one end of the universe to the other. For the little boy, nothing else in the world existed, except his will to stay on the bars, the little girl and his love for her and the cruel bars themselves. The world was spinning, jumping all around him, the children's screams and shouts he did not hear. All he saw were the bars, his hands and all he could hear was his own panting, gasping breath. Finally, came the finale, where he would hang upside-down, then climb up and jump down. He began to lift his legs up, struggling with all his might. His hands were hurting and wet with sweat. Higher, higher, his legs reached out for the bar in front of him. And then he fell down.

The little boy thought that he had died. But when he opened his eyes, he saw the other little children above him, all around, their faces and bodies wavering, as if he was looking at a reflection in the water. The little good friend was kneeling beside him and the little son of a pastor administered the last rites. The little good friend punched the little son of a pastor in the face and he cried, no, no, he is not dead. I don't want to friend you anymore, the little son of a pastor began to sob and he ran away.

Is he alright? The little good friend looked behind him and saw the little girl, anxious-looking. She knelt beside the little boy and wiped away his sweat and the sand on his face and arms with her hanky. Go and call the teacher, she said. But no one dared to move, not even the Braves. Everyone was afraid, oh so afraid of getting into trouble. Quick, somebody, go, she pleaded and the little good friend took a deep breath and ran to call the teacher.

Teacher, teacher, he said, my friend, he fell down and he is dying. The teacher screamed and ran into the playground.

Little boy, little boy, how are you? The little girl was still nursing him and he thought, ah, now I can die in peace. But an ambulance came and he did not die.

When he came back to school, his left arm was in a cast. He was also a hero because of his broken arm. But that did not make the little boy as happy as he was. He was so very happy because the little girl was now his friend. Everywhere that the little boy went, the little girl was sure to go. She even carried his bag for him when the little good friend was not around. They sat together in class. They sat together in the canteen. They sat together in the playground. He was very happy.

But the little boy had an enemy. He was bigger and tougher than anybody in the class and he did not like the little boy because he was now the class hero. I would like to break his right arm, the bully thought, but that would only make him a bigger hero. And he took the little girl whom I wanted for my girlfriend. I do not like the little boy.

One day, the big bully caught the little boy alone when the little girl went to the little girls' loo. Hey, little boy, the bully said. I do not like you because you got the little girl whom I wanted for my girlfriend. But I will not break your other arm. I am too nice.

The little boy was very angry and wanted to beat the bully but his arm was still in a cast. Ha, ha, ha, little boy, you cannot tell the teacher that I threatened you because I did not. But one day, I will take away your little girl and I will try and try until

I get her from you. You cannot tell the teacher that because she will laugh at you. Why don't you give her up, little boy? I am much better for her, and the bully walked away laughing at him.

When the little girl came back, she saw that there was something not quite right with her little boy. Little boy, what is wrong? I have something to tell you, little girl, he said slowly. I... I... I love you. And she smiled back and said, I love you too. He was happy again and said, good, then will you marry me? Yes, she said, I will marry you.

The wedding was set for next week and all week, everybody who knew about it was very excited, most of all, the little boy and the little girl. But he was still unhappy whenever he thought about the big bully and what he said. He is big and strong and he has a lot of pocket-money and many nice toys, the little boy thought. I am not big and strong and rich. Maybe I will lose my little girl and whenever he thought about that, his heart became heavy and he would cry. He will always try to take away my little girl and how am I to stop him? I will never have peace. But I love my little girl so much. And when he thought of her, he was happy again.

Soon, the day of the wedding arrived. That morning, he put on his school uniform as carefully as he could so that he would be nice and neat for his wedding.

The little son of a pastor was to marry them and the little good friend was the best man. All the girls were flower girls except the little girl's best friend, who was the bridesmaid. They all brought a few flowers each to carry at the wedding and to throw in the path of the happy couple. The ceremony would be at recess.

All through the morning before recess, the little boy sat with a heavy heart. Everyone was restless because of excitement but he was restless because the words of the bully still echoed in his mind. How long will I have my little girl? How long before I lose her to that bully? He was not happy on the happiest day of his life. Sometimes he turned around to look at the bully who sat behind. The bully would leer at him knowingly and nod and the little boy would turn back quickly to steal a brief glance at his bride to be. Once, when he looked at her, he would be happy. Now, he was saddened. But he thought, suddenly and with angry determination, I will make sure that he never gets her. I will fight. I will not give up.

The bell rang for recess and everyone rushed out to the bald patch under the big tree behind the playground. Everyone quickly took their places and slowly hummed a wedding march. The couple and their train slowly walked up the aisle of sparse grass and dirt, up before the little son of a pastor. The ceremony went on. Finally, the little son of a pastor said to the little girl, do you take him as your lawful wedded husband? She looked at her groom and smiled, I do. And do you, the little son of a pastor said to the little boy, take her as your lawful wedded wife? He looked at his lovely bride and fingered the plastic ring in his pocket, then quietly he whispered in a hoarse voice, I can't. The little bride broke down and cried and ran away with her bridesmaid and flower girls behind her, but to the little boy, they seemed to be dancing madly away as the tears filled his eyes.

Once upon a time, there lived a boy who wanted to see snow. He lived in a very warm country where snow was never seen and he wanted to see snow. He wanted to see real snow, not the kind that you saw in department stores, little balls of expanded polystyrene, scattered all over the shop window displays or the cotton wool that hung from the needles of plastic Christmas trees. He wanted to see real snow, the kind that floated down from the sky and melted in your hand, the kind that was fine and soft and powdery, the kind that you read about in storybooks and heard about in Christmas carols. But the snow that the boy wanted to see was the kind that fell on ground far, far away from where he lived. So no snow for him.

"I wish I could see snow, Mummy."

"Don't wish for impossible things, son."

"But there is snow, isn't there?"

"Of course there is, but it's too expensive for us to see it."

"How much? Maybe I could save…"

"Don't be stupid, son, you can't." So the boy had to be contented with expanded polystyrene balls and cotton wool.

Christmasses came and went. Although there was no snow, Christmas was still fun. Friends and relatives would visit, there would be a lot of Christmas carols, a lot of food and drinks, a lot of chatter and laughter and a lot of presents. The boy enjoyed it all. He enjoyed the shopping trips for new clothes and presents. He enjoyed the parties, the excitement of opening presents and that special feeling of joy which he felt every Christmas. It had something to do with school vacations, bright, sunny mornings, stormy nights, the festive air, the familiar carols and great expectations.

This Christmas felt different. The boy could not understand his feeling that something was not quite right this Christmas. Perhaps it was because he had heard his parents telling friends that there was to be no party that year. Perhaps it was because he had not seen his mother baking the usual Christmas treats. Perhaps it was because there were no decorations being put up. All this made the house seem strangely quiet and gloomy, something the boy had never felt at Christmas time before. The silence was occasionally broken by either sporadic bursts of quarrelling between his parents or intense barrages that lasted a few days. The boy did not know which he liked better, the gloomy silence or the firefights.

Outside the grim perimeter of his house, his friends seemed to be having a nicer time. As he cycled up the avenue, he saw homes with decorations up and the sound of laughter from their insides, the warm, yellow light flowing out of windows bedecked with flowers and tinsel. Sometimes he smelled baking and he would stop to breathe some of the old Christmas feeling in. But a smell only lasted so long. Everywhere he rode, he heard Christmas carols being played or sung and again, the joyful laughter that haunted him.

The boy now rode in the evenings, whispering past those happy houses with the nightwinds, his little bike lamp lighting the way. The nights were getting colder now, and sometimes the streets were wet and glistened with the lights of homes filled with people waiting impatiently for Christmas to arrive. Sometimes a window would appear in a large puddle and all that was reflected in it would be clear: the warm light, the plastic holly, the tinsel, the silver bells, the silhouettes of its inhabitants, and the boy would ride through the puddle and shatter the illusion, and the lights, flickering, wavering, would settle down and the picture would be whole again.

Christmas morning came and they went to Church. Coming home, the boy heard the sounds of Christmas parties in progress all around and in his quiet, little house, he suddenly felt more lonely than ever before. He closed the door behind him and the gloom was complete. Mother was at Granny's and Father had refused to go. Nothing could make him go. Sister was at a party and his father was in the study. The boy found himself alone, so he read the book that Mother had given him. Finally, by mid-afternoon, his father had decided that he would go to Granny's.

The boy wanted to finish his book so he did not want to go. The situation was tense and the boy had no wish to be caught in any crossfires, not on Christmas Day.

His father was home by evening and the boy was swinging on the gate when he came back.

"No one spoke to me except your aunt. They weren't very nice."

"Oh. Where's Mum?"

"She's staying there for the night."

After dinner, the boy watched some TV and then went out to get his night riding jacket. He pushed his bike out of its hangar and taxied past the gate and out onto the runway. He stopped there, turned on his light and checked his brakes.

"Charlie Juliet Ace Sixer Deuce, you're cleared for take-off." He pedalled up the road, faster and faster, catching the nightwinds, feeling the gush of cold air, then climbing, climbing up into the darkened skies. The Spitfire made a gentle turn to the right and he brought her close to the rooftops of the little houses in the estate. The same warm yellow lights, the same decorations, the same happy laughter, the same smell of roasting meat from the barbeque pits below, the same wet roads with their puddles reflecting the warmth and joy of the little houses that lined them. It had been the coldest Christmas ever, even though he had not seen snow, but maybe, he thought, it will get colder and colder until the snowflakes fall.

Round and round he flew, the cold air biting his cheeks for he had left his canopy open. And then, for the first time in his life, he saw snow. Lightly it fell against his plane, blowing into the cockpit. Snow, I am seeing, touching and tasting snow. So cold it burned, so he shut his canopy and flew about in the falling snow.

Far below on the ground, people were beginning to feel the first drops of rain and they all rushed inside just as the rain began to fall harder and harder, shattering the pictures in the puddles.

Exams were a pain. Wings had come to this conclusion after sitting for his first formal exam. It was the finals for his primary three, the finals that would decide whether he was to be promoted or retained. Wings was not afraid of being retained. No, that would never happen to him. It happened to other people, but it would not happen to him. In that frame of mind, Wings sallied forth to do battle with the bane of schoolchildren, the dragon of all the little Saint Georges and Saint Georgettes, whose fiery breath burned and whose fangs and claws and horns drew precious blood and tore open bloody wounds in report books. No dragon with an ink-bottle for a stomach was going to get him. Nay, not he, not with his twenty-four sharpened colour-pencils in as many colours. Nay, not he, with the gold-tipped fountain pen. Nay, not he with the rule of stainless steel and sharp-pointed geometrical drawing instruments. Nay, not Wings.

His white and green steed had arrived to bring him to his first day of combat. Day after day, for seven days, Sir Wings gallantly rode forth to mortal combat. He fought bravely and well. I have no wounds, thought he. No wounds, I think. I know. But the dragon's wounds always showed later. For another week after that vicious battle, valiant knights sat around and waited for possible wounds to appear. All sat in tense and impatient silence. Some were already in despair, they knew that the dragon had wounded them and the pain had already begun. To those knights, knowledge was pain, knowledge was death. Knowledge that the dragon had got them. Some grew fatalistic and were calm. Some grew so fatalistic that soon they were beyond all hope of help. But Sir Wings, his faith pointed in an opposite direction. The dragon could not get me. I have slain him. And so believing, he sang and he danced and he feasted away, spending his days in absolute gaiety. *Next year, next year, another dragon to slay, but that is still a year away.*

Wings sat there at his desk, unbelieving of what he saw in the report book that lay open before him. It could not be true, but it was. There it was, clear as day, on those damning pages. Wings forced himself to smile, but the muscles of his face felt weak. So did his limbs. Slumped there on his chair, he stared vacantly out of the window.

There was his name, at the top of the page. Primary Three A. Then came the subjects and their corresponding marks. All the way down, they were blue, very, very blue and the lowest mark read eighty-five percent. To someone else, it would have been reason enough for a weeklong celebration. To Sir Wings, he had slain the dragon with no wounds to himself, but there right at the bottom were the three little words that pulled the plug out from his bathtub full of joy. All the years before, Wings had savoured ecstasy at the little phrase, "first in class". This year, it read "third in class". Wings was no longer the top knight at his parents' round table.

Wings opened the door for his mother when she got home that evening.

"Well, how did it go?" she asked.

"Bad news, I got third," he tried to sound nonchalant. Maybe she won't notice.

"That's very bad. You didn't study hard enough. I'm very disappointed with you." Her voice was stiff and formal.

"But I passed everything," he protested.

"That's not good enough. I'm not signing your report book."

That night, his parents had another argument. Wings could not hear what was going on. Ordinarily, he would not have bothered much, one quarrel was like any other. That night's was different. Wings was afraid it might be about his lowered grades. He wanted to go upstairs at least to hear what it was about, but his courage failed him. As a younger child, he had often sat in a corner of the room crying as he watched and heard his parents fight. He could take no more of that. He took some comfort in the fact that they no longer argued in public, like the time they did on the front porch with all the neighbours watching. At least now he did not have to answer the questions of nosey neighbours.

The next morning, he found his report book on his desk. His father had signed it. That was a relief and a burden off his mind. He had been wondering for most of the night what he was going to tell his form teacher the next day. And so began a new philosophy of life for Wings where it concerned his family. So long as his own life ran smoothly enough, he would not let their quarrels bother him. It was their business, not his. Involving himself in their matters only hurt him. From now on, Wings would be detached from all that. Satisfied that he had at last found a solution to his parents' bickering, Wings went down for breakfast.

It was one of those nights his father had to go out to the union office. Wings was at home with his mother and kid sister. They were upstairs and Wings was downstairs in the living room watching TV. When he was home, his father would watch with him and they would make comments at some detective's ineptness or laugh at some bumbling British comedian. Tonight as he watched alone, Wings was quiet.

Wings watched most of the programmes within his nine-thirty bedtime limit. He never asked to be allowed to watch later, because there was only the news and that bored him. The rest of the shows were prime-time programmes and Wings liked them all except the occasional episode with quarelling couples and broken homes. They were far too close to Wings' own truth to be comfortable to watch. When his father watched with him, they would both become silent and Wings would sometimes leave the room. Happily, there were none tonight.

"Wings, come up here." It was his mother.

"Why? I'm watching TV," he called back.

"Just come up here, son, I want to talk to you."

Wings did not like the sound of that, but he knew he had to go.

"I'm coming." Reluctantly, he turned off the television set and went upstairs.

"Yes?"

"Come here and sit down." Wings sat down on the side of his mother's bed.

"Now son, you know that I love the both of you very much, right?"

"Yes."

"Do you love me?"

"Yes of course. Why?" Wings felt his muscles tense.

"No, I just wanted to ask you." No, it was not that. There was more to this. Wings knew his mother well.

"Wings, do you want me to be happy or sad?" She had a note of resignation in her voice.

"Happy, of course."

"You see, son, your Daddy makes me very sad." She said it in a matter of fact way that made it sound even sadder.

"Why? What does he do?" Wings had noticed that not all their quarrels were started by his father.

"He treats me very badly, boy." There was a wetness in her eyes.

"But he doesn't beat you."

"Son, you don't have to beat someone to be cruel to them."

"Oh."

"Your father is a very cruel man and I can't bear him anymore. You don't want me to suffer, right?" Wings heard a sniff.

"You want me to be happy?" Wings nodded in bewilderment.

"Would you hate me if I went away?" This was something totally new and Wings did not know how to answer his mother. He did not want her to be unhappy, but he did not want her to go away either. He would not hate her, but he did not want her to go.

"You love me right? You want me to be happy?" This time her words were choked with sobs. Wings could not bear it anymore.

"No, no, I won't hate you. I want you to be happy, but do you have to go away? I don't want you to."

"No son, I'm not going away, don't worry. But listen, son, even though your father treats me badly, you must not hate him because he is still your father. You must love him too. You must love the both of us equally. I won't go away because I don't want to leave the both of you. But if I go, you will not hate me alright?"

"Yes," he muttered and she hugged both her children. Helplessly lost, Wings saw his mother and sister crying. Not knowing what else to do or think, he began to cry himself.

Stop, stop and let me catch my breath, Wings screamed, but no one heard him because he screamed inside himself. His mind was in a whirl and he was dizzy with the madness that raged outside and inside his head.

Mother was coming down the stairs, bags in her hands, his father was shouting behind her and she was shouting back. The students whom his mother gave tuition to were packing up their books and things, trying to get out of the house as soon as they possibly could. Oh boy, what a night! The things I'll have to tell Mum and Dad and they won't ask me about work and best of all, what a short night and no more tuition for at least another fortnight! They disappeared through the front door in double quick time, murmuring goodbye to Wings who held the door open for them, staring at the stairs and staring at his parents and seeing nothing. His legs and arms had all gone weak and he was suddenly feeling so hot that he broke out in sweat. But his sweat was cold.

"Wings! What are you waiting for! Get into the car!" his mother shouted.

"Wings don't! For God's sake, please don't!" his father pleaded with him. Wings stood frozen to one terrazzo tile. He could not have moved even if he had wanted to. Suddenly, Wings understood. This was to be the end, the real end. Everything else had been a mere preparation, a mere rehearsal for this, the last episode, his mother's Grand Finale. Wings began to cry and his chest began to hurt.

"Wings get into the car! Now!" But Wings stood where he was. I can't leave you, Daddy. I can't. He wished with all he had in his child's heart that it was all a mistake, that his mother was not leaving, that something could be settled before anything else happened.

But as far as his mother was concerned, Wings wished in vain. For her, there was to be no going back to her tormentor, only onwards to peace and freedom.

Wings looked up at where his father stood. Maybe it was his tears, but to Wings, his father suddenly seemed so old. The father looked down at his son. Daddy, Daddy, please don't think I want to leave you, please! But Wings was dumb. No words came. His father's eyes glistened with tears and they were collecting on his bifocal lenses. Wings felt his mother's hand catch hold of his and pull him out of the doorway. When his mother bundled him into the front seat with two soft bagfuls of clothes, Wings saw his younger sister already in the back, huddled into a corner and crying into her blanket and a dirty ragdoll.

Wings' father ran out onto the porch as his mother started the engine. The headlights came on and blinded him. He stopped and looked on quietly as his wife backed the car out of the driveway with his son and daughter. Wings saw his father in the glare of the headlights, arms by his side, fists clenched in helplessness. Wings saw the headlights, tiny pinpoints of bright yellow light on his father's spectacles. Wings waved, hesitantly, slowly. "Bye, Daddy. I love you, Daddy." But his father could neither hear nor see him.

"It's okay if you don't want to tell me anything, son. It's quite alright," his father said. Wings kept silent in the backseat. His father's tone was one of dejection and Wings did not like it.

"Is your mother seeing anyone?" his father asked again.

"I don't know. I don't think so," Wings replied. He had thought about it. He had seen Mum getting out of a car with his kid sister when the little brat had to be taken to the doctor. A man had been driving the car, but Wings did not know who he was. He had never seen him before and had not seen him since.

"Is that the truth, son?"

"Yes." Wings had no other answer. His father looked thoughtful and grim and Wings noticed that the car was moving faster.

"Hello, son, how was your day?"

"Oh, alright, Mum."

"So what did you make your Daddy buy you this time?"

"Oh, nothing, we just saw a movie, that's all."

"Good. Don't keep asking him to buy you things. He'll get very tired of it."

"Okay. I didn't, but she did."

"I didn't!" the kid sister screamed.

"Alright, you two, don't start a quarrel. So Wings, did your Daddy bring his girlfriend?" Her voice was casual.

"Er, no. I didn't know he had one," Wings replied. That was odd. If Dad is as bad as Mum says he is, how on Earth could he get himself a girlfriend? Wings could not reconcile the two points. He was also getting tired of the questions and answers game that his parents played with him and his sister. Daddy played when they went out. Mummy played when they came home. Wings felt like a little squash ball that was getting thrashed around.

Wings sat alone in the attic. The radio sat on the table in front of him. He put on the headset and began tapping on the morse key. Di-di-di da-da-da di-di-di. Outside, a full moon slid out from behind a cloud and her beams shone happily on his back through an open window. The light killed the luminescence of his radio's indicator needles. Wings felt his hackles rise. Have to get this through. Our Father who art in heaven. Di-di-di da-da-da di-di-di. Holy be your... Wings froze. The sound of boots stomping up the stairs. He flung the codebook into the fireplace and jumbled up the transmitter's frequency knobs. He drew his Colt and ran for his secret exit. As his fingers fumbled with the latch, the attic door's lock was blown open with a burst of AK-47 fire. The door burst open just as Wings freed the latch on the trapdoor.

"Traitor!" his mother screamed from the attic doorway.

"Double agent!" his father yelled as he emerged from the secret escape tunnel. Behind each of them stood a firing squad, one with AK-47s and another with Schmeissers. Without a word, his parents stepped aside and the firing squads opened fire. The force of the fire sent Wings' limp body crashing through the window and down to the rooftops below. And the moonbeams shone happily on his back as his blood ran down the roof tiles and down the drainpipes.

"So when will you be coming home, Dad?" Wings asked.

"Two years' time. It's not too long," his father replied. Not too long. But it was time to him. Time enough to forget. He looked at his son. But not this one. Will he be alright without me here? Well, he had not been around for a year already. They seemed to have done quite well without him. The man smiled to himself and shook his head. His son walked on beside him in silence.

"You'll have to promise me you'll look after your sister," he said after awhile. Wings winced at the mention of his kid sister.

"Ah, she can take care of herself, she's sneaky enough," Wings muttered. Sneaky, yes, that was true of all kid sisters.

"Now, come on, boy, don't say that. You'll only make me worry. Now, tell me, can you do it?" he persisted. Wings saw that he was not going to get out of it.

"Oh, alright," he finally agreed. Grudgingly, of course.

"And your mother too," his father added.

"She's old enough to take care of herself," Wings was puzzled. This was a new concept to him.

"Well, you'll be the man of the family once I'm gone," he explained.

"Oh, alright then," Wings replied in a nonchalant way. All this close relationship stuff was starting to bother him. It made him feel very uncomfortable. I hate ties. I don't like commitments. I want to be alone.

"Hmm." His father nodded, not entirely convinced by his reply.

"Do you really have to go away to study, Dad?"

"Yes, son." More than you will ever realise, the old man thought to himself.

A fortnight later, Wings held on to his father's hand as they walked past the airport's automatic glass doors. His uncles were hauling along his father's luggage and they seemed quietly solemn as they approached the baggage check counters.

"'Well, kids, I'll be gone soon," he turned to Wings and his sister. "Study hard, ya? Be good and don't give your mother any problems, okay?" Wings nodded and so did the kid sister. She looked as if she was going to burst into tears at any moment. Wings' face held no emotion. They sat together for what seemed like forever as Father made his round of goodbyes to his cousins, finally hugging his ageing aunt. Then came the voice, so strange and so hollow, echoing throughout the departure hall, calling all passengers, calling all passengers, British Airways to Heathrow, Heathrow.

He bent down so that he could see them eye-to-eye. When I come back, they will have grown. He hugged them. When I come back, will they still be here? Will they remember me as their own father?

"Don't forget to write, okay?" He kissed them both and Wings saw him stride quickly through the departure gates, followed by an airport uncle.

"Your daddy loves you very much. He'll miss the both of you a lot," said the uncle who was driving them home. Maybe I ought to be crying like she is, but I can't. There's nothing in my eyes, Wings thought. Kid sister was flooding the airport and their grandaunt was soothing her. Wings saw his father turn to wave. He waved back, and then his father was gone.

Dear Wings,

How are things with you and your sister? Is everything okay at home? How is your mother? I hope everything is okay.

It's very cold here in Leeds at the moment, so I stay indoors most of the time. I haven't gone out to walk in the parks and gardens for quite awhile. Also, I'm preparing for my examinations and this leaves me little time for leisure. How are your studies getting on? Study hard son, your PSLE's just round the corner and you'll have to do well if you want to get into a good secondary school. How is your Chinese now? Has Mum got you and sis a tutor? Don't worry about fees. I'll tell my bank to pay whatever fees you need. Let me know when you need it. Enclosed in this letter are some pictures I took in the summer. I was in Edinburgh then, visiting one of my old tutors. Did you get my postcards from Edinburgh? It's really a lovely place in summer, but I guess I'll never get used to the climate here.

I suppose you know that those are pictures of a rhino and kangaroos. Over here in England, they have these do-it-yourself laundries. There's a picture of me with a machine.

Please tell me more about how things are at home and at school when you write again. You don't seem to have very much to say about these two places. Are you having problems? If you are, please let me know. Are they treating you alright?

Tell the little girl to be good and to keep up her piano playing. I was very happy to hear that she got a distinction for her grade two examination. That is something to be proud of. Why did you stop playing the piano, boy?

Music is very beautiful and doesn't the sense of mastery and achievement mean anything to you? Anyway, tell her that the next letter I write will be addressed to her and will exclude any references to you. (We have to humour little sisters, right?) I thought she would like postcards better, but she wrote to tell me that she was old enough to receive proper letters!

Well, I've got to go now. Be good and take care of yourself and your little sister.

Love, Daddy

Dear Dad,

Everything's okay at home, so don't worry. Everything's okay at school, so don't worry about that either. I suppose Mum is OK and so is SHE.

Mum has been talking about getting us a Chinese tutor but I told her I'd rather not. Would you like a Chinese tutor?

Anyway, I hate school because it's boring. The other kids are OK and they are the only thing I like about school. Mathematics is giving tons of problems, but no sweat, I can take it like a man.

I was going to tell you that I won a prize at sports day, but I lost.

I swim sometimes now, with my classmates, and we have lots of fun because after the swim, we hang out at this hawker's centre and eat ice-kachang and hang around the emporiums and shopping complexes. Don't worry, none of my friends smoke and neither do I.

By the way, the other night I had a quarrel with

uncle. It's nothing important really. It's just that he insists on being so stupid. Anyway, we'll be moving out once Mum gets a new flat. She's been looking for one ever since that night.

The Brat has been getting sick pretty often these days. Her piano playing must be finally affecting her. I've got used to it now so I don't throw up anymore when she plays her pieces.

Don't worry about my final exams. I've been studying for them and I don't think they're as bad as people like to say they are. I am not afraid.

Well, I'm running out of space. And I've also got to get to school in half an hour. Bye for now and good luck for YOUR exams. They'll probably be harder than mine.

Love, Wings.

The streets were quiet, deserted. Only an occasional rat scurried through the debris, gnawing at fingers that could sometimes be found on a human hand. Blood flowed down the gutters and the rats splashed gaily through the rivers of red and brown. Sunshine filtered through the haze of unsettled dust, lending the streets a dreamy, romantic look that could have once sold postcards.

Out in the fields, there was no grass, just endless miles of churned-up mud. Everywhere was the smell of rotting bodies, alive with maggots. In the trenches. Out of them. Barbed wire, stretching for hundreds of yards. Sandbags, lining the tops of trenches, as if they had been there a thousand years.

The sergeant sat in his trench, brushing the dried-up mud off his rifle. It was the resistance fighters' last stand before the Red Tide swept across the plains in their armoured chariots.

Losing, as far as the sergeant was concerned, was inevitable. He fought, because as a poor peasant boy, he had nothing else. This was it. He had lost his friends — Eddie, the best sergeant he ever had, Keith, Mike — his crops, his home to the Red Tide and the metallic treads of their armoured juggernauts. Now, far, far away from his home which lay miles within enemy territory, the sergeant prepared himself for battle.

He turned the magnetic mine in his hands and felt the slight roughness of its surface. So easy. Get yourself under a rolling tank, prime this, slam it onto the tank's belly, let the tank roll on and boom. A knot somewhere in his stomach tightened. He could not imagine the pain if a tank crushed a man in the soft mud.

Retreat, retreat. Draw the tanks into the city, the killing ground. He did not want to guess at the probability of his being there for the final phase of the battle. He sighed and stroked the wooden stock of his rifle.

"Sergeant Wings! There is a man here to see you. He says he is your father," a young private called out as he came running up to Wings. Wings nodded and stubbed out his candy cigarette. Father. I have not seen you for so long. Ever since you went into exile. From your country. From me.

The old man stood outside his black car, braving the cold winds to see his son sooner and better when he came. Wings strode up the hill, the wind whipping his hair against his face. For a moment, neither spoke as they stood before each other.

"Papa," Wings said and the old man smiled.

"We must talk, son." They got into the car and it bounced along the little lane towards the village.

"It has been a lonely two years, son."

"I know, Dad."

"You must understand that. Living alone is not easy." Wings looked at his father's haggard face. I have been alone too, father.

But I have adjusted to it. I like it now, the aloneness. Perhaps you have grown old and set in your ways. Change is harder for you.

"Wings, please understand when I tell you this."

"I understand, Dad." You took another wife, father, and never even told me. Didn't you think that I would have wanted to share in your happiness? To be there at the renewal of your life? Or was it because I belong to the past?

"I have married again, son."

"I know."

"How?"

"Word gets around."

"I'm sorry."

"No need to be."

"You have nothing against it?"

"No, Dad. I wish you all the best."

"Really, son?"

"Really." The old man smiled and put his arm around his son.

"I have to go back now, Papa."

The old man watched as his son walked down the slope, his weapon slung easily over his shoulder. He is growing to be a man, the father thought. At least he understood. But will I ever understand him? He has become a stranger, so odd. So distant. And the half-light in his eyes. The boy turned to wave, then quickly disappeared into the network of trenches. The old man turned back to his car, opened the door and got in.

Wings looked up from his trench and saw his father's car move laboriously down the lane. He watched it till it disappeared into the distant haze. He turned back to face the plains, squinted against the sun and heard the first low rumble of approaching tanks.

PART TWO

Wolf Whistles

"And every time he shuts his eyes he sees himself as a very fine fellow — so fine as he can never be … In a dream …"

(Joseph Conrad, *Lord Jim*)

1

THE boy stood alone in the field, with its bald, brown patches of earth showing through the coarse grass. The sun was low in the sky already when a tiny black speck flitted across the darkening blue. The movement caught the boy's attention and he tried to bring it into focus. But the speck stayed unclear, a pulsing black dot with a flickering shadow around it.

"I know you are a sparrow," the boy whispered to himself. But I cannot see you. Perhaps it is the failing light, the sun is setting. But he knew better. He turned to look at the goalposts at the far end of the field. White against the green of the Kalidasa fields, they should have stood out sharply, but they were blurred, like everything else.

He refused to give his knowledge voice. Saying it would have made it irreversible, but so long as he kept his silence, there was a chance yet that it might not be true. I cannot see — and even the thought was hard to bear. Looking out into the distance, he saw the sun sink slowly into a row of black trees.

He shut his eyes and the strain behind them eased. Perhaps one day, all will be clear to me again. But now, he had to make his way home for dinner. It was almost dark when he reached his front gate. The family's maid was on the doorstep, one sandal on her foot and the other in her hand.

"I was going out to look for you. Your dinner will get cold. Come in quickly, boy," she said. The boy had been staying out late these past weeks and she wondered what he had been doing. He never came home dirty and he always came home quiet. But tonight, she was glad that she had been spared the trouble of going out after him so she asked him no questions.

He sat down and ate his dinner quickly and quietly. The television set was on but he hardly paid any attention to it. His younger sister sat transfixed by the flickering images which he could not make out from where he sat. Their parents had not come home yet and family dinners were rare because the children were not expected to wait.

Dinner downed, he went upstairs to bathe. He splashed cold water over his eyes again and again and tried to open his eyes in a basin of water. His eyes smarted, but the coolness was refreshing and for a brief moment, the bathroom tiles all seemed clearly defined.

That night, Wings knelt down to pray.

When Wings was nine years old, he thought of a wonderful way to die. Not every nine-year-old boy can think of a wonderful way to die, so he took some pride in that. In fact, most would not even think of dying, let alone in a wonderful way.

But Wings knew how to die.

He wanted to die in the cockpit of a fighter jet, screaming through the air like an angel of steel. To die in aerial combat, a heat-seeking missile to turn his angel of steel into a ball of orange flame and debris. How else could a fighter pilot choose to die?

He did not want to be run down by a car on the streets. He did not want to die with sleeping pills like his mother had once tried. He did not want to die of old age, caged in a body weakened by time. Wings wanted to go in a final burst of glory, doing what he loved best, in the airplane he would love more than anything else. Brought down by another man, like him, who would be scared too, but determined. A man who would love his airplane and his wings as much as Wings did his. Brother on wings, and he would be the better pilot. Anyone lesser would have gone down in his gunsights.

Unfortunately for Wings, but happily for the rest of the World, God got wind of his plans and promptly grounded him. Thou shalt not fly. The order came down like a thunderbolt and God's heat-seeking missile found Wings first and the boy found himself with myopia.

It is very difficult to say when, but there came a day when things became less clear and it was not the mist nor the stuff that sometimes collects on morning eyes. The blackboard in class got harder to read. Maybe it's the light. Maybe I'm tired, Wings told himself. Something copied wrong and he gave his father the excuse about his vision. He began testing Wings' eyes, making him read car licence plates from a distance. Wings suddenly realised he couldn't. But then again, who read car licence plates from a distance everyday besides traffic cops? Wings began to worry anyway.

Then came the school health visit team. It is said that people under stress do not read eye test charts very well. Wings was under stress. He wanted so bad to pass that test, more than any other test the school had set. Predictably, he failed. The most important test and the only one he ever failed in primary school.

Some people accept their fate, though Wings often wondered why. Some accept their lack of height (Wings never said short) and some accept the fact that they are not the most attractive people in the world. Wings had grown up compact, average-looking and with a touch above average intelligence. Which was OK with him. After all, the perfect height, the perfect figure, the perfect face, the perfect mind were standards that changed with the times anyway. But Wings knew what perfect human vision is — 6/6, 20-20, no more, no less. He had lost that, or maybe he never had it.

The day his glasses came was the day the nightmare came true. He'd been telling himself all the way to the optician and back and through the wait for the things that it was all a bad dream and that God was only joking and every night before he slept, he'd tell himself that he would wake up and see perfectly well again. But he did not. He put the crystalline chains around his eyes and the world jumped into sickeningly sharp focus — a sharpness he had never cherished before. But Wings' world, the one inside of him, went dark.

"That's it son, you'll never fly now," his father said. The words cut deep and the world suddenly blurred again as he felt a wet heat rise up in his eyes. Wings turned away.

"So?" There was nothing else to say.

2

BESIDES piano lessons, which Wings had to endure because his mother did not want him to grow up to be a Philistine like his father, Wings had to attend ballet lessons too. He had no part in the lessons of course. It was his sister who was trotting around in a white miniskirt and tapping a tambourine not always in time with the music. Saturdays were often spent at the academy because his mother took them out to lunch before lessons and sometimes for a bit of shopping after.

Had Wings been older, he would have enjoyed those afternoons. Where else could one find so many generally pretty and generally graceful females in one aging bungalow? As he sat in the parents' waiting room with his mother or as he wandered along dark wooden-floored corridors, gaggles of girls ran by, their noses held high for improved air-intake as they passed the grubby little boy. Senior girls, sleek in their black leotards glided past, pointed shoes slung casually over slim shoulders, peering patronisingly down pretty noses at the kid in the shadows.

Wings disliked them all. He was destined to forget his childhood aversion for ballerinas and had he remembered, he would have been spared much heartache.

But at the age of nine, Wings had a major crisis in his hands. He had lost a dream, now that he could no longer fly. Up till then, everything in his life had been directed towards the earning of his wings. Now, he felt like a bird caged by his shortened range of vision. I cannot fly far because I cannot see far. Life was now a shutdown runway with nowhere to go but back to the hangar.

His mother had noticed the change. The boy had stopped building Lego airplanes. He kept away from model airplane shelves in toy stores. The aviation books in his library at home were gathering dust. There was a part of her that was relieved he could not fly. She had no wish to receive her son's body in a flag-covered casket. She had to find him a new interest in life.

"Son, would you like to start dancing too?" she asked him as they headed north for home one Saturday. It had never occurred to Wings that boys dance too as he had never seen any at the academy.

"I'm a boy."

"Yes, I know dear, but boys do take ballet lessons. The girls must have boys to dance with. Look at Nureyev."

"Who?"

"Never mind. It's good exercise and it will help you develop good strong muscles and a very nice posture."

That got Wings vaguely interested as she knew it would.

"Why don't you look at the brochure, it's in my bag there."

He dug around and found the leaflet. He did not read it because his attention was caught by pictures of a boy and a girl in ballet-student attire. The girl's outfit was familiar to him because his sister wore that.

"Mum, the boys don't wear pants."

"Rubbish, son. The drawing isn't good. The boys wear tights."

"Tights?"

"Yes, those black things the senior girls wear."

"That's pantyhose!"

"Something like that," and she knew she had said the wrong thing the moment she finished.

"Nope. I'm not doing anything without my pants. I don't want to dance in pantyhose. That's for girls."

And so, what might have been a brilliant dancing career ended before it began because an ex-fighter jock would not wear girls' underwear.

But even fallen angels must soon learn to live amongst ground-crawling mortals and Wings' mother began to worry as he began to cycle aimlessly around the estate. He needed something to give his passion to. If Wings had been in his teens, she might have suggested a girlfriend, but even that would have been a far from perfect solution. She did not even bother trying to convince him to give his love to the piano. It was hard enough dragging him to weekly lessons. His father would be no help, she thought. An uncultured academic, the man's main quest in life was for knowledge. Even as a boy, he had never indulged in games. The only time he had turned from his books was to court her and when she had been won and walked down the aisle, he promptly went back to study.

"Son, don't you have anything else to do besides pretending your bicycle is an aeroplane?" she asked him one morning as he prepared to fly the Dawn Patrol.

"Yes, sometimes it's a tank."

"No, boy, I meant like why don't you play football or something?"

"Don't like it."

"If I can get Dad to bring you to the pool every week…"

"He's too busy. I already tried. Besides, I want to be an eagle, not a fish."

"Come down to earth, boy."

Wings knew what his mother was getting at, but he gave her a blank stare.

"Why should I? I like it up here."

Everything that was ever worth achieving was born as a dream. The message was clear in Wings' mind. He had read that in one of his books. Flight for man began as a dream. The Montgolfiers, the Wrights, the Lindberghs, Fokkers, Messerschmitts, Yeagers of this world. They dreamt — and did. But Wings was feeling like an Icarus. As he watched the running and shouting boys in the field below chase a little black and white ball between goalposts, he felt more isolated than ever. Why don't I like what everybody else does? Why do I feel so funny when I try to be like them? Perched at the top of the slope, he was like an eagle watching the crows at play. Same outside, he thought. But different inside. Maybe I'm a sissy. No, can't be. I refused to dance in pantyhose. Why did you have to make me different — no why did you let me know I'm different. Was happy when I could see OK. Never thought I was different. Didn't care anyway. Wings couldn't answer his own questions. He waited a little longer and since God did not seem to be answering either, he climbed into the cockpit of his Spitfire and flew home slowly.

"Ever thought of being a cub scout, son?" Wings' mother asked at breakfast one morning. Wings had given it some vague consideration once, but flying schedules had been hectic then and he had not given it deep thought. His mother had been talking to some of her friends about Wings' inactivity and they had suggested the Boy Scouts. She herself had been in the Girls' Brigade, but she did not want Wings in the Boys' Brigade because it would mean going to church and she and her husband had neither time nor use for religion at the moment.

"Scouts would be good for Wing Cheong. He'll have boys his own age to play with and a lot of things to keep him busy.

He'll be so busy trying to earn his achievement badges he won't have time to daydream. And as he gets older, he'll have to look after the younger boys."

"He doesn't look after his sister."

"Dear me, that's different. I think boys, and scouts especially, have very different ideas about brotherhood. It will be good for your boy."

"I will ask him. I can't think of anything else."

"So how, son?" The boy looked thoughtful. But he always looks like that when his mind's not here, she sighed to herself. He nodded.

"Good. You're about the right age. There's a unit in your school. Why don't you look for the notice board and go see the teacher in charge?" Wings nodded again. A reconnaissance mission. Fly into hostile airspace. Land behind enemy lines. Spy. Evade and escape to friendly forces. It was a simple enough mission. Wings was ready.

3

THE next day at school, Wings went hunting for the troop's notice board. It was not hard to find. It was a very primitive and makeshift-looking thing adorned with knotted ropes and twigs lashed together with thread. The softboard was punctured with tiny pinholes and cracked and peeling paint was the insignia of Baden Powell's Scouts. It did not fire his imagination. There was a scrap of paper tacked to the board and it read:

GARDENING NEXT SATURDAY,
PARADE AT 9.00 AM. AKELA.

So that was what Scouts did. Dig around in gardens. Wings was even less impressed. Weeding the school gardens was not Wings' idea of a good way of spending a perfectly good Saturday morning. But Wings had already decided to do a little scouting himself. He would be there next Saturday and would see for himself what sort of people weeded gardens on Saturdays when there were much better things to do like cruising on his bike.

"Scouts," said his father, "are people who go first into unknown places to bring back information or to prepare the way ahead so that others may get there safely. Sometimes, they will look for water, for good hunting grounds, safe campsites, maybe even make trails for people to follow. In war, scouts spy on the enemy. But to do all this, the scout must be very independent, very observant, brave, smart and cunning. He must also be very quiet and very calm when in danger." As he warmed to his subject, the literati in him awoke. "The scout will see, but he himself will not be seen. He will hear, but not be heard. The scout may strike but he himself will not be struck. He is like the knight in chess," he said as he moved his knight in a left flanking movement. He made a melodramatic sweeping gesture after he put the piece down. "Going where no man has gone before, full of courage and very dangerous. Check." Wings stared at the chessboard. His father pondered awhile. "And deadly. Mate."

Wings had simply asked his father for a dictionary definition of scouts. But he had given the boy a full sales pitch and Wings was agog with the new information. He had never seen scouts in that light before. Up till then, they had only been gardeners to him or car washers (he had seen some of them on Job-Week). He had also unknowingly lent the mystique of the knight to the Scouts. The Scouts were not quite there, but they had now come very close to the essence of the fighter pilot Wings had always hoped to be. The romance, the gallantry of that loveliest of chess pieces, the Knight. The stealth, the elusiveness — see but not be seen, hear but not be heard, strike but not be struck — of a ninja assassin. The man had been looking at the chessboard as he spoke. If he had been watching his son, he would have seen the sudden spark in the boy's eyes and the change in his expression from concentration to dream mode.

As Wings rode the bus to school on Saturday, he went over his plan mentally. All the planning had been done mentally anyway so that there would be no damning evidence on paper.

He had everything he needed in a little satchel slung across his skinny body. All he lacked were the cyanide pills if he ever got caught. But he did not intend to let himself get caught.

The plane drew close to the drop zone and standing at the door, Wings felt the bitter morning cold as the wind lashed his body. Then they were over the DZ and Wings jumped. He floated down in darkness down the slope of the school's driveway and landed in a quadrangle of grass. Hurriedly, he gathered his chute into a silken bundle and buried it beneath a bush. He reached into his satchel and drew out his Colt .45 to check his rounds and cocked it. One does not jump with cocked weapons. He slipped it into the holster hidden in his jacket and stepped out to disappear into a passing crowd of peasants.

Moving towards his objective, he looked around for a place from which he could see the parade square and the school gardens at the same time. There was a convenient hedgerow in front of a toolshed. The shed was on a little rise and it overlooked the parade square and some of the garden. Wings did not make straight for it. That would have been too obvious. Instead he took a longer route around the gardens, jumping in and out of drains to keep out of sight. Finally reaching the toolshed, he positioned himself comfortably in a dry drain and peeped from below the hedge to check his field of observation. Yes, he could see most of what he had come here to watch. He settled down to wait.

He had been in position an hour when his stomach rumbled for a post-breakfast snack. He checked his watch. There was still time for a bite. He took out a Mars bar from his bag and leaned back to enjoy his fighting rations. The .45 was within arm's reach and his ears were tuned to high-sensitivity mode. Which was why he had chosen the Mars bar. It was not crunchy and thus did not interfere with aural reception.

The bar was half-gone when he heard the sounds of enemy

troopers falling in on the parade square. Quickly, he wrapped up the remains of his rations and put the binoculars to his eyes.

There were seven rows of men, each row with an unequal number of men. Wings reckoned that each row was a patrol and the unequal numbers must have been due to men lost through capture or death. At the head of every patrol stood the leaders, who stood out because they were usually taller and wore more badges. In front of the entire troop stood two women in uniform. One of the patrol leaders stepped forward and called the troop to attention. He was a somebody here, Wings thought. Look at all those badges. A scout carrying a folded flag marched up to the flagpole. Through his binoculars, Wings watched the boy fumbling with the knots while the troop waited impatiently for him to be ready. At last, flag fastened, the troop began the national anthem, with the red-faced boy trying to raise the flag at such a speed that it would just reach the pole's top on the last note of the anthem. He was too slow however and the anthem's final note was followed by the squeaking of a rusty pulley as the scout covered the last two feet. Wings laughed softly from his hiding place.

"Alright boys, go and change into your T-shirts and come back here in ten minutes and I'll tell you what to do for gardening today," one of the women said. That was probably Akela, Wings thought. The boys melted away into the school building and the parade square was empty again. He kept his binos trained on the woman and did not notice that the other one had gone.

Janet Tan was new to the school and the troop. She had just finished her training at the Teacher's Training College and had been posted to this isolated country school in the north of Singapore. Not that she was complaining, because it was fairly near to her home. But she had never thought she would have to look after cub-scouts. A choir or a dance troupe would have done better with her, she thought. An only child, she knew nothing about little boys except that they were dirty, rude, rough and devious. That described her own cousins rather well. Oh, how she wished she had been given a girls' school. At least they would have been familiar.

She walked *tappitytap* in her black uniform court shoes up to the toolshed to unlock the door for the boys. At the door, she tried the keys in the bunch and the third one clicked the lock open. She went inside to count the tools the boys would need. There were no lights in the shed so she stood away from the door, letting the light from outside fill the shed. Suddenly, she heard a grating sound, saw the shed darken and felt her heart sink when she realised that she was shut in. Too shocked to say anything, she ran to the door but could not open it. When she found her voice, she shouted but no one answered. It was fifteen minutes before she heard the sound of shuffling feet outside and shouted again. Someone lifted the latch and the door slid open.

"Oh, er, Miss Tan what are you doing here?" asked the scout.

"I was locked in. Someone closed the door when I was in here." The boys outside laughed and she became suspicious.

"Was it you, Justin?"

The scout's eyes widened. He quickly shook his head and the other boys laughed again. Janet Tan smiled too.

"You're doing weeding today, Justin."

Wings sat in the school tuckshop breathing hard. Dressed like a local yokel, no one would notice him. He could not believe what he had just done. He had almost been caught by an enemy officer, but he had heard her coming and dodged round a corner just in time. He had realised a little too late that it was not a good idea to be hiding near a toolshed when enemy troops were planning to do gardening that day. Quick thinking and fast movements had saved him from getting caught. He had sneaked round to the door when the officer was inside and bumped her off with his silenced .45. The door was quickly closed to avoid arousing the suspicion of passing sentries. (Actually, he had shut the door because the path up to the toolshed led directly to the door and she would have seen him fleeing if she had turned around. Also, he had never locked a teacher into a room before. It was really quite exhilarating.)

Still feeling quite proud of himself, he bought himself a drink and settled down to watch the peasants working in their fields. Today was the first time that he had taken a really good look at the scouts. He did not like their uniform. That jersey-thing they wore was a bit too much like something from a girls' school. It had no buttons. And the scarf — was it really necessary, especially the red stripes that made it look like a candy cane? He also objected to the shorts, which were rather long. The cap was a redeeming feature and so were the badges. They were special. Every badge meant that one could do something well, that one was getting somewhere in life. They were things one could work for and the results could be worn on a shoulder for the world to see. Why boast when one could quietly flash a badge? The badges also meant that Scouts did more than weed gardens on weekends. This must have been a bad week for them. His mother said they went on hikes. They went camping and had campfires with the Brownies (which was no big deal to Wings). Enid Blyton said they had adventures. Baden Powell promised a grand life. Wings remembered the senior Scouts on the parade square. Tall and commanding. The younger Scouts snapped to attention on a single word. And the Scout who was a Somebody — how did he get to be Somebody? A magic was being worked out in his mind — everything his parents had told him, what he had read and what he had just seen today — it was a potent spell his imagination was casting on him. Was this where dreams and the real world met? Once he could only play the adventurer, but this was for real. These boys actually did those things that hitherto had only been dreams for Wings.

He looked for the older woman in uniform. She was standing in a corner of the nursery supervising a few boys with watering cans and a garden hose. Wings was about to go up to her when the other woman whom he recognised as the one he had locked in appeared from behind some orchids. It was a critical moment, but Wings told himself that she had probably not seen him. He got his courage together and decided to go for it. .45 and other equipment safely out of sight, Wings stepped boldly up to the woman he felt was more likely to be Mrs Akela. He kept his eyes to the front to avoid meeting those of Janet Tan's.

"Excuse me ma'am."

"Yes, boy?"

"I want to be a Scout."

4

WINGS' mother was overjoyed. His father was amused. His sister was disgusted. It was written all over her sulky face as Wings suddenly found himself the centre of attention of family and friends. The kid sister found that hard to swallow as she had been the family star up till then. She could not understand why Wings was being given so much attention just because he had joined a pack of dirty, rowdy, backwoods boys. She saw him whisked off to Sand's House, home of the Singapore Scouts, to be outfitted. She saw him return with all the paraphernalia that made up the exterior of a Scout. She heard the interested and excited voices of friends and relations who dropped by and talked scouting with her brother. It will not last, she told herself. It had better not.

She looked at her own white ballet tunic with the baby pink belt. Now, wasn't that a lot sweeter than that grubby khaki thing her brother had just bought? I can dance, she told herself. All he will do is sing stupid campfire songs and act out stupid things. She looked at her piano books. They say I'm talented. I can play the piano too and I passed grade one with distinction. He hasn't even taken his first exam.

I'll be a famous pianist and dancer when I grow up. He's

only going to be a *kachang puteh* seller. It was a comforting thought and it helped her to forget Wings' sudden and short-lived popularity as she played and thumped the ivory scales to stardom.

It was with great relief that she heard her son's decision to be a Scout. At last, he would have a direction in life. It would also mean the end of daydreaming and a never-ending moroseness. She immediately got in touch with Mrs Han, the troop's teacher-in-charge to make it official. Once she said yes, Wings could be a Scout, the excited mother whisked him off to be uniformed before his interest waned and he changed his mind. She knew the little boy well enough. He had an extremely short attention span and quickly lost interest in anything if nothing was happening. He could sit with his Lego bricks for days on end or spend entire afternoons drawing airplanes or reading or pretending his bicycle was a Spitfire because something was happening in his mind. But the moment something failed to fire his imagination, he promptly left it alone. This boy is going to have problems with girls when he grows up. Fidelity is not going to be a virtue, she sighed. Solve one problem and another comes along. Never mind. I shall burn that bridge only when I come to it, she thought.

My son the Scout, his father mused. I was never a Scout. There was no time. The books, always the books. Yet have I suffered from the lack of something other than books. No, no. The books. I am here today because of the attention I paid them. Is there not the building of character too, when a boy forces himself to sit by his books instead of running in the gutters with the other boys. My face in a different sort of gutter — one between the books. Ha, yes. And a man shall leave his parents and cleave unto his books. Good. Selling cake on the streets — builds character like no ECA can. Poverty teaches more than any uniformed group. Hunger coaches and disciplines in ways no man in a track suit can on the running tracks and playing fields. Empires won on the playing fields of Eton? Bah. Same boys lost the empire. If only they had grown up on the streets. Sun would never have set on the Union Jack. But my own kid out on the streets. No. Poor? No. Hungry? Never. Too young for the university of life. But when indeed are we ready. Ah, well. Better the Scouts and the discipline of being in uniform. Yes. Better and safer than the streets at any rate.

Wings was overwhelmed by all the attention and did not know what to do with it. Why does everybody suddenly want to talk to me? He became a passive participant, hearing words of praise, yes, joining the Scouts is a really good idea, words of exhortation, you must really try your best to be a Commissioner's Scout, maybe even a President's Scout when you're bigger, words of warning, but really, boy, don't forget to study, a Scout must really be good at everything including Chinese and Mathematics, words describing the glory of being a Scout, and when you hear that last bugle call when the sun goes down, you must be able to tell yourself that you have done your best, and knowing so, rest easy.

"I heard you're joining the Scouts, Wings," an aunt said to him one evening. "I brought you something that might help you," she said as she rummaged in her bag. She was the first person who had brought something more than words. She came up with a thin paperback, with pages yellowed and spotted, and a cover that had seen a lot of handling. Wings wondered what it was. She put it into his hands. The cover was green with a curious pattern. Wings looked closer and realised that the pattern was really a black and white photograph of hundreds of Scouts standing in formation, stiffly at attention. It had been coloured green presumably because of Scouting's association with all things wild and wonderful. And in dark red, Wings read the title: *Scouting for Boys*. At the bottom of the cover, in smaller print was the name of the man who had written the book.

"Robert Baden Powell. Auntie, this is the Founder," Wings said excitedly.

"Yes, boy. This is the very first book he wrote for his Scouts. It's like a bible for Scouts." Up till then, Wings had only heard the word bible used in one context — the book one finds in church. That was a holy book, where everything in it was supposed to be true and like a street directory to virtuous living and the pearly gates. He ran his fingers reverently down a yellow page.

"Thank you, Auntie. Where did you get it from?"

"I was Akela once." It was only then that Wings realised Akela was not someone's name but a title.

"What does it mean, Auntie?"

"Mother Wolf."

Wings laughed. "My, what big teeth you have!"

"All the better to bite you with, rascal."

Wings looked at his aunt with new respect. She was no longer just any old aunt. She had been Akela — Mother Wolf and leader of the pack.

5

WINGS stood at attention in the Saturday morning sun. He was on the parade square which he had watched a fortnight ago. From where he stood, he could not see very far ahead as the Scout in front was much taller and all he could see was the coat-of-arms on the back of his scarf. He could not move his head around either as he was supposed to be at attention. Moving his eyeballs left, he could just make out his toolshed hideout above the caps of the Scouts that side of him.

The flag was raised and the anthem sung, followed by the pledge. All this Wings was familiar with. Then in a single action, all the older Scouts raised their right arms halfway up, with only three fingers showing. Wings tried to follow, but it felt awkward trying to hold his pinky down with his thumb. And in one voice, they began to recite the Scout's Promise:

> "We promise to do our best
> To do our duty to God
> And the Republic of Singapore
> To help other people
> And to keep the Scout's Law."

Wings was lost. The troop gave the Scout's three-fingered salute with Wings a moment late. The Somebody Scout turned around smartly and gave them the command to disperse. The troop turned sharply to the right, marched three steps, punched their right fists into the air and shouted something unintelligible.

"What did you all say?" Wings asked the tall Scout in front of him. The Scout looked down from his height.

"That was Latin. We said '*nulli secundus*'."

"Oh. But what does it mean?"

"You mean you don't know?"

Wings shook his head.

"Well, you better know now and remember it. It means second to none."

"What's second to none?"

"Us, stupid."

"Why don't we just say 'first'?"

"Wouldn't be the same, dummy. It's like poetry you know. You say things in fancy ways to make it sound better. Besides, I don't think anyone here knows how to say 'first' in Latin."

Akela's voice rang down the corridor and Wings saw the new Scouts scampering to her. He could tell they were new. They were all about the same size as he was and all their uniforms were bare of badges.

"You better go too, brat," the Scout said. Wings ran.

They were herded into a classroom and Janet Tan called out their names amid the general chaos. Wings thought it was a bit too much like school.

"All right, boys, I'm going to tell you which Six you're in. When I call your name, come up here and get your woggle. Did you all bring your scarves with you?" There was more squealing and shouting and shuffling as the new wolf-cubs scrambled to get their scarves.

Six? Woggle? Scouting had a language all its own and Wings was lost, but he did as he was told. His woggle was grey so that meant he was a member of Grey Six.

"This is how you roll your scarf," Janet Tan said as she demonstrated. Idiotic thing, she thought. Really so hard to get exactly three stripes on each side. But she succeeded. She put the scarf around her neck and slipped a woggle up the two ends till it reached her throat. She felt consoled as she watched the little boys struggle with the operation. Wings thought it was a terribly dangerous thing to wear. It was so easy for an enemy to throttle you with your own scarf and woggle in a hand-to-hand fight.

"Okay. Your Six is like your gang. It's called a Six because that's how many of you there are supposed to be. But there's too many of you, so there will be more than six of you, alright? Every Six is called by a colour and that's the colour on your woggles, alright? Any questions, boys?"

"Can I change colour, teacher?"

"No." She opened her file again. Now, to brief you gentlemen on your career development paths.

"Fine. I will now tell you something more about Scouts. You are now cub-scouts. Wolf-cubs, er, baby wolves and Mrs Han and me are like your mother wolves, okay?" There was a restrained giggle from the back of the class followed by a high-pitched howl. A chorus of wolves began. She ignored it.

"A Six," she said as loudly as she could without shouting, "is like a wolf pack and your leader — we call him a Sixer — is like your big wolf brother."

"Who's afraid of the Big Bad Wolf?" a boy in the corner sang and the wolf-cubs dissolved into chortles. Wicked little things. Wolf is a very appropriate metaphor, she felt. Only a man could have created such an organisation and given it such a name.

"No, boys. Scouts are supposed to be good wolves." And

I am a sheep in a wolves' den. She tried to smile but gave up the effort.

"If you are good wolves and earn your badges, you could become an Assistant Sixer or even a Sixer one day with your own wolf pack." Motorcycle gangs probably grew up as Scouts. Where else could wolf whistles come from? No, that wasn't fair. Her boys were quite lovable sometimes. They just sapped her energy and she did not have very much energy today.

Wings saw her trying to smile and giving up and he felt a little sorry for her. The cubs were still relatively well behaved. Maybe it was the older Scouts. Maybe wolves were like dogs — cute and adorable as puppies but horrors when grown up. Wings felt a slight twinge of guilt over the lock-in incident. Maybe she can see grown-up wolves in us. He noticed for the first time that she was rather pretty and young. He felt a little worse. Heroes could lock up ugly evil old witches, stepmothers and suchlike. But not pretty country lasses. The cubs were starting to make a lot of noise again but she was immobilised. Well, I never scored well for command and control at TTC. She found her voice after a minute.

"Wolf-cubs, please keep your noise down. There's more that I have to tell you. Scouts are supposed to be polite and well behaved. You'll find that in your Scout Law which you'll have to learn for your first test."

There was a general protest. Wings had heard about the tests so the news did not bother him. But to the other boys, tests smacked too much of school. Janet found herself smiling. I will not be the only one to suffer here, you little horrors. This is where the Empire strikes back.

"And you must pass them if you want your badges." Gotcha where it hurts, monsters. That should make you toe the line. She looked around with a feeling of peace within. She turned the page of her briefing file.

"Now, I'll tell you the history of the Scouts," she said with a sudden sweetness in her voice. Once upon a time, there was a Big Bad Wolf named Robert Baden Powell who never wanted to stay home in his family's den, but was always running about outside in all seasons and in all kinds of weather … and set a bad example that millions of boys follow till this day.

6

ANOTHER fortnight passed. The new wolf-cubs were not yet weaned from Akela. But they finally earned their first two badges and their rightful places in the troop. Once his uniform had been bare save for his district patch and his unit number tapes. The troop was 1010. Ten-Ten, the older Scouts said, meant that whatever the troop did, they did to perfection and would always aim to score full points. Ten upon ten, just like in school. We promise to do our best. We promise to be the best. Failure is not in our creed. *Nulli secundus*. Akela had a lower-keyed interpretation of ten-ten.

"It's like the hands of a watch, boys. When the hands read ten past ten, they look like a smile. And Scouts must keep up a smile no matter what happens, which is Scout Law number eight."

Wings understood what she meant because he wore a Mickey Mouse watch, but there were some puzzled wolf-cubs trying to find a smile in digital faces. Wings' relatives had not bothered with fancy interpretations. They had simply bought 4-D with it and when the number did not win (in spite of the fact that failure was not in the unit's creed), most of them had lost interest in Wings' new life. His kid sister had been right. His glory could not last.

He looked at his new badges with pride. There was the World Scout badge, round and purple over his heart. There was the badge of the Singapore Scouts on his cap. He had good reason to be proud too. Most cub-scouts only learnt the promise and five laws. But 1010 boys learnt all ten laws as The Founder had laid them down. They lived in a decimal world where everything had to come in tens if possible. Janet Tan had wanted to tell them it really looked more like a binary number that meant vacillation because it would have read 'yes-no-yes-no' to a computer. But she did not have the heart.

"1010 Scouts take it all the way. Besides it's our number. Our Ten Commandments," said Benjamin the Somebody Scout. He carried a squiggly staff with the head and tail of a snake carved on it. Wings did not know his Bible very well, but what he could vaguely remember of the stories made him see something strangely Mosaic about Benjamin.

There were two slices of a large log that hung high on a wall in the troop den. The Scout Law had been burnt onto them, five aside, with a soldering iron and varnished. Benjamin, the only Scout in the troop who wore a gold arrow on his sleeve, had taken the tablets down to the classroom and taught them the Law.

"A Scout is to be trusted. That means you must never lie or cheat and never break your promises or let other people down.

"A Scout is loyal. That means you got to be on your friend's side at all times. You must defend your troop no matter what.

"A Scout must help other people. That's easy so I won't explain.

"A Scout is everybody's friend and a brother to every Scout. That means that you must not make enemies and not quarrel, especially with another Scout.

"A Scout is polite to everybody.

"A Scout is kind to animals. You must not kick stray dogs or bully kittens or shoot birds. But it's okay if you kill animals for food or if they are dangerous.

"A Scout is obedient. He got to take orders from those bigger than him.

"A Scout keeps smiling no matter what happens.

"A Scout is thrifty which means you can't waste money. Save whatever you can.

"A Scout is clean in thought, word and deed. You can't say bad words. You can't think dirty things and do stuff like touch girls. That's all." There, he had done it. He could now forget it until the next time he had to renew his Scout's Promise.

Janet Tan wondered what Benjamin had that she did not. He was only twelve but the wolf-cubs had sat through his lesson in absolute silence and with total attention. He was not tall for his age and he was a little pudgy. But he was *The* Scout as far as the wolf-cubs were concerned. The badges said it all. Every cub wanted to grow up to be Benjamin. She sighed. I suppose I'd worry if any one of my boys wanted to grow up to be me.

"Alright, boys, today is the day you join your Sixes," Mrs Han announced at last. There was a cheer and the boys got up and ran out of the classroom amidst the clatter of falling chairs and the scraping of tables roughly pushed. They fell in outside still chattering excitedly.

"Always the same isn't it," Mrs Han said to Janet. "Even wolves must leave their mums. There's just a part of them that we can't reach."

"But they come back when they're grown."

"To women, yes, but not the First Lady. And in the meantime, they must run with the pack."

"Call of the wild," Janet whispered to herself. Not a memory buried in the musty pages of literature texts. No, alive in my heart, memory of a boy I could not hold. She was not the only one who lost him. They had found pieces of his Skyhawk in the South China Sea, but they had never found him.

Outside, Sixers and their Assistants were shepherding their new wolf-cubs to the respective Six Hideouts for their initiation rites.

7

WINGS sat with Peter, his Sixer, under the shade of a frangipani tree. Broad oval leaves were scattered around. Some were brown and crackled when stepped on. White-yellow flowers dotted the ground. The shade was not complete and beams of sunlight came through, falling on their faces in a patchwork of light and shadow. Boon Ming, the only other recruit in Grey Six, was being shown some of the things the Six had made and photos of what they had done. Wings was going through the interview part of the initiation. He had heard something about Grey Six. The other Scouts called them Saint Peter's Greys.

"Why do they call you — I mean us — Saint Peter's Greys?"

"I'm Peter, I'm the Sixer and we're Grey Six. That's why."

"Why are you a Saint?"

Peter laughed.

"Why do you think I'm called Saint?"

"Because you're good?"

"You know the Law?"

"Of course. That's how I got my badges."

"Will you remember it?"

"Sure. Aren't we supposed to?"

"Not everybody does, Wings."

"Do you?"

"Yes, Wings. And I like to remind people of it. And if you want to remind people of the Law, you have to follow it, see?"

"Is it hard to follow?"

"Sometimes."

"You follow it all the time?"

"I try."

"Do you always make it?"

"Mostly."

"What happens when you don't?"

"You'll feel awful if you're a good Scout. That's how you know you've broken the Law. Nobody has to tell you."

"What if you're not a good Scout?"

"Then it really doesn't matter anyway."

Peter was scratching something on the ground with a stick.

"But the Law is kind of funny because it means different things sometimes and everybody has his own way of looking at it."

Wings looked blank.

"You won't understand now because you're new. You will later, if you stay on and become a Sixer."

That seemed such a long way off. Wings could not imagine how he could see the Law in any other way than how Benjamin had said it was.

"So what do I do now, Peter?"

"Does God exist?"

"Of course." Wings wondered what God had to do with the Scouts' version of the Ten Commandments.

"How do you know?"

"My Grandma said so."

"Maybe she lied."

"She wouldn't lie. She's not like that."

"If you believe in God, you must believe that all men are evil inside. Nobody's perfect. Not even your Grandma. She could have lied."

"She wouldn't!"

"Did she tell you about Santa Claus?"

"Yes…"

"Does Santa Claus exist?"

"That's different!"

"Did it feel good to believe in Santa Claus?"

"Yes."

"Does it feel good to believe in God?"

"Yes."

"What makes you think it isn't just another one of Granny's tales? Something she told you just to make you behave?"

"So many people believe. They can't all be wrong."

"Many people didn't believe that Jesus was God's son. Yet you say they're wrong."

"The Bible says it's true."

"Do you believe in the word of God?"

"Sure."

"Why?"

"Because my Grandma said so."

"Have you ever read it yourself?"

"Er, no."

"Then how do you know it's true?"

"It's true!"

"What proof?"

There was a long silence.

"Do you believe, then?" Peter asked.

"Urmm…"

"You may believe because I say so."

8

BASIC was over and it had not been anything to write home about. There had also been lessons on the Promise and Law. In between lessons and tests, there had been songs, none of which made a very deep impression on Wings. When was the real action going to start? Wings had joined for adventure, not for sing-along sessions. The novelty of being a Scout was starting to wear off.

Boon Ming however, took great delight in learning campfire songs. "Well, it's better than gardening," he said in consoling tones to Wings one morning. Wings shot him a dirty look and the plump boy carried on with 'Ging Gang Goolie'. Janet saw Boon Ming stick his tongue out at Wings as he turned back to join the singing. A quarrel might break the monotony of things, she thought, so she watched the pair. But Boon Ming was singing with gusto and he had quite forgotten about his patrolmate's slight. Wings was singing under his breath and his hands were merely going through the motions of 'Father Abraham' had seven children and seven children had 'Father Abraham'. He was looking out of the window and slouching in his chair and thinking of his bicycle.

Janet walked up behind him and put a hand on his shoulder.

Startled, Wings jumped in his seat and looked around quickly. "Are you alright?" she asked softly. Wings' eyes went up her necktie to her face. Oh no, he had avoided her successfully all these weeks. What did she want? Had she found out?

"Is something wrong?" she asked again. Wings shook his head quickly and mentally resolved never to lock teachers in toolsheds again. Boon Ming was distracted and turned around too.

"He doesn't like singing, Miss Tan," he said.

"Why not? These are Scouts' songs. You learn them so you can sing them at campfires or when you're hiking."

"I know that, that's why I like singing them," Boon Ming said.

"Why don't you like them?" she asked Wings.

"I just don't. Singing's very dull." His mother had once told him that guilty people never dared to look the righteous in the eyes. He was trying very hard now to out-stare Janet Tan. Why is this little boy looking at me like that? She nodded her head.

"Don't worry. Singing isn't the only thing Scouts do. There's a campfire a week after you join your Sixes. Then there's a short hike at the reservoir, a weekend camp in school, some lessons in Scout craft like tying knots and of course a bit of gardening. That's how we serve the school. The rest of the time you'll have to prepare projects for your tests to get your badges."

"Okay."

"Feel better?"

"Yes, Miss Tan." She smiled at him and walked away.

Boon Ming watched Wings curiously. After a minute, he spoke.

"I know! You like her."

"Who?"

"Miss Tan. You like Miss Tan!" Boon Ming hissed into his ear.

Wings was aghast. "No, I don't!"

"Sure you don't. You were staring at her. You sure look like you like her," he giggled.

"I don't," Wings said fiercely.

Boon Ming was unconvinced. He smiled magnanimously.

"Don't worry. You're my buddy and patrolmate so I won't tell anyone. Alright, man, now we've got a secret!"

"We don't!"

"I thought you didn't want anybody to know."

"It's not true, idiot! There's no secret when something isn't true."

"You don't trust me. And I thought we were brother Scouts. Scouts' Law number one says a Scout is to be trusted. You can trust me and I can practise keeping the Law."

"Fat fool!" Wings was exasperated. How on earth could he possibly tell Boon Ming the real story behind his stare?

"That hurt," Boon Ming sniffed indignantly. "But like a true brother Scout, I won't take revenge. Your secret is safe with me."

"Boon Ming! I don't like her! I hate her!"

"What are the two of you arguing about?" Janet's voice suddenly sounded behind them. Wings felt his guts suddenly dropping to his butt. But Boon Ming, though slow in everything else, was a quick-witted fat boy.

"Ooh, er. Wings hates his sister, Miss Tan."

She gave them a puzzled frown and walked away. She remembered a TTC lesson. At the time, she thought it only applied to secondary students, not P3 cub-scouts. If you teach pupils of the opposite gender (the lecturer had simply refused to say sex), a number of them will surely become infatuated with you, especially if you are an attractive person. Young boys tend to have crushes solely on the basis of a lady teacher's appearance. Girls, being creatures of greater depth and maturity (at this, the largely female class of trainee teachers applauded) go for qualities that would make a man attractive to women of any age. She had turned to the handful of sniggering men in the class and said, which would mean you lot won't have problems of this nature. Janet smiled as she remembered.

Boon Ming had turned around to check on her and caught her smiling. His mouth went straight for Wings' ear.

"Hey, Wings, I think she knows!"

"What? How?" This is impossible, Wings thought. I'm acting as if it were true.

"She's smiling at you."

The blood shot through the capillaries of Wings' face. Boon Ming turned around again and looked thoughtfully at Janet. She was looking elsewhere now, so he was safe.

"How old do you think she is?"

"Stuff it, Fats."

"Campfire's burning, campfire's burning, draw nearer, draw nearer, in the glooming, in the glooming," Boon Ming sang as he and Wings carried a bench to the field.

"Why don't you save your voice for tonight?" Wings grumbled from his end of the bench.

"I'm getting my voice ready. Tonight I'm going to sing! I'm going to dance!"

"You are weird. Why did you become a Scout then? Should've joined the choir or the dance group," Wings panted.

"I wanted to, but my Dad said it was sissy. He wants me to be a man when I grow up."

"Does he know what you're doing here?" Wings put the bench in position.

"I don't tell him. He thinks Scouts are like soldiers. You know, foot drills and sneaking around and all that stupid macho stuff."

"That's what I joined for. Not to sit around log fires to sing dumb songs."

"Uh-uh. I don't like to sweat unless I'm dancing," Boon Ming said as he loosened his woggle.

"But the only kind of dance we do is them funny action songs. Three little ducklings I once knew or one elephant began to dance, up on a spider's web one day," Wings suddenly laughed.

"That should be your song, Boon."

"I ought to beat you up for that, but I'm saving my strength for tonight."

The 1010 unit's Scoutmaster put a torch to the kerosene soaked wood and declared the campfire open. He had been a cub in 1010 and had come back twenty years later as a teacher and their master. In the glow of the firelight, he looked with pride at his boys, faces orange and the darkness that lay behind them, outside the circle of warmth.

Wings sat huddled between Boon Ming and the Tall Scout who had turned out to be the Assistant Sixer of St Peter's Greys. Nathan was a lanky Indian boy of Brahmin descent. His family had become Catholic two generations ago, but his father would not let any of his children forget their Brahmin heritage.

"Remember, Nathan, your ancestors were Brahmins, the leaders of their community. So whatever you do, you must be an example for others to follow." 1010 was just the place for him, Nathan felt. *Nulli secundus*. Winning is our way of life. Defeat is not in our creed. It felt good. He was going to take over the Six when Peter graduated from Primary School. But now, winning and being the best were far from his mind as he watched the fire. It gave him a kind of peace that he could find nowhere else in his life. Here, with brother Scouts, in a circle round a campfire, Nathan could rest from being the best.

Boon Ming was singing 'My Bonnie' tunefully and soulfully. He looked beyond his side of the fire to the other side. In the flickering firelight, he saw a face and felt something move in his chest. "My Bonnie lies over the ocean, oh bring back my Bonnie to me. My Brownie on the other side of the fire, oh bring o'er that Brownie to me. To me!" He was feeling romantic and he would have danced to her side had propriety permitted. But no, he would have to wait till the dances came and he would lead a line and stop right in front of her. His heart revved up in excitement.

Wings looked up at the purple night sky and realised that the moon was full. Round and white and bright. There was a funny feeling in his gut as he stared at the moon. He felt a restlessness welling up in him. There was something he wanted to say, to do, but he did not know what he wanted to say or do. I want to scream at the moon. I want to run with the nightwind, faster than the night. I want to break something. I want to shout at the moon, let everything come out. But people wouldn't understand. They never did anyhow. I want to cry but what for. For everything here inside that I can't let out. But what would I say to Nathan, to Boon Ming, to Miss Tan. No tears anyway, eyes are dry. His hands gripped the edge of the bench and every muscle on his tiny frame went tense. His mouth was sealed shut and his eyes were fixed on the white orb. He could vaguely hear the singing, but the words had long since become unintelligible, just a roar, like the wind that swept grey clouds past that white moon. Wings wanted to fly away fast, but where would he go.

It was time for action songs and Wings was brought back into the world outside himself as Boon Ming struggled to get up. Peter, who was master of ceremonies, looked in surprise as his recruit ran up to him the moment he asked for volunteers to lead the 'Baby Elephant' dance.

"Me, Pete!"

"Do you know the song and the actions?" Peter checked.

"Spent two weeks preparing for this campfire, Sixer. I'm ready!"

"Yo, Dumbo," someone yelled and the ring came alive with laughter. Peter grinned. Boon Ming looked the part. But the boy did not mind the heckling. *Wait till I get going. They can laugh all they want. But there's a Brownie waiting for me on the other side.* The song began and Boon Ming began the 'Baby Elephant' dance. He paced himself carefully so that he would wind up right in front of her when the song ended.

"And he called for another elephant to dance!" The verse ended and he was smack in front of her. He smiled shyly and beckoned to her. But she was shy and she shook her head in terror. The other Brownies squealed in delight and pushed her into the ring. Nathan covered his face and rolled on the bench in stitches. Wings was watching to see what would happen. She finally joined Boon Ming and the pair ambled round the ring, Boon Ming with a Cheshire smile. Ten 'Baby Elephants' later, the song ended and the line broke up. Boon Ming returned to the Grey Six bench obviously quite thrilled with himself.

"Practice pays off, buddy," he said proudly to Wings.

"Yes, you do have a cute wiggle, Dumbo," Nathan snickered. "But I must say you're very brave for a new Scout. Your turn next, Wings."

Wings looked up in horror. The rest of the Six had crowded around them and they were egging him on.

"But…" Wings began to plead. He felt a sudden coldness in all his limbs.

"You can't get out of this, Wings. All our new guys have to do this. Don't tell me you're scared. Scouts got to be brave, man," Nathan shook his head sadly.

Boon Ming saw the sheer horror in Wings' eyes and saw his opportunity to kill three birds with a single wiggle of his derriere.

"Can't you all see that he's not ready? Not everyone can do this stuff on his first night out, you know." Yes, yes, he, Boon Ming, would do his buddy, Wings, a good deed and earn his eternal gratitude. He would also earn his Six's respect for coming to the aid of his fellow Scout. And most of all, he would get another chance to pick up that Brownie again.

"Come on, Wings, what say you? I'll do it for you, buddy."

Nathan felt it was most unnatural and his eyebrows came together in deep suspicious thought. One of the P4 scouts, Eng Kiat, shook his head vehemently and Nathan acknowledged his advice with a nod.

"Nope. As Assistant Sixer, I feel it's best for Wings to do this himself." He patted Wings on the back. "Go, kid. Do it for the Greys."

Wings got up and he felt his legs tremble. Boon Ming stood up beside him.

"Lemme give you some tips." He walked Wings out of earshot of the Greys.

"This is what you got to do. Move at just the right speed so you get to that Brownie over there, the one I picked up first just now. Once you've got her, move at just the right speed so that you can pick me up."

Fear was too strong in his mind for him to realise what was going on in Boon Ming's head, so he agreed. The song began and Wings, the first 'Little Duckling', went on his way. His movements were awkward and he had trouble pacing himself. He had also forgotten the words of the song in his fear, so he did not know exactly where to stop. But as Boon Ming's luck would have it, Wings ended up exactly in front of the desired Brownie. She screamed. No, no, this could not be happening to her twice in a single night! Her friends were in fits and pushing her forward. She was a fey little creature with an Elfin face and Wings regarded her with pity.

"It's okay, you don't have to do it again. Just get somebody else," he said gruffly (how else could one speak to girls?) The Brownies teacher laughingly caught hold of a fleeing fairy and made her join the dance. Wings wondered how she had got her fairy's wings. Nothing short of a 747 could have got her off the ground. But the captain of a plane is always kind to his passengers even when they're carrying excess baggage. They carried on. As he took off, he remembered Boon Ming's instructions. This time, he remembered the words and his timing was better. As he approached the runway, he noticed Boon Ming signalling frantically. He was furiously shaking his head with a look of disaster and pointing energetically at Nathan. The rest of the Six, however, were smiling calmly and pointing at Boon Ming behind his back. Wings smiled and gave the thumbs up sign. Boon Ming looked relieved. And then the cargo plane landed right in front of him.

"I delivered! What more do you want?" Wings protested in the boys' room.

"Don't shout! They can hear us from here. There's echoes," Boon Ming hissed. He was still breathing hard from his recent encounter with a Brownie of larger proportions than himself. He leaned over a sink.

"Come on, man, I was so scared when I started I wasn't really listening to you."

"Some friend you are. I kept your secret. I could be trusted. But you couldn't be trusted to do something important for me. You got no sense of honour. And you're not loyal either."

"I already said why I did it. If I'd known what you really wanted, I would've made her join me instead of that fat Brownie."

"You know what it's like following the behind of a fat Brownie?"

"Look, the skinny one was scared and she'd done it already. I couldn't force her. Besides, everyone was pointing at you. I didn't know you were scared. Just thought you were shy," Wings said in a tired voice.

"You're blind. That's what's wrong with you man. Shortsighted, that's why you can never fly." The words were barely out of his mouth when he felt himself being yanked around by the scarf and a woggle suddenly pushed up tight against his throat.

"What's the matter with you?" Boon Ming gasped.

"You can say anything you want to me, you can call me any filthy name you know, but you will not say that to me."

He saw the mad eyes burn behind the lenses, burning into his, and then he saw the water well up to put the fire out.

"Okay, okay, I'm sorry, Wings." He felt the pressure drop. Wings washed his eyes. Boon Ming wandered over to the door. There were voices outside. He dashed in, whispering loudly.

"It's her! It's her! They're going to the loo!"

"No, don't tell me you're gonna peep."

"Of course not. I'm going to wait for her."

"And then?"

"Talk to her and get her phone number."

"How about the other Brownies?"

"You can divert their attention, just like in those spy movies," Boon Ming whispered excitedly.

"And what will we tell Nathan, we been here too long already."

"Say we were shitting."

"That's lying."

"Good cause. Did captured spies ever tell the truth when questioned?"

"When tortured."

"Peter won't do that to us."

The two boys stood quietly outside the girls' room. Boon Ming was watching the door. Wings was staring blankly at the wall when he saw a shadow start to grow on it and heard a familiar *taptaptappitytap* of black court shoes.

"Oh no," he groaned. They whipped around to see Janet Tan walking up the path to the ladies.

"Don't rat on me and your secret's safe with me," Boon Ming said softly.

"What are you boys doing here?"

"Fire was a bit hot. We're here for fresh air, Miss Tan," Boon Ming explained.

"Fresh air outside a toilet?" She folded her arms. I could make life very difficult for you, boys. Then she noticed Wings staring at her. He was very tired of everything that had happened that night. The campfire, the moon, the dance, the fat Brownie, Boon Ming's love affair and now this toilet business with all its lies. He looked doleful and yes, probably innocent, Janet thought. Besides, he's making me feel very uncomfortable, the way he looks at me.

"Go back to your Six," she commanded and they scampered off. Just then, three Brownies came skipping out (how else do they move?). Janet laughed softly to herself. Silly boys. If they had told me the truth I would have introduced them.

The boys had not gone far down the path when they shot behind a tree and crouched low. Wings put his head around the side of the trunk to scan for Janet. She was nowhere in sight but the Brownies were.

"Bogies one, two, three, at twelve o'clock," Wings announced.

"Speak English, idiot."

"They're headed for us, three of them with your girl in the centre. What's the plan?"

Boon Ming whispered urgently into his ear. As the Brownies drew near, Boon Ming suddenly got out from hiding.

"Hello, Brownies, are you lost?"

"Why should we be? This is our school too, you silly scout," the Brownie on the right said.

"Well, it's dark. I thought maybe you were lost," Boon Ming offered.

"No, we're not lost and will you let us pass," the left Brownie demanded. Boon Ming was looking straight at his heart's desire.

"What's the password, fairy?"

"I'm an elf!" she corrected.

"Well, what do you know! That was the password! You can pass, elf," he stepped aside for her.

"Elf!" the other two shouted immediately.

"I said that was the password. Past Tense, numbskulls."

His Brownie giggled. Right then, a low growl came from behind the other two Brownies and Wings jumped up from behind a bush, his scarf over his nose and mouth. The two girls screamed in unison and fled back up the path with Wings after them.

"Never fear, elf, I'll protect you! Let's run this way!" Boon Ming said to his Brownie and they ran laughing down the other way. Wings took no more than ten steps after the girls when he heard a toilet flush. He turned around and ran back after Boon Ming. Mission accomplished. Now to return to the safety of the Six.

"Wings!" Her voice cut through the night like a cold wind. He turned around and saw Janet with two crying Brownies. She looked stern and the Brownies looked like they wanted to get even.

"Why are you scaring little girls at night, Wings?" Janet was a tall, young woman and had once been a cadet sergeant in school. She could look mean if she wanted too. She looked fiercely down at Wings. This is probably the most entertaining part of the campfire, she thought. Wings only came up to her chest and was forced to look up at her. He saw his moon.

"It's a full-moon night, Miss Tan. And I'm a wolf-cub," he tried to explain. She looked incredulous. She sent the Brownies back to their troop with the promise that she would deal most severely with Wings and his elf-napping accomplice. She sat down on a stone bench so that she could see the boy face to face. Wings had given up trying to look her in the eyes. This time, he was guilty and they both knew it.

"What are the both of you trying to do?" she asked gently.

"I can't tell you. I promised on my honour." Wings tried to look at her face but it was like trying to make the same poles of two magnets face each other. Her being pretty did not help Wings either. It made him more shy, especially after Boon Ming's insinuations.

"But I promise you it's nothing bad, ma'am," Wings continued. "On my honour."

Janet eyed him thoughtfully.

"Can I trust you?" she asked him quietly.

He nodded.

"Don't do it again," she smiled.

He grinned back in relief.

"And by the way, when Boon Ming lets you off your promise, I'd like to know what you were really trying to do."

"Yes, ma'am!" Wings laughed and ran back into the night.

9

LIGHT came through the canopy above, long, narrow shafts of yellow morning sun, spearing through green foliage, making the leaves glow, dappling the jungle floor with pools of light. Shrieks of birds and the soprano screech of things unseen, cutting through the heavy, wet air.

Dark patches on his jersey worked like camouflage, where sweat, skin and uniform met. I am a chameleon, Wings thought. I am changing my own colour. I am the jungle, the jungle is me. The damp air stuck in his nose and sweat dripped into his eyes and he could feel the heat building up beneath his scarf. His forearms were sticky with drying sweat and his palms ached from gripping his spear too tight. It was an ordinary Scout's staff, an old broomstick, sharpened at one end.

He felt something light brush across his face. Long, silken threads of a spider's web, they stuck and would not be brushed off easily, especially mixed with perspiration. He wiped at it with the back of his left hand, his right still tightly clenched around the shaft. He had been afraid when they began, but now he was only edgy and more tired than scared.

The patrol was moving at a snail's pace through the jungle. Moving in a kite formation, in total silence save for the sound of black gym shoes cracking over dead leaves and twigs, the group advanced. Nathan was right in front, at the apex of the kite with his spearman, Eng Kiat. Peter was just ten paces behind, with Boon Ming and Wings on either side of him. On each flank was a pair of Scouts and another two brought up the rear.

Nathan had his eyes focused on the ground, looking for the telltale paw marks of their quarry. Impressions in the mud, mud on leaves where they should not be, broken branches at knee or thigh height, perhaps black hairs caught on thorns or bark of trees. Where are you, cat? Where have you run to? Where you hiding, cat? Come on now, Puss, come to Nathan and all will be okay. Take you home, back where you belong, cat.

Wings licked his lips, sticky dry tongue over dry and flaky lips. It had been more than two hours since they started out and two and a half since he last had a drink. And the sweating, he had lost everything he put in then. He was thinking of water, water, water, in long chilled glasses, burning cold down his throat and killing the heat inside him. When was Peter going to call for a rest? He was breathing heavily because of the humid and hot air and that long slope they had just ascended. The straps of his patrol pack were starting to cut into his shoulders and the right cheek of his butt was feeling bruised from the bouncing of his water bottle. Peter was probably feeling worse. He was carrying a pack, his own water and the fishing net, rolled up and secured to his pack. Well, if Peter could do it, Wings would too.

Boon Ming was frowning as he waded through the heat, the occasional undergrowth and spiders' webs. Dratted cat. Why did it have to run away? Dratted Peter, dratted Six, why did they have to be so civic-minded? Couldn't another Six have taken on the suffering? Misery is the jungle and everything in it, especially me, he felt. He looked across at Wings, who was also frowning, drops of sweat channelled down the brows and down the nose and dripping onto his lip. He saw Wings stick his tongue out to catch the falling droplets. See what a cat-hunt can do to a Scout? He even drinks his own sweat. Hike, they said. Bullshit. Tiptoe through the lallang, can't even talk. Should have said I was going home. Why didn't I think of that? Now this. Maybe I won't even see home again. He quickly brushed the thought out of his mind.

Adventure, Eng Kiat thought as he picked his way almost silently through the bush with Nathan. He kept his spear pointed to the front and kept his eyes ahead, looking askance at the shadows to see into them better. He swept his eyes and spear point periodically to his right and left, over Nathan's thin back. Come out cat, be a man and face St Peter's Greys. I want you, cat.

There is danger in this, but is there any other way to do it? Did I have any choice but to do it? And if I get my men hurt, what will I say to Sir, to Akela, to Miss Janet? But we are not cowards. Perhaps I shouldn't have brought them, but no way to do it without them. Right for us to do it. The Founder would agree. Even if we don't succeed, he would have approved. This is what Scouts were born to do. Would anybody else understand?

Wings had been looking at Peter when he suddenly noticed the eerie silence. The air hung still, not a single blade of leaf moved, not even those near the sky. The birds seemed to have all gone away. The party was over and the silence, like that of a city street at daybreak. Nathan noticed it too — their footfalls were getting too loud. He signalled the Six to stop and crouched on the trail with Eng Kiat, spears out and eyes peeled. The rest of the Scouts did the same and began moving slowly towards the centre of the kite, taking care not to make a sound, still facing outward with spears at the ready. Nathan and Eng Kiat pulled back slowly, not looking backwards, except for footing. The Six formed a tight defensive circle around Peter and the two recruits.

"She's here, Sixer," Nathan whispered. Peter nodded. Wings felt a sudden heat rush through his body and his limbs trembled at the surge of adrenalin. He could feel his heart running away and his temples pound. He was not tired anymore, body tensed and primed for action. He felt alive, a feeling that he had not felt for a long time. It was like the time he locked Janet Tan in the toolshed. Like the time the lorry had charged past him, only an inch away from hitting his handlebars. Like the way he was starting to feel every time he spoke to ... from out of the shadows in the surrounding jungle, she spoke, a low, feral snarl that seemed to come from every bush and tree.

"Get the net," Peter commanded. Wings released the pack straps and the net fell to the ground. He opened it out, a ten foot by ten foot-square, in the middle of the defence circle. Bushes and undergrowth got in the way. He could not spread it properly.

"Problems with the net, Sixer," Nathan said. "Don't think we can set it up properly here. Not even with the weights."

"We'll have to lure her in then."

"But she won't come, not with so many of us here."

There was something that Peter had neglected to tell his men. The net was never meant to be a trap. It was meant to be thrown at short range to entangle the cat, disabling it long enough for them to tie it up. But the cat had to come close enough for it to be thrown. It had to be lured into a close quarter fight. And St Peter's Greys were the bait. Eleven gladiators versus one cat. Eleven spears and a net. Another snarl sounded through the bush, this time louder, but still the cat kept out of sight. Peter cursed softly, breaking Scout Law number 10. All he had to know was where the cat was, then he could position his men. He went through the plan mentally. Find direction. Face cat's direction in a horseshoe shape, open side facing cat. Two scouts holding net at bottom of horseshoe, ready to cast it. The rest to engage cat in combat and fix its position long enough for net to be thrown over it. Subdue cat, secure and sling net on spears. Reach base and become heroes.

There was another snarl and a rustling in the bushes to Wings' left. Peter turned to face the sound and gave his orders.

"Straight line, face left." The Six moved silently, without a word in reply. Another snarl, this time clearly from the left and much louder. It was almost as if the cat was giving them clues to its presence, playing with them, daring them to a fight, challenging them. Catch me if you can. Wings felt his stomach go funny. It was not an altogether unpleasant feeling. He wanted the cat to come out now. He wanted the fight to start there and then and be over fast. All had their spears facing forward, except Peter and Nathan, who were holding the net.

"Horse shoe, not too close to each other," Peter said calmly. The boys were nervous, but no one showed it. Besides, no one really had any idea what they were up against. They all knew it was a smaller cat. They all knew it was black. They all knew it was savage and had teeth and claws to back up the threatening snarl. But Peter had said it was even smaller than a German Shepherd. And there were eleven of them. They could catch a stupid cat.

"Remember, don't stab it unless it tries to claw you or bite. We got to take it alive." But every man had already resolved to stab if the cat so much as turned its face towards them and opened its mouth.

Boon Ming thought of his Brownie as they waited. At least they had found the stupid thing. This would be something to tell her. She would be impressed. He, Boon Ming, was a Brave. He had gone hunting for a predator and found him. We'd better catch it. That would make the story better. He thought of his father. Maybe he'll be impressed too and won't worry too much about my manhood.

A roar broke the silence of the jungle.

"Behind us!" Nathan screamed. The cat walked calmly out of the shadows, as black as night itself, its coat glossy in the light, muscles rippling with power with every step, totally fluid, totally casual, big, black, beautiful, its baleful green eyes staring imperiously, contemptuously at the shocked scouts. From nose to tail, she was almost four feet long. She turned to face them. The scouts backed two steps. She gave a low, threatening snarl. They backed another step.

"Pete, what do we do now?" Nathan whispered, too afraid to take his eyes off the cat.

"Straight line, boys, and face her."

The scouts looked at each other, waiting for somebody else to make the first step. Nobody moved. Peter glanced around and sighed. He did not blame them. It was all he could do just to stop his legs from shaking too. Well, if they would not move forward, they might move back.

"Horse shoe, back off slowly." He stepped back slowly with Nathan. The men on the flanks did not move as the center moved to the back. The manoeuvre left Wings and Boon Ming at each tip of the horseshoe, closest to the cat. Too late, Peter realised his mistake. He had left his recruits in danger. And the stance the cat was taking — it looked like it could spring forward. The recruits could see that too. They kept their spears pointed at the cat. Boon Ming began to whimper softly. We're all going to die, he thought. And nobody will find us because that stupid cat will eat us all. Tears filled his eyes as he contemplated their death, their posthumous awards for valour, their troopmates hearing their coffins to the final resting place, 'The Last Post' mournfully played by the bugler, his parents feeling sorry for what they had driven him to do as they collected the Singapore flag from his Scoutmaster. He was surprised to find himself strangely satisfied with his funeral arrangements. And the Brownie, yes, he would expect her to cry and never marry.

"Back off, Greys, very, very slowly," Peter said in a low voice. Eng Kiat did not move. His eyes were fixed on the cat and he waited till Boon Ming had shivered past him before he moved. Wings saw Eng Kiat take Boon Ming's place on the point and was filled with a sudden respect for the boy, who was only a year older than Boon Ming and himself. The Scout behind Wings had no such ideas. The cat spat and made a high pitched roar and sprang forward. The Scouts screamed as one and dashed to the rear, tripping over roots, dropped spears and each other. The cat landed where Wings had been standing and licked its lips as it eyed them. It was a singularly sinister action. The boys were now huddled into a tight knot and the net could not be thrown because someone was sitting on it. The cat walked slowly towards them. Eng Kiat watched it steadily, eye to eye as it sauntered up. He raised his spear and waited for the cat to come into range. Wings saw him ready himself for the throw. He edged over to Eng Kiat's side. If he missed, he would need a spearman to protect him from the charging cat. Wings' movement left Boon Ming exposed, so the tubby boy began scrabbling around for a spear too. Eng Kiat let out a bloodcurdling scream and threw his spear, but the cat was agile and dodged the shaft in time. Yet the action caught it off-guard and it took off into the jungle in surprise. The Scouts cheered. Eng Kiat picked up his spear and ran after the cat. Whooping in excitement, the Six followed him.

"Scaredy cat!" Boon Ming shouted, having quite forgotten about his funeral preparations. The Six came to a little clearing, but there was no sign of the cat. They were all feeling braver now, having 'won' their first encounter. They were no longer in formation nor in pairs. They were enthusiastically stabbing at the bushes surrounding the clearing. It was covered with grass and Nathan could find no tracks. He did not have to.

It is one thing to pursue a fleeing panther. But when the same panther is charging at you with its fangs bared and making all sorts of frightful noises as it comes, you flee. This was exactly what happened when the cat charged. The Scouts scattered and the cat found itself alone in the clearing with a choice of eleven scents to follow.

Peter was in a quandary. His men were all lost and he did not know how to get them all back. Shouting would attract the cat. Moving around to round up his men might be too slow to save some of them. But there was no other way. Spear at the ready, he moved slowly forward.

He hoped the panther was not downwind. He was heartily regretting this cathunt. The next animal that escaped from the Mandai Zoo, he would leave to the zoo people, unless it was something harmless like a penguin.

He had wanted to provide his boys with some real adventure. He had called them together on Friday to tell them what to bring and they had set off immediately after Saturday's meeting which had been a dull singalong.

This was a real man's job, and Peter was starting to feel inadequate. Maybe we're only phoney Scouts, not like what the Founder wanted us to be. Scouting's history was full of boys who had taken on what even men had quailed at and failed to do. The Founder himself had hunted game. They were doing or had been doing the same. They were now being hunted by their quarry.

Sure gardening was a contribution to the school. Selling flags helped society. But wasnt there a good deed that provided some adventure too? That had been on his mind when he saw the paper on Wednesday. And the cat was also last seen in the forest reserve not far away from their school. It was a long shot worth trying. Now they had found the cat and maybe they would lose their lives for that.

Wings looked frantically about him, looking everywhere for a pair of green eyes, rounded ears and a small powerful head, listening for the telltale rustling of foliage because the cat would make no other sound. He was also lost. He knew the school was due south, but where was north? He could not see the sun because of the canopy and the shadows were unreliably messy. He wanted to shout for help, but feared that it would only work as a cat-call. He wanted to cry too, but he remembered the Law: 'A scout smiles under all difficulties.' He tried but it felt unnatural so he gave up. It was Law 3 that had got them into this awful mess. 'A Scout is helpful and useful' and as the Founder had always said, the greater the personal risk involved, the more noble the act. Wings did not feel noble then. He was feeling extremely sorry for himself. Maybe the Laws are impossible to keep. No, no, I am discouraged. 'A Scout is kind to animals.' Yes, but there was a certain panther he wished dead now.

He was to wish that even more when he met the said cat ten minutes later. He came to a part of the jungle where the trees were spread further apart and thirty feet away from where he stood, he saw her standing perfectly still. Wings froze and watched her, jet-black coat glistening in the afternoon sun. Don't look my way, please, please, don't. But she did. She turned her head and those yellow-green eyes caught his. He could not, dared not look away. Her eyes held his steadily, unflinching. A low growl escaped her throat. I see you, she seemed to say. Then she turned away and walked off. Wings breathed out slowly, so that she would not hear him and return.

He heard a shuffling sound in some bushes in front of him and saw some leaves move. He crept closer and heard a sob. He was relieved. He had found a fellow Scout.

"Hey, who's there?" he said in a low voice. The leaves parted and he saw a P4 Scout. His face was tear-stained and he looked at Wings in relief. He wiped his eyes and sniffed, regaining his composure.

"Let's go find the rest," he said and they set off. It was not long before they found Peter and Nathan, creeping towards them.

"Glad to meet you," Kim Leong said to Peter. "I found this recruit." Wings looked at him in surprise but decided to keep his mouth shout. This was no time to chase credit. The four moved on. They felt better as a group and walked more confidently.

Eng Kiat was alone when he saw a black shadow slink through the trees. He took a few quick steps to put himself behind the cat. There was a little breeze and the cat was moving into the wind. It was probably following a scent from downwind. He decided to follow it. The cat would lead him to another Scout who would also need his help when the cat found him.

This part of the jungle was more open, with less canopy and tall trees to trap air. The humidity was not so bad and there was more light. Eng Kiat felt better as he stalked the cat. It stopped near a tree and began to poke around it. It looked up and appeared thoughtful. Then it stood up on its hind legs and rested its front paws on the trunk. Could panthers climb trees? Eng Kiat did not know. But he was certain that there was a Scout up that tree. If the panther could climb, it could attack whoever was up there, safe from Eng Kiat's spear. It had to be now or never. Yet, if he tried to scare it away, the panther would have found him. And if there was no one up that tree to help him… Eng Kiat forced the thought out of his head and charged at the cat with his spear, shouting with all the power in his lungs. Surprised, the panther took flight.

"Anybody up there?" he asked. There was a swish of leaves against uniform as Boon Ming climbed down laboriously.

"I've never climbed a tree before," he announced proudly. He did not realise that the panther had been under his tree. When Eng Kiat told him so, his face went pale and he was quiet. There was more noise from the trees around.

"Monkeys or Scouts?" Eng Kiat asked Boon Ming. Two Scouts dropped to the ground, grinning in relief.

"How long were you going to stay up there?" Eng Kiat asked. They were about to answer when another boy sneaked up a rabbit path, spear in hand. Five, Eng Kiat thought. Where are the other six? But they had heard his yell and were making their way towards him. Peter's group had found the other two.

"Eleven. We're in luck. Nobody's been eaten," Nathan said. Peter set his compass for due south. It would take them quickly to the road, where the cat would not pursue them. All they had to do now was make it to the road.

They did not bother with stealth this time. If the cat did not hear them, she would see them and if not, she would smell them. Panting, they ran through the jungle, dried leaves crackling and twigs snapping underfoot, sweat pouring down their bodies in the steamy tropical heat, hands grabbing for handholds, feet tripping over roots, not stopping to even brush webs from their faces, just watching the compass needle and running, running, running away from the cat they had come to catch and even as they fled, she followed and they knew because she let them know every now and then when they heard her voice and she was always close, close, her voice, just behind them, not far, stalking them like prey, escorting them out of her jungle, until they collapsed on the concrete of civilised sidewalk, line where their two worlds met. And she, with the soft snarl of a triumphant goodbye, she left the would-be heroes to their world and returned to hers.

And even as they picked themselves up, counted heads, checked equipment and salvaged their lost pride, Wings could not help looking back into the jungle, where those jade eyes with the yellow light had stared right through him. She was shot a week later and the boys in the Six had cheered. But Wings, he went back to the jungle's edge, where his world met hers, to say goodbye and shed a tear in private.

10

THE dirt felt uncomfortable under his nails, the sun shone down with malicious delight and the smell of grass was strong in his nostrils. A caterpillar walked past him, all its legs moving in a coordinated wave. Wings felt an urge to drop a stone on the wriggling patch of colour, but its wave-motion walk thrilled him so much that he could not. The stone hovered above the promised butterfly, which probably did not realise that its short life was hanging in the balance of Wings' fingers. The stone shaded it from the sun as Wings followed it, using the shadow as a bombsight. The caterpillar moved on, burning its feet on the hot bricks of the flowerbed.

Wings heard it long before it appeared, a low throaty roar that got louder and louder, but he kept his eyes on the caterpillar. Death from above. The stone was held aloft by five fingertips that were slippery with sweat. The roar got louder. Wings was listening to it. The voice of angels, like a harmony, more than one voice. A heavenly host, thunder rolling before them, like a carpet for their feet. I hear you, but I will not look at you because I will cry if I look at you. Louder, they called. and his grip loosened on the rock as he concentrated, fighting the urge to look up. And then they were upon him and his resistance broke and he threw back his head, face to the sky just as they passed overhead, five in perfect formation, a kite and a tail, Hunters black against the blue of sky. Take me with you, but the scream could not break out beyond his throat and they banked to starboard, growing smaller and smaller, taking only the thunder with them.

The caterpillar had gone on without the shade of the rock and was probably feeling a bit miffed. Wings looked down again at the little creature and picked up the fallen stone. His heart was hardened and the shadow fell on the caterpillar again. Yea, though ye walk on the flowerbed bricks in the shadow of death ye shall fear no evil from a naughty wolf-cub. Wings flung the stone away into a patch of earth. You will grow up to be beautiful, ugly thing. But that is not important. You will grow up to fly and ride the breezes. Which I can never do. Live to fly. I will not take that away from you, like He has taken away my wings. I am Wings, but I am forever a caterpillar. He felt a dry bitterness in his mouth.

Janet had heard the jets coming too. She had watched her boys drop their trowels and shears and watering cans to look up at the sky. She did not want to look. She had seen Wings staring intently at the flowerbed, holding a rock above the bricks, eyes to earth when all were watching the sky. And the angry despair when he suddenly looked up. She had lost control too and turned in time to see them bank as one into the distance. She had felt a familiar aching but forgot it when she saw the boy throw away the stone. She remembered a test two weeks back for the wolf-cubs' Bronze Arrow. He had brought her a balsa glider looking a little flight-worn. The test called for a balsa paddleboat powered with a twisted rubber band. She had not wanted to pass him. Then she had followed him into the school field and watched him launch it. It had flown straight and true and floated down to land sliding on the damp grass.

"Did you really build that yourself, Wings?"

He had looked a little hurt.

"Yes, but before I became a Scout.'

"Do you still make them?"

"No."

"Why not?"

"What for?"

She had wanted to ask him why again.

'So do I pass?"

"Yes, Wings. You pass."

He had gone to pick up his glider and had come running back to her.

"Flies well. Maybe you can make me one someday."

"Don't think I want to. But you can have this one."

It sat on her shelf at home now, beside a plastic Skyhawk someone else had once built for her.

"Wings," she said softly to herself.

11

"HOW do you like the Scouts, son?" his mother asked a few months later. Wings looked up from the book he was reading to see if she wanted a reply. She was looking expectantly at him.

"It's alright. I don't mind it."

Always non-committal, she thought to herself. What does he really think or feel? I should know, but I don't. He does not talk much now to either of us, except his sister and quarrels don't count as communication. She thought of her husband. Yes, quarrels don't count as communication. Who does he talk to now? There must be someone. Who does he trust? The question was painful because she realised that asking it meant she knew he did not trust her. But she was consoled. Well, his father cannot get to him either. The chubby boy — Boon Ming — but what does another nine-year-old know about life? Even I am not sure anymore. Yet at nine — don't you think you know the world?

She looked at the book he was reading. *Scouting for Boys.* She had opened it once to have a glimpse of what her son was reading. There was a code of conduct and campfire yarns that showed how each law was lived by. A collection of adventure stories, she had once thought. But no, they take it as something more. She had come to realise bit by bit and with a vague sense of uneasiness that she and her husband had been replaced by a book. When parents fail and the child has no reference point, no anchor, no proper system of values, a teacher must provide them, a school must take over. That was her job. She did that for forty children everyday. But her own son was lost to her. He turns to this teacher, some Englishman he has never seen and who has been long dead, but whose voice lives on in those yellow pages. He finds another family in a wolf-pack of uniformed boys and teachers they call mother-wolves. I always knew that you would have to go someday, son, but I never thought it would be so soon. But it is our fault, boy, I guess you had no choice but to find another family. Even when my own father left, I wanted something that would not change and always last. Baden-Powell, you have it down in black and white and you're no longer alive to change anything or betray your sons. Betrayal. It was a strong word but she would not spare herself. But when you shatter a little child's world, it is betrayal. And I will have to betray my children soon. What is the betrayal of a husband or a wife? Both grown-up people who can look after themselves and who knew better than to trust so completely. The more you trust, the more broken you will be when the time comes for betrayal. My son has lost his innocence. He has learnt not to trust. And he has learnt not to trust me. That night she wept

In his own room next door, her husband heard her stifled sobs. He wanted to know why. Once he might have thought of comforting her, but that time was past. Now he only wanted to know why. How do you comfort a woman whose heart is cold against you, who will not share a room, let alone a bed with you? If she wept, he told himself, it would not be for him. It was for their children then, those sobs. He could hear no anger in them. Ah, yes, no anger, then he would be right.

Those tears were not for him.

The girl. Perhaps too young to understand. But the boy? He played, he laughed, he talked and it sounded normal. But something was not quite right. What did he talk about? He talked about school, about lessons, about how he hated maths and Chinese. He talked about his teachers, his friends, his Scout troop. What they did, what he did, saw, heard, said, tasted, touched. But never what he felt. Yes, that was missing. The boy does not talk about his feelings. Yet he must have them. What does he do with them? The man turned inside himself. And me, how do I handle my feelings? Or have I lost that capacity to feel? No, no, no. I feel. But where are the feelings now? Back of filing cabinet in my heart somewhere, there, but where I cannot see them. Better to keep them out of sight anyway. Out of sight, out of mind, out of pain. But the filing cabinet is getting filled with those feeling files — how do I destroy them, retire them? Close them and throw them away. Does my son do that? He is young. Maybe his filing cabinets have much more space for junk.

I am a Scholar. Objective, trained not to trust feeling, but rely on things that can be measured in physical terms or defined clearly in the abstract. Look at me now. Broke my Law once, relied on a feeling, most unreliable one called Love. Look at me now. But I am Literati. I find feeling again in words, feelings writers bury in words, long chains of words that only have meaning when in that order, in that combination, each triggering the others, layering, qualifying, adding, subtracting, multiplying and dividing. Ha, I am forever the teacher for here am I in mathematics again, pure, hard objectivity. And my son. What do I say to him? Never trust your feelings, boy? But so young. Do not, cannot disillusion him. But what we are doing — pah, actions speak louder than words. We are showing him that love is wrong and that feelings were created to be hurt. And you were not born for that, son. He turned off the study lamp and the yellow light gave way to darkness. I am tired. Good. Then sleep must come fast and I will not have to cry for long before the black peace comes.

Wings was getting ready for bed when he remembered that he had not prayed for some time. He sat at the edge of his bed with his feet on the rug. He had knelt there often in the past and prayed with his face to the window, the purple night sky. Sometimes he had closed his eyes. Sometimes he had kept them open. Always, he listened, but he never heard a reply. The memory of prayers marked 'return to sender' was fresh in his heart. It kept his knees from touching the rug. You never listened anyway. I haven't called You for some time and things aren't any worse.

His mind wandered and he saw a face with bright, laughing eyes. He could almost feel her fingers in his hair as his mind went into playback mode. He shut his eyes to cut out the world around him to concentrate on the memory and image. A trembling, fragile peace and happiness he knew was fleeting. It went the moment he opened his eyes. I know if I close my eyes, you will be there again. But I can't. Can't let you into my world like that. Every time I stop the concentration, I lose you. You never stay. You're just like everybody else. Don't want to ever like you. Don't want to trust you. Don't want to need you. Won't love you. I wish the world was different. I wish I could make it mine so I could change it and make it the way I wish it. I wish I could stay in my own world forever and keep you with me. But you'll never stay and I don't want to be alone there. Goodnight, Janet.

12

BOON Ming sat on the steps of the school porch, waiting for his mother to drive him home. He looked at his test card with a satisfied smile. Under the heading 'Bronze Arrow', every space carried a signature. He was now qualified to wear a Bronze Arrow patch on his sleeve. And with a Bronze Arrow, he could also start working for his Proficiency badges. Then there would be the Silver Arrow next year and then the Gold, with more Proficiency badges in between, and finally, the coveted District Commissioner's Badge that Benjamin now wore.

Wings sat next to Boon Ming on the steps. He too held an open test card in his hands. He had earned his arrow too, but he was not smiling. The cubs had to have their new status sewn on by the next meeting. Wings was wondering how he was going to manage that. First, the badges had to be bought from Sands House and that was all the way in town. Then they had to be sewn on. Wings could not go to town on his own. He would have been glad to try, but his parents would not have heard of it. He depended on his parents now. They could not simply walk into the store and buy the badges. The test card had to be shown as proof of the achievement. One of them had to be committed to do it, but Wings was getting tired of his father's

'I've got to work late' and his mother's unreliable 'we'll see'. He wanted something a little more sure.

"Man, we're going to have our badges on next week. Can't wait for it! Wait till the Brownie sees it, then she'll know I'm going to go far," Boon Ming said. Wings kept his eyes on his card.

"But everyone passed and got the arrow, Boon."

"I'm not just anyone. I'm going to be District Commissioner's Scout, just like Benjamin, only I'll have more Proficiency badges than him."

Wings looked up. He could not imagine anyone with more badges than Benjamin.

"Look, Wings, it isn't hard. We're Primary Three now. Next year, we'll work for the silver. When we're in Five, we'll go for Gold and when we're Six — District Commissioner's Badge!"

"What if you fail?"

"Wings! Failure is not in our creed."

"That doesn't mean you can't, Boon."

"What's the matter with you? You're such a … such a … wet blanket," Boon Ming spluttered as he remembered the phrase he had just learnt at English lessons.

"I mean, what makes you so sure you're going to get past silver? Have you ever counted the silvers in P4? Not everyone has a silver."

"Have you noticed that all P5s have a silver?"

"Look, Smart Aleck, have you counted the number of P3s and P4s and P5s? There's less and less as you go up. Nathan told me. He said those who don't make silver by P5, they all leave. And those who aren't going to get gold in P6 leave before they even try. And even if you get gold, you think you can get the Commissioner's badge? And all those Proficiency badges, do you think there's enough time to win them all?"

"Enough! Thank you very much for your discouragement.

Just because you don't believe in yourself doesn't mean I can't believe in me."

"Sorry."

The two Scouts sat in silence. Boon Ming glared at Wings, who was looking straight ahead and did not see the dirty look. But he's right — the guys who don't make it leave. But why should I be one of them?

"Aren't you even going to try?" Boon Ming suddenly asked.

"Don't know."

"We're supposed to do our best."

"What if it isn't good enough," Wings said as he remembered himself telling his mother, again and again that he had done his best, and always, that curt reply, it wasn't good enough.

"Won't know until we try."

"I guess we can always leave."

"I thought you love the Scouts."

"Wouldn't it be too painful to stay?"

"But your Promise…"

"No Law against it, Boon." Wings felt very, very old and tired. He wished Boon Ming's mum would hurry up and drive them home.

13

THE Scoutmaster watched his boys on the parade square, ranks of khaki-clad boys standing at attention. The Founder would have been proud of my boys. He could see himself again amongst them. My shorts would have been baggier and longer, though. The sun has not changed, the light, it looks the same, the long shadows, nothing has moved, except the trees that have grown up and the boys who have gone away.

His eyes went beyond the grassy slopes and the fence that surrounded the school. Little road and the forest that begins from a kerb. Crossing the road into adventure. My father has never found out. And yet I will not let my boys do it. Their parents would not like it. But he hoped with all his heart that they would try it anyway. How can a boy grow up to be a man unless he pushes against the boundaries of boyhood and discovers for himself what anything is about?

The trophies in the Scout Den gleamed dully in the light that came in thin, flat shafts through ventilation slits. Tarnished bronze, silver, gold. Fading black and white pictures of grinning boys, squinting against the sun, impeccably turned out, standing in perfect formations, their names below passing on with time into nothingness.

I promised to do my best. I came home to this den, to a family of wolves that was new to me, but here in my old home. I came back to lead them to greater things. But such things are only possible if every man gives his best and pushes himself beyond what he thinks he can do. I have pushed them hard. He heard a single, solid thump as sixty right feet stamped in unison on command. That is good, but for the Scout, there must always be better. They have learnt it well. They push themselves, at least their leaders do. It has taken years to make them this way, to give 1010 this pride. Now, they will not let it be taken away. I am glad.

There was a tap on the doorframe and Benjamin stepped in. The Scoutmaster raised his eyebrows at him.

"1010 ready for parade and inspection, Sir."

"That's good, Ben. Drill today?"

"Of course, Sir, the competition is only next week, Sir."

"Have they all got their arrows on, Ben?"

"Yes, Sir, their uniforms are alright. You can inspect them now, Sir."

"How ready are they for next week?"

"We'll keep the shield another year, Sir."

"Good, Ben, I'm sure you boys won't let the troop down."

Benjamin felt something tighten in his stomach. There was always that odd chance of an upset. One of the newer Scouts might make a mistake and break a total silence with a mistimed bang. Or he could fumble with a command and give it on the wrong leg, throwing everyone into a messy confusion. There was a price to pay in everything and Benjamin often wished that he was not Benjamin.

Wings watched the Scoutmaster stride into the sunshine, a tall athletic man, just turned thirty. He was in his Scouter's uniform, khaki, like the boys, but he wore a green tie and beret. Wings was afraid of him, though there was no seeming reason to be. He was never harsh, but always spoke to the boys quietly and with great gentleness and dignity. Yet Wings feared him. There was something in his manner which often made Wings wish he was sterner — and more human. Why doesn't he scold us like Akela? Janet doesn't scold us much, except when we've been really bad and we just laugh at her anyway.

He could not understand his feelings. Maybe it's because Mrs Han and Janet are women and they only scold us for being naughty. But Sir. He never says anything when we're naughty.

But it was something every Sixer, Peter included, understood.

"That's just it. He doesn't say anything."

"Yes, but he doesn't even seem angry."

"Because he never is."

"Then why is everybody scared of him?"

Peter sighed and patted Wings' back.

"Because no one wants to disappoint him."

"I don't understand."

"No one dares to fail."

"Failure is not in our creed," Wings quoted.

"Basically. Nobody wants to fail because nobody wants to disappoint him."

"But I'm not scared about that when it's Mrs Han or Janet."

"That's because they don't make you feel bad when you fail."

"But he doesn't do anything!"

"It's very hard to explain, Wings, you have to see for yourself. The next time we lose something, I'll show you what I mean."

1010 lost the drill competition for the first time in seven years. It was not a new Scout's mistake as Benjamin thought it might be. It was not even Benjamin's fault. It was Nathan's. He had been in the front row and it had made him extra nervous. He had brought his foot down a moment too soon and it had sounded very odd on the silent parade square, silent save for the snickers of rival units. That mistake had unnerved the poor Scout even more and he had cut down a salute too late. With all the other boys moving with precision, Nathan's error had been all the more obvious. He cost them two points and they had lost by one.

"It's okay, Nathan," Mrs Han had said to him later. He had been almost in tears, but an Assistant Sixer could not cry.

"It could have been anyone's mistake," Peter said consolingly. The younger boys in the Six did not know what to say to him. The rest of the troop would not speak to him. He had let them all down.

Benjamin fell in the troop and called them to attention. He turned to report to the Scoutmaster and saluted him smartly. The Scoutmaster's face was passive. It held no anger. Wings watched him closely.

"Gentlemen, I know all of you tried hard and I would like to thank you all for the effort you put into training. We've done our best, but I'm afraid it just wasn't good enough. I'm sure you'll do better next time. Bring our shield home next year. That's all. Benjamin, you may fall the men out."

Wings had seen the pained expression on his face and suddenly realised why they were all so afraid of him. He had seen the same look on his mother's face and had been terrified of disappointing her until he had grown immune to it to save himself the pain. He had been afraid of disappointing her because she had meant the world to him. Why was he afraid of the Scoutmaster? He was not mother. Akela would have been a more likely candidate. But if all Scouts were brothers, then 1010 was a family. After all, Akela meant mother wolf. By the same reasoning, Scoutmaster was father. But he was more than that too. He was 1010. He was *Nulli secundus*. He wasn't just the Scout everyone wanted to grow up to be, like Benjamin. He was their world, if he was unit and motto. And he was a representative of Baden Powell, Chief Scout of the World. Wings' mind was tripping over itself as he tried to work out all the complex possible relationships.

The Scouts fell out in silence and went to get their bags to go home.

"Nathan — it's all his fault," Boon Ming muttered. Wings looked at him.

"Well, we were all nervous, Nathan a little more that's all."

"Big deal. We've failed anyway. I feel like scum. The Scoutmaster was awfully disappointed. Did you see his face? I would've yelled at everyone, especially Nathan."

"Come on, Boon. Let it go. It's over."

"No way. The next time our name is in danger, we'll have to leave the guys like Nathan out. Man, if only I was a Sixer."

"You're not, so forget it."

"You've forgotten something, Wings. We're 1010. We don't lose anything."

"You know that's impossible. We all have to lose sometime."

"Only losers think that way."

"We thought we'd win today, but we lost anyway." Boon Ming did not reply.

"We can't let it happen again," he said at last. Wings shrugged and stood up when he saw his mother's car.

14

JANET counted the boys as they boarded the school bus. She knew that each Sixer would be counting his men and his Second would be helping him, but she liked to be sure. Her boys were trustworthy, but still, she trusted herself most.

"Greys all here, Miss Tan, all eleven," Peter reported. She nodded and he disappeared into the chaotic depths of the bus. That was the last of them. She looked around the carpark for stragglers and saw none. Mrs Han's bus was already crawling off. Janet skipped on board and told the driver to carry on.

She looked around for Wings and saw him next to the emergency exit at the back with Boon Ming. She smiled at him and he smiled back shyly.

"She likes you, I told you, didn't I?" Boon Ming whispered.

"Nothing wrong with that, idiot."

"Oh, and you gave her your plane too. How come you didn't give one to Mrs Han and one to Scoutmaster?" Boon Ming insinuated.

"She asked for it."

"I asked for it, and you wouldn't give it to me. And I asked first too. You reserved it for her."

Wings looked at Boon Ming with annoyance.

"So what if I did?"

"Hey, you admit it! You like her don't you?"

Wings felt the heat in his face grow. This would take courage.

"Yes I do. She's my friend." Boon Ming's eyes grew wide.

"You're in love with her," he said with mock astonishment.

"No." No, no, no. It was a bad idea. She was his friend now, but what if he left? Would she still be? What if she left? No, he couldn't let that happen. Best to avoid it. She was his friend, nothing more. That way, no pain.

Janet watched the two boys talk. You remind me very much of another boy, Wings. Why are you all this way? She felt a sudden urge to ruffle his hair and put her arm around him. He was so much a little boy. But his eyes were grown up behind those lenses. And it wasn't just the things he said, but the way he said them. Mrs Han had told her about his parents. They were a popular subject in their estate and Mrs Han was a distant neighbour who was close enough to subscribe to the estate gossip. There was even a neighbourhood bookie taking odds on how long more it would last. And the way the betting went, any bet for more than a year was a pretty long shot.

Janet's parents had stayed together, but the children had not. There were nine of them, too many to feed. Janet was the youngest daughter and her grandparents had brought her up. As a little girl, she had often wished that they had been rich or at least middle-class. The family could have stayed together then. Her grandparents had been kind, but they had taken only her and the loneliness had made her want something more. But now, there was Wings. His family could easily afford living together. There was only him and his sister. But still they could not. I'm supposed to be old enough to know, but God, I still don't understand.

The bus slowed to a halt and a wild whoop drowned out the protest of aging brakes. Out of the front door, the rear door and the emergency exit, wolf-cubs came tumbling out, running to form up in Sixes. Benjamin and the Sixers and Assistants hustled the boys together. He called them to attention. Then on command, they punched their right fists into the air and shouted, "*Nulli secundiis!* " That's what I call arriving in style, Wings thought with a smug smile. Morale at its peak, the boys trotted off in formation to the playing field.

Wings gasped when they reached the field. He had never seen so many Scouts in one place before. The field was khaki with flashes of white and red of scarves, row after row after row of Baden Powells boys, brothers by the law they shared.

"This is going to be some fight," Nathan said. Wings saw Peter frown at him for just a moment before he quickly turned away. The Scoutmaster was already there. His necktie fluttered in the breeze and his eyes were hidden behind green shades. He cut a dashing figure and his boys felt proud of him. After all, amongst Scouters, he represented 1010. He walked up to them.

"Ready for the fight, boys?" he shouted above the noise. The boys responded with a roar. Fighting spirit, that is good.

"How you going to do today?"

"We're going to win!" Eng Kiat shouted and a chorus of approval followed.

"And win big!" Benjamin added, not to be outdone by a P4. The mob agreed again.

"That's right. I want every man to give his best, whether you're playing or cheering. I want you to go out there and play hard, but play clean too. You are 1010 boys. You are the best. You are second to none. Let's show them why!" The boys cheered again and started their war chant which was adapted from a Jewish folk song. Janet could never make out the words and neither could most of the boys, but it sounded very threatening when said loud and rhythmically. This was the part of games she did not like. Mrs Han had grown indifferent to it, but the Scoutmaster's locker-room pep talk always made her feel uncomfortable. It was not the memory of Saturday afternoon matinees of American football or basketball teams with salty old coaches and their locker-room pep talks. But it was the whole, what was the word now? Ethos? Ethos of the thing. Michael had loved it. The game, the challenge, the fight, the rituals, the team spirit. He had taken all that from the rugby fields to the skies. The simplistic attitudes of taking it to the limit and living on the edge. Me against the world. Us against the world. Michael had lost and so had she.

Wings had stripped to his troop T-shirt and shorts and Peter was putting on the warpaint for his boys. Two black stripes of Kiwi on each cheek and a V on the forehead between the eyebrows. The games began. Who could build a flagpole fastest, set it up and raise their unit flag first? Who could pitch a ten-man tent in minimum time? Make a table and bench out of nothing but rope and straight, thick branches? Build a cooking pit and start a fire before the rest? In lieu of food, a single representative from each unit took off on a lonely run with a fifteen second head-start, pursued by lone pursuers from every unit, trying to catch dinner before two laps were run. The boys evacuated their teams from one end of the field to the other in all sorts of positions. Knotting one-metre lengths of rope with every knot they knew to get a single rope stretching a hundred metres. Throwing water-filled balloons at a row of Scouts from other units, every hit by your team scoring two points. Clearing a course of obstacles where only solid teamwork could get a Six through, being all tied together with short lengths of rope. Trying to drag the enemy team into a stretch of mud in a tug-of-war.

Wings got up from the mud, weary. Splattered and muddied, he ran his dirty hands through his sweaty hair. His arms ached and his hands were still smarting from rope burn. The two top teams would be slugging it out in a pushball match to decide the winner of the Scout Olympics. 1010 would not be in that match. The rest of the boys were sitting around the scene of their latest defeat, faces blank, minds empty, bodies drained. Their supporters' voices had grown weaker with each successive defeat until at the tug-of-war, they could barely be heard. Benjamin looked around at his weary warriors. He leaned on his staff and looked out at the field where play was just beginning. What promised land? We lost everything except getting up the flag first. I'm glad we won that. At least my game won. No one can say I didn't do my best.

The Scoutmaster walked through groups of his defeated elite, silent and with a frown. Boys straightened up as he walked past, not wanting to look sloppy even in defeat in case he singled them out for blame. But he did not have to do that. As it was, every Scout was blaming himself in one way or another for the unit's loss.

Wings watched his back and suddenly felt an intense hatred for the man. At once, he felt guilty, but the feeling did not last. Who was he to try to make them feel bad? He did not even let his own mother do that now. Wings hated the feeling of assigned guilt, when someone deliberately makes you feel worthless. Peter noticed his anger.

"What's up, Wings?"

"Why does he do that?"

"I don't know. All I know is that he does it. Maybe he hopes that by making us feel like shit, we'll try harder next time and win."

"Is winning so important, Pete?"

"No, but it is around here. Haven't you noticed?"

"Why?"

"If you want to be *nulli secundus*, you have to be the best and that means you can't lose."

"Why must we always be second to none?"

"I wish I knew Wings. But that's something you can't change. It's always been that way. It's like telling a dog not to bark but to chirp instead."

His hands hurt, so he went to a tap to wash his wounds. Janet and Mrs Han were tending to the boys' wounds nearby. Wings waited till Janet was free.

"Tug-of-war?" she asked as she took his hands in hers.

"Yes."

"Hurt a lot?"

"I can manage." She dried them and wiped his wounds with an antiseptic swab. Wings felt the soothing cold of antiseptic and the light touch of her hands. He felt himself relaxing as he surrendered to her attention, putting himself in her hands. Amid the mud, the dirty, smelly bodies, the shouting and general chaos, he found a little peace with Janet. She noticed too that she treated him a little differently. We don't talk much, but it feels like the kind of silence that only people who have known each other long and well can share. And even the way I touch him or talk to him, always gentler. How do you make me, boy?

"Feel better?" she asked when she had finished dressing his wounds.

"Much," he smiled. She smiled too and pushed back the strands of hair that fell across his brow. You would have made Michael a good kid brother. And he would have been everything to you, like he was to me. Maybe Michael was like you. She felt her heart ache.

"You'd better join your Six, Wings. Peter will be looking for you. We're going back soon."

In a sad, ragged line, they shuffled back to the waiting buses and slumped into seats, hardly speaking to each other. They looked out of windows, took sips from their canteens. Wings clenched his fists to feel the exquisite pain in his palms. Boon Ming was grumbling unintelligibly. It was a long ride home.

15

"I'M going to make more money than you, Wings," Boon Ming said one morning. Wings looked at him and laughed.

"You can try, Fats, but I don't think you can."

"You think that just because I'm fat I can't work, right?"

Wings laughed again and nodded vigorously.

"Let me tell you something, smarty pants, my dad said that my grandma wants me fat because that's a sign of prosperity, plenty, wealth and Mercedes Benzes," he said with an extravagant sweep of his chubby arms. "And," he paused for effect, "I know it's all true because my grandpa's fat and he's got all that, and two wives even."

Eng Kiat and Nathan were rolling out of their seats and Mrs Han was starting to notice them. Peter frowned at his men. They sat up straight with unrepentant smiles.

"What's more, if grandpa isn't proof enough, my dad will do. He's got his own company, he pays a lot of tax, he's got loads of credit cards and cheque books and stuff and gold watches. Okay, so maybe he hasn't got a Benz, but he's got a Jaguar. And he's fat, fat, fat!"

"We know, Boon," Nathan said in a weary tone. Maybe the fat kid is too young to realise it, but he is very tiresome when he talks about his family. He looked around the room at the other Scouts. No doubt plans were already being made in their devious little minds. Where was the easiest work? Where could they get the most money? Could they get a free ride? Nathan felt a slight flush of shame. He had thought all that once until Peter had set him right. Job Week's for trying to make as much as possible for the Singapore Scouts, doing an honest day's work for fair wages. It was learning how to be independent, not relying on others to give you what you should be working for yourself. It was not a time for trying to outdo each other, seeing who got paid most, who got the best jobs, who got the most for doing the least. Peter had been an Assistant Sixer then and Nathan wished that he could have done just as well. He had tried his best to be the Second that Peter had been, but no, the distance that was always between himself and the younger boys, and of late, the entire troop, had been too great. Blame it on my Brahmin heritage. The year was three-quarters gone already and he had not done very well. His promotion was in the balance. Nathan, Nathan, this is going to be your last chance to do well before the year-end assessments. It will look bad if a Brahmin does not become a Sixer.

The same thoughts were in Peter's mind as he listened to Mrs Han brief the boys on Job Week. This would be the fourth time he was hearing it. Funny how the more we hear something, the less we remember of it. His mind went back to the first time. How eager he had been. But now, in spite of the pep talk he vaguely remembered giving Nathan the year before and the one he would give his own boys later, Peter felt tired of it all. Those values Mrs Han is talking about. How many understand, and how many will keep them in mind when we're out on the streets alone? It's all gone wrong, like everything else. Even me. I've gone wrong too. He knew he was no longer doing it for any altruistic reason. I want to make as much as possible because I have to, because I am a Sixer and a P6. I cannot do worse. And Nathan's got to do it good if he wants to be Sixer after me. He looked over at Nathan and found the other boy looking at him with a sorry face. He knows it and it's killing him. We've all gone wrong. He didn't have to look behind himself at his men. I have seen all that already. They will all be lost in the end. Peter bit his lip. I'm sorry, BP. I couldn't bring my brothers up right.

Benjamin was not worried. He would have his usual accounts. He had prepared his father way in advance, as he had every year and the old man had gone out to secure the accounts for him. He would be working the usual places. They always gave him a little more every year. Inflation, they explained as they laughed. Benjamin had no idea what that meant, but he knew it meant that every year, he earned more for doing the same. Besides, there were also the new accounts. He wondered what his father had got him this year. His father would be giving him his appointment list by tomorrow night and Benjamin would have to write it all down in his planner. His father had given him that. Benjamin was a busy boy with a hectic schedule and loads of responsibility. What better training for a boy who will one day take over the family business. That had been his explanation when his wife had asked, "Why buy a $200 planner for an eleven-year-old boy?" A company car and a driver would be Benjamin's for a week, taking him to his various appointments. And carrying so much money around, it was better for the boy to be accompanied by the burly Mr Singh, who doted on Benjamin because the boy was well-behaved and polite in spite of everything he should not have had at his age.

"Well, Wings, how did the week go?" Janet asked at the end of Job Week. It had been five days of mostly walking for him, Eng Kiat and another couple of Scouts from Green and Blue Six. Wings had made $2 at home for sweeping the whole house and another $2 for washing an uncle's car. The rest had been earned walking long miles through the estates of Sembawang and Seletar. Usually a dollar for each cupboard of shoes polished or each compound swept. Weeding a garden normally brought $2, but it was hot, sweaty, dirty work that lasted too long. Besides, the Scouts did it once a month in school anyway. But there was no choice. They welcomed whatever work they could find. The Job Done sticker was far too common a sight and even houses with no stickers often had no work. And worst of all, they had seen two Scouts from another unit selling the sticker to a housewife. It was frustrating and depressing, especially after Eng Kiat and he had turned down several outright donations.

"We can't take donations, ma'am," Eng Kiat had explained to one householder. "We have to work for it."

Eng Kiat and him had paired off while the other two hunted together. They would divide up an estate and meet again at mealtimes. There, at lunch, across the table, they would compare their takings and whenever one team told of a job they had found, the other wished that they had chosen that side of the estate.

"Twenty flat. How much did you manage, buddy?" Eng Kiat had asked Wings as the sun set on Friday. Wings did not have to look at his card. He remembered every job and every wage.

"Sixteen flat. Is that okay?" Wings asked.

"Yep. Most P3s make about that. I'm five dollars behind the P4 average."

"Will you get into trouble, Kiat?"

"No. We did our best. We didn't skive, so it doesn't matter. Bad luck this year, that's all."

But for Wings, it had been an adventure like no other he had ever had. Wandering into places he had never been before, looking after his own meals, walking long dusty roads with friends, drinking from a canteen. He had enjoyed being on the road more than the work or the money, although it was satisfying to see the job card signed, and that anticipation as a householder's pen hesitated over the money column and the inevitable disappointment.

His greatest moment had come however, when one of his father's friends had dropped by for a visit late one evening. Wings had just come home and was eating a late, cold dinner. His father had explained Job Week to his friend and he had been impressed.

"Hm. You know it takes a lot of guts to knock on a stranger's door and ask for a job," he had said in reply.

Wings had felt his spirits take a sudden and steep climb, the needles in his mental altimeter spinning out of control.

He told her everything.

"Good. I'm glad you enjoyed it so much in spite of the tough parts. You're growing up, Wings," Janet said. But what had he said he enjoyed? The wandering, being on the road. He had not said it was the meeting of people or the satisfaction of honest work. It was a need for adventure, a feeling of independence and self-reliance, freedom from all things that kept a man in one place. You really are like Michael, Wings. I hope you never break somebody's heart like he broke ours. His parents' and mine.

The Scouts gathered in the den and the Scoutmaster held up the list of his top-grossing Scouts. Most of them already knew who was on the list because rumours had spread fast.

"The best P6 earnings were from Benjamin. He totalled almost one hundred and fifty dollars," the Scoutmaster beamed with pride. He was especially happy because it was Benjamin, whom he had helped to bring this far as a Scout. He has my spirit, the Scoutmaster felt, and he thought of Benjamin almost as a son.

"Best P5 earnings are from Jeremy of Green Six with fifty-seven dollars. Just fifty cents behind is his brother, James." James scowled suddenly at his brother. They had ended the week with equal earnings. His brother had done the dirty on him. He must have added that fifty cents on his own. Jeremy returned the scowl with a smug smile.

"Best P4 is Kim Leong with forty-five dollars, and..." the Scoutmaster paused to see if the troop was paying attention, "...the best P3 has actually done better than the best P4." There was a cheer from the youngest wolf-cubs, who had been waiting for this moment.

"Fifty dollars from Boon Ming," the Scoutmaster announced above the general commotion. Boon Ming smiled broadly from left to right and winked at Wings. Wings raised his hands in mock surrender and mouthed okay, okay, you win. Boon Ming could not read lips, but he guessed the message.

"But it isn't worth being fat for," Nathan said later. "How did you do it, Tubs?"

"My dad plays golf see, so I caddied for his friends every morning or evening the whole week and they paid me ten dollars each time. And they always bought my meals too."

"Wow, you mean you had to carry all those clubs around?" Eng Kiat asked.

"Well, no. All the bags are on a kind of trolley so I push them around. And sometimes we have an electric cart so I just ride along."

"What would they need a caddy for if they've got an electric cart?"

"Oh, I do things like set up the tees and balls and bring clubs for them. You know, clubs are either woods or irons and they all have numbers, so whenever they need a particular one, I bring it to them."

"That's all?"

"Yep."

"You're disgusting," Nathan said. Boon Ming had made more than him.

"Well, you win still. You did make more than most of us. But it really has nothing to do with being fat. Your dad just knew the right folks that's all," Peter said. Boon Ming agreed, but his mind was already running way ahead. This was a damned good start, as his dad would say. He had got himself noticed. All he had to do now was keep it up and make sure the right folks saw it. He had been watching Benjamin and had guessed his secret of success. He felt happy. He was on the roll now.

Wings was happy for another reason. He had a friend now, one whom he could talk to about anything. She had time to listen to him and he could tell her things he never could tell other people. But she was a grown-up. Would she always be there when he needed her? It was a nagging doubt and one he could not clear his heart of.

16

IT had been a long, hard day of play, but the cubs took a long time settling down. It was not their first camp, but getting to sleep the first night out was still hard to do. They called out to each other in the darkness, voices floating on the night air from tent to tent, giggles muffled in air pillows. Sixers' voices followed, telling them to shut up and sleep. Voice by voice, the cubs signed off, until the night was silent and nothing rode the airwaves save the light snores of tired Scouts.

Wings kept his eyes closed, not tightly, because that needed concentration and would only keep him awake. He was still conscious when the last voice faded into a murmur and all he could hear was Boon Ming's breathing and the songs of the crickets. He sat up and moved to the door. Raising the flap he looked out into the blue darkness and saw the black shapes of other tents, lined up in neat rows. The night was inviting. Wings had been afraid of the dark when he was younger, but now, the night was his friend and he welcomed it. He savoured the solitude it brought, when he could walk abroad in his imagination. The darkness was another world when the light left and when reality was left unlit, things that hurt could not be seen. It did not matter if they were there. They could be forgotten for a time. When had he discovered that? The night like a dark movie theatre, a blackened silver screen for him to run the home movies he made in his head on. That special hour or so before sleep came, the grey zone between waking reality and the dreamtime he had no control of. He waited for those hours of the half-light, when daylight, neon light met the night and died in her arms. Those dying moments were what he lived for.

Grass beneath his sneakers as he crept silently away, cold air blowing in his face. He pulled up the zipper on his track top and breathed in the cold. He shut his eyes and let the wind blow on against him. It was a good feeling, letting the cold wind blow on your face while the rest of you is warm in a track suit. He opened his eyes. He loved the night too because then, he could get away from his glasses. There was not much to see. Night is felt. He walked without purpose, but an empty field was boring, so his feet took him to the school hall. It was really nothing more than a very large roof supported by columns and the only walls stood around a wooden stage. He felt concrete beneath his feet and knew he had found a path. He was soon in the hall and though he made no sound, he could feel an echo. He could not see the roof but he could feel it there. It felt distinctly different from an open field. He climbed up onto the stage and suddenly threw his arms wide open, the way he had seen rock stars do it on TV. He could almost hear the roar of the audience, the screaming adulation. Then he went over to the rostrum, put his hands forcefully on the edges and pretended to be his principal. He brought his palms together and raised them to the roof. I am a preacher and I am asking God to let me see perfectly again so I can fly. But he already knew the answer to that. His fists came down hard on the rostrum with a thump and an angry sob broke past his throat. I am alone in darkness. I can cry.

She started when she heard the thump and her heart began to run. Janet wanted to run too, back to the tent she shared with Mrs Han, but she had to look. She had heard tales of the school spirit and it had nothing to do with cheerleaders. But it might also be her boys playing the fool when they should be in bed. Convinced it was the latter, she made for the hall.

His tears had formed a watery lens on his eyes and for a fleeting moment, he saw a shadow move against the grey grass. He knew he could not be seen on stage. He had not been able to see the rostrum. He kept perfectly still.

Janet picked her way carefully in the darkness. The thump had sounded like flesh on wood. The nearest wooden furniture was in the hall. As she drew nearer to the stage, Wings recognised her silhouette. She was tall, athletic, with short curly hair. Wings could not decide if he should come out of hiding. But her eyes were growing used to the darkness of the hall and she avoided looking directly at anything she wanted to see. Looking at the side of the rostrum, she saw a small figure standing still.

"I can see you," she said. Her voice echoed and the loudness frightened her. Wings was wondering if he could convince her to leave quickly if he growled. Then he remembered that he liked Janet and did not want to scare her for nothing. Besides, she liked him too and probably would not scold him for being here.

"I saw you long ago, Miss Tan."

"Wings, you naughty boy, what are you doing here?" she asked, relieved that it was one of her boys.

"Couldn't sleep."

"Are you alright?"

"Yes," he said as he jumped off-stage.

"You ought to be in bed," she said sternly. She felt for the light switch and clicked it on. A single dim bulb came to life at one end of the stage. Wings' eyes hurt from the photo-shock and he blinked. Janet saw the tear-stains on his face.

"No, you're not alright. What's wrong, Wings?"

"Nothing." She sat down on a wooden bench and pulled him in front of her. She put her hands on his shoulders gently and looked at him.

"Then why did you cry, boy?"

"I didn't!" She traced a finger lightly down a tear-stain.

"If you tell me why you hurt, I can help you."

"You can't."

"Let me try." Wings looked skeptically at her. There's nothing you can do. He thought a while longer and realised that there was no more harm she or anyone else could do.

"I wanted to fly."

She remembered he did not bother much with singalongs. His mind was always somewhere else. She remembered his sad face when she had caught him and Boon Ming outside the toilet. His strange excuse about being a wolf-cub at full moon. She nodded.

"And then I couldn't see so well and I had to get glasses. And I couldn't fly anymore."

The jets he had refused to look up at. The gliders he had refused to ever make again. And then she realised at once, both the aptness of his name and the sad irony it contained. She nodded and sighed. "I understand." At least half of her did. I thought it was your mum and dad who made you cry. But it's this, the loss of a dream, that's all it is. Unless the dream was all you had. She made him sit beside her. When things are bad, where do we turn to? To our dreams, inside ourselves or to the future, outside. Flight — it had been the only way of escape he had. It had been the future he hoped for, something to go on for and in one sweep, both were lost. Her heart ached for him and he looked so small and lost beside her. She put her arm around him and stroked his hair.

"What did you do after that?"

"Nothing, not until I became a Scout." He looked up from his sneakers. "But it isn't really the same, I guess."

"No two things are. Why does it hurt you so much still?"

"Because it meant a lot to me. There was nothing else I wanted. I even knew how I wanted to die."

Janet was surprised. "You knew how you wanted to die? Wings, you're only nine. You shouldn't be thinking things like that."

"How else can a pilot die?" That disturbed her.

"How did you want to die?"

"With my airplane, shot out of the sky." She could feel a tingling run up her nose to her eyes, but she fought them back.

"Why Wings?"" she asked in a small voice.

"Because I wouldn't be happy dying any other way." He sounded so matter of fact. Michael had said something like that once and she had hit him, and besides the pain, there had been the anger when he died.

"But Wings, a lot of people hurt when you die like that."

"But everybody dies. Can't I choose how if I can?" She couldn't answer him.

"Wings, there was a boy I knew who was just like you." She smiled wryly at him and told him her own story of a man who loved to fly. The boy she had met in college, who left her twice a week for a Cessna at Seletar. The boy who chose to fly a fighter jet instead of going on to university. Whose proudest steps were those he took as he marched up to get his wings. Who shot through the clouds riding on a flame and a prayer. Who lived and enjoyed living. Who laughed and talked and cried with her. Who loved her with a passion and died in the embrace of another woman called an A-4.

Wings was silent throughout. "I'm sorry," he murmured when she finished.

"It's alright. You see, Wings, when we lose something or

someone we love very much, it's only human to hurt, even if it's for a long time. But we have to learn to let them go and carry on with our own lives. Michael wouldn't want me to be sad forever. He'd want me to go on with my life and that includes loving someone else." That was hard for her to say, but saying it forced her to accept it. "I know you can't fly anymore, but there's so many other things you could give your life too. Yes, nothing will ever be the same, in the same way that no one can ever be like Michael. But that's how it is, Wings. You have to learn to let it go and carry on."

"I know, that's why I'm here, but when I say it hasn't been the same, I mean it hasn't worked out well."

"Wings, everything that might have been always works out better than what is. Do you understand?"

"Yes. Don't dreams ever come true without some kind of catch?"

"I don't know," she whispered. Maybe a dream come true for one person means a shattered one for somebody else.

"Wings, I know it sounds very cruel to say this," she stopped. Yes, she had to say it. "But I'm glad you won't be a pilot, especially if you want to die flying."

Wings was taken aback and angry.

"Why?" he demanded.

"Because I wouldn't bear it if anything happened to you too. I don't want you to die the way Michael died. They never even found his body. You're my friend too. I don't want to lose another friend that way."

Wings stared at her and tried to understand what she had just said. Didn't friends share each other's dreams? Then he tried to imagine getting his 6/6 vision back and then losing it again. No, no. Twice was more than he could bear. He understood.

"I don't think it'll ever happen to me, so don't worry."

She smiled and hugged him.

"You'll be alright, Wings. It was a lovely dream while it lasted, but when you wake up, life goes on. Understand? Don't waste your life feeling sad about something that's lost. Promise?"

"Okay," he said.

"I want a Scout's promise."

"I promise, on my honour."

"Good boy," she said. Now to learn my own lessons and make that promise to me. Let go, Janet. It's time to carry on living. She felt her heart running again. They talked a little while more, until the boy was tired and could barely keep his eyes open. He fell asleep with his head on her shoulder and she let him lie there for a while, her arm around him. I'll have to wake you up soon. She kissed him lightly on his forehead and whispered, "Thank you, Wings."

17

WINGS put on his freshly ironed uniform with care. It had lost its newness and the khaki was now a lighter shade. But Wings did not mind. It was softer, not prickly anymore and it meant that he was now an old hand. He liked the 'seasoned trooper' look, especially the number tapes that were beginning to fray and the creases in the leather belt. A veteran 1010 Grey, he was on his way to a new unit

He looked in the mirror to check his turn out. What would the boys here be like? Spit and polish, the way 1010 had been, always fighting to win, usually at the top of everything? It had been an awful way to live, but out of 1010, it was something to brag about.

Peter had left when they had gone back to school that year. His time was up and he had moved on to secondary school. Pete had been sad when he left, Wings remembered, but not because he was leaving us. He recalled the time he had first joined, how Peter had told his tenderfoot to trust in him, to let him explain and interpret the Law for him. Saint Peter, they had called him. And Peter had been good. But not as good as Peter wanted Peter to be. Wings was sorry, because he felt Peter had done okay. I tried to keep them true, but I couldn't even stay true all the time myself, Peter had said. How much more could he have done? Wings held nothing against him. I suppose I must find meanings for myself now.

He would not be able to ask Nathan for help. Nathan was gone too. He had been shamed. Yes, he had failed too. He had not been made Sixer of the Greys. Someone else had and Nathan could not live with that. He had resigned the week after the promotions were out. Did it really matter? No, Wings could not say yes. But the troop, that was a different matter. To them it mattered, but only because they made it. So Nathan was gone.

I really am alone. Even Boon Ming's turned funny. All he can think about now is how to get on. How to pass the tests, how to do well in the eyes of the Scoutmaster, how to get his badges. That's all that matters. Doesn't even talk about that Brownie he tried so hard to get. And now, there would not even be the comforting familiarity of 1010. I suppose I can blame Mum for that, he sighed.

It had happened sooner than he had expected. His mother had acted with sudden swiftness, deadly determination and devastating finality. It had taken his father by surprise. It had taken the neighbourhood bookie by pleasant surprise because no one had made bets for the first month of the year. It had taken his grandparents by surprise too, when their daughter had suddenly appeared on their doorstep one evening with two children and a pile of bags. Taken totally unawares, nobody had known what to do to help her or stop her or anything, which was what she had intended. Wings had just ridden in his mother's wake, following her limply into a new way of life.

It had been a major event, by most standards, but Wings knew that if he were to survive it, he had to get on with business as usual. They had moved to a new place. His mother, who had seized possession of the car in her *Blitzkrieg* departure ("well, he got the house, so he gained in the end, didn't he?"), had driven him and his sister to school every morning. After school, they had gone home to their father. Actually, it was an empty house as he had to carry on with his life and work. They had lunch with Eddie and his family and had spent the afternoons studying and playing there. Their father taught in the afternoon, so by the time he got back, the childen were gone, whisked back to their grandparents by their mother.

At school, life had been the same. One change at a time, Wings thought. Easier to handle. But there had been the neighbours' questions when Wings and his sister were out playing. At school, the teachers had asked, especially those who lived in the same estate. The other students had not asked, because they were all too young to really know. Wings had still come to school, so as far as they were concerned, nothing had changed. The neighbourhood children had seen nothing different too. Before the Event, Wings had played with them in the afternoon. He still had. They did not play at night, when he was gone, so they had not missed him.

Wings had stayed on with 1010, attending meetings as usual for those first two terms. Life had not got worse. It might even have got better. There were no more quarrels to listen to night after night. The uncertainty that had hung over their heads — would she leave or wouldn't she? — that was gone too now. Both parents treated them better, trying to win their affection and loyalty. Their grandparents were kind. It was a pretty good life.

But Wings had known that it would not last. There had been talk about changing schools. That meant leaving the estate, the school and the troop for good. And Janet.

She is my friend, but not in the way Boon Ming or Peter or Nathan or Eng Kiat are, he thought as he slipped the woggle up his scarf. What I say to her, they can never understand. But Janet can. Yet why should I trust her? She's a grown-up and grown-ups can't be trusted. And she's a woman too. That's worse. But she's the only one who doesn't have to be second to none all the time. He saw again her face, with her smile and bright laughing eyes that he had seen go red only once, the time she talked about a boy called Michael. She never says that what I tell her is stupid and she's always kind, even when I think she doesn't understand at all. She never laughs at me. He could almost feel her arm around him again and he remembered thinking that it was such a long time since he felt like a child. He felt safe with her. He had trusted her when he put his grazed hands in hers, when he had come out of hiding in the dark, when she had persuaded him gently to tell her why he cried. And she hadn't let him down. No, not yet. But maybe she wouldn't. What a hope. But another part of him knew he needed her in a way that he hated to admit. He wanted to trust her. No, that would not do. He would not give in to that. But his heart would not take no for an answer. How hurting it would be if you did not trust her. She trusts you. But I won't hurt her. Would she know that? Difference between what you should do and what you want to do. He wanted to trust her, at least one person in the world. I surrender. I wish I didn't need you, Janet. I really wish I didn't. But he did. And something in him knew that if he had to need anybody, it might as well be Janet. Maybe she's the only one who really cares.

She had missed him the week his parents broke up. She had mentioned his absence to Mrs Han and she had told her the story. When she got home, she had tried calling, but Wings was no longer at his father's house. That night, she had wept for her little friend and wondered if he was all right. She had found him the Monday after.

"Hey, didn't see you last week. How have you been?"

"Okay."

She had bent down and said softly, "I'm sorry, Wings."

"What for? It wasn't your fault."

"I'm sorry it happened to you."

"It was going to one day anyway."

"You feel alright?"

"Yes. I'm okay. Don't worry about me."

"I can't help it." They had been silent for a while.

"Wings, anytime you feel bad and need somebody, come to me okay? I'll take care of you."

"I know. You're my friend."

"And you're mine," she had smiled as she roughed up his hair.

Talk had grown into plans and those grew into certainties. By the end of term, Wings had known for sure that his time was up.

"Janet, will you still be my friend when I'm not here?"

"Of course, Wings," she had said in surprise. "Are you planning to go somewhere?"

"Wasn't my idea. My mum's going to send me to a school nearer home." He had tried to sound as if it happened everyday.

"When?"

"Next term."

"You've got my phone number and address and I've got yours. Real friends can't ever really be far away from each other."

"I guess, but I won't see you again and we can't talk to each other like this anymore." She had looked at the little boy and felt a twinge of pain. With him far away, how could she watch out for him?

"Wings, the means aren't important. It doesn't matter if we talk face to face or on the phone or in letters. What's important is that we do talk. And I want you to call straight away if you get into any trouble. Do you understand?"

"Okay."

"Are you going to be a Scout there?"

"If there's a troop." He had not been excited about it. 1010 had been a lot of fun, but it had been a let down too. Perhaps he had expected too much from scouting. But Baden Powell, all those things he wrote about, surely those were true? And the Law he had engraved in his heart — was it only a standard for people like Peter and him to feel guilty by? Maybe it had all been just a hope. Something Baden Powell had wished and had put into words to make it real. Then this would be as much a dream as flight. And as a dream, it don't come up to scratch with flight.

She had taken his hand in hers and he had felt the soft, smooth warmth of her palm, her fingers gently closing around his.

"I care, Wings, don't forget that. No matter what happens, you've got me to run to, okay?" She had hugged him and thought, we must be a sight, Akela and her little wolf-cub, both in uniform.

"Goodbye, Wings."

"Bye, Janet."

Bye Janet. He sighed. Must not think too much about them all, 1010 and Janet. Think of now, think of my new school, my new troop, my new life. Yes, think about these.

He had already thought plenty about his new school. Most of the kids lived within walking distance, amongst the filing cabinet Housing Board flats. The rest came in school buses, from other satellite towns of filing cabinets. Where were the cars in the driveway? The cars that had stretched out of the school and all the way down the country lane outside his old school? Absent, like a lot of truants. Wings walked too, because his grandparents lived on the highest floor of a nearby point-block. He had figured the kids' parents had cars too, but did not send them to school because they could all walk. But someone had set him right on that.

"You mean your father has a car?"

"Yes, but not anymore. My mum took it from him. Does your father still have his?"

"Ah, he has it for half the day, and at night, someone else takes it," his new classmate had explained.

"Does she return it?" Wings had asked with his mother in mind.

"Ya, sure. Otherwise I can't come to school."

"What do you mean? Your dad doesn't bring you to school. You come in a taxi."

"That is my father."

Wings had also found out that the simply-dressed women who came at recess with food and drinks for the screaming and crying PI kids were not servants or nannies. He had met a tearful PI babbling incoherently and had taken the chance to do his daily good deed. He had thought the woman waving frantically to the little boy was his nanny until he had screamed, "Ma!" and broken away from Wings.

There was also no forest. The school was surrounded by roads, high buildings, low buildings, unfinished buildings, provision stores, coffee shops, hairdressers, wet markets, hawker centres, playgrounds made of metal piping and concrete, hardware stores and neighbourhood police posts. Where did the Scouts go to hike? What did they patrol? Where would they camp?

Wings would find out today. He did not know what the Scouts here were like. He did not know what they did. He had not made the attempt to scout them out the way he had once done. He was accepting the Promise that he believed all Scouts took, that he would be a brother here as he had been at 1010. Different place, different people, but we are all Scouts. He was taking that leap of faith Baden Powell compared to jumping into a lake without checking out the temperature first. Shouldn't one look for rocks? The question had bugged him ever since he had read that yarn, but he decided it was not the point. Don't worry about things like temperature. A little cold won't hurt you. Take it like a man. Wings often wondered how many silly Scouts had taken a header into cold water only to hit rock bottom.

He held his breath and took the plunge.

18

Dear Janet,

Hi, it's Wings again. How are you and things at 1010? I've joined the Scouts here and they are rather boring. I went for the first meeting last week. All they did was some drill (which wasn't very good) and then they sang some songs after (which I never liked doing anyway.)

At 1010 if we weren't doing stuff like singing or marching or gardening (which we do here too), we did things for our tests and badges. Remember how big we thought Benjamin was with all his badges? I'm the only one with an arrow here. Not even the P6 boys have arrows and most of them leave at the end of P5 anyway so they can study for the PSLE. Boon Ming would love it here. He told me last week that he had just two more tests to pass to get his silver arrow.

Actually that isn't so good. I mean, even if a Scout was ready to take a test, the teachers aren't ready to test them. At 1010 we could take tests every week. Here it's always 'maybe next week' or 'we try to have it once a month' and we often never do. At least that's what the other boys say. I'm in Red Six now and even my Sixer doesn't have an arrow.

Anyway, my new unit is more like a boys' club than a Scout troop. We called you and Mrs Han Akela. Now our teacher is just Mrs Lim. And our Scoutmaster isn't really a Scoutmaster. He's just an old boy of the unit. By the way, we are 2400, which our Scoutmaster says is midnight in Army time. We don't hike or camp or anything like that very much, so say the boys, but they play a lot of football, which I never liked anyway.

Do I sound like I'm unhappy, Janet? But I don't really feel unhappy. And I don't feel happy either. It feels like in-between. I'm here and that's it.

Things are all right at home (home means here now) and I see my dad once a week on Saturdays or Sundays. My mum is awfully busy with her business so I don't see her very much. There's a man she sees now too. I think my dad sees someone too. But I'm not telling either of them! I'm too young for all that so I don't see anyone. Have you got a boyfriend yet?

School is not as bad as I thought it would be. I've made lots of friends. They're different from the kids back there. I haven't got any really good friends yet, maybe because I'm odd or something. They say I talk funny. They talk funnier but there's so many of them and only one of me so I can't tell them that. They also say I'm rich, because they found out my mum has a car and I used to have a servant. But didn't everybody? And some of them don't like me because of that. Some of the Scouts didn't like the arrow either. The Scoutmaster too, I think. Yep, I'm not very popular although a lot of people know me. Sometimes I wish I was the nobody I was before my parents divorced. I don't like being famous because of them.

It's a rather sunny afternoon and I'd like to go downstairs to play. But there isn't anyone around to play with. It wouldn't matter if I had my bike, but it's been left at my dad's house and my mum won't bring it over because she says I'll ride all day and not study and I'll probably ride on the roads too. My mum knows me well!

There's nothing very interesting on TV in the afternoons except Chinese movies and you know I can't watch those. I'd rather read a book than subtitles. They change too fast. Don't say do your homework because that's done and I won't do anymore than I have to. Would you? And I can't write to you every day either because I won't have anything to tell you and because I haven't enough money for the stamps. (And they say I'm rich!)

Do you know I can see all the way to the harbour from my window? I do that sometimes. We're so high up nothing blocks the view and it's windy and everything. I saw some American ships come in one day and they were so big and grey I could see them from here. And I saw the aircraft carrier. I couldn't see the Tomcats, though, but I saw their wings flashing in the sun. But talking about that makes us sad. I still wish I could fly, Janet. And living so high makes it worse because I can look down at everything and everybody, as if I was flying. But I can't. I feel like a bird in a cage being hung out from a window.

Well, I guess I'll end here. Thanks for being my friend, Janet. It's nice to tell someone things you can't tell anyone else. I miss you.

Love, Wings.

She folded the letter carefully and slipped it back into its envelope. She felt a heaviness about her as she added it to a small stack of similar envelopes.

"I miss you too, Wings."

19

HE sat bathed in the warm yellow glow of his study lamp. The rest of the room was dark and by his bed, the luminous hands of his alarm clock shone nine o'clock. His grandparents were watching television. The kid sister was staying with some cousins for the weekend. Mum was out on a date. He did not mind being alone. Of late, he had learnt to enjoy his own company. Not that it was of his choosing, to be alone. No, circumstances had taught him to.

The gun lay on his desk, stripped, with its parts neatly laid out. He held the anvil, scraping off the black stains of gunpowder carefully with a teaspoon.

The wind blew suddenly at his curtains and he felt the rush of cold air. Rain tonight. Sleeping will be good. Shuddering, he stood by the sill and looked far out at the city lights. All the way up here, I can see everything. I am a bird. The first raindrops hit his face and he pulled the windows in. It was starting to rain at night.

But he remembered the weather two months back had not been wet, just humid and heavy. They had followed the silent trail by the water's side. It was narrow, so they had walked in Indian file. The sky was blocked out by the clouds and the water was green and still where no wind blew.

A terrapin's shell broke the surface of the still water. There was a shout further up the column and boys rushed to the waterside to see the terrapin submerge and swim quickly away. They marched on. They'll like the squirrels, Wings thought. And those little frogs, the size of a thumbnail. Maybe a grass snake would show itself. Or a monkey. He suddenly felt a longing to be back with his old unit. He had not appreciated any of these before but the 2400 boys, with their excitement and fascination with everything that breathed and moved with its own life, they were helping him see them again. He felt a vague pride too. This had all been his. It still was, really. It felt like taking new friends home and showing them the rooms, your toys even though you didn't live there anymore.

The squirrels came and this time the boys kept still and did not get too close, having learnt from their encounter with the terrapin. Bushy tails trailing, they ran up and down trees and one came onto the path. The boys crept closer.

Let's catch him, one of the boys had suggested. But Wings had stopped him and said it was a wild thing and had a right to be free, that it would be unhappy caged. So what, the other had shot back, it doesn't belong to you. Got your name on it? Show me. Think your bronze arrow means everything is yours? Wings had kept his silence at the familiar taunt. The boy quickly picked up a rock and hurled it at the squirrel. His aim was bad and the squirrel got away.

Down the trail in the clammy heat, one of the boys in his Six had asked to borrow the binoculars Wings had brought. It was deep inside his pack, the Scouts were moving fast and Wings was getting weary. He had given his patrolmate a curt 'no'. The Scoutmaster had heard the conversation and had strode up alongside later to give Wings a little speech on sharing what one had with those who did not. Wings knew there was no need to try to explain. They had decided early on that Wings, being better off, was probably spoilt and selfish.

But why should I be extra nice just to prove them wrong? If it had been anyone else, no one would have said anything. If someone else had said leave the animals alone, they would have listened. He sighed as he polished the contacts of the batteries that drove his gun. Maybe I am stubborn. And maybe that is why I am alone.

Even in our games, I am the outsider. He put in a magazine and heard a solid *click*. Standing up, he leaned back against the wall in a fighting stance, ready to whip around the corner.

He could feel again the roughness of the wall through his uniform as he pressed himself against it. Two weeks back. He was breathing hard as he stood there, feet spread and knees bent for stability. His hands gripped the Heckler and Koch tightly, small, black with a lethal weight. Chin Meng squatted beside him, the sweat dripping off his forehead onto the concrete.

"Get up," Wings said. Chin Meng sighed and struggled up. Wings bent low and took a quick glance around the corner.

"Move!" Wings dashed across the open space to the cover of the next building. Chin Meng followed reluctantly. As they cleared the grass patch between buildings, a short staccato burst of an M-16 on auto broke the silence and Wings knew he had made a mistake. Chin Meng screamed and Wings took a quick glance around and saw him fall on his knees on the grass. Wings cursed and looked around frantically for the hidden gunman. Sound, sound, where did it come from? Loud, but the damn echoes. Almost no difference. Close, he's close. Then he spotted the slim black barrel of the M-16 protruding over a balcony. Wings dashed out from cover again, firing at the gunman to keep him down. The gunman had not turned his fire on Chin Meng to finish him off quickly. He had been waiting for Wings to come back for him. Two kills, but he had not reckoned on

Wings spotting him. He now kept his head down as automatic fire came directly at him.

Wings hauled Chin Meng up to his feet. The P3 was small, so Wings carried him in a fireman's lift. He had stopped firing for a moment. One, two, three, four, the gunman counted the silence. Was the damned agent waiting for him? No, he'd be busy with his partner. Wings had already started running when he heard the clatter of an M-16 handguard against concrete balcony. He spun around and was almost toppled by Chin Meng's weight. The gunman appeared and promptly ducked as a volley of machinegun slugs came his way. Wings ran for cover.

"Idiot," Wings said. The boy had tripped over a root. Chin Meng rubbed his ankle as Wings reloaded their weapons.

"We're running out of ammo," he said grimly. Where else could they get ammo? The nearest store was two blocks away at Block 89. He felt for his coin purse. There was no comforting weight or jingle. He'd spent too much on the gun itself. Saved two whole months for it and even then, the week had been on a really tight shoestring. He checked the time. There was only half an hour to go. No, buying ammo now might turn out pointless. He had one more roll of caps. Chin Meng had half. That's the price one pays for being trigger-happy. Of course, they could be dead before twelve o'clock.

A shrill whistle sounded and the echoes ran around the concrete blocks. It was the Reds' signal to regroup. Chin Meng got up to go, but Wings pulled him back. Not right, there were twenty-seven minutes more to go. They had been watching their patrolmates assembling when guns opened up from the blocks around them. The Reds had tried to return fire, but they were pinned.

"Give me your gun," Wings demanded. Chin Meng handed it over reluctantly. What if they came for him? He'd be alone and unarmed, but he gave it up.

With a gun in each hand, Wings ran off, disappearing into the maze of grey concrete. Go around, get behind them, at least one group and blow them away. He felt a strange sensation in his stomach, not unlike the first time he had opened the pages of a porno magazine. There was a tingling in his arms and his heart was pumping fast. He flanked the building and got round to the back. It was a point block with only one stairwell. He ran up, two steps at a time, his black gym shoes hardly making any noise. The noise of exploding caps got louder as he neared the third floor. Then he could smell the burnt gunpowder. They saw him come but it was too late. Even as they turned, he was in firing position, facing them, suicidally squared, knees bent, sitting low, a gun in each hand, a smirk on his lips and then the explosions and smoke, one set coming fast as the motor drove the caps under the pounding hammer and the other going as fast as he could squeeze the trigger. Through the haze, they saw him open his mouth to laugh and then the ringing echo in the corridor and his face disappearing in the acrid smoke.

Game over. Blue Six had cheated and won. Red Six ambushed and massacred. Someone had revealed their whistle signals to the Blues and they had used the knowledge well.

"Some of the guys say it was you who let the secret out," Chin Meng said.

"I heard."

"But I believe you," Chin Meng said.

"Thanks, kid." Wings felt old. He was older, in more ways than just years. He had fought in the forests of Sembawang. Some of the boys called his arrow 'Wings' Jungle Warfare Badge'. It was meant to be derogatory because the implication was that he was a country bumpkin come to the city. But he was a veteran of Saint Peter's Greys, a member of the elite 1010. It was something they could not boast of, say what they may. That was often the only comfort he had. He had not bothered to prove his innocence. *Maybe I am proud. Maybe I'm just tired.* He had walked home alone

Must buy ammo before next week's game. He squeezed the trigger and it had a comforting solid click. He checked the oil level. There was no purpose for the oil. It was heated in the barrel to produce smoke for added realism. She had been smoking from the barrel when he had slain the Blues. A housewife had opened her door to investigate the commotion and she had seen him, machine-pistol smoking in his hand and she had screamed and he had laughed wickedly before disappearing into the haze and down the stairs.

He laughed again in the silence of his room. But it was forced and awkward. *Have I lost the ability to laugh? I should be happier here,* he thought. *I am a P4 going on 5 and the only one with an arrow. I am Somebody, even if I'm not quite Benjamin.* But he did not feel that way. *I am not really one of them. Not family, just a visitor, at the most a cousin from the country visiting his relations in the city slums.* That was sticky, because he had become a Scout not just to fill the spare hours that the loss of flight had left him with. He had joined with a vague hope of finding somewhere and something to belong to. He had never felt like an outcast at 1010. He was a true son, though not a filial one because he had not felt the family spirit of *nulli secundus.* That had set him apart. And now this. At least the older rift was his own fault. This? This was because — he could not decide. *Is it me or them? How can I be like them?* He did everything they did. He had stopped bugging the teachers to give more tests for arrows. The Scoutmaster had told him straight that there would be no tests for silver until everyone had had a chance to go for bronze, which he already had. Proficiency badges were out too. The Scoutmaster wanted his boys equal.

So there was nothing to do but attend meetings, do a bit of half-hearted drill, sing a few songs, do gardening or clean the school grounds or wash the toilets. We're the school janitors, the gardeners, the furniture movers, the paper-pickers, the toilet washers. Our reward is football after meetings and gunfights in the housing estates. And the buildings, the playgrounds are always the same. He vaguely remembered a man named Baden Powell and the dream he shared with a million boys around the world. Here, at 2400, the dream had died. I must bring it back, but what can I do against all of them who couldn't care less. The spirit of 1010 had not been completely true to Baden Powell, but at least their actions had been. They were Scouts, almost like the good fellows Baden Powell had written about.

All this, he had told Janet in his letters to her. And she, in return, could not help him much. The book, she always wrote back, read it, Wings, and remember what you are supposed to be. The Law, the values that stood behind them. Her little boy was lost and she could not reach him, could not help him. There had to be something more she could tell him, besides hang in there, kid, learn to adjust to them, learn what's good about them, like not having to be second to none all the time. Remember your own Promise and the Law you share with all those true Scouts all over the world through all time. It broke her heart to read his letters, the loss of one dream after another, his heart going back to the world of his daydreams, flying away from a world he had come to hate. Wings, Baden Powell, he didn't lie to us, because the world and people were really that way, in his time and in the places he went. He did all those things and he wanted us to enjoy doing them too. But how do you tell a child that the world changes, often for the worse without teaching him to be a pessimist and a cynic? But Wings, we live in a different time and place and all things change over space and time because people are always changing. She tried practical suggestions. Think of the city as your forest, how can you adapt to survive in it? Can you get around it the same way you could run through the forest, knowing every track and fallen tree? Could you help a stranger there? You might not need to make fires anymore, but can you put them out? How did you get jobs for Job Week when you were out here in the country? It will be harder in the city because people are more wary. Same principles, she told him. Baden Powell gave you those you can use anywhere, anytime in life, not just here and long ago. Use your imagination, boy, think of all the ways you can keep your Promise and Law.

He remembered Peter and that morning under the frangipani tree when they had talked about the Law. You may believe because I say you can. And Peter had tried his best, only to see his efforts come to nothing.

I am now on my own. There's nobody left to tell me what it means. Not even Janet. I have to decide myself. Do what I think is right. The responsibility overwhelmed him. But hadn't he been making his own mind all the time. But that was different. Then, he did what he wanted. Now he had to decide what was right and what was wrong and then do the right thing. The P4 year was drawing to a close and it was almost certain that he would become Assistant Sixer of the Reds. He'd have to do a lot of thinking then, for himself and for his boys. One year to learn and practice before I take command. He saw Benjamin again, and Peter and Nathan. He saw them from a hilltop, from behind a hedgerow, through the flattened perspective of field glasses and he wondered how he would measure up.

He put the last bits of his gun together and carefully packed away the weapon and the cleaning kit. There was something thrilling about the illicit possession of the weapon. He could only guess at the punishment his mother would mete out if she ever found out how much it had cost him.

As he placed the gun carefully into the drawer, he reached for an envelope and drew out a photograph. It showed a young woman and a boy, both in uniform, both smiling, she behind him, her hands on his shoulders, her head against his. It seemed a world away and an age past. Wings suddenly felt more alone than he had in weeks. Outside, the rain had begun to fall in sheets.

20

THE year drew to a close. Wings took a bus to the heart of the city. Christmas was coming and there would be a million people out on the streets, doing their shopping, dragging along their hordes of little wailing children. Wings had nothing to buy, or rather, no money to buy anything with. But to town he had to go, as if the bright lights and the decorations and the Christmas carols could work together to warm the days that were getting colder with the rains.

He remembered a Christmas past, but it was already two years ago, he thought. But even a big street is the same as a little avenue. Everywhere, people are happy or at least they are trying to be and the joy is doubled in the reflections on the wet pavements and slick black roads. Laughter amid the jingle bells and thousandth Noel and certainly no silent nights with the clinking of glasses and the singing of carollers. Little lights winked at him from store windows covered with spray-can frost, streamers running through polystyrene snow. The smell of the street, smoke and gutter and hamburger joints and back alleys filled with rotting binfuls of yesterday's food.

Home to me now, this. Wings strolled casually on. With his bus pass, town was a free ride away and he went often. And now, this season more than ever, he needed the town. He saw in the windows, shelves, display cabinets, racks and boxes, things he would someday own. Faces flashed by him, one like the other before it and the one that would follow. There were pretty girls, but he knew he was too young. Someday then, when I'm grown up, I shall love somebody and belong to her and I will come to town to buy her a present. He was ten going on eleven. How long more? Four, maybe five years? Too long — God, will I even be alive by then? Maybe this Christmas you make me a promise, a present, huh? Don't kill me until I find love and let me live awhile to enjoy it. Ah, depressing. He wished he had money. Spending made him dizzy, it made him feel better and the more he spent, the better he felt, because one is worth what one buys for oneself. But he knew it would also bring on the guilt. Oh the beggars who sat outside the department stores. He would give them a coin or two, maybe more, if he had spent a lot. But today, he would only feel sad for them because he was not buying anything.

He looked wistfully at the rows of model airplanes on display. Someone had put them together and painted them. They stood in neat rows, an Air Force in miniature that would command the airspace in little boys' hearts. But he could not look long.

There is nothing I need, he thought, so there is no reason to buy. No reason except to make me happy for a while. He took his eyes off a Swiss knife and carried on his way.

He was looking at some soft toys when he heard a familiar voice beside him say, "Any Christmas wishes?" He turned around and she was smiling at him, the way she always had.

"Janet!"

"Hi, Wings, how have you been? I got your card last week, did you get mine?"

"Yes, just two days ago."

"Are you with your mother?"

'No, I came alone."

"Do you come alone often?"

"Yep!"

"Why?"

"There isn't much else to do at home." Wings took a careful look at her. She seemed different. He could not tell why.

"How have your holidays been?" Then she took his hand and squeezed it. "Are you okay?" He nodded. She raised her eyebrows at him and he nodded again with more emphasis. She knew it was not talk he needed, but her presence in his life and there was nothing she could do about that. She wished with all her heart that she could spend the rest of the day with him, though even that would have helped him little

"Would you like to have tea with us, Wings?" she asked as she pointed to a smiling man waiting by an escalator. Wings had been about to say yes when he followed her finger to its mark. He felt a familiar aching in his heart.

"No, thanks, Janet, I'll have to start for home in a little while."

"Well, take care of yourself, Wings. Be good and have a merry Christmas, dear," she wanted to cry and she knew he could hear it in her voice. She hugged him and bent to kiss him quickly on the cheek and she was gone, her heels clicking against the marble floor. She turned to wave and they sank into the ground as the escalator took them down. He knew then why she looked different. She had found somebody to love.

"Happy Christmas, Janet."

21

THE Sixer was relieved. His Second could now take care of all those little details that he had once used to. Attendance, the weekly funds, taking names, form-collecting and stuff — all that would now be done by Wings. The Sixer wore his new double bars with pride. And a brand new bronze arrow too. He looked askance at Wings, who was walking down the row and calling off names. Well, country boy, we're equal now and I'm Sixer, which still keeps me a step above you.

"Your scarf, Seng Huat," Wings said. The boy looked back calmly at him. "Who are you to tell me that? You're only Assistant Sixer." Wings was about to tell him it was his job anyway, but he already knew what 2400 boys were like. They went by the book whenever it was convenient. Where does it say you can check our uniforms? And if Wings did something they did not like, it was 'there are unwritten rules — understood, one what, you English educated also so stupid'. There was no reasoning with minds so small, he thought. Once, he would not have cared, but now, he felt obliged to explain.

Chin Meng rescued him. "You're in the wrong anyway." Seng Huat scowled and muttered some obscenity in Hokkien. Kim Seng came to them and asked what was going on.

"He's not Sixer and he's checking our uniforms," Seng Huat said petulantly. Kim Seng looked at Wings. He knew there was nothing wrong with what Wings did, but he felt vaguely threatened by this boy who had possessed an arrow since P3.

"I'll do it next time," he said coldly. Wings glared after him and Seng Huat smiled, quite satisfied. The other boys were silent, but the Sixer had already given them tacit permission not to obey Wings if it suited them.

A week later, Wings was leading half the patrol down a dirty alley. Kim Seng was with the rest of the patrol on the other side. Between them were two rows of shophouses and a little lane. Green Six was coming down it and the Reds were organising a hasty ambush. Wings reached his alley end and quickly positioned his men. Kim Seng did not appear and Wings began to worry. Chin Meng made a quick check round the corner.

"Hey, Wings, I can't see Green Six."

Wings squinted across the killing ground and Seng Huat suddenly appeared round the corner with the Sixer and the rest. As Kim Seng tried to form them up into a firing line, Wings felt an angry heat rise in him.

"Shit, they stopped to buy drinks." He would have to talk to Kim Seng about that.

"Wings, I still can't see them," Chin Meng reported. Wings looked across at Kim Seng and Green Six suddenly jumped into view from behind the Red Sixer and his men, guns blazing and Red Six died in a thunder of caps and smoke.

"What the hell were you doing?" Wings said angrily to Kim Seng later. "Why did you have to buy drinks when we were supposed to be moving into an ambush position?"

"Don't forget who's Sixer," Kim Seng said. He knew it had been a mistake to let Seng Huat go into the shop. The Green Six Second had spotted him and they had cut round to the back when Seng Huat did not appear from the storefront. There was no defence.

"I haven't forgotten, but maybe you have. You can't just act like a Sixer. You've got to do the right things too," Wings said. He knew he had the advantage this time and he was not going to let it pass like he had before. The boys listened in silence. Seng Huat thought it was a good thing. If he played his cards right — yes, he could get away with anything. He had gone into the store against orders, but Kim Seng had not admitted that because it meant that he could not control his men.

Kim Seng smarted from the last remark. "Don't act smart and think too big, boy. You think just because you come from some high-class unit, you can push us around. Don't look down on us because you got arrow first and because you talk better."

Wings recognised the old us-against-him line and the usual below the belt references to his old unit and education. He was about to reply when Kim Seng sneered, "And if you're so good why didn't your last unit keep you?" It was more than Wings could take and he suddenly found his knuckles in Kim Seng's solar plexus. His mouth gaped wide as he doubled up and sank to the floor. The other boys looked on in horror. Chin Meng bent down to help him up. Wings stepped back and viewed the scene in silence. A Scout is a brother to every other Scout. He had broken the Law and he realised with a twinge of guilt and sadness that he would do it again if ever he had to.

Red Six was out on patrol again. Kim Seng led the boys while Wings covered the rear. Hunting for Yellow Six, moving carefully through void decks, expecting fire from behind every column, around every corner, from every balcony, every window, every stairwell. They were spaced out, five paces between each man, so that the whole Six would not be caught together if someone opened fire.

The sound of piling floated from a distance, like artillery shells fired at regular intervals. Occasionally, a helicopter thundered low overhead. The small streets were busy with cars, vans, pick-ups and cycles, ferrying their loads of humans and poultry and fish and vegetables and the carcasses of pigs. People crowded the warm shade of corridors, forcing Red Six out onto the pavement. They stared at these boys in uniform, their weapons in their hands, moving in a line, going nowhere in particular while everybody else had somewhere to go.

They passed a vagrant sleeping on a table-tennis table on a void deck. The man was so still. He might have been dead for all Wings knew. Kim Seng was looking at his watch and around the blocks. He wanted to hurry and throw caution to the wind. Just find them and fight, he could have screamed, but he knew better. That way, you made mistakes. He glared at Wings' back. And I cannot make mistakes in front of him.

There was an uneasy understanding between the Sixer and his Second. They hardly said a word to each other unless it was work and absolutely necessary. Both never mentioned the other, both did their best to win the loyalty of the boys in their charge. And that meant getting the job done. It was good in that way, Kim Seng had to admit. Red Six was doing very well compared to the other Sixes. We are just not happy with each other. That's all. But they did what they were supposed to do.

Wings did not like the cold war between them. But it will only be for a year and then they are all mine. He was never one to pick a fight too, and this keeping on his toes was rather tiresome. He wanted to relax again, to be the carefree Scout he had once been. But not when one has men. When one is responsible for so much. And the aggression that he had recently learnt to give vent to was a new and exhilarating thing. He had been brought up never to fight. He had always clenched his fists and walked away, always frustrated, always aware of the consequences faced by boys who decide to fight. Points of no return, setting the wheel of trouble in motion, watching it spin and come slowly to a stop and praying for a favourable outcome. Violence, he knew, was not the best way to settle anything, because it always raised more dust. But sometimes, it is the only way. He looked at Kim Seng. Some people are too stupid to learn any other way.

There was a sudden shout from the lift lobby and a splash two seconds later. The vagabond jerked awake with a shout when the water-bomb exploded in his face. He sat up dripping wet and muttering incoherently, feeling for his belongings in a small plastic bag.

There was laughter down the corridor and Wings ran towards it, gun raised. Kim Seng had not seen the bomb and was puzzled. Had Yellow Six attacked? Where was Wings going to? He gave the order for the Six to follow Wings.

They found Wings standing still in the middle of the void deck, facing a group of five boys, all about their own age.

"It's none of your business. Don't be a busybody," the boys' leader said in Hokkien.

"Why did you do it?" Wings persisted in English. The waterbomb could not have hurt the old man, but he could not help the anger. A defenceless old man. He wanted to get even.

"He was sleeping on our table. Looking for trouble, is it?" the leader asked threateningly.

"You're looking at trouble, son of a bitch," Wings spat the words out. The boy knew just enough English to understand.

"You want to fight?" the leader asked. Kim Seng was worried. They were reaching the danger point. Once they began, there would be no turning back. Wings did a quick assessment of numbers. Five against eight, but they had four P3s who weren't of much use. Kim Seng, Seng Huat, Chin Meng, himself. The boys looked rough and only Seng Huat had any semblance of roughness. He realised that their machineguns were stupidly impotent in this situation. What weapons did the roughs have?

Then with unexpected speed and viciousness, the five suddenly rushed the thin Red line. The leader came straight for Wings. It was not his fault. He had never learnt how to read Scouts' badges of rank. He sent his fist around in a hook and caught Wings neatly in the jaw. Wings staggered from the shock while the boy did his best to conceal the pain in his knuckles from the bone-to-bone contact. Another tough had got Kim Seng by his scarf and was strangling the Sixer with the woggle. Chin Meng kicked him in the groin and he bent over in agony. Seng Huat had his arms pinned behind him while the other boy punched him in the belly. The fifth one chased the fleeing P3s.

Wings blocked his opponent's flailing arms while Kim Seng and Chin Meng went to help Seng Huat. They saw the two Scouts running up and they let go of Seng Huat and backed off.

"You lose!" the leader shouted as the Scouts withdrew. Wings' jaw was starting to turn purple and Seng Huat was swearing revenge as Kim Seng and Chin Meng helped him away.

The P3s had fled and dispersed and were eventually captured by Yellow Six. The vagrant had disappeared during the fight.

"We'll get them next time," Wings said and he began to make plans. I promise. Scout's Honour. I promise I'll get you.

A fortnight later, the usual firefight game brought the Reds back to that part of the estate hunting for Green Six. Wings had told them to bring a change of clothes. They now blended with the residents and could not be spotted from a distance. But Wings had another reason for getting out of uniform.

"Playing with your toy guns again?" the voice was familiar. Wings whipped around to see the leering face of an old enemy. Wings smiled back. The Six had heard the voice too and turned around to face the boy. His gang appeared around the corner.

"Want to get whacked again is it? Who told you you can come back here?"

Wings slipped his gun into his satchel and brought out half a metre of chain. The rest of the Six did the same. The P3s would not run away this time. Kim Seng had given them a dressing down for their previous desertion. There was a metallic click and a blade flashed in Seng Huat's hand. He had told his brother about his beating and the older boy had supplied him with a switchblade, smuggled home from Thailand.

Wings swung his chain around slowly.

"We have some old business to discuss."

The other boy spat on the ground. He was not going to apologise. He watched Wings and his chain warily as the P3s moved around their flanks. "What do you want?" he demanded as the Reds moved in.

Wings felt a sense of power as he swung his chain around lazily. He did not mean to use it, but the sight of this cocky ruffian cringing was satisfying. He remembered the emaciated vagrant, the wet, wrinkled face, the defeat and resignation in his blurring eyes. Wings felt the anger again. Then before he could stop himself, he stepped forward and clipped the boy neatly on the side of his head and grazed his temple. The boy screamed. The Six moved in for their pound of vengeance.

Wings shouted for a halt and the five boys were forced to their knees, arms pinned behind them. They remembered what had been done to Seng Huat and grimaced as they waited for a similar fate. Already, the bruises on their limbs and backs were beginning to show and ache.

Seng Huat had kept his knife when the fight began. He now walked down the row and stopped in front of the boy who had punched him two weeks ago. He clicked open the blade and grinned menacingly at the trembling boy. He caught him by his hair and jerked his head back. He watched the tears well up in the boy's eyes, savoured the moment and then with a quick movement, slashed the boy's long fringe of hair off. He did the same for the rest. A boy began to cry.

"Let these girls go," Kim Seng said. He turned to the leader.

"Don't forget. There are a lot of us. If you ever disturb even one of us, all of us will look for you and next time not so easy."

The boy nodded. They got up hesitantly and moved back slowly two steps before fleeing round a corner.

Wings heard their slippers on the concrete and the crying and saw them in his mind again as children, ten, eleven-year-old boys like himself. He felt sorry and his heart was guilty. But I had to do it. For what? Justice. And revenge. For who? The old man they tormented. And for me. But honestly. Which of these? Wings did not dare answer. He could not find anything of the sort in the Book. And there was a growing sense of certainty that Janet would not have approved. He laughed to himself and tasted a bitterness in his mouth. What would she care now? She will be gone soon. It's time I start doing things my own way for me. She'll be too far away to help — or to care anyway. His heart ached at the thought of her, but he pushed it out of his mind quickly. Of late, Wings had become very good at that.

22

Dear Janet,

Hi, it's Wings again. Thanks for the Christmas present. I got it only after New Year's Day. I suppose it was the rush that made it late. Anyway, I like it a lot, though I can't understand everything in it. It's a rather funny kind of fairy tale — have you read it yourself? It has to be a fairy tale because of the things that happen in it. There's a little prince with no mum or dad (okay, mine aren't around all the time, but they are somewhere, if you see what I mean). A planet so small one can see many sunsets in a day just by moving the chair. And cooking breakfast over a volcano. And all those funny people he meets. Is this some sort of fable, like Aesop's? There's the fox that wants to be tamed. Janet, why does he want to be tamed — so that he will wait for the Prince and feel sad when he doesn't come? I'd rather not expect so that I won't miss. Maybe you can explain it all to me someday or maybe I'll find out for myself when I grow up. My mum says that fairy tales have another meaning for grown-up people. Maybe it's true.

Congratulations on your engagement too. Yes, I remember seeing him at the department store. He looks alright, so I suppose it's okay if you marry him. Let me know when you've fixed a date. I shall send you a wedding card. It's nice to know that things are going well for you. I miss you quite a lot now, and I guess I'll miss you more when you're in America with your husband (he'll be by then, right?). Don't forget to write to me once in a while and be sure to tell me when you've got kids. Will they become Scouts and Brownies too?

By the way, I always thought you had finished school already, how come you're going back to study again? I hope it's optional because I don't want to spend too much of my life in school. My dad keeps going on about university and I haven't even sat for my PSLE. My mum's such a nag too, when it comes to work. The way she nags me now, can you imagine what she'll be like by the time I get to Sec. Four? Studying and parents take all the fun out of school.

Oh yes, I haven't been a terribly good boy or Scout lately. I got into my first fight the other day. My Sixer can't admit a mistake and he keeps insulting me. Anyway, no one reported it because it happened outside of school and because I think they are a little scared of me now. It makes things easier in a way. They don't talk back when I tell them to do things. And they disobey the Sixer as often as they disobey me. Yes, Janet, I know a lot of it isn't right, but it's the only way I can get things done. I think I'm beginning to understand what the difference is between 1010 and 2400. At 1010, everything we did, we did to win. Over here, we just want to get things done and over with. And play football afterwards.

Sometimes I miss my old friends from 1010, but I don't know if they'll accept me as I am now. I don't think

I'll really ever be different to you because you know what I'm really like. But they don't. I mean Boon Ming and all of them. I'm sure they'll say I've changed and become worse. So I got no home here and no home to go back to. When I grow up, one of the first things I'm going to buy is my own house. And I will live there myself and do as I like in it. And anyone who doesn't like what I do or the way I do them can leave! I'll let you visit me and I won't kick you out no matter what you say because you're a good friend.

Time is really starting to move fast, though I don't really know why. Are the days longer in the North? They say when you enjoy yourself, time flies. But I'm not enjoying myself, so why, Janet? Everything seemed to last longer when I was in 1010. I was a P3 and it felt like forever and I had so much fun. Then suddenly I was in P4 and I changed school. Half-year here, half-year there and I'm in P5 and an Assistant Sixer. Gosh, I mean I'm what Nathan used to be! And all those dreams we had about being like Benjamin, well, they sort of disappeared into the air. I don't think about badges anymore. I still wear only a Bronze. Hope you aren't ashamed of me. But somehow, it hasn't been important around here. How has Boon Ming been doing? We hardly call each other now and when we do, there's so little to say. Of course, I haven't seen him since I left 1010. Is he on his way to Gold? According to the plans we made, that's where we should be now.

But plans somehow don't always turn out the way you hope. May yours all work out. I really, really want you to be happy forever, Janet. Well, I've got to go to bed now. School is less than ten hours away. Don't worry too much about me. I'm learning how to take care of myself.

All my love, Wings.

23

Dear Wings,

It's been awhile since I've heard from you. What have you been up to? I'm quite surprised at some of the things you've been telling me. You've grown up to be rather naughty, Wings. It's really not necessary to hit anyone, you know. Don't do it anymore, okay? I don't want you to get into trouble.

I know there are a lot of things that are making you unhappy, and I wish that there was more I could do to help you. And it will be even harder when I go away. But Wings, remember the Law you once repeated to me when you were younger? That Law can still be used now. It means the same things it always has and if you follow it, it will see you through all the bad or sad times in your life.

I know how it is. Lots of people who promise to obey it never do. But that does not mean you have to go the same way too, Wings. Think about it. Baden Powell never meant it to be a Law that one boy insists another boy follows. It's not for me to remind you to do this, that or the other. The Law is something to keep in your own heart. Do you know what I mean when I say it's got to come from within? It's self-discipline and it's a guide to living decently.

Enough of that. I suppose you will get tired of reading my letters if all I do is scold you and tell you to be good. But I can't help it. I care a lot about you.

I'll be leaving in a fortnight's time and these few weeks I've spent rushing around to get my winter clothes etc. My wedding's really going to be very simple, so there isn't very much to do. The money that would have been spent on the dinner and partying is going to pay for our first year's fees.

I'll be getting married at the registry next week and there'll be a dinner at home for both our families. And that's about it. I would have made you come if I had gotten married in church. You know, every girl dreams of getting married in a grand way in a lovely wedding gown in a lovely church. I did too once. But I guess it's who you marry that's important, not how or where. I hope you're not hurt that I didn't send you a wedding invitation. As you can see, there's going to be no ceremony to attend.

Wings, I shall miss you terribly when I'm gone. Will you miss me too? I want you to write often and tell me what you've been doing and don't hide anything from me because I want to know how you really are. Yes, you're probably thinking that I'm too far away to help anyway. But remember that there is always someone who cares and who's thinking about you and wondering if you're okay.

Sometimes I wish I didn't have to go, because it means leaving friends like you behind. But even if you can't see me, Wings, remember what the fox said about not seeing with the eyes but with the heart? Yes, I've read that book so many times. I've had it ever since I was a little girl and it's my favourite book, even to this day. That's why I got it for you. I wanted to share that story with you because it is such a beautiful story of friendship and of the things that really matter. And as you grow up, you'll find that it's not just a fairy tale for children. It's real, and sad. But even in the sadness there is a kind of hope and a gentle peace. The kind only real friends can share.

Wings, no matter what happens between us, or if something happens and we never hear from each other again, remember that we're always friends, please?

The picture we took together is going with me. And by the time I come home again, I'll expect you to have grown and changed. But I hope you won't mind — you'll always be the little friend who cried because he could not fly, the little boy that I've grown to love so much.

Goodbye, Wings. Please take care of yourself.

With all my love, always,
Janet.

24

THE bus roared into the bus-bay, screeched to a halt and the doors hissed open. Wings ran out, not even looking as he dashed across the road to the glass doors of the passenger terminal building. He ran up the moving escalators to the departure hall. Television screens stared greenly at him and he looked for the flight number and the corresponding check-in row.

He ran on, dodging the trolleys and the people with their luggage and families in tow, long lines of tour groups, couples hugging, kissing tearful goodbyes. Wings felt like crying himself. Would he ever find her in this crowd? Was he too late? He reached the counter where she was supposed to be. He scanned the line quickly, but there was no tall, familiar figure.

He was sweating, even in the cold air-conditioning. Maybe the flight has been delayed. He ran to find another TV screen. No, it was on schedule. Could she be late? No, that was unlike her. The cafeteria. He ran all the way up the stairs. The lift was too slow. There were pictures of old airplanes hanging on the walls of the cafeteria, but there was no sign of her. He ran back down stairs. Where has she got to pass? Only one place. The departure gates. Short goodbye, but I must see her before she goes. To hold her one last time and tell her I love her and I'll miss her. There were groups of people saying their goodbyes. He raced from group to group, hoping that she would be at the centre of each one. But she was not. God, if you are there, please let me see her one last time. Please.

Last call, last call, he heard the voice that echoed hollowly and sadly through the building. He saw people running and then there was no one else in a hurry. Observation deck, he thought, even though he knew he would not see her from there.

He ran for the escalator and strode up it, wiggling in between people and luggage. The deck was long and he did not know where to stand. Then he saw the tail of an SQ plane. Wings was silent. The 747 was awesomely huge. A sleek, shiny, white whale with wings. The towering tail fin, blue with its yellow bird marking. Wings stared at the flying whale that would take away the woman he had come to say goodbye to.

"Janet," he whispered. He was still breathing hard and his gasps began to turn into sobs he could not control. Tears gathered in his eyes and he let them roll. Don't take her away from me, Jumbo, please. But the plane had already begun to roll slowly to her runway, to get into take-off position, airframe vibrating, engines swallowing air that Wings would need twenty years to use. Stop, please.

He wiped his tears with the back of his small hand. Fresh tears grew on the small, trembling body leaning on the railing. He was beyond caring who saw him now. The fading whine of Rolls Royce engines came back to life and changed into a low, powerful roar. He looked up and saw her on the runway, faster and faster, airframe shaking as her wheels ran over the black strip. Her nose tilted up, her engines pushed and her wheels left the ground and she climbed. Wings watched as she rose, suddenly weightless, no longer the lumbering giant of the ground, several hundred tons of steel suddenly becoming feather and bird-flesh, infused with bird-spirit, her winking lights fading with the roar of her four engines into the darkness.

"Bye Janet. I love you." When he had finally let himself say those words, she was no longer there to hear them. There was no one on the deck when he decided to go home. It did not matter. There was no school tomorrow. He curled himself up in the backseat of the bus, turned his collar up and let his tears dry in the nightwind.

Wings sat atop a slide, watching the birds fly from roof to tree to lamppost to grass and back into the afternoon sky. It was quiet for a Saturday afternoon, but Wings reckoned that everyone else was at home studying. They should be. The mid-year exam's just about now. I ought to be home too, doing maths or Chinese or something. But he could not spend a Saturday afternoon like this at home before the books. He had stolen the keys and crept out. He knew he would face something later on, but what the heck, this is worth it and I might die before I get home anyway.

As he sat alone on the slide with the wind in his hair, he remembered how Janet had run her fingers through it, the cool feeling of air against scalp, the roots bending over with her hand, the electricity of her touch. Wind, you are nothing like Janet. He tried to imagine Janet's touch again, but the feel of cold, smooth stone of the slide and the rough rusting metal anchored his imagination to reality.

Wings shut his eyes and tried again. Once this had been so easy. He could have even seen Janet next to him with his eyes wide open, felt her hand in his when only wind not her fingers wound around his. He could not shake the reality.

How does one fly? What had Peter said to the Darling children? Think lovely thoughts, think lovely thoughts, he whispered to himself and promptly stopped when he realised that people would think him mad if they heard him. He also realised that his thoughts were no longer lovely. He could feel again the bicycle chain in his hand, the feel of chain hitting stone, hitting flesh, hitting bone. The anger when he saw the old man wake up bewildered and defenceless. The satisfaction when his fist sunk into the Sixer's gut. The thrill of watching the punks cringe, the fear and tears in their eyes, totally, totally at his mercy.

Janet, have I even lost you in my dreams? I cannot even hold you here. He opened his eyes. He looked at the blue skies, the blocks of flats that towered up into them, the green patches of grass amid the concrete, the barriers around the saplings, the drains, the brick of pavements, the mosaic-skinned dragon with its dirty spout of water. Shut, open. Shut, open. Concentrate. But the worlds within and without were starting to look alike.

25

SHE has not written for some time now. I think she will not write again. She must be busy. She is a student, a wife, maybe by now, a mother-to-be. She will not have time. That is the best reason.

Or maybe she no longer loves me or cares about me and I am no longer her little friend.

Little friend is not so little now. I am like a puppy that has grown into a dog and I am not cute or adorable or cuddly like before.

Maybe it is my fault. I never had to tell her all those things we do — or I do. But I told her because she told me once never to hide anything from her because she really wanted to know. She knows now, and maybe she doesn't like what I've been telling her. That makes it my fault. But I can't lie to her. She's the only person in the world I can tell the truth to. Other than you.

Her letters, they came less and less often and each was shorter than the last. Shouldn't have complained. Now they don't come at all. I look in the mailbox every day, hoping and hoping that there will be an envelope with the red and blue edges. *Par Avion* — by aeroplane. The aeroplanes I love so much. One took her away and now, they are not bringing news from her.

But it gives me something to look forward to when I get home from school. The disappointment doesn't last because I sleep early and when I sleep early, there isn't time to hurt. Except when I dream of Janet. I don't like dreaming about her because it never turns out well and she always leaves again.

I look at our picture every night before I sleep and I say a prayer for her, just in case things like that actually work. I wish she knew I'm thinking about her. And I don't even want to wonder if she's thinking of me. Probably not.

Should I tell her about Job Week and what we did? So different from that first time two years ago.

We got our jobs from Seng Huat's dad and Chin Meng's grand-auntie. Chin Meng's grand-auntie is a professional mourner and that's the job she got us. It is kind of sad, when you die and your family has to hire professional mourners because they can't cry for you themselves. But then again, I wouldn't cry for anybody now. You have to feel pretty bad to cry and I don't feel terribly much now, not for anyone I know, even Janet. I'm writing this with dry eyes. Tears would only make the ink run.

Anyway, there we were, dressed in dark clothes, our uniforms left at Chin Meng's place. You don't really have to cry, his grand-auntie taught us. You just have to sound like you are and keep wiping your eyes with a towel so that your dry eyes won't need explaining. And because the towel is rough, all that rubbing will make your eyes go red anyway.

Chin Meng's grand-aunt is really good about this. Many professional mourners are not obviously sad. They talk loud, they gossip, they play mahjong. But she was a real pro. Her company all looked genuine too. I could tell who the real friends and relatives were. They were looking happy and normal. I thought I would feel sad at a funeral, with everybody around me crying and someone lying in a wooden box dead. But no one was wailing and when Chin Meng's aunt gave the signal to start, I still couldn't feel anything because I knew we were fakes. And that was when I thought of the poor old woman in the box, with no one to really cry for her, all alone in death and surrounded by living people who were all dead in their own ways. I was angry at them all and sorry for her and that's when I began to cry too. The boys saw me, and I guess they caught it too and began to cry, real tears too, though I'll never know what each of them was crying for.

We got ten dollars each for a day of weeping, with lunch and dinner and supper and all the packet drinks we could drink. And I used to get a dollar for sweeping whole basements. The money felt odd and I was afraid that when 1 got home, it would have turned into those hell-bank notes they burn for the spirits.

Seng Huat's father runs a gambling den in Jalan Besar, which is only several bus-stops from our school. It is illegal, of course, and that worried me quite a lot. But if it had been legal, we would have been unemployed. Besides the money was good and we weren't earning it for ourselves anyway. It was going to the Scout Association, some of it to our unit and some of it to charity. We weren't stealing or cheating or anything like that. People who walk into gambling dens do it with their eyes open, which was also our job. Kim Seng, Seng Huat, Chin Meng and me were lookouts and we were looking out for the Police.

The four younger boys, Seng Huat's dad did not trust. So he gave them a job in the den as errand boys. They would run out to buy drinks or cigarettes or food. They each made about twenty dollars in tips by nightfall. We had been promised fifteen for our job, but Seng Huat's dad gave us a bonus of five to make it equal and for bringing the luck that kept away the cops for a day.

The third day's work was the most exciting, at least for the four of us older boys. Seng Huat's father had a friend who ran another place nearby. He did not want any of the younger boys. It was in a sort of dirty hotel where air-con is an extra.

I don't make my own bed at home, and neither did any of the others. So we got there early and one of the regular staff showed us how to. Our job was to change the sheets every time the guests left the room.

There was one woman who took a little longer to come out. I went in with the sheets and I saw her tying the sash on her robe. She had on a lot of make-up, but there were lines on her face. Her hair was long and black and glossy and her long nails were dark red. She asked me who I was and what I was doing there. I told her I was a Scout on Job Week, trying to make some money. So am I, she said. What do you do? I asked and she gave me a funny smile and a five-dollar note. I can't give you anything else, she said in Cantonese, you're too young, and she walked out.

If I had known then, I wouldn't have asked. Seng Huat told me later at lunch and they thought it was very funny that I didn't know what was going on. Well, I mean I know how it's done, what's got to go where and all that, but that's all. It was odd, how could a woman let a stranger do that to her body — not once in her life and not even once a day, but every hour she took a stranger inside her.

The corridor was empty later. All the rooms were full. We heard loud grunts from behind door 27. Kim Seng suggested we take a peep. It was a door with glass ventilation slits at the top. We gave him a leg up and he was grinning when he got down. They held me up next. The customer didn't see us because his back was to us and the girl couldn't too because he was probably blocking her. He lay on top of her, his buttocks bouncing up and down between her open legs, grunting as he went. She was lying very still, like a limp ragdoll, her long black hair spread out on her pillow. I climbed down. The boys took their turns.

Just before Kim Seng was about to go up again, we heard the man groan loudly. We split.

We got twenty dollars for that day's work and we did not bother the rest of the week. It had been an easy fifty dollars and I didn't wonder why people did it that way. The only things that bugged me were people. Like the old woman in the box, the poor man who had a little money and who lost it in an hour, the woman with the long, black hair, with the sad smile, lying dead still with her legs apart.

How can I tell Janet all that? But I've always told her things like that and maybe she hates me now because of it. But it would have happened sooner or later. After all, I'm really not important to her. It is the only ending I guess, the way I always knew it would be. Doesn't matter. She's gone now and I can't do anything about it. I can't pretend to be someone I'm not just so she'll keep writing and liking me. Tell me the truth, she said. I did and she's gone.

Well, it's been three years now, since I became a Scout. And here I am now, P6, Sixer of the Reds. And all the time that has passed since then, I haven't even used well.

All those things I wanted to do, they never turned out that way. P6, a Sixer and still wearing my Bronze. The coloured threads are wearing out. My arrow is fading. There are no proficiency badges. All those hopes of being like Benjamin, a Somebody Scout, I lost them all. People here don't even like me.

I met Boon Ming at the Sands House the other day. It's been so long since we've seen each other. He hasn't lost any weight. His arrow has changed to Gold, his sleeves are covered with the red triangles of proficiency badges. He's become Benjamin, the Benjamin we all wanted to be. The leader of the tribe. I am a leader of a tribe too, but one that even God has forgotten. He looked at me and I know he looked at my sleeves. What did he think when he saw them empty, I would like to know. He was polite. It is in our Law, I think. Can I say he's changed? Maybe he has always been this way, only it didn't show earlier 'cos it takes sleeves covered with badges to bring it out. Or maybe it really has changed him. Or maybe it's just me. He could be the one who's normal and me the one who's changed. Did I feel smaller than him? Yes, of course. Look at him. He has kept his promise. I can barely remember mine.

That Law I learnt, almost forgotten now. We never needed it here. But was it something we ever needed anyway? We wanted to be something better than ourselves, so we gave us the Law. But what's the point, because no one wants to obey it.

But Janet, she says it can still be used. The principles, the spirit of the Law, she said. But she left, just like everybody else. How can I trust her now?

I am here today because I lost a dream and had to find something else to do with my life. I don't think it's made any good difference. I am still going nowhere. Wasted time.

There must have been some good, but I cannot think of anything good. Friends? There are people I know, that's all. Purpose? There was none, because in the end, I never got to learn those things Scouts are supposed to know. But I learnt how to look after myself, how to be independent, how to survive, not just in the jungle but out here in the world. That can't be bad, even when it means the things I've been doing and seeing. Is that still being a Scout? Would I have learnt all that anyway? I know I can be a gardener if I'm jobless. Maybe that's what it's all about. Being on your own and being able to look after yourself no matter what. If that is so, well then, maybe I am a real Scout after all. Maybe more than Boon Ming with all his badges of proof. My tests come every day, with everything I do.

And that time I shared with Janet. My happiest ever. I still haven't heard from her and I'm going to give up hoping. Maybe something happened to her and she can't write. Or maybe she's okay but she just doesn't want to write anymore. Maybe she's just lost my address. But I write it down for her every letter I send to America. I still love Janet and I don't want anything bad to happen to her, even though that means she's not writing because she doesn't want too. Gosh, that hurts. But so long as she's okay, I guess even that is okay with me. I just wish I knew for sure.

I heard jets this morning, as I was on my way to school. I still feel like crying and I still don't want to look up. I suppose I haven't got over that yet. Will I ever? Get over flying and Janet? God isn't fair. He took away both, didn't even leave me with one or the other.

Mum gave me a new pen and this diary for Christmas. She said it's because I am now a leader of men. I am writing this with my new pen and I will write one last letter to Janet. I've given her so many last chances, but this is it. This is the absolute last. She'll probably laugh, so what.

Wings sighed as he put the full stop on the sentence. So what. His pen nib hovered above the page but he could think of nothing more for now. It was like having a trip switch that shut his thoughts off when they got too painful. Besides, he knew he should be thinking of his new boys. They would be coming any moment now. He closed his diary and slipped it back into his knapsack. He took out an old, battered book and turned its yellowing, dog-eared pages to the first chapter. Chin Meng, his Second, was standing outside the door of the classroom.

"New boys ready for interview, Sixer," he reported. Wings nodded. He felt a pleasant shiver of excitement as he remembered his first meeting with Peter. It was his turn now. His old copy of *Scouting for Boys* lay on the desk, opened to the Promise and

Law. He looked at it and read the familiar words once more. We need to remember that, he thought. He shut his eyes, and for a moment, he saw again the morning light shining down through the leaves and branches of the frangipani. He smiled, for he saw that the memory was good. We must remember that. Yes, must try to remember that.

PART THREE

Where the

Boys Were

"… the youth shut up from
The lustful joy shall forget to generate,
and create an amorous image …
In the shadows of his curtains and
in the folds of his silent pillow."

(William Blake, *Visions of the Daughters of Albion*)

1

"WHAT do you need sun-tan lotion for?" Boon Kim asked as he watched Krishnan spread the oil over himself. "Aren't you dark enough?"

Krishnan did not reply at once. The oil was smooth and his skin was warm from the sun. His eyes were closed and the world was red as he faced the sky. The smell of the lotion made heaven complete and he did not want to waste a moment of it answering the questions of fools.

"Lotion doesn't make you darker, idiot. It's to protect you from sunburn while the sun makes you darker."

"Sorry Krish, I am so stupid," Boon Kim laughed. Krishnan turned to lie on his belly and Boon Kim poured a trickle of sand down his spine.

"Never mind, afterwards you die," Krishnan murmured as he slipped into sleep.

Boon Kim turned to his left where Har Tow lay. He was wearing an enormous pair of women's shades that stood out on his hooked bridge and against his pale, skinny body.

"Eh, want to play volleyball or something?" he asked hopefully.

"Go away, I want to sleep," Har Tow said from behind his

shades. He could feel the sun on his body and he could see himself beautifully tanned. Too bad about the muscles. Why couldn't people get muscles the way they got suntans?

Muscles need work. He sighed. He would have to be satisfied with a tan.

"Doesn't anybody want to do anything besides sleep?" Boon Kim asked exasperatedly.

"You can borrow my binos and watch girls," a voice from Krishnan's right said. Johnson rummaged in his haversack and brought out a Zeiss.

"Here," he said as he tossed it over Krishnan to Boon Kim.

"Where you get this, man?"

"My Dad's. He uses it to watch his horses," Johnson said as he settled back to sleep.

"Not using it today?"

"No Singapore races today. Too lazy to go all the way up to Malaysia. He won last week anyway."

Boon Kim put the binos to his eyes and focused. He scanned the shoreline from his right slowly all the way to the left. He saw little children on the sand by the water, their mothers with their jeans rolled up, wading in with them. He turned around and looked inland and watched people cruise by on rented bikes. Nothing interesting. His gaze returned to the beach, where girls were more likely to be and less likely to be fully clothed.

Then he saw a pair of them walking slowly from the left. They were in swimsuits and were carrying beach stuff — portable music, towels, beach bags. They were tall, leggy, tanned and Boon Kim noted, well developed too. He was disappointed. They were probably too old. Sixteen? Seventeen? He sighed wistfully. They were out of reach. When? When? When would he ever be able to go for something like that? He had taken long longing looks at the girls in the Pre-U wing of his school, but they had been looking at the Pre-U boys, not at little Sec. One runts.

They walked past him and his binos followed the wiggle of their rears. One was larger, the other tighter with a muscular curve. Then suddenly, something shot into his field of vision and hit the tighter bottom. The girls looked around in surprise and the one with the tight bottom bent to pick up a little shot glider. A small figure ran up to point to the glider and the girls laughed as they handed it back.

"Wings, you dirty rascal," Boon Kim said under his breath. But he had to give it to Wings. It was a very good variation of the old bump-into-her tactic. He had very good aim too.

But what was happening? Wings was not chatting her up. The girls were walking on and Wings was going back from where he had suddenly appeared. Torn, Boon Kim decided to watch Wings. He had trotted to an empty stretch of beach and was loading his glider on the launcher for another flight.

"How to believe this guy?" Boon Kim grunted to himself.

Har Tow was unloading food from the bags to the table by a burnt-out barbeque pit. Krish dug around for the condiments and utensils. Boon Kim was spiking their drinks with beer.

"Enough, enough," Johnson warned. "We won't have enough for the rest of the day."

Wings freewheeled and braked hard near the pit. He had been sent out to buy batteries for their cassette player. He tore open their plastic wrapping and began loading them into the player. That done, he turned to his own haversack and brought out a tape. The next moment, the frantic beat of drums and the screeching wail of distorted electric guitars cut the air.

"Hoi! What the shit is that?" Boon Kim reeled. Everyone was looking at Wings.

"Mildly heavy metal?" he offered apologetically.

"Not even mildly, man," Johnson laughed. "Give us Radio

One. They play a lot of sentimental requests this time of day. Besides, you never know what news you can pick up, you know, like who's interested in who." Wings began searching for the station.

"They announce that?" Har Tow asked in surprise.

"No, but you can guess from the requests," Krishnan said.

"*Wah lau*, Har Tow, which century you living in, boy? Tch, I can't wait for the day some beautiful girl dedicates a song to me," Boon Kim sighed.

Wings found the station.

"…and this song is also going out to Simon of Victoria 2C from his admirer, Jeannette of St Anthony's 2B, with the message, stay cute and…"

"Milksop," Wings said in disgust.

"Did you hear that?" Boon Kim almost shouted. "I know the guy! How come he's getting requests already?"

"Well, he is Sec. 2, and we're only Sec. 1," Krishnan suggested.

"Eh, come on, guys, don't worry, next week we'll be Sec. 2!" Har Tow consoled. "Bought all your books yet or not?"

"Trust you to think of that," Wings laughed. He was disassembling his glider and packing the parts away in its box.

"Don't you think of anything else?" Johnson had been watching Wings.

"Yes, too much."

"What do you mean?"

"When I think too much about other things, I go flying. Gets my mind off them."

"You're very strange, Wings."

Wings smiled and shrugged.

They were lolling about on the bench, Cokes in hand, sentimental requests dripping like treacle from the twin speakers of their mini boom box. The sun had slipped behind the clouds at lunchtime and had not come out since. Probably up to some hanky-panky with the moon, Wings thought.

"Ever thought of getting a girlfriend?" Boon Kim asked in general.

"No, not yet," Har Tow said. "My mum and dad say it's not a good time. Study first, get good job, get established and then have all the girlfriends you want."

"Standard advice, lah," Krishnan said. "For me, I'm really scared that they might go and arrange a marriage for me."

The boys laughed.

"Set man, this guy so lucky, father and mother can actually go out and find him a girl. Eh, don't forget to invite us, okay?" Johnson said.

"You think it's good. Huh. They'll sure find me a girl with personality and character."

"What's wrong with that?" Har Tow asked.

"You see, Prawns, when we say a girl has personality and character, it usually means she has nothing else," Wings explained.

"Hm, since when you became an expert on this?" Boon Kim asked.

"Eh, so how, all want to get girlfriends this year or not?" Johnson interrupted.

"So easy is it? You forget we come from a bloody boys' school," Krishnan reminded him.

"Then we must look for other ways. Can't just give up like that," Boon Kim was looking at a group of girls walking past.

"If anyone of us here can get to a party with girls or gets a chance like that, inform all and share share a bit," Har Tow suggested.

"Not a bad idea for a monk," Krishnan noted.

"Dunno how, but certainly must try," Boon Kim agreed. "I'm starving for some action. I'm almost fourteen and I haven't touched a girl."

"So fast want to touch. Must get first," Johnson set him right. "Then you can touch all you want."

"Ah, I don't know. Don't like the idea," Wings sighed.

"Eh, you gay, ah?" Boon Kim edged away.

"Shit, no," he punched Boon Kim. "What I mean is, at fourteen, the only kind of girls we can get are other fourteen-year-olds. I'm sure no one here is going to date some kid just out of Primary Six. And these fourteen-year-olds, if they're really so hot, don't you think the fifteen and sixteen-year-old boys will do better than us? I mean if you were a Sec. 2 girl, would you prefer a Sec. 3 or 4 boy or a Sec. 2 punk?"

"Dunno, I've never been a Sec. 2 girl," Krishnan laughed.

"Don't be an idiot, you know what he means," Har Tow said.

"Yes, and do we really want fourteen-year-olds? I mean, they're so," he paused for effect, "undeveloped." The boys burst into laughter.

"Consider it an investment and watch your interest grow," Johnson suddenly giggled and rolled off the bench in hysterics.

"I don't want to die waiting for things to develop," Krishnan added and burst out laughing, slapping Johnson's back.

"Yes, gentlemen!" Boon Kim stood up on the bench and gestured grandly. "A tit in hand is worth two in the making!"

"Enough! You're all so gross. Women are not sex objects," Har Tow scolded them.

"So what are they?" Boon Kim asked innocently.

"People, asshole," Har Tow glared. But he could not control his laughter either.

"Look at it this way, guys. At fourteen, we are men, but they are only children," Wings observed sagely.

"I know, lah, you only think of Playmates and Pets of the Month as women. Wank with them every night, right?" Boon Kim asked snidely. Wings punched him playfully.

"Not every night."

It was dusk when they mounted their bicycles and headed for Johnson's house. The sea had turned grey, the sky, violet and the wind was in the skinny branches of the trees. As they coasted down the bike path, Wings felt at peace with the world, but there was something in his heart, a feeling of great restlessness that had been plaguing him of late. But the feeling that made him feel like shouting and just freaking out, where did it come from? He looked up for the moon. No, not full yet, just a silver sickle caught in the ethereal trailing webs of cloud. No, I don't know why. He breathed out slowly and concentrated on the tail-lights of Krishnan's bike.

2

SUNSET over the Gardens but Wings did not want to go home for dinner. Not yet. There was something very dreary about evenings in his house. It got very dark, but it was no use turning on the lights because the dull fluorescent tubes made no difference against the fading light outside. There would be nothing on TV, except maybe the cartoons, but Wings no longer watched them. He had given them up since they had stopped making him laugh. There would also be his sister to bicker with and when his mother came home, there would be more criticism. Trying to please her, that was another thing he had given up trying to do. But he toed the line. That was the only way he could remain solvent and not starve at lunchtime.

School had been on for three weeks now and he realised that he had not been keeping the new academic year's resolutions. There was the undone homework. His books still looked very new. But then, he had not touched them. That shout-at-the-moon feeling he had had just before school started, it had not gone away and he was feeling restless still.

The sky had turned deep purple and the street lights had come on. They lined the roads of the Gardens dimly, with hardly enough light to fill the long shadows, the pockets of darkness in the hollows of doors, windows, ventilation slits. He walked down the alley, the darkness familiar to him. I can walk with my eyes closed here and there would be no difference. He struck a match, the quick orange flickering lighting up his fingers and palm, the sudden glare making him squint. He breathed in deep and the tip of the Camel flared vermillion. He flicked the smoking match away and breathed out.

He reached home just as their maid was clearing away the dinner dishes. He was lucky tonight. His mum was eating out and she was not there to see him come back late. He bolted down his dinner and went for a quick shower. Turning on his bedside lamp, he looked over the balsa skeleton of his latest project. It had been two months since he had last touched that airframe and he was beginning to wonder if he would ever finish it. Someday, when there was less work. He realised a little guiltily that he did no work. Then what? The lethargy, the feeling that he simply couldn't be bothered anymore. He sighed and looked out of his window across the street.

The lights in the opposite house were on. A dog barked. Turning off his bedside lamp, he sat silent in the dark to watch the light from the window across the road. For a long while, there was no movement. Then a shadow moved to the sill and another black blot moved behind it. The shadows blended, darkness cleaving unto darkness and the flick of an electric switch blacked out the window. Show over, he turned on his bedside lamp. He had not seen his neighbours in the same light ever since the first time he had seen them come together.

He wondered what it was like, shared sex. He often wondered too, if that was where his restlessness came from. Hormones, nothing but biochemicals, and not some philosophical existentialist reason. If that was all, then the solution to his problem was simple. Maybe all I need is a woman. He thought of the whores he sometimes saw on his way to school. In the dim red neon of their cubicles, they excited him. He had looked in once with the boys. But in broad daylight, together with the everyday and commonplace, he had found them repulsive. There is beauty in the darkness. He flicked off the fluorescent tube and turned on the yellow nightlight. Beauty in the darkness. He unlocked his bedside table and took out a tattered magazine. Heart racing, he felt a lovely knot tighten in his belly as he opened the pages and then the delightful shock of pleasure when the pictorial began. Maybe all I need is a woman and if I can't have the real thing, I guess this is the next best. But it was a good second best because lately, it was the only thing that could take the restless feeling away and send him quickly to a deep, dark sleep.

He woke late the next morning and there was light in the room, reflecting off the white walls painfully into his eyes. He almost died. Throwing off the blanket, he ran to the door and to his great relief found it bolted. He picked up the magazine from the floor and locked it away. As he fumbled for his towel, he suddenly remembered what day it was. Tuesday, first workshop practice of the year and he was going to be late. He showered, dressed, gobbled his breakfast, put on his basketball boots, grabbed his haversack, mounted his bike and pedalled like crazy.

Arriving at the workshop in poor shape but with high spirits, he braked and rims screamed against rubber pads as his hair stood on end. He had arrived in style, and as he dismounted, he looked around to see if anyone had seen him come in. The carpark was empty and quiet. Pre-National Anthem silence. The band struck up and the song began in a hundred different keys. Wings sat down outside Metalwork One to wait. Another year of misery. But Workshop was not so bad. Something nice too about making something for yourself. Funny kind of feeling. Boys would die if they knew. Feelings get in the way.

The mumbling that passed for singing ended and he waited for his class to appear. But no, instead of boys in white shirts and khaki shorts, a sea of sky-blue pinafored girls appeared. Wrong workshop, was the first thing that crossed his mind, then before he could think anything else, the boys appeared, all nineteen of them against the sea-sky legions of at least a hundred and eighty.

Boon Kim came up and grabbed his arms.

"Wings! Girls!" he screamed in a whisper.

"I can see that," Wings said.

"We said we wanted girlfriends and look at this!" Johnson exclaimed quietly. "Maybe there is a God after all."

"Eh, no Indian girls, lah," Krishnan mourned.

"Guys, we must do something about this," Har Tow said as he looked around nervously. Wings was in shock. He did not know what to make of it all. Only last night, he had thought a real live woman was out of his reach for the time being. And then to be faced with this the next morning. He suddenly felt very, very afraid and Johnson's comment on God did not help much. Can't be Him, Wings thought. God never gives anything good so easily.

"They'll have to fight over us," Boon Kim sniggered. Wings was more realistic. It was nine to one, a heavenly ratio, but convent girls aren't all pretty, contrary to what is said about them. Closer to Earth, then. Three to one. Take away the frigid ones and that left one point five to one. Take away those already reserved by others quicker off the mark and that left zero point five to one, or two to one in the girls' favour. Wings had learnt early on that when life gives you lemonade, extract the fructose and the sucrose and you will still get lemons.

"So what do we do?" he asked softly.

"I'm sure they're as interested in us as we are in them," Har Tow observed thoughtfully.

"So what do we do about it?" Wings asked again. His brains had suddenly been purged.

"Strike while the iron is hot, make hay while the sun shines, make love while the night's young," sang Boon Kim.

"How?" Wings' thoughts were beginning to get focused.

"We'll figure out something later, no sweat, now we have to make trays, not love," Johnson said as they moved to their workshop.

"What about me?" Krishnan whined. "My parents will never let me intermarry."

"Ai, stop talking," the class monitor (and leader of workshop group two-thirteen) squeaked. No one obeyed orders instantly, and even those with nothing to say made an obligatory murmur before there was silence.

The boys were abnormally cheerful and hardworking, full of life and vitality. Wings figured it had something to do with mating rituals. The male has to show positive traits that will enhance species perpetuation, thus encouraging the female to mate. The pigs he had known the year before had graduated to swineherd status, working hard to impress the shepherdesses who surrounded their sty. Wings remained the lonesome cowboy, filing down some shoes for his horse. Girls made him very conscious of himself and he did not like the feeling. Pulse rate too high. Too much sweat. Tongue too dry. *Acne vulgaris* too. Their presence was exciting but it was all too tense and he was extremely glad when class was over. Having checked and signed for his tools, he made a hasty exit to the cool and calm of the bike shed. The long ride to school would calm his shot nerves. As he coasted down the driveway, he felt the tension slip away. God bless bicycles. It was going to be a tough school year.

3

WINGS had gone from the workshop straight to school because he was on library duty. There were two duties he liked best — the baggage check-in counter and the customs counter. All he had to do was shove a bag into a pigeonhole and hand out a number tag or look officious and check books for the proper date of borrowing stamp

"You'll never get promoted that way, Wings," his day-leader said. Wings took out the Walkman headphones from his ears and said, "Huh?"

"You'll never get a promotion if you only do bag and customs counter, Wings," the day-leader said again patiently.

"Doesn't matter. I like what I'm doing. Besides, I don't have to think and I can listen to the radio or I can read or maybe even do homework," Wings explained.

"I don't believe you about the homework. But what I'm trying to tell you is that you should have a little more ambition."

"Come on, man, 1 have ambition, more or less. I just don't want to be a day-leader or chief librarian or anything like that," Wings said as he turned off his radio. It looked like it might be a long conversation.

"I'm telling you as a friend and as someone who's older…"

"And smarter?"

"Don't try to be sarcastic. This is for your own good. I heard you just quit the NCC."

"Yes, and so what?"

"Why?"

"I don't like doing drill every Saturday. If I wanted discipline, I would have stayed at home with my mum."

"But I thought you liked airplanes and isn't that what NCC Air is about?"

"Ya, they only call it NCC Air but they're as ground-bound as turkeys."

"What do you mean? Don't they do anything with planes?"

"No. What they've been trying to teach us about airplanes, I already know. And I don't like going for classes where instructors don't show up. They also said we'd do shooting but we only draw rifles for arms drill, which is shit. They said we'd build airplanes and go for joy rides with the Air Force. It hasn't even happened for a lot of Sec. 4s. They make promises they don't intend to keep. And I don't like Sec. 3 and 4 jerks telling me what to do when I'm quite sure they don't really know what they're doing either," Wings said bitterly.

"But where's the meaning? You can't just walk around Orchard Road every Saturday and watch movies and girls at MacDonald's. You've got to do something with your life. You're going nowhere. You got no purpose, that's what's wrong with you."

Wings looked at him from the side of his eyes. "That sounds very familiar, Jinks. I'm sure I've heard that before."

"A rolling stone gathers no moss," Jinks the day-leader said sagely.

"Nonsense, Mick Jagger's made millions."

"Don't try to be funny. You know what I mean."

"Mean? Meaning? Meaningless! Meaningless! All is

meaningless!" Wings announced in his best quivering prophet voice. Heads turned. He laughed wickedly.

"Shut up you ass, this is a library," Jinks said as his face turned red. "You know what I'm talking about. You got to give your life to something to make it meaningful."

" 'We are born, we copulate and we die.' Shaw, I think. 'Mothers might as well give birth astride graves'. Beckett. Life is only that bit of light between dropping out of the womb and into the grave. Why bother, brother?"

"You'll get your 'A' in literature, but you're going to screw up your life," Jinks sighed at last. And I'm not even fourteen, Wings thought as he watched the back of his day-leader disappear among the shelves.

Har Tow came up to the counter with his bag. He carried a large shoulder satchel that was reinforced round the sides so that it would stand straight and not damage the books inside. It even had a pocket for the beaker of water Har Tow carried all the time.

"Hey, Wing Cheong, here's my bag," he announced as he dropped it with a heavy thud on the counter. He brought all his books to school.

"Don't you pack it for the day's subjects?" Wings grunted as he heaved the bag over into a pigeon-hole. Wings was disciplined in that respect. Heavy bags do not make for easy riding.

"No. Might need them so I can study when we're free."

Wings laughed out loud. "You're such an ass." It was not true. Har Tow was the class brains. The boys called him prawn-brains because at the tender age of twelve, they had already developed a vague sense of irony.

"Hey, Wing Cheong, you know the girls we saw today? Wow, I can't wait for next week to see them again." His eyes shone. Wings' eyes widened. This was Har Tow speaking.

"I didn't know you liked girls."

"Don't all men?"

"No," Wings said in all honesty. He had found a book on homosexuality tucked away in the statistics section of the library the week before.

"Well, I'm here to get a book about it."

"On what?" Wings was getting alarmed and amused.

"Sex, of course."

"No! Not really!" Wings' laughter carried into the library through the bag counter door and the day-leader was walking out to stop him. Har Tow was turning livid.

"Not that kind, I mean. I just want to know about women and things like how they feel and think and what they like in men. Come on, Wing Cheong. I already know how it's done."

"Cut it out!" Jinks warned and stalked back to the Borrowing and Returning Counter where all the fast-tracking career librarians were stationed.

"How?" Wings challenged.

"You mean you don't know? Well, I don't know everything of course, but I do know that there are at least sixty-nine different ways of doing it," he said proudly. Wings shook as he tried to control his laughter.

"By the way, you rushed off so fast after workshop. There's something I'm supposed to tell you. We're having a tech team meeting at recess. And I hope you haven't told anyone about our luck. We want to keep them all to ourselves, understand?" Har Tow looked serious. Wings nodded back with mock seriousness.

"It's not funny, Wing Cheong, this is a state of emergency. We're going to war. See you at recess."

The bell rang for recess and boys charged out of the old grey granite building for the tuckshop or the green field. Twenty boys made their way to the stop butt of the air rifle range. They went behind the wall, out of sight and hearing of the rest of the school.

"Okay, everybody here?" Boon Kim asked. He counted heads and made sure that all belonged to Tech Group 2/13. He nodded to Har Tow who cleared his throat and began nervously.

"Alright, all here. We can start. Okay, now everybody here knows about this morning. There are about 180 girls and only 20 of us. I think this is the beginning of good times."

The mob cheered.

"But as we all know from history, even in good times, there will be problems and conflicts."

"Get to the point," a heckler said and was immediately hushed. As class brains, Har Tow commanded some respect. Regaining his composure, he continued.

"Ah, what I think we need, guys, is a Code of Conduct that will govern our behaviour towards these girls and towards each other. After all, most of us are new to this."

There were suppressed giggles, but no one interrupted.

"I've been doing some thinking and I've come up with a set of guidelines. I mean, it may not be perfect, but I think most of you will agree. And if there's anything, you know, that you're not comfortable with or if there's anything you'd like to add, we can all discuss it right now."

"So tell us," the heckler said. The mob nodded in agreement.

"Right." He fumbled for a scrap of paper in his shirt pocket.

"Prepared speech," Boon Kim whispered to Wings.

"Gentlemen…" The mob cheered.

"Gentlemen, I have a dream that one day, we will all find our perfect mates, the Eves God created for each of us in Eden, taken from our sides so as not to be above us or below us but beside us, within our arms to be loved, cherished and protected by us, as He meant it to be, one man one woman unto death…"

"Who's better at this, Wings, you or Har Tow?" Boon Kim nudged Wings in the rib.

"Ow, that was my Eve, twit. Better at what?"

"Talking cock."

"Oh, him, I guess. I just talk dirty."

"I will now list the Laws of our Brotherhood. The First Law is this: one man, one woman. No Brother shall tackle more than one girl at a time. This is to give all Brothers a fair chance of finding love.

"The Second Law is this: no Brother shall cut in on another Brother's girl even in the tackling stage. Once a Brother has reserved a girl, no one else is to compete. Once they are steady, no need to say. No one is allowed to *sabo* in any way. If possible, we must help each other.

"And the Third Law is this: no Brother is allowed to go for the ex-girl of another Brother. This is to prevent ill feeling and suspicion amongst Brothers. It also supports the Second Law."

"Wah man, better than Shakespeare," Krishnan noted. He was a debater and hoped to someday become a lawyer. He listened carefully. He had never heard Har Tow to be so profound. And certainly never so eloquent. It is wonderful, he thought, the things womankind could inspire mankind to do, from eating apples to giving speeches.

"Did you think up all this in the library just now?" Wings asked out loud.

"Yes," Har Tow admitted.

"I hope that's all," someone shouted from behind.

"Yes, these are the three main Laws for now," Har Tow said.

"Thank you, Har Tow," Boon Kim said as he got up to take over the meeting again. Wings always wondered at the way Boon Kim could naturally take command of any situation. He wished he had Boon Kim's confidence and charisma. Even Har Tow got some respect because he was smart. Krish could talk and Johnson had the money. But he, Wings, what did he have? Nothing. It was depressing, especially now, when he would need all the confidence he could get.

"Okay, guys, so next week starting, we have to decide who to tackle and *chope*. Obviously, first come, first serve. Try to find out names so that we can be sure who is taken and who isn't. If there's any clash, we'll settle it here like gentlemen. Maybe it's better if you all choose more than one first so that if you clash, easier to settle. Eh, but this doesn't mean you can try for more than one. Remember, this is only for the *chope* period, okay?"

The mob grunted in agreement.

"Remember, first come with name, first served. So you got to move fast. Must speed also because we only have one year. This year or nothing, okay?"

"Wah, man. Pressure," someone murmured. The bell rang for lessons.

4

HE plucked the guitar strings without thinking. E, A, D, G, B, E, the notes rang sadly and hollowly in the dim tungsten light of his room. He had argued with his mother — no, the argument had to be a two- way thing — she had scolded him then — for what? Being late? Being untidy? No, that would have been okay. But she had taken him to task for being him and being like his father. These days, she had taken to scolding him for that whenever she'd had a bad day at work. But Dad's a mugger and I can't even stick the thought of study. He's got purpose and I haven't. How the heck could we be the same? Well, at least she did not beat him anymore. He laughed. I'm too big. Probably afraid I'll hit back. She had threatened to smash his half-finished airplane instead. The memory still made him angry. He had slammed his bedroom door in her face.

Probably no money for a fortnight at least, he thought. Once, he would have been worried. Now, no more. He had recently found a way to stay solvent. The magazines he had paid so much to the *mama*-store manager for, he had turned them into an investment. He had set up a small business renting them out to classmates and 'recommended clients'. And for those who wanted to own the things but did not know where to get them nor want to run the risk of getting caught, well, Wings would provide a 'skinrunning' service. There was a commission of course, and he was always careful to conduct transactions out of school. He'd achieved 'favoured trading partner' status with the *mamak*-store owners and he got to see a lot of girls for free.

Girls. He sighed a cloud of smoke. Hm, won't pinch mum's fags anymore. He did not like the menthol slims. He had to decide fast on one at the next workshop session. But what to look for? He had no ideal woman in mind, not even after the hundreds of pin-up girls he had met at night in the skin-mags. Nothing turned him on. He had just been scared that first day. I don't know what I want. How am I going to choose without any criteria? He knew he could always look around the day itself and decide on the spot. But that's so haphazard. And what if there are a few? How does a guy choose? It was a familiar problem. He often could not decide which centrefold to dream with. I will ask Boon Kim tomorrow but now for some comfort. He put away his guitar and took out a magazine.

"Your standards are too high, that's why," Boon Kim said when Wings told him of his problem. "You cannot expect a fourteen-year-old girl to look like a Playmate."

"I know, I keep telling myself that. But I'm just not interested in any one of them. I saw them, yes, I felt excited, okay, but I didn't feel like I had to have any one of them. Do you understand?"

"Something wrong with you, boy?"

"No! I have all the proper responses when I'm looking at grown-up women. But nothing happens when I look at a kid."

"Wings, these girls are not kids. They reached puberty even before you and me. Man, they can be mothers now! And I suppose you can be a father now, can't you?" Boon Kim's eyes narrowed to slits.

"Of course I can."

"It's your brains, man. You've been wanking with those grown-up women in the magazines until nothing else can get you up."

"I'll kick you there…"

"Listen, man, what's in those magazines and videos, they're not real. It's all dreams and imagination. But this, what we have in our hands now, this is the real thing man. Flesh and blood and hair and skin, you can touch it!"

"I haven't tried."

"Your problem is dreams. Don't think, Wings. Touch."

Wings tried again to remember the girls but all he saw were blue of sea and sky and the chattering of girlish voices, that stayed in his ears, but with no words, just waves of sound, like the sea-sky blue. What do I like in a woman? He tried to think. He never even had a favourite Playmate. How was he to know if she had long hair or short? Curly or straight? Dark or fair? Tall or slight? What colour eyes? What kind of face? Cup size? No, there wasn't. No ideal woman in his head. Boon Kim was wrong. My standards are not too high. I don't even have standards. Then what was it? Ah, the skin. Uncovered, unprotected, naked, vulnerable skin and flesh that lay beneath flimsy clothing. To see what cannot be seen. Another human being totally open to your gaze, like the unwrapping of a present, take away the bows and ribbons and the shiny, satin wrapper to touch the ultimate gift beneath. The fascinatingly beautiful ugliness of female genitalia, the colour, shape, texture of skin and muscle, the line of thigh joined to curve of hip and gentle mound of groin, the light diffused through hair, long line of limbs going on forever in grace, breasts full and probably soft and warm, to be cupped in hand with nipple between the fingers, the lips glossy wet, elegant curve of brow like vortex drawing you into pools of eyes to drown in throes of orgasmic release. It was then he realised that it was not any particular woman he wanted. It was Woman he loved, Woman the Creation, the Art. And sex was the only way he could be part of that art. I am in trouble. Maybe I should forget about girlfriends and just paint nudes or something.

Wings was not the only one who did not know what he wanted in a woman. Har Tow, as he came to hear of his friends' problems, had subdivided the boys into three categories: those like Wings who desired the Universal Woman (and sex), those who liked a subset of women definable by a matrix of characteristics and those who wanted a particular individual. He had to get them all to the particular individual stage.

"We should have a systematic system for selection," he said to Wings at the Library door and promptly went in to invent one. He came up with a three-category prioritisation system.

"First, very easy, you list all the physical things you want in a girlfriend, then you put them in order of importance. Take the five most important ones.

"Second, you must decide how smart, how class and how rich a girl you can handle.

"Third, think of all the personal qualities you want in a girlfriend and list them according to importance. Take the top five.

"Once you've done all that, comes the real hard part. Put all 13 points in descending order of importance. Subtract the last three and bang, you have a list of your top ten priorities to help you choose a girl."

The boys spent the remainder of the week struggling through the exercise, going through much agonising soul-searching, especially at the prioritisation part. Wings was totally lost. Everybody could come up with an ideal woman, but he could not. Some, like Boon Kim, failed at the priorities.

"Why so much theory, Wings? I just want a hands-on session!" The two boys laughed. Yes, hands-on. Theory was well and good, but it only took place in the imagination. After all, did one buy a bicycle solely on a list of technical specs? No, to really know what you want, you have to ride a lot of bicycles, Wings thought. Only after you ride and find what you want, can you quantify those wants and turn them into technical specs. I need to ride, he decided. But then again, girls aren't exactly bicycles. Problem unsolved, Wings mounted his ten-speed on the long-awaited and dreaded workshop day and rode forth to meet his destiny.

5

WINGS coasted into the bike-shed earlier than any of the boys. As he was locking up his ten-speed, he heard the low whine of a Mercedes engine and thick wheels crunching through the gravel of the driveway. He looked up and saw three doors open, one in front, two behind, and three girls in blue got out, dragging bags and files with them. He froze in the shadow of the shed and watched. The doors slammed shut with heavy thuds and the whine picked up again as the heavy car eased itself forward and out of the gate.

The enemy had regrouped in the meantime and was making their way across the landing zone to the safety of the tree-line in Wings' direction. His tongue went dry and he gripped his padded handlebars as he felt the familiar ache in his palms and the warm wetness soaked into the foam grips. They were getting closer and he could make out their faces clearly even in the dim of daybreak. The one on the left, he noticed, was plump and cheery, laughing as she spoke. The one in the centre, she was tallest, had come out from the front seat, had short bobbed hair, was on the thin side and carried a netball. The right one was small and slim and had long, flowing hair that caught the morning wind. Wings still had no ideal woman, but the small, dark girl with the flowing hair and the intense expression of brows and eyes, she caught his imagination. Just then, they passed the bike shed and they looked in because he had let his chain slip in panic and it made a loud clank. For a brief moment, the girls and Wings stared at each other, then they began to giggle as they moved on. Wings felt his face go hot.

It was seven o'clock already but still too early for the rest of the workshop people to arrive. This was an opportunity, he knew. It would be difficult with too many people around. But now there were only three. He had a good excuse to talk to them, after all they were all early. And there was someone who was interesting. All he had to do was walk up to the stone bench where they were seated and say hello, how come you're so early too? It would be an excellent start and he would have an excuse to talk to them when he met them again. The thought was exciting. Should I act now, he thought. An old familiar feeling crept over him and he remembered a playground nine years past, when he had stood on the fringe and looked in on a group of girls just like he was doing now. He had not been able to act then. Why? Because he could not make his jelly legs obey, that was why. And they were not obeying now either. Yes, no, yes, no, go, stop, go, stop. He was immobilised. There isn't time, it's got to be now or never, before the hordes arrive. Would there be another chance next week? Wings did not want to bet on it. And next week would be too late. Anyone who isn't blind will spot her and *chope* her and then no chance. Come on boy, you've got to act now, now, now. What if they laugh at me? But there isn't anyone around to see or hear that. But how will it feel, me dying here all alone under that withering fire. They would not be alone for long. As his heart beat wildly and all his limbs trembled in fear, anticipation of action and his indecision, the enormous SBS transporters were winging their way to the workshop with reinforcements. He heard the sound of flaring engines as they came in to land, air brakes screeching as they came into the landing zone, hiss of exit ports opening and the thunder of feet as the sea-sky legions dismounted and advanced to reinforce their threatened sisters. He saw the first few breach the gate and his heart sank right down to his basketball boots. I've lost.

The boys too were all early for once, so they could spot the first girls arriving to the last and assess every one of them. Some of the boys were smarter. They stationed themselves at critical points, where the girls were sure to pass so that they could have a look at every one of them. One such place was the main gate.

Loitering uneasily there, they pretended nonchalance, chatting amongst themselves with eyes alert, following the girls and giving them a quick once over with the ten-point priority table. Many a boy felt his heart torn when a girl fit his priorities and he had to decide whether to tail her further for more information or give up his position at the gate and the possibility of something better coming along.

Others were more practical. No matter who they chose, they reasoned, there would always be something better. So, the first girl that matched their requirements was pursued for a deeper intelligence probe. They were not being noble of course. The other half of their philosophy said that if something better came along, it would only be natural to discard the old for the new improved model. As it was with their fathers' cars, it also was with their females.

Johnson and Krishnan had chosen higher ground for observation. They stood on the balcony of the second floor of Woodwork Two and watched the girls through Johnson's father's racing binoculars and Krishnan's mother's opera glasses (replete with glass jewels).

"We'd be too far away from the action, what if we have to

make decision to pursue and *chope*?" Johnson had asked when Krishnan had suggested the balcony.

"Don't worry, lah. Very few of them have enough guts or sense to decide on the spot and *chope* now. Most likely, they will all spot a few and then go back and discuss and trade. Basically, everybody doesn't want to make the wrong choice too early. They all also want to see every girl before deciding," Krishnan pointed out and Johnson was convinced.

Besides the gatekeepers and the high ground observers, there were the patrollers who walked in groups of two and three, all over the compound. From his bike shed, Wings watched them patrolling. He could hear the voices of the first three girls not far away. Only a hedge between us. He caught a glimpse of her face through a gap and sighed. We might have been talking now, you and me. But now I guess we won't ever.

"How are we going to learn their names?" Johnson mourned. "Why can't they wear name tags like some decent schools do?"

"Well, you could always eavesdrop and maybe catch a name or something. Or you could look at their files or bags or pencil-boxes. That's what they write them for. For guys to read," Krishnan said knowingly. He had no worries. Whichever Indian lass he targeted, he was quite sure he would be the only one to lay claim to her.

"Ah, silly us," Johnson suddenly said. "Their names are on their aprons!"

"Oh, yah, forgot that," Krishnan whispered. "But what if she's not in a nearby class? How will we ever get to see her apron?"

Before Johnson could think of something, the bell rang for assembly. The boys sang with gusto, bent on drawing attention to themselves. The headmaster was pleasantly surprised. He had not heard the National Anthem sung that way for ages even though the boys were flat. Some girls looked around and tittered.

Immediately after assembly, Boon Kim got the boys together to see if anyone had made progress yet. Nobody had had the courage to do more than look. Wings felt a little better. He was not the only coward. The next possible phase of action was three hours away, when workshop ended. It will be a good time to work up some courage, Wings thought. Faint hearts never won dark ladies with long flowing hair.

The hours went by, with boys trying to make trips into girl country with excuses like needing to go to the loo or needing the drill. The boys with the benches at the border between technical group 2/13 and the rest of paradise were the luckiest, but as luck would have it, most were also cowards and the most daring thing the bravest of them did was smile vaguely at one of the girls who immediately bent her head to avoid his gaze. Johnson was somewhere in the centre, sharing a bench with Har Tow. Boon Kim and Wings were beside them and Krishnan shared a bench somewhere near the border.

"Between the last bell until a bus comes that goes to the convent, how much time do you think we've got?" Johnson asked Har Tow.

"Ten minutes here, ten minutes at the bus-stop maybe. Say twenty minutes."

"More like fifteen," said Wings.

"What size groups?" Johnson asked.

"Minimum three, I think," Boon Kim replied. He had been watching grouping trends the whole morning.

"Make that five or more because they are all probably going back to school, which is different from coming from different places," Wings pointed out.

"Pessimist," Har Tow noted.

"Realist," Wings said.

"Probably right too," Boon Kim acknowledged. "Never mind today, even if we don't find out any names, we can still observe their grouping habits. Let's hope they got tendency for movement to hawkers' centres."

"Roj," the boys agreed.

The bell rang. Packing up began in earnest and the sea-sky legions started flowing out. Tech Group 2/13 regrouped quickly to see if the situation could be exploited.

"Hurry up," Johnson pleaded, "follow your heart's desire!"

"Names, don't forget, we want names!" Boon Kim reminded as the boys split up.

Wings looked for the girl with the long flowing hair. He kept watching for her even as he ran to the bike shed. He quickly unlocked it, saddled up and waited, one foot ready to push down hard on the pedal for a quick take-off. She never appeared. The workshop grew quiet and deserted. I must have missed her, he told himself. He cranked up and the bike whizzed past the gates. As he saw the bus-stop, he slowed down to a crawl and started searching for the hair that marked his target. There was a sharp horn blast behind him. He looked around and saw an SBS transporter bearing down on him. No way out, his thigh muscles strained hard, the bike accelerated and he was making warp speed in two seconds from the blast. He could only glance to the side as he shot past the bus-stop, but everything had become a blur. The transporter flared to a halt in the landing bay and he slowed down to look behind. Sea-sky blue in confusion as they scrambled aboard the mother ship. He could not see her.

"Power down to cruise," he muttered as he freewheeled despondently. Maybe she's back there somewhere. He made a lazy U-turn and his legs pumped the bike back to warp speed to the workshop. The watchman was closing the gate. Where else? He rode down every minor road that turned off the main. He checked the bus-stop on the other side, raced to the hawkers' centre, circled it like a hawk, but she was gone. Oh, but he had time on his hands. He flicked the derailleurs on to maximum, biggest gear front, smallest gear back and pedalled furiously, the analog speedo telling him he was nearing 35 km/h. He got to the convent in fifteen minutes, excluding time spent at lights (it is stupid to beat lights in the city, especially at cross-roads). Where are you, girl? He lapped No-Man's land once before putting his bike on a heading for his own base. He had not found her, but at least he had worked off the adrenalin. His legs were feeling tight and he was breathing hard. Slow ride back, now. The bike chain skipped gears.

"Power down to cruise."

Recess came and the space behind the stop butt was packed with boys talking excitedly, shouting at each other, negotiating, bartering. Har Tow raised his arms for silence and the marketplace quietened.

"So how? Anybody *choping* a girl?"

There was much shaking and nodding of heads. Wings did not move. That girl. He could have asked. He had been so close. He had not even taken a peek at her file or pencil case for a clue. Now someone else would probably name her and he would not even be able to tell if it was her.

"To be fair to those who dared, we should begin registration now," Boon Kim announced. It was hard to say that, because he had not found out the name of his girl. But Boon Kim was fair, at least when he was not playing rugby.

Those who already had names agreed enthusiastically. Those who only had a face in mind resisted weakly. Wings was silent. He was still kicking himself.

"Okay then, we will start listing. Index number one will name up to four girls he likes. If anyone of you has the same girl, we will settle it right now in everyone's presence. If there is no challenger, he must decide which one of the four he will choose," Boon Kim explained.

"If no decision is reached by the parties involved, we will settle it for them and our decision is unbiased and final," Har Tow declared as Lawmaker.

"But what if you have vested interests, wouldn't you decide in your own favour?" Krishnan asked.

"Coming to that. In order to preserve the integrity of this court, I, Lawmaker, Boon Kim, our leader, Krishnan the Judge and Wings the Whip will have last choice."

Wings looked up at the mention of his name. He had not been paying attention. The mob clapped and cheered. Some were genuinely impressed by this show of unselfishness. It sounded very much like something from a Chinese Language Reader. Some thought Har Tow and his court very stupid, which was to their advantage. A few thought maybe the court was gay.

Har Tow and Boon Kim had anticipated the problem of settlements and had both agreed to stand last in line to make up the court, Har Tow being Lawmaker and Boon Kim the acknowledged leader of the Tech Group in this business. They included Krishnan because his interests were different and thus neutral. Wings, they wanted because he was a friend to both and would give fair judgement should Har Tow and Boon Kim need settlement. But they had not had time to tell the two boys.

Krishnan accepted it without question.

"All the Indian girls are mine anyway."

Wings was shocked and did not know what to say. Well, so it didn't matter whether I knew her name or not. Someone else would have beaten me to her anyway. And what if no one had picked her, would she have wanted to have anything to do with me? Probably not. He sighed. Just as well I'm the Whip. I'm neutral. I'm normal, I can want. But there's no one to want back.

Wings turned off his ears as trading began. He was out of the race. There was no point listening to see if anyone had targeted her. He would not know. She had no name. You are just a pretty face with long dark hair that catches the wind. I heard your voice, saw you smile and remember the sound of your laughter.

Trading came to a close when the bell rang and nine boys had a girl each to begin work on. Seven had another week to find their accounts. Four made up the temporarily celibate court. Wings walked slowly behind the mob as they headed back to class. He kicked at the grass and a tiny tuft flew up with a clod of earth clinging to its roots. He watched it as it arced through the air and landed softly two feet ahead. He stopped to look at it closely. The grass belongs to the earth and the earth belongs to the grass, but I belong to no one and nowhere. He looked at the grey granite of the school building. Hm. Maybe I should become a Franciscan monk. Good way to leave the world without killing myself. He walked on to class.

It was funny, he thought, how he had started with absolutely nothing in mind and now he had a face he could not purge from his memory. Wings spent the rest of the week trying to forget her. He remembered a childhood story of a man who was told to sit on a hill and not to think of the word 'hippopotamus'. How did he solve that one? Time had faded out the solution and only the problem remained. Get out of my mind, he pleaded with her smiling face, but she ignored him and laughed, her long hair streaming across her face.

He turned to old friends, the Playmates he had forgotten for a while. Yes, you are a comfort. A fantasy is better then a reality that can never be. At least, if the fantasy don't work, you can always tell yourself it was just a fantasy. But the comfort his glossy girlfriends gave was not enough. It helped him get to sleep, but she came back in his dreams. The dreams, they were different each time and most times he could not remember very much of them, but the feeling they left him with was common. It was a sickening combination of heat and sweat and heartache and a sinking feeling of utter despair. Fan blowing across his back, chilling him as the sweat dried. Fan clicking away into the night which was always young when he woke up from those dreams and he would try to sleep but no, the heat and sweat and sickening feeling of defeat, they kept him awake and he would have to reach across the bed for his darlings again. Comfort me one more time tonight, girls. It's bad.

Tuesday came again. He had one last hope. Maybe she was not on the list. Maybe no one will spot her this week. It was a vague hope, but it was enough to send Wings speeding early to the workshop. He parked and waited. He went through his lines. Hi, I saw you all last week too. How come you come so early? My name's Wing Cheong, but my friends, they all call me Wings because I like airplanes. What are your names? And if he managed to claim her as his area of interest, he could keep up the morning meetings for another couple of weeks to sound her out before trying to ask her out. Yes, she probably won't go out alone with me. So I'll ask all of them. She won't feel so odd then. Then maybe after a couple of months, when we really know each other, maybe she'll agree to go on a solo date with me.

Mum gives me fifteen dollars a week. Can do movie and lunch at Mac's with that. No more books, tapes. I can cut the Camels. Damn, no more planes too. Keep some for bike repairs. Woah, no savings. And even if there are any savings, I'm sure she has a birthday. And even if she isn't Christian, I'll bet she'll expect something at Christmas. And there's Valentine's. This is going to cost a lot. Nothing left for me.

He looked across the empty carpark. Is this a good idea? Sure, I can guess what Har Tow and Boon Kim will say. Don't worry about having nothing left for yourself. She'll give you more than you had to give up. It's worth it. But what if she doesn't? And who knows best what I need other than me? I mean, who even bothers to look out for you?

These were disturbing thoughts and he tried to brush them out. He was trying to do a very important job that would need all his concentration. Would ten dollars a week be sufficient funds for the conduct of a romance? Concentrate. Where is that car? Ten dollars doesn't go very far for me. How on earth can two live as cheaply as one? Going 'dutch' is out. She'll go with the guy who can settle all the bills. Always the case. He heard the roar of an SBS transporter as it flared into the landing bay. Would she mind travelling by bus? Or does the guy who can afford cab and expensive places win. He felt his enthusiasm waning. The sun was coming up and the rays were gathering strength as they sliced through purple clouds. It's money in the end. Looks too and I haven't got either. Even if girls went for brains, it wouldn't help me. He saw the first flashes of blue as they came through the gate. So what am I doing here? I can't win anyway. He sat down heavily on the kerb. The tension faded and he felt drained. Nothing to be afraid of now. It's over. Don't have to do it anymore. She's not even here. He sniffed and stood up. I don't care. They can have her.

As he walked out of the bike shed, he heard a familiar laugh. Before he could stop himself, he turned towards the sound. She had stopped laughing and was smiling when he saw her face. She recognised him and was about to smile at him when she realised that he was glaring at her in anger. Confused, she looked away quickly.

He watched her as she walked away. You're just like all the rest. Just like all the rest.

6

HER name was Karen. That much he knew. Johnson told them right after he had seen the keychain hanging on the zipper of her bag. Wings felt his heart sink again to his basketball boots. Lately, his heart had been hanging around there a lot. Johnson had been pretty gleeful after that and it took a lot of control on Wings' part not to snap at him. As it was, no one noticed Wings' mood especially Johnson who declared he was 'in love' to every one of the Tech Group boys.

Johnson's surname was Ang, which put him at the head of the Tech Group list. He was the first to name her at the next meeting and there was a general idea that if Johnson had picked a girl you wanted, you might as well give up because he was handsome and rich and bound to win anyway. Johnson himself had some doubts about his looks and only he knew that his father kept him on a strict allowance. But he was not about to let that become general knowledge.

No one else named Karen. Wings did not listen to most of the proceedings after that. The dreamtime feeling he had been getting of late, it came to him in the afternoon and he leaned against the stop butt feeling hot and sick with a sense of panic. Karen, so that is who you are. Karen with the flowing hair and the intensely dark eyes. Karen of the dawn and the laughter in the cold morning air. Karen, Karen, Karen.

He felt a sudden anger with everything and everybody. He was angry with Har Tow for creating the Law. He was angry with the Law that now stood in his way. He was angry with Johnson for beating him to it, through the Law. But he knew he had no right to be. After all, he had accepted the Law too. And he could not be angry about being made the Whip. He could have declined, but his self-defeating attitude had led him to accept it without question. And was it not this very bad attitude of his that had cost him Karen? No, he told himself. Har Tow is innocent. So is Johnson. The Law is here to protect us from each other, prevent bad feeling between friends, to make sure that no woman will ever come between friends. To protect us from people like me.

It made him feel worse, but he felt that he had got his priorities right. Friends and loyalty before girls. I must keep the Law, especially now that I am Whip. And what did the Law say? Do nothing to *sabo*, everything to assist. Not only must I not *sabo* Johnson. I must support him. That is what a friend must do. And I must do this because he is my friend. I am honour-bound.

The bell rang.

Honour. Scout's Honour, Friend's Honour. He remembered ten laws he had once inscribed on the fleshy tablets of his heart. The laws, they were good. BP never meant to put those who obeyed at a disadvantage. It was just that the laws worked too well for people who did not obey them. Only nice boys, it seems, played by the rules and only they got hurt in the end. Wings felt the bitterness rising up in him as he took out his mathematics text.

Friend's Honour. He pushed it out but it came back and he did what he could to keep it out of the main area of his mind, until he could hold it off no more. Sir, I need to go out. Why, you have just come back from recess. No, Sir, my stomach feels funny. Which wasn't a lie — isn't the stomach the seat of all emotions? Wings dashed out to the toilet and shut himself inside a cubicle, slamming the door and shooting the bolt shut. And there he stopped holding back and the tears, they ran down his face as he remembered the death of friend's honour. An image of a young woman in uniform with her arms around a little boy in the same khaki shade, her face to his. Friends, were we? Where are you now, friend. You left when I needed you most. She had been silent when he needed her voice. I blame you. For what, Wings could no longer remember, nor did he want to. And the tears stopped flowing and he was too tired to cry anymore. He hit the tap again and again as it squirted and stopped, squirted and stopped in a spasmodic attempt to save water. In the mirror, water ran down his face in streamlets. Where is the water, where are the tears? No difference. Very good, except the eyes are a little red around the rims. But they won't even notice. Trigo requires one to look at the paper.

Was it better then, he asked himself as he worked through the problems, to believe in bases and heights and angles, radii and diameters and circumferences? I might even believe in pie-value and logarithms and I will trust in my set squares and protractor and compass. These are constant. But Laws, he remembered, they fail only when those they are meant to govern disobey them. Had there been anything wrong with BP's Laws? Even if Janet had failed me, it was no reason for me to fail somebody else. Hadn't Pete kept on teaching those Laws to us, even when he saw them being broken all around him? And didn't I do the same when I was Sixer? The memory of failure was painful. That was why he had never gone back to the Scouts. But hold on to your Honour.

He looked around at his classmates, especially those from Tech group 2/13. The feeling of anger and rebellion surfaced again. Why should I follow a set of rules simply because you do? If I want Karen, I will take her. I don't care what you say or do to me. Who are you to tell me I cannot go for her. She is no more yours than mine. At the thought, he winced. No more mine than yours. She doesn't belong to any one of us. None of us can lay any claims on her. Unless we play by the same rules. And the claim is only valid amongst us. Who else would respect it? She doesn't belong to any of us. An old doubt came back. If there are no rules, we fight just like that. No consideration or etiquette, just: best man wins, strongest survives. He looked up from his triangles. Will I win? The old answers came back. No. Haven't we been through this before? Why look for a fight you cannot win on even terms anyway? Between me and Johnson, who would win? Johnson, of course. He's got the money and the face and he does better in his studies too. He'll get further than I ever will. So what's the point. He's the better man, full stop. And he's best equipped to survive in this world, with or without the Law.

Wings sighed. Well, if I can't win, I might as well back a winner. Like the game he so disliked. Football. If you can't score, pass the ball to a team-mate who can. And even if you didn't score the goal, your team still wins. And why lose a friend over a woman? You could lose both. Make two friends instead. The power of positive thinking. Wings snorted and his maths teacher looked at him quizzically.

"Yes, Wings?"

"Nothing, Sir."

7

WINGS was at his desk drawing a map of Malaysia. It was a tricky business, getting that middle bit of the peninsula just fat enough. He would normally have simply traced it from the atlas, but he had to draw several maps on a single page this time, each to show the distribution of a particular crop.

The sun shone through his window and the road outside looked hot, light glinting in the droplets from the shower that had stopped only an hour before. Was it his imagination or was that steam rising from the ground? He yawned and went back to his map. Can't even blast a bit to keep awake, he grumbled to himself. His sister was practising for her grade six exam and his mother had made the rule that when sis practised, bro did not blast his cassette player. Wings abided by the law. After all, his mum had bought the player for him.

Should be riding, he thought. The Gardens are very nice to ride around in on a boring Saturday afternoon. The roads were peaceful, except for the little brats on their ubiquitous BMX bicycles. But their older sisters who walked the dogs, yes, they were something else. When I reach seventeen and get to junior college, I suppose that's when life will really start.

But at the rate I'm going — he stared at Malaysia — will

I ever get there? Better work harder. I can almost see the Promised Land. Wings had just seen his father that morning and as always, they had discussed his schoolwork.

"Are you coping, boy?"

"Barely."

"That's no good. This is the year you get streamed."

"Yes, I know."

"You need tuition?"

"No!"

"Okay, okay. But why aren't you coping?"

"Ah, just no mood most of the time."

"What do you mean no mood? Study shouldn't be dependent on moods. It's supposed to be a regular affair."

"Ideally."

"So why isn't it for you?"

"I haven't the time, Dad."

"Hullo! What do you do with your time? Too much ECA?"

"No, I quit the NCC and the Library doesn't take much. It's just like there are so many other things I have to think about."

"Like what? At your age, studies should be the first thing on your mind."

"Ah, I know."

"Then? Been going out to play too much? Riding too often?"

"No. I ride to school, don't tell sis. She'll only tell mum. I get enough riding every day."

"So what then? Bad company?"

Wings had laughed. To some of his friends' parents, Wings himself was bad news.

"Business been bad," he had murmured. His father had ignored him. Another silly comment, nothing more. But business had been bad. A rival skinrunner had started business in school and he had access to some really hardcore stuff. Must have a talk with *mamak* soon.

"You got a girlfriend?" his father had suddenly asked. The question had caught him off-guard. But he had bounced back quickly, true to form.

"No such luck." Which was the truth.

"Well, don't start now. You've got plenty of time. Wait till you get to college when you're more mature; the girls will be too. Relationships will be more meaningful."

"I'll keep that in mind."

"How's your sister?"

"Keeping as well as ever. She just got on the Prefectorial Board. I think she has an eye on the Head Girl's job. She's aiming for a distinction for piano this August. Hopes to get into the A class next year. Getting good grades of course."

"You got a fast-tracking kid sister."

"Hm?"

"Are you proud of her?"

"Nope."

"Why?"

"Little Hitler."

"Don't tell me you're jealous?"

"Whatever for? I'd rather be me than her."

"You can do just as well, you know."

"Couldn't be bothered."

"Tch, what kind of attitude is that, son?"

"What's the point?"

"Maybe you don't see the point now because you're young and headstrong, but you will later. Why don't you act in faith? Try to do it right now? You might like the rewards later."

"And what if I don't?"

"Okay, let's look at the closest reward — JC. You do well enough at your 'O' levels and you get in to enjoy all the fun of JC life. Is that bait enough?"

"I'll think about it."

"That's so noncommittal. Motivation, ambition, drive — you know, people always say I got too much of these. This must be retribution, a son totally without."

Wings had laughed. "Yep, I'm just a beach bum. Just want to ride my bike, sit under coconut tree, listen to radio, sleep, eat and drink Bacardi and Coke."

"Son! Even the Hippies in the 1960s had university education!"

"Was it very useful?"

There was a knock on his door. He got up to open it. It was his mother.

"There's a call for you."

As he walked out to the hall, she looked around his room and saw the open books by his desk. She smiled to herself in relief. At least he was doing a little work. He had grown distant and more and more of a stranger. Sometimes it felt like having a boarder, not a son. She saw the clothes on the floor and frowned. And this boarder-son has too many of his father's bad habits. His only redeeming trait, diligence in study, the boy had not inherited.

Wings picked up the phone and a familiar voice sang hello. It was Johnson. Wings felt something catch in his throat as he said hello.

A fortnight ago, Johnson had got his break. The tall girl Karen hung out with had thrown her netball to the chubby girl before going to the toilet. The chubby girl had missed and the ball had dropped into a deep and narrow drain. Johnson, loitering nearby as he had been doing for weeks, seized the initiative and tried to retrieve the ball for her. Besides, he was thin enough to do it. The chubby girl was not. He took his time so that the tall girl would see him in his chivalrous act. Two mouths speaking well of him to Karen would be more convincing.

"Oh, I'm Johnson by the way. What are your names?"

"Han Mei," said the fat girl.

"Mildred. Thanks for saving my netball."

"Oh that's all right. See you all next week."

"Sure," they said and walked off giggling.

Ever since then, he had been trying to find a way to get closer.

"I need advice, Wings." Wings frowned. This could be more than he could take.

"Why ask me? This is all new to me too." Keep an even, casual tone. Noncommittal.

"Ya, but you're the one with all the ideas." Protest, subtly.

"Har Tow too, John."

"Yes, but not for something like this. And Har Tow's a bit dreamy. He might cook up something too fantastic."

"OK, so what exactly is the problem?" Assist, support. Even if reluctant, I must be honestly helpful.

"Well, I've made contact with the group, now I need to know how to get their confidence and Karen's so she'll go out with me."

Going down, Wings thought. His heart would be passing many basement levels.

"Okay, besides the ball incident, what else has been happening?" Stay cool, he told himself. Remember the Law. Remember your Honour. Remember Johnson is your friend. Do not *sabo* — the temptation to give wrong advice was strong. Assist, support. Johnson needs it now.

"Right. Last week, we passed each other, all of us, because they always walk together, and we waved and said 'hi'."

"Pretty good, I must say." But not for me, he winced.

"Yes, but what's next? I could go on doing this forever, man!"

"Ah. Let's see. They come very early to workshop, did you know that?" Wings felt the pain as he gave away the information.

I'm helping him win the girl I want. Bite the bullet, the pain won't last forever. Two friends now. Two.

"Alright. Should I go early next week to catch them?"

"Yes, you must. And you can use an opening line like, 'oh hi, you girls are very early too' and because they already know you, they won't mind talking to you." I can't believe what I'm doing. That was my line and I just gave it to Johnson. He comforted himself. What the heck, I won't be using it anymore.

"You think it'll work? Sounds a bit too easy."

"You want a complicated plan, talk to Har Tow."

Johnson laughed and then his tone got serious.

"There's something else I wanted to ask you, man."

Oh God, he knows, Wings thought.

"You've been rather moody these days and I just been wondering — are you okay, man?"

Wings was silent.

"Hey, you still there or not?"

"Yes."

"Is it because you haven't found a girl? Relax, man. There's still three terms left."

"No, it isn't that." It was not a lie. He had found someone. He just couldn't get her, that's all.

"You want to talk about it?"

"No, it's something I have to take care of myself. Nothing I can't handle."

"Sure, ah?"

"Yah, I'll be okay. Just need a little time."

"Well, you can always call me, you know." The guilt feelings hit.

"I know, thanks a lot, John."

"What are friends for? Thanks too for the advice."

"Yes. Well, I got to draw maps."

"Eh, basket, that reminds me I haven't done mine. Huh,

thinking too much of Karen already. Okay, so see you Monday, man."

"Ciao." Wings put back the receiver. He went back to his room and sat by the edge of his bed, staring at the balsa skeleton of his unfinished airplane. He sat there for a long time and did not notice the light fading until his maid called him out for dinner.

8

WINGS and Krishnan were strolling down the mall. Krishnan had on his shades ("genuine Ray-Bans, bro, see the sticker?"). Wings did not wear shades because of his glasses. Early on, he had made the choice. Either look at the girls or look cool. He had thought of prescription sunglasses with photogray lenses, but he knew his mother would never hear of it, though she had a pair herself.

"Oh man, look at that," Krishnan murmured.

"Where?"

"There!"

Wings looked and hmmed in agreement. Krishnan sighed. "Isn't it great, the bachelor life?"

"No complaints yet."

"Hey, Wings, can I ask you something?"

"What?"

"How come you didn't pick a girl from Tech?"

"I dunno. Didn't see anyone I liked, I suppose. What about you?"

"I don't fancy any of the Minachis there either," he said sadly.

"How about the Letchmis and Jeyantis?" Wings asked in his best imitation of Krishnan's Indian accent.

"Also no go lah."

But two Indian girls had approached him to buy tickets for an Indian Cultural Night that their school's Indian Cultural Society was putting up.

Wings could not believe his ears. "You mean you're going to a concert packed full of Indian girls, probably all to yourself."

"Looks like it."

"Dey, maybe they also got plans for you."

"What do you mean?"

"Like we eye them, right? Maybe they're looking out for you too."

"Possible. After all, there are too few eligible men in the local Indian community."

"But they are starting young…"

"Come on, in India, children already can get engaged. By the time fourteen, married already. Fifteen, got baby, dah."

"You got sperm yet or not?" Wings asked bluntly.

"Sure, I'm a man already. As you can see, while you all are asking people to go out with you, they are asking me to go out with them."

"You have a big ego, Krish."

"Amongst other things."

"Won't they be glad when they find out."

"They already know. Why you think they interested in me?" They laughed out loud, ignoring the stares of passers-by. Krish was quiet for a while (quite unusual) and Wings' mind went back to Tuesday. He had been riding slowly out of the bike shed. His eyes had been on his derailleur levers. The cable that controlled his rear gears was fraying. He had heard a sudden scream and had triggered his brakes immediately.

"I'm sorry…" he had begun. Then he had looked up. "Karen."

She had been either still too stunned from her near accident or because he had known her name. She had not replied immediately.

"Are you okay?" Wings had asked gruffly.

"Oh, I'm alright. Yes." She had looked at him. "How do you know my name?"

"Oh-ah, it's on your file."

"I'm not carrying that file today."

"Don't be difficult," he had said rudely. "So long as you're alright, I shan't bother with you. Next time watch where I'm going."

He had pulled away before she could say anything else.

"Penny for your thoughts, bro."

"Huh? Oh, nothing."

"Dreaming of a princess, eh?"

"There isn't one."

"Do you wish there were?"

"I thought you said the bachelor life was great."

"That's what I said. You don't have to agree."

"Krish…"

"Yep?"

"Nah, forget it."

"Okay. Hey, look at that."

"Krish…"

"Hm?"

"Never mind."

"Wings, isn't that something? Now she can be my baby any…"

"Krish…"

"You do that one more time and I kill you."

"Okay, okay. Look, man, supposing you and I saw that girl at the same time."

"Uh-huh."

Wings stopped. Should I tell Krishnan? Up till now, nobody

knows. What if Johnson found out? How would he feel? How would it affect us?

"You promised to go on."

"Okay. Now, supposing both of us like her. Which of us should have her?"

"She's Chinese. My parents won't hear of intermarriage. I guess she's yours. Congratulations. Now I dare you to approach her."

"Wait, Krish. Supposing it was okay for you to go for her. What should we do?"

"Easy. Both try, best man wins. All in the game."

"What if I was scared and I didn't dare try and you made the first approach but you aren't serious yet. Would it still be okay for me to try?"

"Wah lau eh, why do you make life so complicated? You watch too many Chinese serials is it? I guess that would depend on how much progress I've made, but if you were my friend and a gentleman, I think you should back off if I've already started. I mean, I might have developed some feelings for the girl by then."

"Should I instead be trying to help you?"

"That might be expecting too much of you, but if you can make yourself, you'd be quite noble. Why you asking all this?"

"Just trying to see how our Law works, that's all."

"Don't tell me you planning on *potonging* somebody's *jalan*."

"Course not! No such thoughts at all." Wings panicked. Had he said that a little too vehemently? He swore never to bring up this business again to anyone else.

"How are the guys doing, besides us?"

The last Krish had heard, the cyclostyling machine at the workshop had broken down. Group reps had been instructed to make copies of lesson notes themselves. Boon Kim had appointed himself assistant to Tech 2/13's rep and had eventually met all the other reps and assistants. He was working on a rep who was an air-head, but a very pretty thing named Georgina who had matured somewhat early.

Boon Kim, being a good buddy, had introduced Har Tow to the girl's assistant. She was a demure, quiet girl named Violet and according to Georgina, the class brains too.

"Just your type," he had told Har Tow before introductions had been made. Johnson had made friends with a group of three girls and was getting on fine with them, including Karen.

"I should think so. I taught him how." The boast hurt, but it was the only way he knew how to deal with pain. Take it head on. Then pretend it doesn't hurt.

"I say, if you're so good with advice, why don't you get yourself a girl too?" Krishnan asked in amusement. Wings did not look amused.

"Look at me, man. No advice in the world can help me."

Krish looked at his friend. "Come on, lah. What's wrong with you? You're as normal as anyone. What's the problem?"

"Krish, look at Boon Kim. He's an athlete, a rugby player. I mean, he's somebody. Look at Har Tow, he's smart, gets the book prizes every year. Then Johnson. The guy has everything he wants. There's nothing he can't have. And you, you're on the Debating team. You win Best Speaker prizes. Your career has been planned from here to Law School and Inns of Court. Then look at me, Krish. What have I got?" Wings was despondent.

"So that's your problem," Krishnan said quietly. He looked at Wings, but he did not know what to tell him. Wings was not handsome the way Boon Kim was, with all the brawn. He wore glasses. He had acne. He was not at all like Har Tow. Wings was near the bottom of the class. And yes, his mum had a business of her own, but it was nothing like what Johnson could command. And the gift of gab bit — yes. Wings was okay with them, but when teachers made him speak in class, he froze.

And he had never spoken to any of the Tech girls.

"But you can draw and make stuff better than anyone of us can," Krish finally said. "You may not be into studying, but you solve everyday problems faster and more simply than we do. You ride better than anyone I know. And you're such a damn nice guy too." Wings sighed.

"Don't you see, Krish, the things I have don't count for anything. It's not normal they're looking for. It's Special. What I got, they don't mean anything when a girl has to decide who she wants for a boyfriend. Not even nice. And Krish, believe me, I am not a nice guy."

"I tell you something, bro," Krish said slowly. "You think my gift of gab helps me? Yes, okay, sure it does in many ways. But it also makes a lot of people hate me. You know what they say about Indians being smooth-talkers and fighters and all that. It's true, sort of. My dad and uncles, they wouldn't survive as lawyers if they weren't. But Wings, people do not like me because of it."

"Sorry man, didn't know that."

"That's okay. And Johnson. Do you know how many people want to beat him up just because he comes to school in a Jaguar and wears expensive basketball shoes? What about Boon Kim? Some guys in the team don't like him, say he's a showoff and he's coach's pet. And if you think it's hard for him to stay on top, what about Har Tow? You know his parents never let up on the homework and the tuition? This girlfriend thing is his first attempt at living a normal life. His mum and dad don't know, of course."

"Thank God I'm normal? Krish, don't you see that even if the world hates you, you can always tell yourself you're special. You can run away and hide in that. But where am I to run to? I got no place to hide and nothing to comfort me with, except maybe a dream and a dirty magazine."

They looked at each other for a long time in silence, then turned away to look elsewhere when it became uncomfortable.

"You got a problem."

"I know."

"You need to solve it soon."

"I know."

"And I don't know how to help you, bro."

"That's okay."

"You need something to prove you wrong. No words can change the way you feel."

"And what's that?"

"You need a girl who'll love you for you full stop, nothing else. And when you find her, I think you can be more sure than all of us that she wants you for you. Because you're normal. I guess you just got to wait."

"I wonder if it will be long."

"How long can you wait?"

"How long should I?"

"I don't know."

"Me neither."

9

THE afternoon heat had left the sand, and in the cool of evening, Wings walked barefoot along the water's edge, grains of coarse sand slipping between his toes as water ran over his feet. The wind was up and he could see the brightly coloured sails of windsurfers over the dark green water. Children were running past him, adults calling after them. Wings walked further on to get away from them.

He had been walking up and down the beach for almost two hours now and he was beginning to wonder if he was stupid — and dishonourable. A silly whim had sent him on a bus to the beach. There was a reason of course and it made him feel like a rat. Karen lived around those parts and there was about a chance in a million he might meet her on the beach. Well, he told himself, it's only a chance in a million. No need to feel guilty. His legs were sticky with salt water and he felt warm even in the evening breeze. Sunburn.

His radio had been on all that time and his headphones were beginning to feel uncomfortable in his ears. Saturday afternoons had nothing but request shows, one after another. He had heard dedication after dedication and he felt a vague sense of loneliness when he realised that he did not have anyone

246 THE STOLEN CHILD

to dedicate a song to and that there was no one to dedicate one to him. The DJ was not sounding terribly sympathetic either. He had heard a late night show once, and someone had asked for a song for all the lonely hearts out there in this world tonight. That was the closest he had ever come to getting a dedication. He switched off the radio and pulled out the headphones. The FM receiver sat neatly in his hand and its weight gave him a feeling of security. Heaven in my hand. Such comfort just to hear another human voice in the dead of night, the magic of FM stereo coming through two little miracles in your ears, the antenna umbilical cord putting you in touch with some humanity. He wrapped the headphone wires around the receiver and popped it into his pocket.

He turned around to look at his footprints in the sand, a pair in a long line, getting washed away in the break of white-green waves on rough sand. Karen, don't I wish you were here with me. He looked down the beach towards the more deserted side and he saw a girl walking by the water's edge, the waves rolling around her ankles as she moved.

If only you were Karen. I wish you were Karen. The wind blew her hair wild and it whipped back in long strands with the wind. He followed her from a distance. If you were Karen, what would I do? First, I wouldn't walk. I'd run. Yes, I'd run up to you and call your name. But would you know who I was? You'll probably look at me, not recognising me and ask me who I am and how I know your name. And maybe you will remember the day I almost ran over you, and all the times I forgot to smile when you looked my way. Then what will you say to me? Wings felt a familiar sickness rising up through his gut. There was a pleasant aching in his belly, the kind he felt before a race or an important test or exam, the kind he had felt in the bike shed when she had only been a hedge away.

What if you are Karen? I'll never know, just walking behind

you fifty metres. What if you never look around? I'll never see you and I'll never know if you might have been Karen. There are no Legions of Seasky blue here and here the sea is green like the glass of a Seven-Up bottle. No Tech Group 2/13, no Johnson, no Laws, no Court and I am no Whip, just Wings. He began with long slow strides, sloshing through the water till he was on dry sand, running with languid lengths up the beach to the girl in front. They can do the century sprint in sub-ten seconds. Theoretically possible for me to cover fifty metres in five seconds, but acceleration through water and over sand is slow, make that seven, but I don't want to shock her, make that ten, but I don't want to be out of breath when I reach her, twelve, but she's also moving at the same time, make that fifteen. And he was drawing alongside her.

She heard the footsteps of a sandrunner, his toes digging into the sand for traction and the slap of his soles on damp packed sand. She turned as he passed, looked him straight in the face and they both recognised each other. She smiled.

"Karen!" he gasped, surprised.

"Hello," she said.

Karen sat at her desk with homework laid out in stacks before her. The study lamp was the only light in her apartment still on. Her parents had gone to bed and her older sister would not be home till after midnight. The comprehension was done, but the pages of the composition book were still blank.

Fourteen was a funny age to be. Technically, she realised that she was a woman. That had been three years ago, the first time. But then, the boys had not paid her very much attention and she would not have had anything to do with them. She was still not too keen on them, but they were there and she had no feelings against them. She knew she enjoyed the attention she had been getting of late from that guy named Johnson and that strange boy named Wings, but she did not really know what to make of it. Johnson, she could guess, but Wings was something else altogether.

Johnson talks to me at workshop, he's very polite and very nice and he talks to me on the phone. Quite fun. Is he going to ask me out alone? She looked at the photo frame on her desk, three girls in Seasky blue in the belly of a pink ceramic pig. Mei, Mildred and me. Does getting to know boys mean leaving your old girl friends behind? We've been through so much together, ever since Primary 1. Will having boyfriends break us up? When you go out with a guy, it means less time with the girls. He'll want you to spend time with him. Look at Sis, she used to go out with me all the time until boys came into the picture.

She flipped the pages of her English Grammar book. Can't get anymore work done tonight. Maybe a break will help. She popped a cassette tape into the player and set the volume low. She walked about her room picking up magazines, books, clothes and soft toys. No good to lie down. I'll fall asleep. She went back to her desk as the tape came to an autostop. The click was loud in the silence and she winced, hoping it would not wake her mother.

She leaned back in her chair to think about Johnson and how they had met. Mei and Mildred knew him because he had rescued Mildred's netball from the drain. He had been friendly after that and they had been friendly in return. They had introduced her to him when he came up one day while they were waiting for workshop to begin. He had come up to them every week after that and Mildred and Mei began to make fun of her because he seemed to pay more attention to her. She could not be very sure, but she thought that Mei had initially felt some resentment about that because it was she who had first met Johnson and probably felt she had some kind of right to him. But the feeling passed and she was soon back to her normal self. Friends aren't worth losing, especially over a boy you've just met. Johnson was a rich boy and generous too. Mei and Mildred liked that about him, but Karen had her reservations. *Maybe it's only because he doesn't really know the value of money.* She thought about the twenty dollars she got each week. Her parents were anything but poor but they kept their daughters on strict allowances. Johnson, however, always managed to pick up the tab. He had asked them all out to a movie once and he had paid for all their tickets. Mei and Mildred were thrilled and they told Karen she should be too. After all, if a boy paid for everything, a girl could have a lot of fun for free and still have a lot of money left for herself. But that did not feel right to Karen and she said so. Maybe you have a point, they said, but Johnson seems like a nice guy. There can't be any harm in that.

There were really so many things to think about that her mind swam. A breeze against her curtains and the distant roar of an airliner reminded her of the beach and the boy she had met there. Wings, the funny boy in the bike shed who had given her that funny look. Wings, the boy who had almost knocked her down on his bike and still rode off scolding her. And he had known her name too. Well, that might have been Johnson's doing. Wings was his classmate after all. But that day, on the beach, he had come out of nowhere. It was a coincidence she could not understand. Had he been there intentionally? That was ridiculous, because the stretch of beach was five kilometres long. It was just too much ground for a lone boy to cover. There were also twenty-four hours in a day. How on earth could he have picked the exact hour she would be there? And why that Saturday? If she had been regular, she might have believed it was intentional, but it was something she did only once in a long while. People who live near the beach don't always long to walk there. How, Wings, how did you find me? Were you looking for me? She did not know. They had talked for quite a while on the breakwater, and it was so easy, as if they had been friends for a long time. He had mentioned Johnson too, and that was a funny thing, because she had thought Wings was out to give Johnson some competition. He had nothing but good things to say about his friend. Is it a set-up? Or am I just a very vain and conceited girl?

Too many questions and no answers at all. It was wearying. But there was something about the boy she liked. He was fun to talk to. He could make her laugh, though in a different way from Johnson. But he was odd. There was that strange look in his eyes and he had avoided looking at her most of the time, his eyes always into the distance, especially at the sky when he heard the thunder of jets.

Oh, it was all getting very confusing. What should I do? Johnson may be trying. If he is, what should I do, how should I respond? And Wings. Is he trying too? It's so hard to tell. And if they both are, what should I do? Will I have to choose? Who should I choose? Questions, questions. Even complex equations were simpler to solve. But maybe that's only because there are solutions to complex equations. But then again, maybe this isn't even a problem. Yet.

She slipped another tape into the cassette player. An hour to midnight. Maybe I'll get some answers then. She could hardly wait for her sister to come home. There were so many things she had to talk about.

10

BOON Kim called a stop-butt meeting. As the acknowledged leader of Tech Group 2/13, he felt duty-bound to see if everybody was doing okay and if anyone was breaking the Law.

The boys gathered behind the stop-butt as usual, but this time, before school started so that there would be more time. Wings lugged his things over wearily. These meetings had become extremely painful, especially when he had to stand and listen to Johnson reporting his progress with Karen.

He looked at Johnson. He was ashamed of the feelings that crept into his gut. I am jealous of you. But Johnson smiled at him and winked. Wings smiled weakly and looked away. Karen had told Johnson about their beach meeting and she had told him what Wings had said about him.

"You're a real buddy," Johnson had said to him later. "Owe you, man."

"S'okay, man."

Krishnan made his report. Most of the boys found his reports more interesting because he talked about things outside the workshop. The Convent's Indian Cultural Society had made him an unofficial honorary member and his presence at functions was much valued, at least according to him. He was learning how to folkdance at the moment and was contemplating learning the sitar. He was already adept at the drums as his father played them. Krishnan helped out the society whenever they held a concert and needed another drummer. He said his folk dancing lessons were coming along fine and he would soon be able to help the girls out at concerts by partnering them. Before Krishnan came along, they had to rely on the taller girls to dance the men's parts. He was, in short, God's gift to the Convent's Indian Cultural Society.

"But have you found a particular girl yet?" Wings asked.

"When you got so many to choose from, it is not easy."

"Indian customs don't allow polygamy," Boon Kim warned.

Krishnan jerked his head from side to side. "I know."

Boon Kim and Har Tow had experienced an unexpected stroke of luck. The workshop had acquired some new drills and all the benches had been shifted after a work improvement team of teachers had decided on a rearrangement for better 'workflow'. The new arrangements put Har Tow and Boon Kim together on the Border. It was all very well, since Boon Kim had found out Georgina had a Sec. 3 boyfriend who played rugby for the Saints. Har Tow had failed with Violet too. Not his fault, he was quick to point out, but her parents did not allow her to know boys. It would affect her grades, they felt.

"So this year you're going to repeat, right?" Johnson laughed.

But Boon Kim had recovered fast and had started borrowing tools from the pretty and leggy basketball forward beside him. After he had borrowed her file, he had gone on to borrow a chisel, a hammer, a plane and more suggestively, a screwdriver. Wings felt it was a sure sign of interest, as he pointed out that any silly girl would have known that he had all those tools in his cupboard and had no reason to borrow hers. On two occasions, she had been unable to open her vise and he had gone to her rescue. He explained things to her and demonstrated techniques. It meant that he had to be very good with his work. Even if he never got Peggy, Har Tow had said, Boon Kim would do very well at Tech. They talked before lessons and they talked after lessons as they walked to the bus-stop. Eventually, they had exchanged phone numbers and birthdays. He called her, but not too often, and because he was rather poor, had picked up bits of scrap wood in the workshop and made her a little model cottage for her birthday. A sure sign of his intentions and domesticability, Har Tow said.

But Boon Kim did not forget his buddy. He told Har Tow that since he had already used the borrow-tools ploy, he had better not do the same. Since Boon Kim, Peggy and her benchmate Sandra were already friends, it was only natural for them to include Har Tow in their conversations and eventually, their trips to the nearby hawker centre for ice-kachang after Tech. From ice-kachang, it went on to Hokkien mee (the bigger the meal, the greater the interest and commitment). It was not long before they decided to go to a movie with lunch at Mac's. Day dates became Saturday night dates and they swapped their canvas sneakers for roller skates and the shop floor for the roller disco.

Johnson began by first thanking Wings. Wings' heart went cold. He did not know what to feel.

"He's helped. Told me how to approach them and it worked. He talked to Karen too, to tell her good stuff about me and test the water for me, too. So everything's going okay for both of us and we've gone on our first solo date. Er, it's a lot cheaper."

"Whip! Not fair, why never help us?" somebody shouted.

"My buddy, that's why," Johnson said. Wings felt like he had been skewered and left to cook over a slow fire. He knew Johnson meant well, but the pain was getting too much to take. He had hoped to forget everything he felt for Karen with time, but no. She called him up sometimes to talk, and lately, talk had become centred on Johnson. He looked away as Johnson sat down and someone else came forward. He turned up to the sky he loved so much, where his heart had first been broken. Then he saw them. A pair of tiny, mosquito-like silvery objects, flashing silently through the blue towards him. No one else was looking. They shot past high overhead without a sound and Wings saw from their silhouette that they were Tigers. Then, as he watched their tails get smaller, the thunder rolled by. His heart soared with the sound and he suddenly felt like shouting, but as the thunder died, so did the elation. *That's where I'll never be.* An old, familiar ache gripped his heart. *Like meeting old friends. But he could handle it. Like old friends, you know where you stand with old heartaches.* A frown crossed his face as he remembered. *Hello, old friend.*

Wings was at the baggage counter after the meeting (as usual) when Har Tow dropped his heavy bag with a bang. Wings smiled and took the headphones from his ears.

"Yo."

"Yo, yourself, Wings."

Wings took the bag and put it into a pigeonhole. He was getting used to its weight.

"What's the problem?"

"What problem? I'm getting used to your bag's weight."

"Not that. I mean the other problem."

"I don't understand."

"There's something wrong with you."

"Who says?"

"Me."

"What makes you think so?"

"Just now at the meeting. You looked like there was something wrong. And another thing that has got us worried.

How come you didn't pick a target? Everyone has someone except you. How come?"

"I'm the Whip."

"We never said Whips can't share the action."

"Well, how else can I stay impartial?"

"Boon Kim and me, we get on fine and the Judge, he's doing okay too."

"Judge's area of interest not the same as ours."

"Ours is the same."

"I know, but we got around that, didn't we? We just took last choice. Noble move."

"You don't like the idea?"

"You never told me about it."

"You wouldn't have been Whip if you had known?"

"I didn't say that. Ah what the hell, anyway. It doesn't matter anyhow."

"Of course it matters. You're not happy with something and I want to know why."

Wings looked out to the basketball court.

"Come on Wings, so what is it?"

"Nothing. Nothing will come of nothing. It's the only thing we can be sure of in the end."

"Don't be an ass. Let me guess…"

Wings stopped him. "Don't bother. I'll tell you myself."

Airplane. I wish I could get into one now and fly away from all this shit forever. Just fly away.

"I did meet a girl I liked," he began. "But the first time we met, I didn't dare to say anything to her. I was too scared."

Wings remembered that first morning he had seen Karen, how she had caught something in his mind, when only an hour before, he had had no ideal woman.

"The week after that, I tried again. But then I began to think. Would she ever love somebody like me? I guess the answer was no. So I gave up. And she arrived and I didn't do anything again."

"Who is she?"

"And someone named her as a target before I could, because I am the Whip."

"God, Wings, I'm sorry."

"It's okay. Even then, he still comes before me alphabetically. Would've lost anyway."

"You forgot negotiations."

"No point. Would have lost in the end. The only thing that changes is when I lose. Sooner, later, I still lose."

"You're really depressed."

"I'll be okay."

"You still haven't told me who."

"I won't. That would only raise bad feeling. Which is what we don't want, do we? Otherwise, why the Laws?"

"That sounds rather bitter. But you can't cut in now. You know the rules."

"I know the rules."

"Everybody's on the roll now. I know how you feel, but she's out of reach now, Wings. Forget her."

"Yes, I know. Though I was really hoping you'd tell me something else. You don't have to tell me that." The progress reports every week behind the stop-butt, they had hurt. An appropriate place. Like bullets, those reports, tearing into flesh and making me bleed. And I am the stop-butt. The pain stops here. No one else need know about it.

"So that's what's been making you so moody is it?"

"It's more than just the girl. It's other things. Look, Har Tow, if he hadn't got her first, do you think she would have gone for me? Why do you think I'm not breaking the laws? Because even if I did, I can't win."

"So why so moody?"

"That's just it. I can't win anyway."

Har Tow looked at his friend in pity. "How can I advise you? Maybe I can introduce you to one of Sandra's basketball team-mates, huh?"

"Don't really feel like it."

"We don't always feel like what's good for us."

"I want to hit something."

"Try my bag."

The day-leader came to call Wings away. As he followed his chief, he felt for his rib. I knew it. They're all there. God forgot to make me an Eve. And that's why I'm alone. Thanks a lot, God.

His room was dark. He did not turn on the lights because he did not want to see anything. The dark shapes and shadows of evening, those suited his mood better. He could smell the dinners cooking from as far as two doors away and heard the laughter of children as they ran along the street or rode their little BMX bikes or chased their dogs and each other. He had heard the cars of people coming home from work, heard the roar of school buses, the televisions with their evening cartoons. He flicked the radio on, but all that was on was the news. He put a tape into his player and turned up the volume to drown out the sounds of the world outside. He blanked out his mind and let the good old rock and roll take over. Cover me, cover me in sound and darkness and the beat and make me forget all the pain. He heard the frantic, desperate wail of electric guitar strings as fingers walked up the high frets, his heart following the frequencies, walking all over the minors with a hollow tension he could not understand but fully identified with. Tell me what I'm feeling. The bass strings pounded away at his subconscious, like a hypnotist easing him gently to sleep. Is the beat the only thing we can rely on is the beat the only thing we can rely on and is it only those empty melancholy minor keys that can tell me anything about what I feel and the screaming of steel strings cutting deep into flesh of fingers we want to scream I want to scream and die. The bassist pounded on and the drums made him feel like he wanted to get up and just let his body convulse with the rhythm, not caring what he looked like because there was no one to see anyway and then the rest note came and the guitars, the bass, the drums, the keyboards went dead and in the total silence, the scream of climax and Wings followed suit, the air forced out of his lungs in perfect pitch unison because he had done this so many times before. Restless spirits lonely hearts restless spirits lonely hearts restless spirits lonely hearts till fade. He fell on his bed, sweat pouring off his body. The tape ran on into silence and the final autostop. The click woke Wings and he realised it was way past dinnertime. He remembered his mother telling him to see to his own dinner because she would be at Gran's that night with the kid sister.

That night he took out his Camels and made himself a stiff whisky and Seven-Up. He sat on the edge of his bed, the cigarette smoking between the fingers of his right hand and the whisky in his left. He had moved the phone to his room and he stared at the buttons as the radio kept on rocking. Only his bedside lamp was on and the dim yellow light cast long dark shadows around the room. This is how I like it, he thought. This is how I feel.

His books were strewn across his desk, gathering dust. He had not touched them for a long while. His grades were sinking but tonight, it did not matter. It did not matter most other nights either.

Seven numbers ran through his mind. Her phone number. He looked at the push-buttons one by one and still could not make up his mind to call her. Karen. Will you answer the call?

Would you be willing to talk to me? He thought about her on the beach. How beautiful you are. What would you do with someone like me? They had walked and talked, all along that beach, right up to the breakwater and they had climbed the granite slabs to sit there and look out to sea. His fingers ran lightly over the plastic buttons. They had talked about school, about Tech. They had talked about the people in the workshop and each other's friends and Johnson. She did like Johnson. And those things that Johnson had said they did, well, he knew now that they were true.

"Are the two of you going steady or something?" The words had come out awkward. It had been very hard to say. She had been surprised he even thought that.

"No, we're just friends." Sure, he thought. A vague hope swelled up but it receded as quickly as the waves crashing against the breakwater.

The wind, as always, had caught her hair and blew it back in long dark streams. Wings had looked at her, the graceful curve of brow and the intense dark eyes, her whisper-soft voice, the lilting laughter. Shit, I am falling in love.

He had walked her home and she had said thank you, almost as if it had been a date. His heart broke as the door closed. Was it the last time he would ever see her like this? No, it was not. He could not get the image out of his memory. It was like a photograph that kept popping out to the foreground of his mind. Karen on the breakwater, hair blowing in the wind, a smile on her face as she looked out to sea and turned to look at him, the laughter in her voice and in her eyes. He saw that picture ever so often, in waking hours as well as the dreamtime.

Now his fingers hovered over the digits she had given him that day on the breakwater. Would she speak to him? Would she be happy to hear him? Would they have a good talk or would she hang up after a few minutes? Why should she talk to me? I'm nobody to her. She only calls to talk about Johnson nowadays. He was afraid and the knot in his stomach tightened unbearably. He took a gulp of whisky and the aftershock was numbing. He took a long drag on his cigarette. And so what if she hangs up and refuses to talk to me? Would it make a difference to me? That would only be a confirmation of what I've known forever. He plonked his glass down on his bedside table, turned down the volume and stubbed out his Camel in an ashtray. His fingers trembled uncertainly over the buttons and then he went for them, with a familiarity that came from punching them over and over again on his calculator keys. He heard a ringing tone and his pulse rate shot up. And then a cut as the phone was picked up.

"Hello." The familiar soft voice

"Hello, Karen? It's me, Wings."

11

THE car rushed along and Wings had his window down. His father looked at him and asked, "Why do you prefer it down? Doesn't it irritate you? The wind blowing your hair all about?"

"That's exactly what I like about it, Dad. It feels like flying in an open cockpit."

"I see you haven't outgrown that."

"Nope. Perfectly good fantasy. Can always run to it when everything else is going shit."

"Things been going shit lately?"

"You might say that."

"Schoolwork?"

"Amongst others."

"So how is it?"

"The first term has passed and I'm not too sure of what we've been doing. And every day, I find I know less and less."

"That's bad, boy. If you don't get a firm foundational knowledge, it's really very difficult handling new information because it's all built on the basics."

"Aiyah, think I don't know?"

"Then do something about it. Hm. Why isn't your mother making you buck up?"

"She's too busy. Business been bad lately." Mine too, he realised. *Mamak* had not been able to get the hard stuff from Sweden. And his rival — where was his source? Maybe I should get another supplier. Must get my ear back to the ground. Been too busy to take care of things lately.

"I wish I was around to kick your ass." Wings wiped his brow in mock relief. His father went on, "Really, you need a firm hand to guide you and maybe spank you once in awhile."

"I don't object to your presence, but corporal punishment tends to have the reverse effect on me. Ask mum."

"Not good for a boy to grow up without a father around," he muttered. Wings heard him.

"Well, it wasn't your fault, was it?"

"I don't know. 1 thought it wasn't. Now I don't know."

"Dad, why did Mum leave you?" he suddenly asked. "Was it because she wanted too much and you couldn't give?"

"What makes you say that, boy?" his voice was very soft.

"I've been thinking," not just about his parents but his own attitudes to women, "different things are important to you and her."

"That's true."

"Are there always differences, I mean, between men and women?" Wings remembered his own reasons for not daring to approach Karen.

"Usually." Wings knew the questions were hurting his father, because his answers were getting shorter. But he had to know.

"Is it always the same differences?"

"You're getting very deep." He pondered his son's question. Was there an answer? He had one, but he was not sure. He did not want his own cynicism to rub off on the boy. You've got a long way to go, kid.

"So, is it always the same?"

"Yah, maybe." He snorted. "Probably." What the heck.

He'll find out sooner or later. This might save him some pain. Besides, at his age, he's not going to chicken out and just avoid women for the rest of his life. No, the young, they will find out for themselves by trial and error. And what better way to learn? He cleared his throat and began.

"It's like this, son. Men, we have to be something. You know, identity. Like a teacher, doctor, lawyer, engineer," he tried to think of something the boy could relate to. "Or pilot."

"And the girls?"

"The women. They're different. They can be something, almost anything you can be, but deep down, they know they will all come back to the same thing — wife and mother. So women, they do not look to be, because that is given them. No. Not to be, but to have. Women want to have and men, we cannot always give."

"I understand."

"Do you?"

"Yep."

"Good. Bear that in mind. Less you expect, less you hurt."

Back at home, Wings studied the plans for his airplane. *I really have to sit down and finish it one day.* He made a list of all the materials he would need and made a rough estimate of costs. He whistled softly. Where would he get that kind of money? No point asking Mum. He considered his own resources. Should he touch his secret savings? No, better not. He could quarrel with his mother anytime and get stranded. No, can't touch the reserves. Well, there really wasn't any time anyway. Rumours of exam dates had been spreading and the latest rumour would leave him exactly half the time he figured he'd need to prepare for the exams. Hm. Problems, problems.

Will you ever fly, he asked the wooden skeleton. *Even if I can't get off the ground, I promise you will. Somehow. If I could fly. Where would I go? Away. As far away as possible. If only*

I could fly. All this shit wouldn't bother me. Just climb into a cockpit, start up, taxi and take off. He thought of Karen. If I had the power of flight, would I need you? No, you wouldn't bother me at all. I could forget you so easily. Take off like a bird and never think of you. If only I had flight. I wouldn't need a woman. A man needs only to be, not to have. Only when he fails to be, does he seek to have. I cannot be a pilot and so I need to have love. But I do not have love and there are no wings for my ego to take refuge beneath. If only I could fly.

The telephone rang and he heard his sister answer sweetly and then her voice became gruff. He knew it was his even before she screeched for him.

"Hey Wings, Boon Kim."

"Ah, what?"

"Eh, you know Johnson's girlfriend, right?"

"Yes, so?"

"What she look like?"

"Well, she's got long, silky hair. Straight. She's kind of dark. She's slim, got dark eyes and a pretty face. About half a head shorter than Johnson."

"Whoops."

"Whatsamatter?"

"I don't know man. Shit, I think Johnson may be two-timing her."

"What?" Wings almost shouted.

"I'm not sure, so don't jump to conclusions."

"Then what makes you say that?" Wings said sharply. His heart was pounding. He was angry with Johnson, sorry for Karen and he had to admit, maybe glad for himself. The last feeling left him guilty.

"Shit, I saw them at West Coast. I was visiting my Grandmother. I was cycling along the shore when I saw this couple. The guy looked damn familiar so I went to look see. As

265 COLIN CHEONG 265

I got closer, I realised it was Johnson and I thought the girl was Karen. So I tried to get closer and surprise them then I realised, shit man, Karen got long hair and this girl had very short hair, you know, like a sportswoman. Could tell from her bra straps too. And she was quite fair and she was bigger size. You sure Karen hasn't cut her hair?"

"I don't think she would. She said Johnson said he likes her hair long. Eh, you sure or not?"

"Damn sure. It was Johnson. I would have said hi, but I was afraid he might be embarrassed so I left."

"But Johnson wouldn't do that, would he?" It was so strange. Under normal circumstances, if Wings had felt nothing for Karen, he would not have felt the need to defend Johnson. But as it was…

"I dunno. This is something we've never handled before, I mean girls, so I don't know how Johnson will act. Other things he's okay lah, but comes to girls, I don't know man. Like my mother always tells my sisters — be careful of men, even the ones people say are good, because when it comes to women, men sure no good. Like they say, 'a prick has no conscience'."

"Boon Kim, you are so full of folk-wisdom. I'm sure our friend isn't like that."

"I dunno. I think it's best you talk to him about it. I mean the two of you have been getting quite close because of this girl, right? Funny actually, because from what I know, girls always drive friends apart."

"We have a Code of Conduct and we stand by it," Wings said simply. What is a man without his honour? And what of honour? It is but a word. But a word.

"I'll have a word with Johnson."

"Okay, keep us posted. I'll inform Har Tow and Krish. But let's just keep it to ourselves okay? I hope you're not going to tell Karen straightaway."

"No, we talk to John first."

"Okay. See you."

"Ciao."

He hung up and sat quietly by the phone for a while. What should I feel? What's right to feel? Happy, because this is the opening I've been waiting for? It could wreck their relationship and I'll be there to comfort her. What Dad said about building on foundations, he's right. I have a firm enough foundation with Karen. And she'll be grateful to have a friend nearby. And when the crying's done and the tears dried, I'll be there, ready to help her love again.

He thought of how fond Karen was of Johnson. She never said 'love' and that was a comfort. But the rest she said. The things they had done together, the time shared. She told him everything and he often wondered why he subjected himself to such torture. Maybe I am a masochist. Maybe this is a mental version of a sex-spanking. There was always that heartbreaking brightness in her voice when she talked about him. And the devastating sorrow whenever Johnson and her had had a disagreement. Her moods had come to follow Johnson's and Wings could tell how she would be feeling if she called at night just by watching Johnson in school in the day. And the rotter was doing this to her. He could imagine the pain she would feel if she ever found out and he felt very angry with Johnson. How could you hurt a little girl like Karen?

He forced himself to stop. It's so easy. Too easy. Too easy to take advantage of the situation. I'm like a bloody vulture, waiting to feast on the results of somebody's misery. But how could Johnson do it? If he did it? And if he did it, maybe there's a reason we don't know. Maybe it was a cousin we haven't met. But he's my buddy and I can't rat on him, even if he has done something wrong. I have to stand by my brothers. He remembered a morning five years back, when he had taken the Promise and Law at his cub-Scout investiture, when he had earned the right to wear the purple badge of universal brotherhood. A Scout's Honour is to be trusted. Scout Law Number One. A Scout is Loyal. Scout Law Number Two. There must have been a reason why the Founder had put those two laws before all others. Honour, Loyalty. I cannot shake those ideals, even now, this far in life. I cannot forget them just because an image of a beautiful woman with long hair says I should and promises me something, I don't know what. And as he forced Karen's face out of his mind, another face drifted into focus. I got a bloody slide projector in my head! The khaki of her uniform seemed so far away. The green tie, the Scouters' insignia. Her smile, the only one he could remember now. Janet. She had betrayed his trust by forgetting him but he had stayed loyal and remembered her. I am forever one of BP's boys. I took the vows and now they hold me for life. Well then, I must stand firm, even in a world that has forgotten its ideals. I am Ronin — masterless Samurai, because BP is dead. Samurai is the same because I cannot forget my vows of Honour.

He stood up. He felt much better thinking of himself that way. He breathed out slowly. This is what I must think. Freezeframe. Stop thinking right here. Forget the rest. Do what Honour says I must. Forget the rest. Remember only the Code. The Code is all. So simple. Follow the Code. Be a man who obeys not his baser instincts, but the higher callings of a Code. And what does the Code say I must do? I must set my friend right. Yes, that is what I must do.

12

WINGS was at the baggage counter when Har Tow walked up with his bag.

"Wings, my boy, we have to stop meeting like this," he said. Wings laughed and took his bag.

"So, ah, have you talked to Johnson?" Har Tow asked softly.

"Yaah."

"So what's going on?" Har Tow and Krishnan only knew what Boon Kim had told them. He had also told them to leave it to Wings to settle.

"He admitted it."

"What? You mean it's true?" Har Tow could hardly believe it.

"Yes. Her name's Lynette."

"Who is she? Is she from the workshop?"

"Yes. But a different class. They do metal when we do wood."

Har Tow got behind the counter and sat down next to Wings. "This is bad."

"Johnson doesn't think so, bro."

"What do you mean? Surely he knows it's wrong."

"He doesn't think so." It finally sank in and Har Tow did not know what to say. He stared blankly ahead. He could not accept the fact that Johnson did not subscribe to the same values he did. He looked at Wings as if he had the answers.

"I told him he couldn't. That even if he didn't think it was wrong, he ought to think of Karen's feelings. And he said he had." Wings paused. "And that's when he told me about himself. You know his mum, she's his Dad's second wife. And you know the lady who drives him to school? That isn't his real mum 'cos she's dead. That's First Wife. And she loves him like her own because she couldn't have sons."

"You making this up, Wings?"

"No. Johnson really doesn't think it's wrong because it's worked out fine in his family. And First Wife, yeah well, she knows about the young woman his Dad keeps at some apartment in town. And she says it's okay as long as his Dad does his duty as a husband and a father. She doesn't mind 'cos he's really good to her even with the mistress and all."

"And that's why he doesn't think it's wrong?" Wings nodded.

"He just said that Karen had to get used to the idea, that's all."

"Will she?" Wings shook his head.

"I think she's very possessive."

"We all have our faults. So what else did you tell him?"

"I told him that by normal standards it was wrong and that maybe he should try to get used to having one girl instead of expecting Karen to get used to the idea of sharing her man."

"What did he say?"

"He didn't like it."

"Then?"

"Then I begged him to stop." Wings was staring straight ahead because he did not want Har Tow to see the tears shining in his eyes. He had taken it all the way. He had gone as low as he could have. He had begged another man not to hurt a girl he had no claim to.

"You knelt?" Har Tow was incredulous.

"No, I just said, 'I'm begging you Johnson, think about

Karen's feelings.'"

"And what he say to that?"

"What's it got to do with you?" The words came out bitter. Wings had almost hit Johnson in the face then, but he had kept his fists down. It wouldn't have helped Karen any.

"Then I told him that if he couldn't be bothered about her feelings then he should think about us and our Code and he just laughed. He said it didn't affect any of us and that we should just let him do whatever he wants."

"He's forgotten that the Code protects him too." Har Tow was solemn. He did not take infringements of his law lightly.

"I think he has. But never mind. I threatened to tell Karen about it and he blew up. I said, 'There you are, if it was okay, you wouldn't be so scared.' And he kept screaming that she wasn't ready. When will she be ready for something like that? I told him that she didn't have to stick around with him and put up with all that. I mean, there are a lot of guys who'd give—" he stopped dead, then he went on, "anything for her."

"And?"

"And he just gave me a real dirty look and said real cold, 'Whose side you on anyway?' That's when I gave up."

"So what you going to do now?"

"I'm going to tell Karen about it when I get home tonight." There was a long silence.

"Wings, I hope you don't mind me asking this."

"No, nothing between friends. Shoot."

"Remember one time you told me you liked some girl but someone beat you to her? Could this girl by any chance be called Karen?"

"You're very tactful. Yes. Karen. The one and only. How did you guess?" Wings turned to Har Tow. The tears had dried.

"You said you were beaten by someone earlier in the alphabet. You're a Wong and Johnson's Ang. Not many people in between."

"So what about it?"

"You're not by any chance still hoping for her, are you?"

"Why?" Wings could not say 'no'.

"Because if you are, then maybe what you're doing now about Karen and Johnson, you shouldn't do because maybe you have an ulterior motive. Vested interests or something like that." Har Tow had thought it over very carefully. He did not want his friends separated by a quarrel over a mere girl. Why had he drawn up the Law, for goodness sake?

Wings was confused. Had he arrived at the decision to tell Karen because that was what he had wanted to do all along? So that he could disrupt their relationship and then home in on Karen? Then maybe the way he had prodded Johnson, maybe he had done it so that Johnson would be negative so that in the end, Wings' decision would be justified. Had he really done all that without thinking?

"God…"

"Look, Wings, maybe you should leave the matter alone and we'll do what we can. Nobody else knows about the way you feel about Karen. Only the two of us and I'll keep my mouth shut. You leave John alone. We'll try and change his mind."

Wings looked absently at him. His mind was still reeling. Did I really mean it that way? Did I fool myself so completely? I even thought I was doing something honourable. It looked good, didn't it? But what was below it? Just a dirty, rotten trick. What kind of a person am I?

"Yah. You're right," he said at last. "I shouldn't do anything else. Leave it to you guys. Whose side am I on? Not John's. Not Karen's. I was on my side, that's all."

He looked at Har Tow.

"Take care of Karen, bro," he said sadly. He sighed. I'm not fit to do it anymore.

13

WHY did God create kid sisters, Wings wanted to know. He had asked himself that question many times before and had always arrived at the conclusion that it was a curse God had laid on every older brother after Cain. He seldom heard his girl cousins complain about their brats. But the boys! Oh the boys had lots to say about kid sisters, all his cousins, all his friends. It proved his theory, he felt. Older sisters had not fallen from grace the way Cain had and were thus spared the curse.

He had not minded her terribly before she learnt to speak, but once she had, there had been no shutting her up. Wings, who never talked back to his mother because she had brought him up with a very hard hand not to, did not like the idea of the brat talking back to him. Besides, she had a way of making him look bad. He had felt none of the much-considered sibling jealousy, but the kid sister had been often used as a reckoning rod for her irresolute and delinquent brother. That made him dislike her more and her smugness about it did not help.

He had just quarrelled with her, as usual, and he really could not remember what it had been about. Neither could he recall the last time they had had a proper conversation. His mother had given him stern warnings about being civil to her and he had shot back cheekily, "Well, at least we acknowledge each other's existence," before dancing out of reach of her hard palm.

His bad mood made studying difficult as his mind was busy plotting his sister's downfall. She had gone out shopping with their mother and their maid after lunch and Wings had the whole house to himself.

Must get out of this mood, he told himself and automatically looked towards his half-finished airplane. He shut his eyes and tried to imagine himself in the cockpit again. Spitfire Charley Juliet Ace Sixer Deuce, taxi up. The groundcrew pulled away the restraining chocks and the plane rolled forward as he gave the Merlin engine throttle. He taxied her into position and waited for control tower's clearance. Charley Juliet Ace Sixer Deuce, you're cleared for take-off. He snapped a smart salute to his crewchief and the plane surged forward. He watched the scene outside the cockpit until it became a familiar rushing blur and the tail lifted off the strip. Airspeed reading 55 knots, ease her up. Gently, he took her on a gradual climb. He pulled in his landing gear and eased back the spade yoke.

This is absurd, he thought as he opened his eyes. I'm groundbound and that's it. With his eyes open, he saw only what was there, real time, real life. With his eyes shut — once it would have been so easy. But now, the slightest lapse in concentration or distraction from the real world would send his Spitfire down in flames. The only time he could really run away was when the darkness covered his eyes and sent everyone else to sleep. The dreamtime, but even that had become contaminated by reality. No, he could not even dream of Karen without feeling stupid the morning after when the light came and when he dreamed, there was a stickiness for realistic detail that he had never felt before. I love you, he would have her say, but the contamination, it would itch like a rash and make him realise the real time truth. She'd never say that. And the dream would turn sour.

And so, what was there left? Compromise. There had to be a compromise between dreamtime and realtime. Something that was halfway real and halfway dream. He knew of only one thing. He unlocked his drawer and looked at the growing stack of magazines. He wanted to laugh when he thought about how important an event your first solo flight was. With these, I am solo all the time. Sex is meant to be shared. That was realtime. So in the dreamtime, we fly solo with a two-dimensional image in a glossy magazine. The women, they exist in the realtime, but not in my mind. But here it is, the compromise existence. They are not here, but they are more than just my imagination. Even if I can't touch them, I can see them without closing my eyes. He picked up the topmost one. The telephone rang.

Karen listened to the ring tones. Normally, she would have hung up by the eighth ring, but now, she would wait till the phone cut itself off. Wings opened the door and went into the hall to look for the phone. Where did that stupid girl put it? He found the phone and said a rude hello.

"Wings? It's Karen." He softened immediately.

"Hi, what's up?"

"I need to talk, Wings. Can you spare the time?"

Of course he could. "Yes. What's wrong?"

"It's John, Wings."

"Why? Did you both have a fight?" He knew what it would be about. He had been dreading this. What am I going to tell her? All thoughts of his Pets had fled.

"I don't know how to tell you."

"Put it in the simplest words possible." He thought for a moment. "No matter how much it hurts." There was silence.

"Wings," she said at last very softly, "I think Johnson's been cheating on me."

"Where did you hear that?" He told himself to keep an even tone. Don't get excited. It will only make her suspicious.

"Mildred told me. People have seen him with this girl from my school called Lynette."

"Can they be relied on?" Stall, say nothing to confirm it.

"I don't know, Wings. Why would anyone want to make up stories like that?"

"Out of jealousy," he remembered himself, "or maybe spite. Lots of reasons." Please don't ask me, girl.

"Wings, that might be so if it was only one person, but Mildred says there have been more than a few."

"Mildred says. Have you heard yourself? Maybe Mildred is doing the dirty on you." He could have slapped himself. No, not everyone is like me. No one is as black.

"Wings! How could you say that? Mildred and Mei are my best friends. How could you even think it?"

"Sorry, kid. I'm bad, so I think everyone else is too."

"Wings, do you know anything?" The crunch had come. The axe had fallen. Wings wished that he had gone shopping too.

"No," he lied. He said it abruptly, forced the monosyllable out of himself. Well, at least he had not lied about Johnson. The lie was about himself. Petty sin. White lie. Don't want her to hurt. Don't want John in trouble.

"Are you telling me the truth?" she asked, her voice breaking.

"Yes, Karen. Would I lie to you? You're like a sister to me." Double lie. I am going to burn in hell for this. He was beginning to see how one lie led to another.

"Wings, I feel so bad. No one knows anything. Either that or no one is telling me the truth. And I don't want to say anything to John until I have some proof. And I can't say anything now and I just can't do anything about it," she began to cry and Wings listened painfully to her sobs.

"I'm sorry, I'm probably disturbing you. Thanks, Wings," she said after a while.

For telling you a lie? His heart ached as she put down her receiver. He stared out of the hall window at the street outside. It was drizzling, the light was muted and all the leaves were a brilliant green where the rain had washed them and the light passed through their translucent shapes.

He picked up the phone and keyed her number

"Karen? It's Wings. I'm sorry. I lied."

Karen sat on the breakwater alone. The water was black, and far out at sea she could see the lights of the merchant ships at anchor. The black water crashed beneath her feet, the froth gleaming in the moonlight. There were no stars for the clouds hung low and the moon, near full, peeped from a gap in the dark mass overhead. She saw a flash light up the grey sky far away and then heard the faint distant roll of thunder. She sniffed and wiped her eyes on her sleeve. There was a couple on the other end of the breakwater, where she had sometimes sat with Johnson.

There isn't anything between us, she remembered him saying. Nothing at all. She's like a sister to me. Why did you have to listen to all those rumours? And what the hell did you ask Wings for? He's been jealous about us ever since we started. Of course he'll have nothing good to say about me. And I'll bet that was the first time he ever heard this stupid story, when you had to tell him. Of course, he'll agree! Get smart, Karen, who are you going to listen to? Other people or me?

Don't be angry, she had pleaded, but he had gone on, indignant that he had been suspected that way. You don't trust me, that's why. You think I'm not being sincere. What kind of relationship do we have if you don't trust me? I trusted you, didn't I? You and Wings are such good friends, always talking on the phone. Trusted you. And him too. And now the two of you come up with this.

Johnson had felt like a bastard. I'm the one who's wrong, but I'm making her take the guilt. But it's the only way I can save our relationship. I'll make it up to her. She won't understand now. She needs time.

She had cried and he had softened the tone of his voice.

"Call me when you think you can trust me." He had calculated the effect of that on her and hung up. Let her suffer a few days. She'll be less likely to ever bring it up again.

She watched the couple down the end and her heart ached. He was holding her round the shoulders and their heads were together as they talked. Hadn't he done that too? She watched as he kissed her and stroked her hair and she remembered Johnson doing the same to her. She could almost feel his hands and lips caressing her neck, his cheek against her breasts and then his tech-roughened palm beneath her tee-shirt cupping a naked breast, playfully pinching. The tears began afresh as she remembered. She had let him do all that because she loved him and he was treating her this way now. She felt cheated and the pain in her heart worsened. What had Sandra told her about this? Don't let them go too far. The sooner you give them what they want, the earlier they'll take you for granted and leave you. Her boy, that innocent-looking one called Har Tow, well, what do you know, Sandra had said, still waters run deep. Why hadn't she listened? You like it don't you, he had murmured in her ear as he stroked her thighs. You like it don't you? Yes, she had said and she had not lied. It had felt so wonderful, to be touched that way by someone you loved. She suddenly felt cheap and used and her tears were bitter. I want to die, she thought as she looked down into the churning black mass. The waves seemed to call her, reaching out for her as she felt the spray hit her face.

Nobody cares, she thought. Then she remembered her parents, watching TV now, and her sister, out on another date. Would they understand? How could she ever explain it to them? And if she ever told anyone, would they still accept her? And the boys, what if Johnson told on her, what would they say? Cheap, second-hand, slut, easy, good-time girl. Who would know and try to understand and still be her friend? She stood up and the wind blew back her hair. She felt the breeze drying her eyes and she rubbed away the tear-stains. She knew someone who would. There was a low, low rumble in the sky as an Airbus passed overhead.

14

"HEY man, how was the weekend? How many times you shake?" Boon Kim said to Wings when they met before school in the toilet.

"None. Coitus interruptus," Wings laughed.

"Come again?" Boon Kim asked, puzzled. Wings always found the weirdest ways to say the crudest things. Wings laughed again.

"What does that mean?" he asked, determined to find out. "Laugh at me just because my vocab not so hot, right? Bloody snob."

Wings was bent over the sink laughing when he felt a hand on his shoulder and found himself jerked up and around.

"Wings!" Johnson screamed in his face as he shook him by his collar. "What the fuck do you think you're doing?"

"What are you talking about?" Wings shouted back although he knew perfectly well what it was about. It was the moment he had been dreading. He did not expect it, but Johnson's palm swung around hard and heavy and found Wings' left cheek with a loud smack and sent him looking the other way. His hand smarted, but Wings' face had gone crimson. Wings put a hand to his face. I got that coming, he thought. I deserve it for ratting. Otherwise Johnson would not be standing now. He turned around slowly to face Johnson.

"Want the other side too?" he asked mockingly. His face showed no emotion, only the five-fingered red mark that Johnson left. Johnson raised his arm, but Boon Kim hit it down.

"That's enough! What are the two of you trying to prove?"

"Stay out of this," Johnson warned. Wings felt the heat rise.

"You'd be dead if he did," he said quietly. Johnson stepped forward menacingly but Wings stood his ground.

"Enough I said!" Boon Kim shouted. He pushed himself in between them roughly.

"What the shit is going on here?"

"He told on me!" Johnson yelled, pointing his finger in Wings' face.

"I warned you."

"I told you to stay out of it!"

"So I couldn't."

"She's my girlfriend, in case you've forgotten. How I handle her is my business," Johnson said in a dangerous tone.

"Not if you're hurting her." Wings did not blink.

"That doesn't make you innocent." Johnson's veins were showing. His face was red and he was sweating.

"Neither are you. You cheated on her." The look of nothing on Wings' face scared him, maybe more than if Wings had turned ugly.

"That's none of your fucking business!"

"It's mine because she's my friend."

"And what was I?" Johnson was near to tears in helpless anger.

"I told you to stop. You didn't listen. And I told you I'd tell her if you didn't stop." Wings was infuriatingly expressionless. If he would lash out, Johnson thought. Hit me, Wings…

"You still got no right."

"Neither do you."

They glared coldly at each other. Johnson's heart was beating madly. Why had he told on him? Why? Were he and Karen that close? If so, what did it mean? There could be only one reason.

"Enough, assholes?" Boon Kim asked. Johnson shook his head.

"No. I just want this prick to know that I know what he's up to. He wants Karen. Why do you think he's been so pally with her? He's using this to *sabo* our relationship. So we'll break and he can take her for himself. Well, you tell him no chance, man. I'm keeping her. She's mine. In more ways than you want to know. And I want him to know that as from this moment we are quits, no more friends."

"The feeling's mutual." Wings thought for a moment and then spat the word out. "Bastard."

Johnson lunged at him but Boon Kim shoved him back. Johnson gave him one last frustrated glare and walked out. Wings watched him go and felt sick. He wanted to cry. He leaned over the sink, but the tears would not come. Damn, why this way. Boon Kim put a hand gently on his shoulder.

"Better splash some water on that cheek, bro."

15

HAR Tow had been with Sandra regularly, even though the mid-year exams were drawing close. We study together, he had protested when the boys made fun of him. Yes, study what? The boys had asked. Biology? Har Tow had been offended by that old schoolboy joke and he acted the part, but inside, he felt a little guilty because it was partly true. Sandra and him, well, they hadn't meant anything at first. They just sat close together and she had begun to lean a little on him and he had started to hold her hand. It was possible because he was left-handed and she, right. So if he was always on the left and she on the right, it was possible for them to hold hands and study at the same time. What a blessed coincidence, he thought. Unfortunately, they had not stopped at hands. Soon, pens too were put down and the freed hands called into play. They had petted, lightly at first, but as the days passed, it had grown more passionate. And because there was no one else at home that time of day at Sandra's house, they had moved to the couch and the work had taken a backseat to the petting.

He had managed to make himself stop from going further because the exams were so close and he had told Sandra they would have to go on hold till the exams were over.

"And we'll continue where we stopped." Sandra, of course, had no intention of letting him go any further, but she said nothing. The experiences of the last two months had changed Har Tow. He found himself thinking more and more — not only of Sandra, but of sex in general. He felt a sudden sense of restlessness that he had never known and a feeling of being held back from fulfilment. The thoughts and feelings disturbed him and gave him no rest. He told Wings in the Library.

"I could lend you a magazine," Wings offered. "Help you get it off. I know, I've had that feeling too."

"I don't do that stuff. The real thing or nothing. No pirate copies for me, man." The boys laughed and the Librarian glared at them.

The boys no longer sat in a group. The rift between Johnson and Wings made it awkward, so they took turns to hang out with Johnson and Wings. Today, it was Krishnan's and Har Tow's turn to be with Wings. Boon Kim was somewhere else with Johnson.

"Aren't you guys going to patch up?" Krishnan asked Wings.

"I can't be bothered," Wings said. And it was true. He was very tired of the whole affair. He was tired of trying to explain himself, justify his actions to Har Tow and Krishnan and Boon Kim and Johnson and the rest of the Tech Group boys. Everybody knew about it. Johnson had seen to that. The Tech Group had taken sides. Even Boon Kim and Har Tow were not impartial. Boon Kim had felt that Wings should not have ratted because men should stand by their brothers no matter what. No girl was worth your friend, he reasoned. Har Tow sided with Wings because he felt that under the circumstances, Wings had done the only thing possible. He had evened things out between Karen and Johnson by letting Karen know exactly where she stood. What happened between the couple later, that wasn't Wings' business. I mean, Johnson knew the consequences, didn't he, Har Tow asked the boys.

But there was the talk. Johnson had made it known that Wings' motives were wrong even if his action may have been correct.

"He wants Karen. Why do you think he hasn't got anyone yet? He was waiting for something to happen, see? So he could walk in and take over."

Johnson had told Karen not to speak to Wings anymore but she felt she could no longer trust Johnson, though she did not say so. She was not about to give up the friendship of the only boy she could trust now. So she had called him to make sure that everything was normal between them and Wings had been relieved.

"Don't expect me to say anything nice about Johnson now," he warned.

"Well, it wasn't nice the last time, but it was true. Just keep telling me the truth, Wings," she had said.

All truths but one, Wings thought. How I really feel about you, girl. He had cried one night for her and his pillow had been soaked and he had kept getting out of bed for the bathroom to clear his nose.

"He keeps saying that they're only friends and that all they do is talk on the phone," Boon Kim said.

"Did you ask him about his intentions?" Krish asked.

"He said he doesn't have any."

"But he likes her. I know he was very fed-up when Johnson *choped* her first. How did he get to know her?" Har Tow asked.

"Oh, Johnson said she said that they met by accident on the beach. They made friends and they've been talking on the phone ever since."

"But how do you tell someone's intentions?" Krish persisted.

"I'll take his word for it. I believe him," Har Tow said simply.

"He has this thing about honour. As long as Johnson

continues to call Karen his girl, Wings will not cut in and he will not *sabo*. But if they split, then I think that's when he'll move."

"Then why does he keep calling her now?" Krish asked.

"Foundation, lah. He is preparing, I think. He knows something maybe even we and Johnson don't know. Johnson says she's quite on with Wings right? By the way, is Johnson still playing doubles with that girl called Lynette?" Har Tow wanted to know.

"Yes." Boon Kim's face was dark. He had been unable to get Johnson off it.

"Actually, sometimes I wish Wings had got Karen," Har Tow said softly. "But he didn't. And there are the Laws to follow."

The run-up period to exams was always too short. Many of Tech Group 2/13 were caught with their pants down. Wings was no exception.

"But you can't call it an unfair surprise," Boon Kim reasoned. "Everybody knew that there was going to be an exam. It happens every year."

"I know, I'm just grumbling. I like to grumble and I like to blame anything but me. That's all." Wings had passed only English, Art and Tech (and not too well either). He had failed Chinese, Mathematics, General Science, History, Geography and Literature (all the way to rock-bottom F9).

"Well, there's always Finals," Boon Kim said.

"Thank you very much," Wings replied glumly. "That's a lot of help."

"At least you got an early warning. May's ending. That means you've got June, July, August, September and half of October to prepare for Finals. A lot of time, what."

"Sounds too much like work. And I'm too depressed to work."

"Why? Still *frus* over Karen?"

Wings ignored the remark. "Do you think if I repeat this year, my tech group will get all the girl classes again?"

"Hope long long."

"Okay then, no point repeating."

"Hey, you're still hot for Karen?"

"No such thing. Like I keep saying, we're friends, that's all."

"Does she know it's affecting your studies?"

"You sound like an agony aunt column. 'Affecting your studies' — do you know how often they use this phrase? No she is not affecting my studies."

"Don't bluff. I'm sure she is. You just won't admit, that's all. Why don't you be honest with yourself?"

"That sounds familiar too — 'why don't you be honest with yourself'. What are you going to tell me next? 'You must be fair to the both of you'? After all, 'you are both young and have a future ahead of you'. 'Go out and make as many friends as possible, both boys and girls.' 'If she really likes you, she'll understand.' Talk cock, sing song, Boon Kim."

"I'm trying to help and you won't listen…"

"Another cliche."

"Wings! Will you stop being an asshole?" Boon Kim was getting exasperated.

"Sorry," Wings said, but he was unrepentant.

"All this about Karen is just a waste of time. She belongs to somebody else. Can't you get that into your thick skull? You no brains or what?"

"From my results, I suppose we could say that."

"Er, sorry. Didn't mean it like that."

"That's okay. I know I'm not stupid. I just got no mood to study."

"Why?"

"Because."

"Because what?"

"Shit, how would I know? It's just a real sick feeling. I just don't feel like studying. No meaning. I mean what for?"

"Get a job?"

"That will come with time."

"No cert no job."

"I'll get the bloody cert and I'll get a job. Don't worry."

"No good certs, no good job, no good money."

"I don't care."

"Look where money got Johnson."

Wings looked at Boon Kim with an expressionless face. He's not looking at me, Boon Kim thought after a few moments. He's looking past me, as if I'm not even here. It felt very strange and he was beginning to feel uncomfortable when Wings refocused his eyes on Boon Kim.

"I suppose so. No money, no talk, and definitely no women."

"Yes, why do you think I work so hard? I just think of the money and all the fun I'll have when school is finally over," Boon Kim revealed.

All the fun. Wings remembered the Saturday afternoon when he had been cruising up and down Orchard Road with Boon Kim. They had heard a familiar voice call out behind them. Turning around, he had seen Johnson first, and then that familiar long hair and the dark eyes. He had felt his heart suddenly being ripped in a thousand different directions. He had never known that such pain could be possible without death. He had wanted to simply turn and run, run as fast and as far as he could away from them, the sight of her hand in his, the smirk of proud ownership on Johnson's face, the hesitant smile of recognition on her lips, probably already offered as a living sacrifice to Johnson. Wings felt the familiar hot sickness flash through all his limbs and his gut. When they had carried on their way, Johnson's arm around her shoulders, he wanted to rip that offending arm away from her sacred flesh and smash

Johnson's face to pulp, turn that smirk into bloody mush, put his fingers into those eyes that insinuated superiority, break the nose held high in a rich brat's cockiness. But he didn't. The rules of civilisation kept him from it. And those rules, they made him angry because he felt that those rules had been created by the privileged to protect the privileged and to keep people like him down. No, those, they are not my rules, why should I live by them. Because there are consequences. Yes. Consequences. Otherwise Johnson would be getting beaten up now. And would she love me for doing that? No. But what difference? She would not love me anyway, so I might as well be satisfied with pulverizing Johnson. But the consequences. The system protects its own. Protects them from the outsiders. That is what I am. An outsider. Will never be part of that mainstream. Everybody's riding Express, but I'm on the Sub-Normal. He had been very foul after that and Boon Kim had been quite shocked at Wings' language and bad mood.

"Cheer up," Boon Kim had said in a vain attempt to help. But Wings had gone into his silent mode, shutting off all input and producing no output. His mind had run on at high speed, in total silence, his thoughts a hopeless confusion, like so much stuff in a blender whirling and cutting, just a heady mixture of anger-frustration-generated adrenalin, negative emotions and deep deep depression. It had not been long before they ended their cruising. Wings' mood had affected Boon Kim too badly.

"And you say you got no feelings for her. What kind of a man are you if you're going to let some stupid bitch do that to you?" Boon Kim had finally exploded. Wings was silent. He had flagged the bus, got on and gone home to the Gardens.

16

THE exams are over, Har Tow realised. It's time to go back to Sandra. And where we left off. He could imagine the feel of her skin, the curve of her hip, her tight bum and sleek thighs. And those lips, soft and warm and wet. Sandra was a good kisser. She was not passive either. She did not just let him kiss and stroke her, she kissed and stroked back too. Har Tow knew he was on to something good because some of the boys had complained that their girlfriends had no more life than Barbie dolls. Might as well have kissed the wall, they said. But even an unresponsive girl was better than a wall and none of them ever puckered up to a wall.

But Har Tow was not satisfied. The petting had left him feeling shortchanged, not that Sandra had had any intention to cheat him. He had always been excited and restless before they got down to it. But when they had stopped to get on with the real homework, the restlessness had always come back. He had borrowed a magazine from Wings in the end (Wings had refused to take the rental money for once) but it had been of little comfort.

"Do you know how to get it off?" Wings had asked him suspiciously. Har Tow had nodded vigorously. Of course he knew. But after he had come, the feeling of restlessness had not gone and it was worse this time because he had felt drained and utterly lonely and depressed.

"There is something singularly incomplete about self-employment," he had said to Wings.

"Well, some of us don't mind being our own boss. You know what the economy is like nowadays."

"Ever considered going into a partnership?" Boon Kim had suggested as he snickered.

So now, Har Tow knew where the feeling of incompleteness and restlessness came from and he had been given the solution. She had been looking him in the face all along except when she closed her eyes to kiss. However, Har Tow was never one to take an answer for a fact. I have to think about this, he told the boys. Boon Kim may be wrong. Besides, as class brains, he felt a little sore that he had missed the solution. Perhaps I can make more sense of it all. There must be a 'why' to it. 'How', we already know.

He went to the library on a Saturday morning (unheard of) and found the quiet reference section unusually stuffy. This was because the librarians were so used to not having visitors on Saturday mornings, especially after exams, and had not bothered to open the upstairs windows.

Har Tow walked downstairs to the first level and found no one, not even at the counter. I could steal some books, he thought, and no one would know. But Har Tow did not fancy anything the library had to offer. Besides, he was not that kind of boy. He walked out of the library and ran straight into Wings' day-leader, who had volunteered for post-exam Saturday duty to chalk up points. Har Tow was glad that he was an honest person and that there had been nothing to tempt him

He went on downstairs to the basketball court and sat at the stone table beneath a shady mango tree. The street beyond the fence was unusually quiet, the canteen practically empty. No basketball pinged along the concrete court and no one cried 'foul' in Chinese. It was a cool, sunny morning and light pierced through the green canopy of the mango tree in slim shafts of gold, dappling the stone table and seats with light. A gentle breeze shook the leaves and they rustled. A lovely day, Har Tow thought. Too bad I don't write poetry. He allowed his thoughts to wander and it occurred to him that much enlightenment happened under trees. Newton had been sitting under a tree when that apple fell. Eve had been under a tree too when she learnt she could gain the knowledge of good and evil by eating apples. Steve Jobs must have taken a bite of the apple too and been deleted from the garden of IBM. But so what? An Apple a day would keep the creditors away. But Buddha had been sitting under a Bo tree when he received enlightenment.

His mind was in-between thoughts (i.e. blank) when he heard a little thud to the left of him. A ripened mango had fallen from the tree. He remembered his Science lessons, still rather fresh from the exam. Some trees drop their fruits and the seeds take root in the soil and draw nutrition from the fruit flesh as the first shoots sprout and leaves bud. And when the seed takes root, it belongs to the ground and the ground belongs to it. They become a part of each other. And the seed grows into a tree to make a long story short.

There was a deeper meaning in all that, Har Tow told himself. He had learnt in Literature that all is not what it seems to be on the surface. Look a little deeper and you will find its true meaning. Yes, yes, like the way make-up and girls' clothes only told a surface story. What was beneath was often less than desirable.

Girls turned his thoughts to love. Is love not like a seed? It drops from a tree or a hand or a beak to rest in the soil. Then it tries to take root in the soil. If the soil is soft and damp and fertile, the seed will grow into a plant. But if the soil is dry and hard and barren, the seed will die and no tree for you. And if the soil is soft and damp and fertile, but choked with weeds, the seed still cannot reach the tender embrace of the earth and will not grow. No touch, no growth. And again, no tree for you.

His mind went blank and when it booted up again, he thought of the seed nestled in the warm, moist darkness of a rich embracing earth. Was there an equivalent for human beings? Could he compare the seed with a child and the earth its parents? The parallel was the first that came to mind. But not quite. Did not the seed grow into a tree, producing its own seeds? Here was reproduction, chapter 12 in the Biology text. Yes, there is sex for some plants — pollen and pistils and other such phallic objects and bees and butterflies for artificial insemination. But where is the contact, the touch? He could only think of the relationship between plant and earth, the seed ensconced in the regenerative darkness of the earth. No, no, then. Perhaps it is not a Parent-Child relationship, but a Man-Woman relationship. Okay, but which is Man and which is Woman? He thought of most of the animals they had studied in science. The nurturer was always the female. Was that not what the good earth did? Did she not take the seed into her warm, moist darkness? And seed, was it not a synonym for semen, the stuff that activated eggs? And after all, wasn't it seed that made the entry and earth that yielded? The skin of the mango and the flesh would fall away and the seed would be taken up by the earth. Its roots would grow, penetrating the warm, wet darkness below. The preposition in operation here was 'into'.

Har Tow vaguely remembered a verse he had come across in his reading, but which he could not remember where from. 'A man shall leave his parents and cleave unto his wife and they shall be of one flesh.' It sounded terribly much like sex to Har Tow. The seed, after all, also left its parent tree to cleave unto the earth and once its roots sprouted, they would be of one flesh (that presumably meant united). And if love was a seed, how else would it grow except through contact between earth and seed? If union was the ultimate expression of love, shouldn't people who loved each other have sex? It was not a matter of should, Har Tow felt. It is really a matter of must.

But only the seed stands to gain anything. The thought stopped him dead. That is true. Love had to be a symbiotic relationship at least, if not synergistic. He remembered the chapter on Ecology. Interdependency. Food Chain. How did the earth depend on the plant? Well, the plant would give it shade from the sun, preventing it from drying up the earth and scorching it barren. It would protect the earth from the eroding forces of rain and wind. It would nourish the earth with fallen leaves that would decay and keep the ground fertile. And the earth would continue feeding the tree with nutrients, helping it to grow and giving it a home, a connection, and bringing their sons up, who would leave in time to find their own bits of earth.

Har Tow could think of nothing else for a long while. His mind boggled in awe and wonder. What a beautiful relationship. What an elegant, practical system. What a lesson for human beings. He looked around him, at the trees, the ground, the carefully tended shrubs, the grass, the fallen mango. He looked up at the sky, pale blue with candy-cotton puffs of cumulus clouds, the sun peeping out behind them in brilliance. He thought of the crystal droplets the cumulus promised, the golden light that would wake the green cells of chlorophyll in the leaves. Wake up, wake up, it's time to make food. And love. He laughed out loud, suddenly in love and at one with all of Creation. Whoever made all this, I salute you. This is not just the work of a scientist or an engineer or an ecologist. You are an artist.

And I am enlightened. Har Tow realised what had been bugging him all these weeks. He could now put his finger on it. It is incomplete because it is incomplete, he thought. I am restless and unfulfilled because I have not finished the task begun. Love must be taken all the way or not at all; without the contact, the union, love will die like seeds on parched ground or seeds kept away from the ground by weeds and thorns. The direction that love must take, it must be towards that ultimate union, which is the first step in that symbiotic relationship between seed-plant and earth.

We are the seeds and they are the earth. Seed must leave tree to cleave unto earth and be of one flesh and love will have meaning. We are the seeds and they are the earth. Earth that will not take seed into her warm, moist, fertile embrace, it is dead ground and seeds must be rescued to be planted elsewhere. Weeds and thorns that prevent good earth from taking the seeds must be removed. If they cannot, the seed must be taken out and planted elsewhere. And when is sowing time? Anytime for us, once the earth is ready. And we shall reap what we sow. When harvest time comes and the fields have turned to gold, when the rose buds open, we shall reap love. Har Tow jotted it all down in his notebook. Hmm. Maybe I can write poetry after all.

On the last day of school, he called for a meeting at the stop-butt. Wings was not there. Being the last day of the term, he thought it a good time to play truant. Har Tow was disappointed. He had wanted so much for Wings to hear his speech. But, Wings or no Wings, he had to do his part as Lawmaker. The mob cheered when he stood up and gestured extensively. He cleared his throat and they were silent.

"I have had another dream…"

17

SHE fingered the small gold band, running her fingertips over the roughness of its intricate patterning. She looked on the inner side, engraved with their initials, 'J LOVES K'. She was saving to get Johnson one in return, the same pattern except a little larger, and with the initials, 'K LOVES J'. I love him, I think, but ever since that business with Lynette, she had been less sure. She had forgiven him after he had relented and promised to have nothing more to do with Lynette. But still, she could no longer trust him.

Karen looked out of her window into the black of the night, and far out at sea she saw the familiar lights of ships, anchored in one of the busiest ports in the world. She found the busy title odd, because she never saw much movement amongst the ships. She looked down, and there was the white line of foam against the breakwater she had sat on just a fortnight ago.

Her gaze returned to her room, her desktop. Only her study lamp was on because her sister was asleep. She liked the yellow light because it made the room feel warm and cosy. She sat with her legs tucked up and rested her chin on her knees. Leaning back, she looked at the photo of Mei, Mildred and herself in the belly of a pink pig. When had that been taken? Only at the end of last year, during the last school hols. Another picture stood beside it now, framed in a gleaming brass heart, shot only last week, on her birthday. She looked at herself in both pictures. The girl was the same, but the clothes, one a sea-sky pinafore, the other an off-shoulder blouse and short denim skirt. One was a child, the other, not quite a woman, but getting close. And only six months in between.

She remembered what she had thought at the beginning of all this dating business. She had not been particularly interested in boys, but she did not dislike them. They were there, and if they wished to pay court to her, it was all right with her.

She remembered her mixed feelings when she had been faced with two possible boys. In the end, there had turned out to be only one. Why didn't Wings? What had all their earliest accidental meetings meant? She had thought he liked her, and he had shown a sort of interest, but he had never been consistent. Sometimes, he had treated her almost with the tenderness of a lover. Other times, she had felt like one of the boys. And every now and then, he had seemed to be on the verge of taking her seriously, but always, something had held him back. Had he only been playing with her? Yet right now, she felt he was the only boy she could count on.

Her confusion had subsided greatly but there were still many unanswered questions that nagged her. Some had grown irrelevant when she slipped into the habit of seeing Johnson and when he had finally declared he loved her a month ago. She had classified Wings simply as a friend who was good to talk to on the phone because he never asked her out after that chance meeting on the beach. She had thought him a suitor, but he never showed signs of pursuit, except the phonecalls, and those seemed trivial when compared to Johnson's persistence in asking her out. It had seemed pretty well-sorted out. Until now.

The questions that had plagued her for a while now came

back with greater force. Wings' awkwardness. People were only awkward when they liked you, her sister had said. Their chance meeting on the beach might not have been by chance at all. But what silly boy would wander a whole day on a beach in the hope of meeting a girl he vaguely knows? Her sister had said that boys in love tend to do silly things. The cards and tapes he sent her too, the sister claimed she could read between the lines of the cards and there was meaning in the songs he chose.

"But every pop song is about love," Karen had protested.

"But have you ever listened properly? Why choose these particular ones? Does it apply to his situation?" She thought about it and it did make sense. It was as if he was using the songs to tell her something he would not say himself. Besides, sis was a final-year English literature major at NUS and had spun a man or two around her long fingers before.

Her suspicions made her a little awkward and wary of Wings when he called, but it had added a new dimension to their relationship. He was a pen-phone-pal with a dash of romance, but it also made her feel guilty when she was with Johnson. Wings and her said very little to each other at workshop, and absolutely nothing when they were in company. Neither had broached the subject of silence, but it had been a tacit agreement, perhaps because both felt there was something illicit about their friendship. Illicit. Johnson had declared love for no more than a week when she had heard about his two-timing habits. And now that the two boys had fallen out with each other, her friendship with Wings had grown even more clandestine.

Her recent thoughts about Wings were sparked by the memory of the choice she had made. She had liked Wings, partly because he was so strange, yet could make her laugh and she did not mind being with him the whole day. But Johnson, who was more normal, could also make her laugh, and they did have things to talk about, though not as odd. She liked his company too. And he obviously liked hers. He had asked her out. She had refused the solo dates initially, but he had persisted and she had relented. And each succeeding time, it was harder to say no, until a call from him automatically meant they had a date. He knew how to make his dates fun. They went to the zoo, the bird park, every garden on the island, they went to Sentosa, to roller discos and high teas. He took her to functions in the night, where fourteen-year-olds congregated to dance in the dark with flashing coloured lights and ear-blowing disco music. They rode bicycles along the beach opposite her house, and he brought her home to play his newest records for her.

It was in his house that the problem began. He only brought her back when there was no one home and they would sit on the same beanbag as the records played. It was there that he had stolen the first kiss from her. He had tried before, on a darkened dance floor, but she had turned away quickly and he had been angry. But he had not tried it again because the public rejection was embarrassing.

That first kiss had not been unpleasant, and she did not stop him when he tried again. The quantity and the intensity of the kisses increased as the time they spent in his house went up.

Johnson kept a mental progress chart on which he assessed his performance and plotted his next steps. First his hands had only held her head, his fingers running through her long hair. But they had travelled down her neck and back with time. His kisses too, came down from her face and lips to her neck and chest and shoulders. Hands went further still, to her hips and around the curve of her bottom, along the length of her thighs. He could not reach further down. So hands decided to explore her inner thighs. From the knee, they worked their way up (or down) the river of eroticism to the heart of darkness between her thighs. But before he even let his hands brush against her genitals, he had first to progress to breast (butt, breasts and genitals in ascending order of privacy). So hands were withdrawn from Down Under and airlifted to the Himalayas (actually, Johnson felt that Karen was on the small side, but then she was only fourteen). Once the mountains had been conquered ('because they're there') and his flag planted by way of a kiss on each pinnacle, Johnson's attention returned to the southern hemisphere.

"Hey, I can get my girlfriend hot," he proclaimed proudly one day to Tech Group 2/13 during a stag outing. Boon Kim heard it and immediately checked if Wings was within earshot. He was not.

"Johnson, keep that to yourself."

"Why shouldn't we talk about it? The girls aren't here."

"Johnson, you tired of living is it?" Boon Kim said darkly and Johnson decided to shut up. But nothing could take the satisfied smile of conquest from his face.

Wings had been incredulous when he read the transcript of Har Tow's speech. He crushed the paper and grabbed Har Tow by the collar. Nose to nose, Har Tow was cross-eyed with surprise at Wings' anger.

"What the fuck are you trying to do?" Wings hissed. His eyes were mad and Har Tow was honestly afraid. No words could come, his eloquence had fled. How do you explain the beauty of love and its ultimate expression to a man about to kill you? Boon Kim had been nearby and had saved Har Tow. Wings himself had nothing to say. His mind was whirling. Had Johnson seduced Karen yet? If not, how far had he gone? Damn Har Tow and his scatterbrained ideas. No, the silly boy could not have meant any harm, but he lived in a different world, not unlike Utopia, and the world Wings felt they all lived in was somewhere between purgatory and Hades itself.

Boon Kim tried to explain it to him. "It's like this. Har Tow believes that sex is the ultimate expression of love because it binds two people together. He told us some story about a falling mango and seeds and earth and some other bullshit."

"Yes, I know, I read."

"So, he advised all of us to try and reach this ultimate expression of love."

"In other words, screw your girlfriends."

"If you want to be so crude, yes."

"It's just an excuse to fuck."

"You don't need an excuse to fuck."

"You're just trying to invent some pretty reason for it."

"Sooner or later, it will be done anyway. Might as well have a good-sounding reason for it. That way, everybody's happier."

"You're hiding behind some noble idea, but what you're doing is shit."

"Wings, tell me the truth. Wouldn't you be doing it too if it weren't for Karen? Would all this matter to you if it wasn't for her? What if Karen had been yours and not Johnson's? Wouldn't you be trying too?"

Wings got up. He had no answer.

"I don't know. But it's all hypothetical. The truth is what is happening now, real-time. I don't like it and I am saying so."

"It's nothing like our three Laws of brotherhood, you know. It was only Har Tow's advice. I mean, like you don't have to do it to be a part of us."

"Three Laws and a bit of advice."

"The common experience and the Law binds us."

"Sounds funny when you say it. Har Tow does it better."

"Wings, if Karen lets him, that's her business, not yours. And if Johnson decides to, that's his business, not yours. Give it up, man, there's still half a year for you to pick up someone else."

Wings shook his head.

"Fuck the Law. Fuck the Brotherhood. This is where I get off."

"You're joking."

"I'm not playing by your rules anymore. I'm an outsider now."

"Wings! We're your friends…"

"Yes, I know. But I'm out of the game. Go ahead and score with whoever you want. I don't give a shit."

"Are you going to interfere?"

"Wouldn't bother." He laughed.

"No, I wouldn't bother at all."

Karen had another choice to make. The first time she had had to choose, she hadn't really chosen at all. Wings had taken himself out of the running and she had chosen Johnson through force of habit. And now, there was again the danger of slipping into a decision which she would not really make, but have made for her. Should I say yes. After the dust from their quarrel had settled, they had gone back to their old ways, necking at Johnson's house, kissing on the beach, and Johnson always trying to get a little more from her each time. She had told him to stop every time, but he had always gone on. At least he went no further, she thought. And everytime she tried to stop him earlier, he'd ask why darling, you let me do this the last time and he would do it as he spoke and she would be helpless because what could she do? He knew she wouldn't do something like scream rape because it meant getting the both of them into trouble. She couldn't fight because he was stronger and so she submitted. But there was a voice behind her ear that said, but why are you so worried Karen? You like it, don't you? Otherwise, why did you let him start in the first place and why do you let him go on? You've been a bad girl, but that's okay, so why keep up the polite fiction of virginity? Enjoy it, it's okay. It's natural.

And now, Johnson had brought up sex. He wanted to go the whole way with her. He had stroked her, stroked her until she had been wet but she hadn't stopped him, not only because his whole weight had been on her but because it had felt so good. Her face went red at the memory of that night on the sand and she was angry with herself, with Johnson, with the whole world for making it wrong and making her guilty. I wish I didn't have to decide.

Would it have been different with Wings? Maybe he wouldn't have forced me into this. She could not answer herself. If I loved Johnson with everything in me, I'd say yes. But I don't. I don't love him enough. No, she did love him, but not the way she would have wanted to, not after Lynette. She thought of Wings and their meeting by the beach. She could hear his voice on the phone, his merry laughing voice that sometimes changed to a wild, almost hysterical abandon. He never forced her to do anything, not even when he had been advising her over Johnson. There was a gentleness in him despite his roughness in person. He made the better friend. But as a lover? What would he have been like? Would he have been any better than what Johnson was now? Who did I think I could love more? I never even chose. I just drifted with the tide and here I am. I can't give everything to someone I don't love with all my heart and don't trust. But if I don't give him what he wants, what will he do? I do love him enough to hurt.

She turned to look at her sleeping sister. She could not decide. I wish I could just disappear and get away from Johnson and everybody and start all over again. She felt like she was trying to rub a blackboard clean, but the chalkdust was refusing to fall away and was just staying on the board, no longer in recognisable shapes of words, but just big smudgy, cloudy, dusty masses that made no sense. She flopped onto her bed and buried her head in the pillows, but still the senseless masses swirled around her. She felt the increasingly familiar wetness in her eyes and this time she did not try to control them. Slowly, they rolled down her cheeks to stain her pillow, and with her face against the cold dampness, she fell asleep.

18

"LOOK, it's a free world, isn't it? If Wings doesn't want to be a part of our Brotherhood, it's his right. There is no law against dropping out," Krishnan said pointedly.

"But we are family," Boon Kim reminded him solemnly.

"You been watching Godfather is it?" Krishnan asked. Boon Kim looked away. They took it for a yes.

"In a way it's like that," Har Tow began.

"What do you mean in a way?" Krishnan demanded. This was disturbing. He was a die-hard individualist and the fact that he had the field of Indian girls to himself was a source of great satisfaction. He did not mind following rules so long as they did not get too much in his way and people did not force them on him.

"Krish, our group can only function if everyone obeys the laws. Once a member drops out, he need not follow the laws. Once others see the freedom he has, with no punishment, others will follow him and we will have chaos."

"Prawn Brains, there is a cost. Don't we ostracise the bugger?" Krishnan asked. That had been made quite clear at the first meeting. A man who disobeyed the Laws of the Brotherhood was excommunicated. It was a verbalisation of a tacit law that operated amongst children. If you are not with us, you must be against us, so we won't friend you.

"Krish, are you going to stop talking to Wings?" Boon Kim asked suddenly. Krishnan was silent.

"That's it, man. Neither will I."

"Obviously, not friending him will not work. And when others see that it doesn't work, they will realise that there is no cost in breaking away," Har Tow said.

"That leaves us with only one solution," he went on. "We must find Wings at all costs and bring him back into the fold."

"Easier said than done," Boon Kim griped. "The guy hasn't been home for three days. We even called Karen."

"He must go home sometime," Krishnan reasoned.

"Thanks a lot. This is vacation time. By the time he comes back, it could be too late. Everyone will know by then and everyone will do whatever he wants." Boon Kim grumbled.

Krishnan thought for a while. "I know something about Wings," he started.

"Don't we all?" Boon Kim sighed.

"No, I mean some of his habits. It could help us find him or get him to look for us."

"You want to put a 'Please Come Home — All Is Forgiven' ad in the newspaper is it?" Boon Kim asked sarcastically.

"Won't work, Wings does not read newspapers. He says it's only bad news anyway," Har Tow offered.

"Will you all listen to me? I haven't finished. Look, Wings is a lone wolf, right? That means he probably has not called anyone and is on his own somewhere…"

"Tell us something we don't know," Boon Kim said. He was getting irritated with Krishnan. Why couldn't he just get to the point? Showing off, he decided. Krish has to show off, even at a time like this.

"Where did his family say he went?"

"They said he was staying with a friend and he went on his bike," Har Tow said.

"Probably a lie. Wings doesn't have any friends other than us. He was a Scout once, that means he could be camping on his own somewhere. Okay, Har Tow, what does he do when he's got nothing to do?"

"Listens to the radio."

"Which channel?"

"Radio One, FM." Har Tow was beginning to see Krishnan's idea.

"So what do you propose, Sherlock?" Boon Kim asked.

"My friend's sister is a DJ for Radio One. The plan is this. Each one of us will send a dedication to him with the message 'call me immediately'. We will send at different times so the chances of him picking us up is greater. We will also send messages using all his other names so it won't sound too fishy."

"When can we do it?" Har Tow asked excitedly. He had never heard his own name on radio before.

"I call my friend now. Who got ten cents?"

They made the call and were in luck. The DJ herself was at home. She laughed when she heard their problem and promised to help. She took their dedications and called up the DJs on duty that day. She herself was slotted for the night shift. An hour later, Krishnan called again to confirm the broadcasts and she reported that it was all systems go.

"Right then, gentlemen, let's get home quick and watch the airwaves."

Wings was watching the seawaves. He had finished his chores for the day and was taking a break before starting to make dinner. He looked at the pile of twigs by his cooking pit and was satisfied. Enough for cooking and a campfire for another hour. The tide was going out, the water ebbing slowly away, listlessly. Wings was feeling like the tide. He had been on a high when he broke away. He had felt like the metre high waves, white capped and growling as they cruised in, hitting the beach with their watery green weight. Now, energy spent, he thought of breaking camp and heading for home and a hot bath. Yes, tomorrow morning. Watch another sunrise, fire coming from the water and over it, climbing into the sky like a slow, slow rocket booster, sending beams through the evergreens behind, beam me up Scotty, beam me up! But no, he was bound to this earth, like the roots of the evergreens, irretrievably bound to the ground. Ashes to ashes. I will be like the twigs I burn. Dust to dust. I will return to the earth that gave me birth. A seed on a wing, finding no place to rest, no earthy embrace, no darkness to dream in. No daughter of earth to call his home. Even the birds must come down to earth sometimes, their flight is but a temporary passport to heaven. Yes, fly free and fly where you will, you must still come back down, return to Mama Earth and her daughters. Was there nothing that belonged to the sky forever? Wings remembered an old dream. And a little caterpillar's promise. And his own broken wings. He looked around. The beach was empty both sides. Behind him were the evergreens and the highway. Before him nothing but sand and sea. Not a soul but his (that is, if one believed in such things). It was as good a time as any to cry, but the tears could no longer come.

Krishnan was getting worried. Two messages had gone out in the afternoon and still there was no reply. The boys were beginning to lose faith in his idea.

"Come on, guys, there are two more shows and two more messages to flash okay?"

He waited with the radio by him through dinner, much to his mother's annoyance. It was fortunate his father had been out with some friends. He would never have allowed that.

The dedication took to the airwaves and hit the beaches in a hundred thousand receivers, but Wings' radio was off. He was running low on power and had decided to save the juice for the night.

Darkness fell as expected (one of the more predictable things in this life). Wings sat by his campfire, watching the embers die. He was about to add more magnesium shavings to start another fire when he decided to keep the remaining twigs for tomorrow's breakfast fire. Early night then. Listen to the radio for a bit, probably won't last more than an hour. Wake up early tomorrow. Breakfast, break camp, ride out at first light.

He zipped up the mosquito net of his tent and lay back on his air pillow. How much more does a man need to be content? BP was right, but he had not taken women into account. A woman was that last thing to make it all perfect. But no, a woman always came with a whole lot of discontent. This was all a man needed, but a woman, oh no, from that first apple in paradise, women were the ultimate consumers. She would want more than he could give. All he wanted was a stretch of quiet beach, she would want at least Orchard Road.

He clicked his receiver on, heard the static and tuned in carefully to Radio One. It was almost clear, the fuzz largely due to his dying batteries. Ah, this is what I call being rocked to sleep. It is a strange experience, sleeping with the radio on, drifting in and out of consciousness, in from silence to rock and roll and out again to silence and sometimes that funny area where the rock and roll becomes a part of the dreamtime.

"And here's a dedication going out to a guy named Wings from his buddy Krishnan with the message 'call me the moment you hear this, it's really, really, urgent'. So Wings, I hope you got that loud and clear. Don't keep your friend waiting now. It could be something to change your life. But it's okay if you listen to this song first before you rush for the nearest phone…"

Wings opened his eyes. The static brought him back into the conscious world. The red battery indicator was fading and glowed dimly in the dark of his tent. Had he heard, really heard what he had heard? Call Krish. He looked at his watch. It was only ten. He could easily ride to a phone booth. He decided to sleep and call when he got home.

When the call did not come immediately, Krishnan consoled himself. Wherever he is, he may not have a phone handy. It takes time to get to a phone. So I must be patient. I wish everybody had pagers. He was patient till 2 a.m. His eyelids refused to stay open and shut on their own accord. Krishnan surrendered. If the phone rings, I am sure to wake up.

Karen had been tuned in to the station too. There was only one person she knew of called Wings. And she knew that Wings had a friend named Krishnan. She had met Krishnan on Orchard Road once. She had been with Johnson. He had been followed by a bevy of Indian beauties.

"My harem," he had whispered to Johnson.

"My concubine," Johnson had hissed back.

Karen had not heard any of it.

Was anything the matter with Wings? Should she call him to see if he was okay? She did not take long to decide. She went to the living room where the phone was. The phone rang till it cut itself off. Either everyone had gone to bed or no one was home. She put the receiver down and curled up on the sofa. Her parents had gone to bed and her sister was out as usual.

If they have to resort to a Radio dedication, Wings must have been out of touch for sometime. And she had not heard from him this week either. Ever since that problem with Johnson, they had been calling each other more frequently and regularly. Johnson did not know, of course, and she had no intention of ever telling him about her continuing friendship with Wings.

Where was he? If he had planned to go on vacation, surely he would have told her. It worried her and what made it worse was that she could talk to no one about it. When Wings was around, she had him to turn to, but now, the problem was him. Wings, where are you? And as she tried to imagine where he could possibly be or what kind of trouble he could be in, a passing 747 whined low and slow on its landing approach. She saw from the balcony, the twinkling lights that marked the plane's extremities. So strange, she thought. Everytime I think of you, an airplane flies by. But then again, it could be because we're so close to Changi.

The roar of a climbing airliner woke him. He got out of the tent to stretch. He felt the cold morning wind in his face and was happy. He thought of Karen. What are you doing now, girl? Probably still asleep. He knew she slept and woke late. Maybe by some freak chance you dream of me, huh? Maybe if I concentrate hard enough, I can project me into your dreams. Will it be a happy dream, though? No, mustn't think about you, girl. He broke camp quickly, packing up his bedding and tent, before starting up the fire for breakfast. He dumped in all his remaining rations. As it cooked, he gathered the cans and boxes, squashed them flat and packed them away. He would leave no trace of his presence.

I never make a mark anywhere I go anyway, he thought bitterly. They won't miss me, I'm sure. But he was missing his buddies already. A man can be alone for only so long and to really enjoy being alone, you have to feel like you're getting away from something. People, I guess. Maybe I shouldn't have done that. Chucked the Brotherhood. And for what? He thought of Karen. Was she worth it? No, I can't do that. Can't decide simply based on what it's worth. Have to decide on whether to follow right or wrong. Or friends. But Karen is my friend too. And who would have been the one who got hurt? Yes, I suppose I chose right. But what a lonely choice. We might have all been sitting around here now, all of us, waiting for breakfast.

He settled down to eat and put the headphones into his ears, but the radio was already dead. Then he remembered that strange dedication. He would check when he got home. Besides, what good news would Krishnan have? He was not anxious to hear bad news anyway. He ate slowly, watching the waves.

No one was home when he got back, but they had left him a long phone message list. The boys had been calling. He stopped at one name near the bottom. Quickly, he threw down his equipment and pressed her number. The phone rang and then he heard her sweet hello.

"Did you call, Karen?"

"Yes, last night, but you weren't in. There was a dedication for you on the radio last night."

So it was true.

"Yes, I heard it too."

"Have you called Krishnan?"

"No, I just got home."

"Where have you been?"

"Oh, I've been camping by the beach the last four days."

"Alone?"

"Yep."

"How could you?"

"I did it, didn't I?"

"But there's no one to talk to!"

"True, but I don't need people to be happy."

"That's rubbish. No man is an island."

"I am a Rock."

"That's a sick song."

"It's my song."

"Wings, don't be like that. Is there anything wrong?"

"It's a bit difficult to explain to you."

"Because I'm a girl?"

"No, not that. Actually it's easier talking about things like that to girls. Wouldn't tell boys."

"So what is it?"

"It's still difficult to explain to you, but not because you're a girl."

"That helps a lot, thank you."

"Sarcasm doesn't become you, dear."

"Shut up, idiot."

There was a silent moment.

"But there is something wrong, isn't there?"

"Sort of."

"So why aren't you telling me?"

"I can't, not to you."

"Is it about me?"

"Whoa! Ego, ego…"

"Shut up or I won't talk to you."

"Sorry. But you are right. It's about you."

"Then don't you think I can help?"

"Karen…"

"What?"

"It's you that's got the problem."

"What?"

"My problem is, I don't know how to tell you about your problem. And I don't even know if I should."

"Wings! If it's my problem, don't I have a right to know?"

"Yes, but there's so much at stake here…"

"What about me?"

"It concerns my friends."

"I'm not your friend?"

"Different…"

"I'll cry…"

"See if I care."

Karen sniffed. Wings laughed.

"Just like a tap. That's what I'll call you from now on."

"Shut up, I was only pretending. Don't you dare call me Tap. If you do, I shan't speak to you again.

If I tell you Karen, will you believe me? What will you think? I am beyond the Law now, but I still have my honour and I promised not to interfere. And how will it look? I say you're my friend too and I want to help you, but they will say that I only interfered because I want to steal you from Johnson.

"Karen, it's really very, very personal. I don't know if you'll ever believe me either."

"Try me. If it's my problem, I guess it's personal. And you've never lied to me."

But I have Karen, I have. Everytime I said I only think of you as my friend. Everytime I said that it was all I ever wanted from you.

"There's always a first time." He stressed 'first time'.

"Never mind, tell me and I'll decide."

"Karen…"

"Wings, if there really was a problem and if you were really my friend, you'd tell me about it and try and help me."

"It will hurt." You and me.

"Even so."

"Karen, do you ever feel that first times are significant?"

"Yes."

"This has something to do with it."

"What do you mean?"

"Remember the first date you ever had with a guy?"

"Yes, that was with Johnson."

"Right. How about the first time you ever let a guy hold your hand?"

"Johnson too."

"And the first time you ever let a guy kiss you?"

"Well, it was so long before I let him hold my hand. I mean, the poor guy's been waiting so long, so you usually let him kiss you soon after."

"I wouldn't let a guy kiss me."

"I hope not."

"Okay. Now, Karen … ah … how far would you let a guy go?"

"What?"

"Er, how far would you let a guy go? I mean like after kissing, what else do you let him do?"

How did he find out? Karen was silent.

"Karen?"

"I'm still here."

"Did you hear me?"

"Yes." She felt the heat rush up her neck to her face. Had Johnson told them everything? I'll kill him if he did. She bit her lip. What was she going to tell Wings?

"Wings, why are you asking me this?" she asked softly.

"Karen, it's important that I know. Trust me."

How far would she go? She remembered asking herself that not long ago, but she had found no answer. At least not with regard to Johnson.

"Well," she began slowly, "I guess I would if I loved him enough."

" 'Would' meaning all the way?"

"Yes." Her voice was very soft.

"Are you sure, Karen?" Her answer had hit him like cold steel in warm belly.

"Yes." Double stab.

"With Johnson?"

There was a long pause before she answered. "I don't know."

Wings was slightly consoled, but his relief disappeared very quickly. *Maybe she already has and is feeling bad about it.*

"Has he asked you to?"

"Wings…"

"Karen, have you done it?"

"No."

"Look, I won't think badly of you or anything if you have."

"I haven't." *Relief. But she could be lying.*

"Okay, but will you?"

"I don't know. If I love him enough, I suppose I will." *Oh no.*

"Do you love him enough?"

"I don't know, Wings."

"Karen, would you mind if I gave you some advice?"

"You're not much older than I am."

"But old enough. And I can see it from a guy's point of view."

"Okay."

"You say you will if you love him enough, right?"

"Yes."

"But what if he doesn't love you?"

"Then I won't of course. That would be stupid."

"But Karen, a guy can say he loves you even when he doesn't."

"But…"

"He can and will say anything to get what he wants. He might even tell you to prove your love for him by doing it."

"But I'd know, wouldn't I? Whether he really loved me or not? Wouldn't I, Wings?"

"Karen, let's say he isn't a jerk, that he isn't lying to you and that he isn't blackmailing you…"

"Blackmail?"

"Yes, you know, when they say they'll leave you if you don't give them what they want or when they ask you to prove that you love them by doing it, or kill themselves if you leave them."

"Oh."

"Okay, let's say he isn't doing all that. Let's say he really, really loves you and means to be yours forever. And assuming also that you love him very much. Would you?"

"If he asked, yes."

"You wouldn't offer?"

"No. That's for a guy to ask."

"Hm. But the answer is yes. Okay. But remember, you are not married, not even engaged. What makes you think you can hold him forever? What if you break up? There are so many reasons why people break up. It could be money, it could be in-laws, it could be someone else in his or your life. Then what happens?"

"But doesn't having made love make two people closer?"

"No. He might decide that you aren't as good in bed as some other Linda, Lena or Lynette." Wings immediately kicked himself for that slip. The name hit Karen like a slap.

"So?" she asked coldly.

"I'm sorry, it wasn't intentional. But face it, it's not a permanent bond, okay?"

"But he can still leave you after you're married, can't he?"

"Yes, I know what they say about marriage only being a licence for mating and it's only hearts that hold people together, not some signatures on a fading certificate." Ask my mum and dad. They could give lectures on it.

"Yes, so what does it matter now or later?"

"Karen, a divorced or widowed woman is not expected to be a virgin, but men expect their wives, if marrying for the first time, to be untouched."

"That's disgusting!"

"Yes, but that's the way it is, silly girl."

"Don't call me that. It's double standards."

"That is not the point. I mean, how will you tell that to your next boyfriend? How is he going to take it?"

"But if he loves me it won't matter."

"Karen, if I offered you two cars, both exactly the same, except one is brand new and the other one is secondhand, which would you take?"

"I'm not a car. I'm a human being. And no two things are exactly alike, especially people."

"Karen, please listen to me. What you say would be the ideal situation, but the world is not an ideal place. I'm just telling you what I already know about it."

"But you're a cynic."

"Cynics become this way only through experience."

"You make yourself sound very old, Wings."

"I feel very old, girl."

"Can I cheer you up?"

"Yes, promise me you'll think about what I said."

"Okay."

"Karen, just don't do it. Don't go to bed till you're legally wed…"

She laughed, "It rhymes!"

"Karen…"

"Yes, mum."

"If you ever feel horny, give me a call and I'll talk you out of it."

"Wings! I'm not a whore."

"Face it, kid. Nice people get horny too. If they did not, nice people would become extinct."

"You are disgusting."

"Uh-huh. Karen, one last thing. If you've done it, forget it, that's in the past. Start over and don't do it again. But if you haven't, don't start."

"You're worse than my mother."

"It's for your own good."

"You even sound like her."

"Karen?"

"Yes?"

"Please take care of yourself. I'd look after you myself if I could, but I can't always be there for you," he said gently. She felt a sudden surge of warmth and if Wings had been there, she would have hugged him and laughed. She had not felt like this for so very long.

"Thanks, I will. Take care of yourself too, Wings."

"That's what I do best. Gotta go now."

"Bye."

"Bye." He held the phone to his ear till he heard her handset click before hanging up. I did my best, but was it good enough? Both sides are my friends, but Karen stands to lose the most. And who do I love more anyway? The answer to that was clear.

19

WINGS rode ahead of the group. He was riding a BMX bicycle with 24-inch wheels, somewhat larger than the one kids usually rode. This bike was in terrible condition, actually worse than Wings' own clanking ten-speed racer, but it handled well and with a little bit of skill and more careful balancing, Wings found he could make it go places and do things he couldn't do with a racer. The bike kept his mind off other things, like this outing and the reason for it.

He stopped and looked behind. The others were cruising slowly behind, many still quite unsteady and some couples on tandems. Johnson and Karen were on a tandem of course, he noted ruefully. Krishnan had chosen not to ride and had stayed behind to help with the marinating. He had come alone too, like Wings. He also knew what it was all about and had warned Wings. To his surprise, Wings had expressed no vehemence and casually accepted the invitation.

Har Tow rode his bike unsteadily because he was watching Wings in the distance ahead. Face it, you can't do two things at the same time, he told himself. His and Boon Kim's date were riding between the both of them quite easily. Boon Kim on the other flank had no problems. Like Wings, he had been riding since the age of seven. He laughed at Har Tow and the boy shot him a dirty look. Boon Kim smiled and turned away quickly. Har Tow thought about their meeting with Wings. He had told Wings their position and Wings had listened to them. He had not argued, he had not fought back. Har Tow found it disturbing. Wings was a rebel, he did not give in so easily. But as Boon Kim said, four days on the beach beneath the evergreens does much to soothe a man's soul. Wings must have found if not enlightenment, at least peace in those days. He had said nothing about Karen, and they of course, did not want to bring her up. And so, they had taken Wings back into the Brotherhood without anyone else even guessing Wings had been out for almost a week

The next difficult part had come when they had to tell him about the holiday bungalow. Boon Kim had an elder brother who was an army officer in national service and he had rented a Service bungalow for a week. Boon Kim had asked for two days and a night and his brother had readily agreed.

"Are you bringing girls there?" he had asked.

"Yes…" Boon Kim had said, for he was not one to lie.

"Hm. Well, I won't ask what you intend to do. I will just assume it's immoral."

"What do you mean?" Boon Kim began indignantly.

"Aiyah, I was your age once too, what. Think I don't know what you're up to is it? Do what you want. Just don't get into trouble. And to stay out of trouble, don't make too much noise and don't do it in public, that's all. And yah, don't go and get anyone pregnant." He had not heard of statutory rape. He rummaged in his drawer and came out with a slim cardboard box. He looked it over before throwing it to Boon Kim.

"They haven't expired. You know how to use them, right?"

"I guess."

"Good. I know I can't stop you if you want to, so I might as well help you do it safely. Remember, this is to prevent sperm from entering a girl, so put it on before you put it in and don't get any of your own body fluids on it while putting it on. And check for punctures before you start. Now, if it breaks because you've been too rough, get out immediately and put another one on. Understood?"

Boon Kim goggled at all the information, so he nodded dumbly.

Wings had not protested when he found out what the outing was really for. He had just asked for time, place and shopping plans. Har Tow had been extremely puzzled though the others were relieved.

"Krish," he had said. "I think you had best stick close to Wings. He is not behaving to expectations and that is dangerous. Keep a close watch on him, especially when night falls."

Krish and Wings had gone shopping for the food and supplies.

"Wings, this is it. You know what this is for, don't you?"

"Yep. The *coup de grace* of Har Tow's Love Campaign."

"Yes, the final big battle. Eighteen men and eighteen targets, because you and I are excluded."

"Yep. This is where it all leads to. Where it all ends. And I suppose the troops will be home by Christmas?"

"I don't know what you mean, but this is the most important outing yet. We need your full cooperation."

"Aren't I cooperating? Aren't we doing all the supporting work for this party?"

"You won't do anything to jeopardise the outcome will you?"

"Krish, where did you learn to talk like that?"

"You know what my dad does."

"Okay, I promise I won't do anything. I will only support and I will not interfere."

Krishnan picked up a frozen chicken. "What do you think, Wings? Whole chicken or just parts?"

"What does it matter? It's all meat to us."

Krishnan missed the barb. "Yes, I suppose parts would be a better idea."

"Where is this place, Krish?"

"Somewhere in Changi, Loyang or something like that. Not really sure myself. A four bedroom bungalow, really big."

"Four huh? Yep, the Killing Ground, all right," Wings muttered.

"What did you say?"

"Nothing. And they are coming, like lambs to the slaughter…"

"Huh?"

"Hey, Krish, since you and me got no meat of our own, maybe we buy ourselves a whole chicken each, huh?" Wings laughed wickedly, but Krishnan did not understand.

"Too expensive, man."

"Yes, I always knew that."

As Wings pedalled on, he went over all those things that Krish and he had talked about that day. Wings had called the whole thing wrong. Krish had asked him why and he had had no answer.

"Why is it wrong, Wings?"

It's a set-up, he had argued, but Krish had said it was no more a set-up than helping a guy and a girl accidentally meet and get introduced. The outing merely facilitated a closer physical encounter.

But the outcome, Wings pointed out. The girls lost their virginity. So would the boys, Krish argued. Besides, it's only a loss if you think about it that way. Positively, it was the ultimate expression of love between two people.

But pre-marital sex is wrong. Says who? Krish had asked. Again, Wings had no answer. He thought about traditions. Was there not something that said women should be given to their husbands pure?

"Chauvinist. Those are double standards created by men who wanted to have fun with women and marry girls who never had other people. That crap only grew out of jealousy, man. Besides in those days, there wasn't contraceptives and abortion so a woman who did it could get pregnant. Which meant that women were safer not doing it."

But wasn't abortion killing? Wasn't killing wrong? And wasn't anything then, that might lead to an abortion, best avoided?

"My dad says that abortion is legal. It is also cheap. Five dollars, the last time he mentioned it."

"Isn't there a law anywhere that says we can't screw before marriage?"

"Not that I know of."

"Then why do I feel like it's wrong?"

"You must be either a sentimentalist or a traditionalist to believe that."

"But…"

"Wings, where do our values come from?"

"The past."

"Yes, usually really past. Those rules were made by people for their situation then, not now. Wings, there are some things we all know for sure are good and bad. Like if I hit you for nothing, that's wrong. If you took my money from me by force, that's wrong. If we forced girls to have sex with us, that's wrong. If we lie or cheat or steal, all that is wrong. And you know why it's wrong? Because we have to hurt somebody when we do it. That's what makes things wrong. But if you do something and no one gets hurt, then it's okay. I mean like, when we wank, didn't people one time say it was wrong? But is it? It don't hurt anyone, that's why now they're telling us it's okay. Last time, there was no contraception or abortions, so it makes sense that a woman shouldn't sleep around, but now, she can and she won't get hurt. Sex would be wrong though if you had some disease and you knew your partner would catch it."

"And is that the only rule in the end? Don't hurt anybody?"

"It's the only one that makes any sense."

"So if you know that there may be a chance that what you do now may hurt someone else in the future, should you do it?"

"I know what you mean, but if everyone knows the score and you never meant to hurt, I suppose it's okay."

Wings did not know what to think. All his life he had searched for that perfect set of laws to live by. There had been his parents' laws — the written laws they had lived by, the unspoken ones that they had broken. He remembered the ten laws of Baden Powell. Those were given to him and he had accepted them as his, but not all who swore by them lived by them. That made it hard for Wings because he always found himself on the losing end. And now the laws of this brotherhood. They had made their own rules and he had accepted them reluctantly as the price of brotherhood. But they had become meaningless after a while because he knew he could survive with or without the brotherhood. They held him to the law because it worked for them. One errant member would lead to more, and the eventual disintegration of the whole and the law existed only within the context of the group. Without it, the law was dead. How fragile our values are, Wings thought. But this one law, the one that everything boiled down to, was it the only thing with meaning left? Don't hurt anybody. It sounded so easy, so simple. All other laws simply grew from this. They named the ways in which one could hurt somebody else. They were the rules of thumb that helped one choose the way that hurt less. But why mustn't we hurt anyone? Because an action will bring forth a reaction. Action reaction, these had nothing to do with morality and values. It was good old physics. Tangible, quantifiable and thus reliable.

Action-reaction, Wings thought. We shouldn't hurt others if we don't want others to hurt us. A murderer kills. Action. Society executes him. Reaction. Wasn't it Gandhi who said, 'An eye for an eye, making the whole world blind'? Don't hurt anybody, perhaps there was meaning in it after all. It enhanced the survival of the species. And that was Biology. Quantifiable, tangible, believable.

The daylight faded quickly, as if in response to the boys' anxious waiting for darkness. Soon the only lights left were the dim streetlamps and the orange glow of burning charcoal in the barbeque pits. Krishnan and Wings fanned the flames which leapt up past the wire grilles. Har Tow touched Sandra's hand and they smiled at each other. Boon Kim was talking softer and closer to Peggy as they lounged on the verandah. Johnson had been extra nice to Karen the whole day and was preparing to cook her food for her.

"Eh, Wings, we're not the only ones fanning the fires."

Wings snorted in reply. Krishnan shrugged. He counted out the shares of food. It was an extremely large party. There were twenty boys and twenty-five girls. Some of the girls had wanted to bring along their friends. Har Tow had no objections.

"So long as they pay."

There were two main pits in the garden, which Wings and Krishnan worked on, and five portables on the low stone wall that fronted the beach. Hardly enough for forty-five people, Wings thought. But I guess eating is not what we're here to do.

His mind had been off Karen for most of the day, except when he looked her way. He had not wanted to look her way because it usually meant looking at Johnson too, which was revolting to him. But now, as he stood beside Krishnan, fanning, his mind was blank and his thoughts turned to Karen. He looked out over the now black beach, darker now because his pupils had adjusted to the fire, over across the water, and saw little lights of ships at anchor. He thought of Karen by the beach, the first time they had ever really talked. He shut his eyes and her face appeared to him as she had then. I've done all I can for you Karen, the rest is up to you. I hope you know what you're doing. It all sounded so trite, so neat to him, but he realised with a sickening feeling that it was true. That is all I can do for you

The fires were ready and people were bringing their food to cook (or burn) as the case might be. Wings and Krishnan walked away to the kitchen to get away from the heat.

"You okay?" Krishnan asked.

"Ya." He opened a can of beer and gulped it down quickly.

"No good on an empty stomach," Krishnan warned.

"Doesn't matter. No mood for nutritional lectures, man."

"You going to get yourself piss drunk?"

"Nope, but it suits my mood."

"She may need you to be sober."

"Don't talk to me about her," Wings said angrily, but he realised the truth in what Krishnan said. Yes, there could be trouble tonight, and he had to be sober if he was to help her.

"I wash my hands of her," he laughed as he rinsed away the soap. But could he really? No, no, I have to be there for her if she needs me. But what the heck for? She is my friend and I said I'd look after her if I could. I care about her. He stuffed a sandwich into his mouth to keep off the hunger.

"Where you going?" Krish asked as he walked out of the

kitchen. "Don't you wanna eat?"

"Later." He picked up the guitar in the living room and left by the back door. He flanked the building where he thought no one would see him, walked across some grass and vaulted over the low stone wall into the darkness.

Karen saw him go because she had been watching the lights of the ships. Hadn't there been another night like this, when she also looked at the ships' lights out at sea, when she had first asked herself if she was ready to give Johnson all he wanted? And the time she had the radio on, and they were playing a song for a boy she knew and what he had said to her the following day. She looked around for Johnson, but he was not at any of the pits. She got up and headed for the part of the wall Wings had crossed over into the darkness.

She could not see much, but she could feel the sand giving way beneath her feet. Then she heard the hollow, melancholy notes of an A-minor chord. She followed the sound. He was changing chords and his fingers picked out a flowing arpeggio. She saw him sitting further down the wall and she walked up to him.

"Hi," she said shyly.

"Hello, Karen." He did not look up.

"You okay?"

"Yep. How about you?"

"So far so good."

"You know where all this leads to, I hope."

"I can guess. Johnson's been preparing me for it."

He did not want to think about how Johnson had been doing that.

"Is he succeeding?"

"No, I'm still as uncertain as I ever was."

"That's better than nothing, I guess."

"What do you mean?"

"At least you've been thinking about it."

"Why would it matter to you whether I did it or not?"

"Because you are my friend and I care about you," he said flatly.

"That's nice to know."

"I don't want to see you hurt."

"I won't let myself."

"Don't."

"Play me a song."

"What would you like?"

"Do you know 'Sometimes When We Touch'?"

Wings laughed. "That sounds appropriate for tonight's activities."

"You're sick."

"There is a silly side to everything in life. Hey, do you know the words? I don't. Can only remember the tune."

"Yes, give me a two-bar introduction."

His fingers formed the first chord and they were away. Standing before him, he could feel the warmth from her body. He listened to her breathe between the words she sang and the breeze blew across the water, across the sand, through the night, through her dark hair. He wanted so much to reach out, to touch her and pull her close to him, to lift her chin for she sang with her eyes down, lift till he could look in her eyes and press his cheek against hers, pink-hot and hold her to him, the feel of her body against his. Soft, softly, you are singing a love-song with me. God, I wish it was for me.

But the song could not last forever. It was one of those that never had an extended remix made for it. Besides, Wings was not sure how long he could keep himself from actually touching her.

"Give me a five," she laughed. He slapped her palm with his and caught her fingers between his. She did not pull away.

"Hey. Before you go back, just remember I'm around if you need a friend, huh?"

She nodded. "I'll remember."

"And like the family planning ads used to say, 'Take Your Time to Say Yes' and it's also okay to say 'no'. Forget all the current crap about having kids while you're young. It's a bad idea for people our age."

"Okay already!" she was laughing. "You have an awful way of putting things."

"Uh-huh. Take care, girl."

"You too." He let her hand go and she slipped back into the darkness, back to where the fires burned.

By half past ten, the embers were dying, cinder vermillion turning to ash grey. The eating was over and a devouring of another kind began. Clusters of people sat on the verandah, on the low stone wall, and in the dimmed lights of the living room. But if heads had been counted, the count would have never reached forty-five.

Har Tow was whispering into Sandra's ear and she was giggling. Occasionally he would nibble at her earlobe and she would brush him off with feigned annoyance. They sat on the stone wall, holding hands as she leaned on him.

Krishnan and Wings were on the patio, talking to the seven extra girls, of whom Lynette was one. She is rather pretty, Wings thought. He wondered why none of the boys had targetted her. Only Johnson. It felt so strange, her being here, after all that had passed. Other groups and couples were scattered throughout the bungalow and the garden

Johnson was walking up and down the beach with Karen. He believed that the way things were going, the rooms would be quickly taken and he did not want to have to wait in line. That would kill the spontaneity of things and Karen might cool off and change her mind in the waiting. So he had taken an earlier stroll on the beach to drop off a groundsheet and some drinks and titbits at a secluded spot. He would take Karen for a walk and by and by they would get to the point and there they would sit for a while and talk. One thing would lead to another and wham, he would be between her slender thighs. And if she did not say yes, well, he had a contingency plan.

Har Tow surveyed the dimly lit room with satisfaction. The normal way to have gone about it was to have had a disco party after the barbeque. Get them going with the vertical expressions of a horizontal desire first. Yes, hip pulses and then the slow sentimentals where bodies got closer and closer until contact and then the pressure against each other building until the unconscious pelvic motions began. Then couple by couple, they would drift from the dance floor to the bedrooms that so conveniently surrounded the living room. But Boon Kim had warned him against loud noise and unwanted attention so Har Tow decided to forego the disco. His troops would have to do without the artillery bombardment. They would have to soften up their targets themselves. Boon Kim had suggested spiking the drinks, but Har Tow and Krishnan had said no.

"Play fair. If you want to score, no dirty tricks," Har Tow had admonished him. But he had allowed beer in the punch. He felt it was fair since everyone would be given notice of it. He also made unspiked punch available, but there were few takers.

It was almost midnight when Wings watched Boon Kim emerge from a room with Peggy, but he wore the smile of a winner. She was looking a little sheepish and was pulling him towards the driveway. Obviously she did not want to see her friends just yet. Funny isn't it, Wings thought. We say it's the ultimate expression of love, but we're still ashamed of it. We say it's alright to do it, but after we're done, we act like it's wrong. He thought of Karen. Is she alright? Has she said yes? They were not in the bungalow. He got up and walked across the patio. They were not on the grounds either. He looked across the stone wall into the darkness. The bastard, he thought angrily. He's got her alone out there somewhere. Quickly, he strode to the wall and leapt over it. Landing on the sand, he looked left and right. He chose left. He took off his moccasins and started running, searching the shadows for Karen.

They had been walking for over an hour, just talking, and she was leaning her head on his shoulder. Johnson took that as a good sign. He steered their conversation towards love, how much he loved her, how much he cared about her and how he would never ever leave her and did she feel the same about him? The beer in the punch had made her feel a little heady and she was sleepy and Johnson was so so warm and his arm felt so comfortable.

"Johnson, I'm tired."

"Well, I've got a surprise for you." He ran and she followed, stumbling across the sand. He came to his secret place.

"Ta da! Drinks, eats and a clean groundsheet to sit on!"

"Good! Give me a drink."

They sat down and he opened a can of Coke for her. He put his arm around her as she drank and she fed him from her can. He kissed her but nothing else. He knew he could not rush her. He could never continue where he left off where she was concerned. Every time they petted, he had to start from scratch. But it did get easier each time as she grew to enjoy it.

It wasn't hard that night. She had been well prepared. Harvest time, Johnson thought. He kissed her and followed his usual route down her body. Nothing irregular, don't want to alarm her, he thought. He had never managed to get her clothes off yet, but does a girl's clothes need to be all off? Course not! He reached between her thighs to lightly touch her genitals. It was something he had never tried with her before. She did not say anything, but a warning signal tripped in her mind. What was it they had talked about all night? Love. It had made her heady and soft and willing, but now, the first alarm had been triggered and she was coming out of her stupor. He reached into the waistband of her track pants and a finger slid down her spine to the valley between the cheeks of her butt.

"Johnson, don't," she whispered.

"Why not?"

"Because I don't like it."

He took his hand away and they continued kissing. But slowly, his hand found its way there again.

"Johnson, stop that. I don't feel good about it."

"Sorry, what would make you feel good?"

"Kissing and hugging's fine."

"Is that as far as you're going to let me go?"

"Yes."

"Don't you trust me?"

"Yes, but you might lose control of yourself."

"You don't trust me. Maybe you don't love me." He pulled away from her and looked at her angrily.

Hadn't Wings said this would happen? A second alarm went off.

"I love you, it's just that I'm not ready for anything more."

"And when will you be? We've been going for almost half a year now. What do you want me to do to get you ready?"

"I need time, Johnson."

"Do you love me, Karen?"

"Yes I do."

"Then show me." Was Wings some kind of prophet? Everything he said would happen was happening.

"Karen, darling, I love you, you know I do. Won't you please let me show you I love you — my way?"

"If you love me, you'll respect me and my feelings."

"You're not being fair."

"Johnson, I will, when I'm ready, but not until then."

"I see. What do you want from me, Karen? Haven't I given you a lot already? What else do you want? Tell me now. We'll go to town to get it tomorrow, I promise."

Karen was stunned. "I'm not a whore."

Johnson knew it was the wrong thing to say. Damn, how could he have let that slip? He tried to recover what he could. "I'm sorry, okay? I didn't mean it that way. Look, do we have a relationship or not?"

"We do." Her voice was hesitant.

"Good. I'm glad we agree on that. Now isn't a relationship about two people trying to make each other happy? All I'm asking you is to let me make love to you just this once. It would make me happy. Don't you love me enough to want me to be happy?" He looked so pained. It had worked other times. He was depending on it now.

"Yes, but what about me? I'd feel like trash after it. Don't you care about my feelings?" Karen was scared. She wanted to get away, get back to the safety of the bungalow. His face was turning black. She had seen that look before, just before he had exploded when they had quarrelled over Lynette.

"It's always your feelings. What about mine? You're a moody selfish girl!" He caught her by her shoulders and shook her hard.

"Johnson! You're hurting me!" Panicking, she struggled to break away from his grasp.

"Why should I care? You obviously don't care about me." His grip was painfully tight and she struggled in vain.

"Johnson, I do," she pleaded. But he was angry and he knew that he had lost whatever headway he had made with her over the last week and few hours. He had to take her now or never.

"Look, Karen, I've invested a lot in our relationship and it looks like it's been all for nothing. This is where I take back what you owe me."

Without warning, he pushed her roughly to the ground and threw himself on top of her. The impact hurt and it was the last straw that made her cry. The sight of her pinned beneath him crying was more than he could take and it drove him to madder heights of desire.

"Think you could get a free ride from me, didn't you? Little slut, now you're getting a ride all right." He kissed her roughly as she tried to push him off her. His hand went to her track pants and in one movement, he pulled them halfway down her thighs. He grabbed at her buttocks and then savagely thrust his hand between her thighs, groping for her genitals. She screamed in pain and the sound shocked him. He pushed himself up and looked around in sudden panic. She kicked wildly in that moment of freedom and her foot found a target. It was not a hard kick, but it was well placed and Johnson doubled up in pain and shock. His jaw dropped open but he could not even scream. She scrambled out of the way as he fell forward, clutching his injured groin. Standing up, she pulled up her pants and ran as fast as she could.

Wings had been on his way back from the left when he heard a faint cry far away from the right. It was a long shot, but it could be Karen. He sprinted over the hard-packed sand by the water's edge. He passed the bungalow and was breathing hard when he saw a slim figure running wildly towards him.

"Karen! Is that you?"

"Wings! Wings!" she called. He ran to her and caught her as she stumbled forward.

"What happened, kid? Are you okay?"

She shook her head as she cried and held on to him tightly.

"Please take me home, Wings. Please."

No one noticed the dawn, when the sun rose out of the grey-green water burning red. The lightening purple sky, the wind that whispered through the leaves of the coconut trees, the smell of salt rising from the water, riding on the wind, the crisp cold cutting through windbreakers.

Wings walked along the shore, sand in his deck shoes, breeze in his hair and the cold piercing to the bone. He listened to the waves, to their rhythmic assault and withdrawal, riding up and pulling back, in and out, in and out. A long night it had been, and he was not sorry to see the sunrays break the darkness to turn black to purple to blue. There were some things, he had learnt, that only the darkness could bring out, for only the darkness would hide them.

Well, at least Karen was all right. That was a comfort. It had been a near thing last night. God, if you do exist, I'd like to say thanks. She was at home now, probably still asleep. Wings had not slept at all. He had walked the beach the whole night, from the time he had seen her safely home. Up and down, up and down. Past the bungalow, past the late night lights.

He was not ready to go back in yet. He knew they would be waking up soon, and he wondered how they would seem to each other, lovers in the morning light, when the darkness could no longer hide them. No, he did not want to see them. He decided to take a long slow walk to the hawkers' centre for some coffee and toast. Yes, that would be good on a morning like this.

Krishnan woke first because he had gone to sleep right after he had seen Wings and Karen off. Of course he had not fallen asleep immediately. He had spent much time tossing and turning, trying to figure out why Karen had been crying and why it was Wings who was seeing her home. He gave up after a while and stretched himself out on the couch in the now empty living room. Too many beers, Krish, he told himself. But here he was, awake and fresh. He struggled to get up from the deep springy embrace of the couch and walked to the sliding glass doors. The beach is so nice in the morning, he noted. Good for a run. He was looking around for his Nikes when he suddenly decided not to go. Wait, they will be getting up soon. I wonder what they will look like and how they will behave. Krishnan had heard much about 'morning afters' and wished to know how they really worked in real life. This should be quite fun, he thought as he went to the kitchen to get breakfast.

Har Tow walked in from the garden with his giggling girlfriend. They looked quite normal to Krishnan. Their clothes were all on and they were still holding hands. Har Tow had been out on the patio the whole night with Sandra and they were still as lovey-dovey as the night before. Krishnan could not understand. Aren't they supposed to be feeling a little awkward? Maybe even a little hostile to each other? But no, they look absolutely normal. He decided that they probably never got round to doing it. Sandra had not let Har Tow do more than neck, but Krish did not know that.

A room door opened and Krishnan looked up hopefully. Boon Kim emerged with a big smile. Peggy took a little longer to come out and she looked around before entering the living room. She hung from his arm in about the same way he might have let a prize fish hang from his rod.

Small groups and couples dispersed around the bungalow awoke one by one and congregated in the living room for breakfast. Some had been playing guitar and singing Xinyao songs till the early hours. Their voices were hoarse now, but still they chatted on, laughing as they sipped on the coffee Krishnan had made. A group had been playing Trivial Pursuit. Someone said that they would have all done better in the mid-year exams if they had studied the same way they did memorising those questions and answers. Well then, Krishnan thought to himself. Not everyone was doing it. And that was what we planned this for. He looked out of the kitchen window. Had the party been a failure? He looked around at the sleepy but happy faces. It doesn't look like failure. Boon Kim was still all smiles, but his smile was losing some of its brilliance as he listened to the talk around him. Was he the only one last night who had scored? It felt funny, being the only one. He looked at Peggy and she was now looking at him with something like reproach in her eyes. He went up to her and touched her arm. She shrunk back from him.

"What's the matter?"

"You lied to me."

"What do you mean?"

"You said everyone was doing it, so it was okay," she said in a low voice. She was trying hard not to cry here.

"That's what I thought, Peg."

"You lied."

He glared at her and stalked out of the kitchen. She put down her coffee and went after him. Krishnan had seen them. Yep, that confirms it. They've done it all right.

"Hey people!" One of the boys shouted above the general noise.

"Let's take a survivors' picture!"

There was more shouting and screams as girls protested.

"Like this? But we just woke up!"

But they gathered on the patio anyway.

"Is everybody here?" Har Tow called out

"Looks like Wings and Johnson are missing," Krishnan said.

"Karen and Lynette for the girls," Sandra reported.

"Ooh, I see Wings has found himself a girlfriend. Wonder what hanky panky he's up to," Har Tow smiled. No one but Krishnan had seen Karen leaving in tears with Wings. He had gone to bring her bag to her and had called the cab for them. He kept quiet now.

"Well, there's still one unopened door," Boon Kim observed.

"Dear me, all four of them in there? How kinky," Har Tow noted and was immediately booed down by the house.

"Johnson! Hurry up and come now!" Krishnan suddenly shouted. The boys laughed at his unintentional innuendo.

The door burst open. Johnson had been holding back for this very moment. He had wanted to make his entry with all eyes on him. Johnson stepped out with Lynette, who wore a look of triumph on her face. Whispers shot like a current through the ranks of the girls.

"Uh-oh, wrong pair," Krishnan muttered to Har Tow. Even he had not stayed up long enough to see this. Har Tow frowned. The air had suddenly gone tense and everyone could feel a kind of static, growing as Johnson and Lynette walked up. He had his arm around her waist.

"Hey come on, let's take the picture. I want this on record. Our new situation, man."

"Yah, okay," the cameraman said. He began making adjustments.

"Where's Wings?" Boon Kim asked.

"I…" Krishnan began.

"Wings? That shit? He left with that second-hand slut I used to have. What's her name now?" Johnson drawled. Boon Kim stared at his friend. He had never seen Johnson act this way.

"Don't you talk about my friend like that!" Sandra suddenly shouted as she jumped up to face Johnson.

"Honey!" Har Tow pulled her back. "Ignore him, OK?"

But she was beyond consolation. The tears were rolling down her dimpled cheeks and Har Tow had to take her away.

"Let's get on with it, okay?" Johnson said suavely.

"What about Har Tow?" Boon Kim asked. He was standing up now, with Peggy by his side. "We're not taking a picture without him and Sandra." They walked back through the living room to the kitchen where Har Tow and Sandra were. Groups began to get up and go. The mood was gone.

"You're a jerk," a girl spat at Johnson as she passed him.

"You're a fat bitch," he shot back.

The cameraman was unscrewing his camera from the tripod.

"Hey, how about one of me and my new girlfriend, huh?"

He looked at Johnson and Lynette. Then he nodded with a sigh.

"Sure. Why not?"

The girls had been escorted to the bus-stop. The boys had stayed behind to clean up, take stock and hold a stop-butt meeting.

"All here but Wings," Krishnan reported flatly. The boys seemed to have lost their spirit from the photo-taking incident and everyone was feeling uncomfortable. No one looked at Johnson.

"Anyone know where he went?" Har Tow asked.

"He left last night and hasn't been back since," Krishnan said.

Johnson snorted but the boys ignored him.

"Okay, I call this meeting to order."

Krishnan reported the group's financial state first and gave a detailed account of the expenditures. He reported that all items belonging in the bungalow had been checked for damage and everything could be accounted for. Everything was in order, the budget, the logistics, the area cleaning. But the reports were long and it was as if they were trying to put off the real reports, the reason why they had all come here in the first place.

"OK, sitreps," Har Tow said finally. There was silence.

"Gentlemen, you were all aware of the reason behind this event and our ultimate objective. Give us a report on whether you achieved it or not. If you have, congratulations, please tell us how you did it. If not, tell us how far you got and what help you need to accomplish it."

The silence persisted.

"We will go by the normal alphabetical order. But before that, let's have a show of hands to see who made it last night."

Two hands rose up. Johnson and Boon Kim saw that they were the only hands up. Boon Kim let his sink a little but Johnson raised it up even straighter with a sneer on his face.

"Are there only two men here?" he said dryly.

The boys looked around at him but did not make any reply. They had grown very tired of him ever since the photo-taking.

"First sitrep. Johnson Ang." He had been waiting for this.

"Well, guys, as you all know, I was going with Karen. But there was this girl called Lynette who started calling me a little while after I had started dating Karen. I told her I was already seeing someone, but she wouldn't listen. She kept calling me up and asking me out. So in the end, just to humour her, I did. Okay, so I went a few times, but it was nothing serious. But she wanted more than just casual dates and she was persistent and finally, I got fed up and I said, 'Okay then, but you'll have to wait for me.' And since you can't keep a girl waiting forever, I decided to use this outing to help me make my decision. If Karen had said yes, I would have stayed with her. But she said no, so we called it quits last night and I started a new relationship with Lynette. And it just so happened that she was willing." The boys had listened in absolute silence.

"Thank you, Johnson."

The mob turned around to see who had spoken. It was Wings. Their Whip was back.

"You heard everything?" Har Tow asked him. Wings nodded.

"And I've heard Karen's side of it too." The boys made way for him as he strode to the front. He glared at Johnson. Johnson looked back lazily. But his mind was racing. What had Karen told him? Had she told him everything? Surely that wasn't the kind of thing a girl would have confided in a guy?

"So you had Lynette waiting around for you, right?"

"Yes. So?"

Wings turned to face him and took a step towards him. "You know, Johnson, the First Law of the Brotherhood says one man, one woman. You broke that Law."

Johnson breathed out in relief. So Karen probably had not said anything. Wings was on a different subject. A charge of infidelity was nothing compared to attempted rape.

"Ya, so I'm sorry I broke that rule. But it was for convenience." Play along, boy, play along. Don't let them ever point in that direction, Johnson said to himself. But he was sweating in the cool of the morning. He had never meant to hurt Karen, it had gone terribly, terribly wrong, but he had never meant to hurt her. Wings was walking up to him. Bastard, he knew how to make a guy uncomfortable.

"So whether one follows a rule or not depends very much on expediency." Wings winked at Krishnan. He had learnt the word from him. Johnson saw the wink and thought, asshole, expediency my foot, he's trying to tell me that if I can break the law, so can he. Well, you can have her. I don't need her now. You can have that secondhand slut. And you'll find out in good time that I had her first.

Johnson was right on one point. Wings was trying to tell him that just as the law was a matter of expediency for Johnson, it could also be for other people.

"So I suppose you won't object to the expediency of this?"

Johnson looked puzzled at Wings and then suddenly felt the wind knocked out of him as Wings slammed his knuckles into Johnson's solar plexus. His breath caught short and before he could recover, Wings sent a right hook against his temple.

Johnson spun and stumbled. The boys cleared the floor and Johnson fell with a thud on the carpet.

"One for Karen, one for me." He had not forgotten the slap in the toilet.

"Wings!" Har Tow shouted in dismay.

Wings raised his eyebrows at him.

"The Law, Wings," he almost pleaded. "The Brotherhood…"

Wings looked at him apologetically.

"I'm sorry. I'll still think of you as my friends, even if you won't. But the Law, the Brotherhood," he said slowly as he looked sadly at Har Tow, trying to find the words to say it all, "I guess this makes me an outsider now."

"Wings," Har Tow murmured. He was near to crying.

"I'm sorry, guys. But I think it's time I left."

He looked at Johnson, a crumpled heap groaning on the floor and a familiar feeling of remorse crept over him. But he brushed it away quickly. He looked up at the silent boys. Krishnan handed him his haversack. He caught Wings' hand.

"See you in school, bro."

"Yah." He smiled and walked out into the driveway.

20

THE wind blew strong and cold and carried the hint of rain to come. He didn't need the wind to tell him that. The clouds said enough. Black and threatening, they spread out across the sky like a canopy and thin shafts of light pierced through to touch the grey water below.

The sand was an insipid yellow-khaki-white, darker where the dirty water crashed against it, running up and then running back to join the sea. Children screamed in the waist-deep water and mothers screamed after them, trying to get them back to shore.

Branches of the trees swayed, their leaves rustling in accompaniment to the beating of sparrows' and mynahs' wings. Chaos before the storm, people taking the hint from the thunderclouds and packing up to go. He watched them all, from the harried parents, the gleeful children, to the people who would leave with only half a tan. Pity. Settled down and then the rainclouds, he thought. Maybe we never really get to settle down anywhere.

He recalled a day when he had stood on this same stretch of beach launching a plastic airplane while his friends baked brown. It would never be that way again, not with all of them.

Something in that made his heart ache, but he knew that they had come too far to go back to that day on the beach. Friendship, he supposed, was like everything else he knew — fragile. Which silly dreamer had said it was forever? Maybe the memory is all we ever get to keep. But even in the knowledge of that, he could not help feeling the pain of loss. Perhaps even more than when Mum and Dad broke up. At least that was their fault. This is mine.

He walked along the water's edge, the headphones of his FM receiver blocking out all sound from the outside and he held a can loosely in his left hand. There were special shows on that day, but he hardly heard them, his heart a million bands away. He walked on to a quiet stretch of beach and came to a familiar wall of granite rocks. He climbed up the breakwater and sat down heavily.

The ships out at sea were still, there was no movement, not even a sampan. Guess everybody's on shore leave. He saw far off to the left, the great grey hulking shapes of American warships, a small carrier group. He looked for the flashing of Tomcat tails, but there was none. The sun was not strong enough.

He looked around, there was nobody in sight. He put the can of beer down and opened the pouch around his waist for his cigarettes. He stuck a Camel between his lips and shaded his Zippo against the wind. He sucked strong and steady and the fag was lit. He looked at the bare rock beside him. That's where she was. The memory was bitter and the beer and the smoke couldn't take the taste from his mouth. Almost a year ago, then. Was it such a short time ago? It felt like years. But then I feel old. They had sat there the first time they met, on this very same beach. He'd been walking along the shore, with some weird hope that he might meet her and he had. That's when they had become friends.

And the last time? After that barbeque thing the boys had

planned. Her boyfriend had almost raped her and he had been on hand to rescue her. What a hero. He snorted and blew the smoke through his nostrils. The wind took it away quickly. Yes, they had met here again, but this time, they had planned it. She had to be comforted see, and who better to do it than the boy who had rescued her? And she had gotten over it and they had gotten more friendly and he had hoped. Hoped for what? I can't say that. I'm a decent boy. Love is a four-letter word. There, I've sinned.

And so is hope. Just as well I didn't. Like why it was just as well he could not fly. I might not have liked it. At least now it is only a dream and it is as good as I make it. And run away to that comfort when reality gets a bit unbelievable.

Just as well. Because she never grew to love him. Always, he was the good friend she trusted and confided in. That was all. Well, at least that still stood.

She had cried that day and she had asked why it had all turned out that way. And he had looked up at the sky for an answer and remembered thinking, silly me, I never found them there. But there had been an answer in his heart, only he had never given it voice because she was innocent.

Love, like flying, Karen, is a dream that must not come true because heaven must always be out of reach to be meaningful. And himself, he so wanted to believe that heaven could be touched. Mum and Dad missed. I mustn't. So he had not told her.

But maybe he should have, I should have told her. Time had made her forget and the pain had worn off. And she had learnt to forgive too. Whatever for. Then Lynette had chucked Johnson for some Rafflesian winger who scored touches regularly on and off the rugby field and always had to try. Johnson had been shattered and it had made him sick enough to be warded. And the news had softened her. His pain had made her forget the pain he had once inflicted on her. She had gone on a friendly visit. Then two. And she was still seeing him after discharge and when he got well enough to come back to school. Well, what do you know. They had got back together.

The beer was flat. He finished the dregs and hurled the can out to sea. Had it all been wasted time. No, he stopped himself. She needed me then. And she wasn't a waste of time. I love her too much to think that of her. So long as she's okay. That's all.

Heavy weather, but the storm had not yet broken. He heard the low powerful roar of Rolls Royces. He looked up and saw the 747 climbing, the shafts of light that had broken through the clouds glinting off its slender polished wings. She will rise above the storm, cruise above the thunderclouds and darkness in the sunshine, escape the tears below. An escape I can no longer be a part of. He could no longer conjure up his plane, Charley Juliet 162. The dream had died inside him. Once he had used it to escape, a familiar heartache to make him forget new pains. Not anymore. And that skeleton at home. Still undone. His mother had been bugging him about it. Finish it or throw it away, she had scolded. You never finish anything you start

They were out today, his mother and sister. At Gran's probably. He had refused to go. No, not today. I don't feel like making jolly meaningless conversation with people I don't see the rest of the year. He'd written his Dad a card and wondered if he had got it. It might not have made it on time.

He felt for his wallet and it felt fat. He felt secure. Hadn't been fighting with his mother the last two months, as bad as he had been feeling, and his business had been doing comfortably. He'd found another supplier in the redder part of town who could get the hard stuff. And videos now. The money was good, but the comfort his make-believe girlfriends gave him was better. He could have had the real thing of course, wouldn't have cost more than twenty dollars, but that first experience he had ever had of them as a Scout — he could never make it with a whore.

He turned the receiver off. The damned dedications were getting saccharine. Worst time of the year to listen to request shows. This and Valentine's. Valentine's. His thoughts went back to Karen. And I thought this would be a good time to tell her. He'd been hoping and they had been getting close when it had happened. They say first loves never die. Which song had that come from? Well, no matter. He'd been saving to get her a present for then. And now. He felt in his pouch for the ring. Round and silver, it flashed in the darkening light as he held it up to his face. Guess I can't give this to you now, Karen. It would be wrong. He felt an impulse to fling it out to sea, just like in the movies. But he couldn't. Hell, it wasn't the money. He'd kept Janet's picture and all her letters. Karen's too. The ring would just go with all the Karen stuff. And, he tried to stop the thought, but it came anyway, and maybe one day she'll get to wear it.

The thought hurt him. I love you, Karen. Happy Christmas, darling. He felt the wet heat rising and fought back the tears and failed. He looked up at the great grey sky. Please, God, if you are there. Won't you ever? But he could guess the answer already. The first raindrops hit his face and the water rolled away with his tears.

"Merry Christmas, God, wherever you are," he whispered bitterly.

Merry Christmas to you.

About the Author

COLIN Cheong was born on 24 April, 1965. He attended Hwa Chong Junior College and graduated from the National University of Singapore in 1988 with a degree in English. He has been a journalist, political analyst, business writer and teacher. And yes, he still rides a motorcycle from time to time.

OTHER WORKS BY COLIN CHEONG

• *Poets, Priests and Prostitutes*, 1990

• *Life Cycle of Homo Sapiens, Male*, 1992

• *Seventeen*, 1996

• *Void Decks and Other Empty Places*, 1996
(Commendation Award, Singapore Literature Prize, 1995)

• *Tangerine*, 1997
(Singapore Literature Prize, 1996)

• *The Man in the Cupboard*, 1999
(Merit Award, Singapore Literature Prize, 1998)

• *The Colin Cheong Collection*, 2011
(a compilation of three novellas and 23 short stories)